The Grimm C

Hidden

By: Lyla Oweds

The rights of Lyla Oweds to be identified as the author of this work has been asserted by him/her in accordance with the Copyright, Designs and Patents Act 1988.

No part of this publication may be reproduced, stored in a retrieval system, or transmitted in any form or by any means without the prior written permission of the publisher, nor be otherwise circulated in any form of binding or cover other than that in which it was published and without a similar condition being imposed on the subsequent purchaser.

Cover Design by

Crimson Phoenix Creations

Edited by

Heather Long and Becky Lynn

Copyright© 2020

All rights reserved

Warning:

This book contains references to past abuse and other dark themes. There are no explicit details, but there are vague references to the events.

Table of Contents

Chapter One 11
Chapter Two 27
Chapter Three 46
Chapter Four 63
Chapter Five 74
Chapter Six 98
Chapter Seven 111
Chapter Eight 128
Chapter Nine 145
Chapter Ten 153
Chapter Eleven 166
Chapter Twelve 177
Chapter Thirteen 186
Chapter Fourteen 195
Chapter Fifteen 214
Chapter Sixteen 231
Chapter Seventeen 244
Chapter Eighteen 259
Chapter Nineteen 266
Chapter Twenty 281
Chapter Twenty-One 290
Chapter Twenty-Two 303
Chapter Twenty-Three 314

Chapter Twenty-Four 329

Chapter Twenty-Five 335

Chapter Twenty-Six 345

Chapter Twenty-Seven 354

Chapter Twenty-Eight 367

Chapter Twenty-Nine 380

Chapter Thirty 398

Chapter Thirty-One 417

Chapter Thirty-Two 430

Epilogue 443

The Author 449

Glossary

Onmyoji — An onmyoji is a practitioner of onmyodo. It's an occult-based science that was popular during the Heian period in Japanese history. The most popular practitioner was Abe no Seimei. Their magic is drawn from the underworld. They are also fortunetellers, tarot masters, and can bind a shikigami to them to act as their worldly familiar.

Shikigami — A shikigami is a spirit guide, of sorts, that is present on Earth through a contract with an onmyoji. They have a human form but prefer to take on their animal shape in this realm. They act as an intermediary between the underworld and this realm on behalf of their onmyoji.

Necromancer — In this universe, the necromancer retains most of their original definition with one change: they cannot summon spirits. Necromancers deal with the physical side of death and the memories that are tied to living and dead things. Because a person's essence is tied to the spirit as well as the physical body, necromancers can dream-hop and manipulate emotions.

Fae — Much of the original fae folklore is kept, including the appearance of the Seelie and Unseelie court. In this world, fae act as the intermediary between this world and the underworld. They live between the two, and their specialty is mediumship—communication with spirits.

Witch — A witch in *The Grimm Cases* and *Alpha* are much like a hearth/house/green witch of today. There are no sparkling spells and wand waving. Witches practice earth-based magics that are quiet, subtle, healing, but also deadly if in the wrong hands. Both men and women are witches.

Wu Xing — The mythology behind both *Grimm* and *Alpha* are based off the practice of the Wu Xing (the Chinese Five elements). Every "ability" falls within one of those elements: the fae belong to the Wood element, the onmyoji are Fire, witches are Earth, shifters are Metal, and necromancers are Water. The properties of their abilities tie in with the aspects of their element within the Wu Xing.

Controllers — In the Wu Xing, one of the five elements controls (overcomes) another in nature, and so it is in this story. To keep one ability set from growing too powerful, their opposite exists. Metal controls Wood, Water controls Fire, Wood controls Earth, Fire controls Metal, and Earth controls Water.

Supporters — The same as the controllers, except with the opposite effect. Each ability can help other abilities grow stronger, that's the generating cycle. Wood helps Fire, Fire helps Earth, Earth helps Metal, Metal helps Water, and Water helps Wood.

Xing — The Xing, as characters, are the backbone of *The Grimm Cases* universe. They are archetypes, elements "manifested" into the world, who are reincarnated every other lifetime to restore balance. They have had many lives and are the leaders of their world.

Er Bashou — The Er Bashou is top-most ranking official below the Xing. Their sole function is to oversee the other officers and to serve the Xing. Officers are sorted into their quintets at the age of thirteen based on the strength of their abilities.

Jiangjun — The Jiangjun ranks below the Er Bashou and is one of the top three confidants of the Xing.

Tongjun — The Tongjun is the third top-most official, falling under the Er Bashou and the Jiangjun. There are other officials under the top three, but these are the ones most prevalent in the story.

Quintet — The more powerful the person, the harder it becomes to control their powers, and the more easily unbalanced they can become. When someone is at that level, they seek balance. So those who have abilities are organized into groups of five individuals who have comparable and complementary strengths.

The Council — They are a group of overseers created by the Xing to help keep balance when they are between their reincarnation cycles. The council is made up of powerful individuals—though no one knows their real identities—who help determine the laws for the rest of the supernatural world to follow. When the Xing are alive, they can actually override a Xing's decision if they think they pose a danger to the general population.

Chapter One

Bianca

Cage

Bare walls made up my prison, leaving me alone with my memories. The past—and the expression on Bryce's face—kept returning to my thoughts.

There was no way I would be rescued, so there was no use in wishing it. The boys would be helpless in this situation, unlike when I'd been kidnapped by Daniel Cole.

They wouldn't be able to circumvent the law.

My parents had complete control, and my worst fears had come true.

They wanted me to get better, but I had no idea what that meant. What did everyone expect?

Knowing the boys and meeting other mediums had proven I wasn't crazy. That the things I saw were real. And this knowledge left my blood boiling at the injustice.

I wasn't wrong! And I wouldn't give in. There was no way I could go through the rest of my life pretending to be someone I wasn't.

A knock echoed through the room, but it didn't surprise me. I expected her to come, after all.

Sure enough, without waiting for a response, Dr. Reed strode into the room, closing the door behind her. Our gazes met, and her confident stride faltered.

"Bianca." She sounded apologetic. "How are you?"

I blinked at her, incredulous. What kind of question was that? Did she not realize where we were? Did she not have eyes?

"Why am I here?" I asked in return.

Her lips pressed together in a line before she responded. "Why are you in a straightjacket? Is that blood?"

"I was brought here from the hospital." I was too tired and on edge to care about manners. "But I thought you knew that."

"Yes." She frowned and pulled the strings holding the jacket closed. "But I thought that they'd be gentle, at least."

"They're never gentle." I shrugged as she pulled the garment off me. "You know that," I added, watching as she set it aside and turned toward me again, this time to check the wounds on my neck and shoulder. "They never are."

I had nothing left to lose, and she might not answer. But it couldn't hurt to ask. "Why is that? Do they hate who I am?"

Dr. Reed froze, and her concern steeled over with something unreadable. She turned her worried, dark eyes from my wounds back to my face. "Pardon?"

My heart thundered in my ears. I'd only suspected, but now…

While I'd been left restrained and alone, I started to wonder. My memories and thoughts intermingled, and conversations from the past began to make sense. Overheard words from dark hallways were finally becoming clear.

They *knew*. So many people had known this whole time. Dr. Reed, the people who worked here, and even Finn. It would surprise me if my parents weren't aware as well.

But why would everyone lie? Why would they keep me locked away?

"I know who I am," I told her, my gaze holding hers. I only wanted the truth. "I talked to Damen, and the others, and…"

Her brows furrowed. "What did Damen—"

"Why were you suppressing my abilities?" I asked. "Why did everyone want me to think I was crazy?"

"Bianca…" Dr. Reed's focus turned to my neck again. "Let me fix this up, and I'll talk to you. All right?"

It wasn't all right, but what could I do? I wasn't exactly in a position to argue. So I remained silent as she fussed around me, ordering a cart of supplies to be brought into the room. I didn't say a word—despite the fact it hurt—when she peeled the dried bandages from my neck. I was trying so hard to be strong, to ignore my discomfort. By the time she finished, I was barely paying attention.

Instead, my mind had drifted.

She hadn't looked surprised. It only confirmed my suspicions. But regardless of the truth, I was still locked away.

Why? Would I ever see the others again?

Finally, the room had cleared out, leaving us alone. She pulled over a small chair and faced me as she sat, crossing her legs and folding her hands into her lap.

"Bianca." Her voice was deceptively mild, considering the turmoil in her eyes. "Can you tell me what you're feeling right now?"

Annoyance shot through me, electrifying my nerves. Before now, I had been numb and tired. But an anger was beginning to swell in my chest.

How dare she ask me that.

"You lied to me." I forced the words out through my fury. "How could you do that? You're my doctor."

How could I ever trust her again?

Dr. Reed grimaced. "You're not wrong." She looked away nervously. "But there are difficult circumstances involved. And concerns regarding your physical and mental health. Those issues go beyond your abilities. This is not about you being the Xing."

That didn't matter—she still should have told me. Everyone was *wrong*. I opened my mouth to tell her so, but she continued. "Have you heard the voice again? The one that used to come to you in your dreams."

The question startled me out of my anger, but she wasn't finished. "Are you ready to talk about your past? You've been with the others, and I know you've stopped taking your medication. It's dangerous for your abilities to go unchecked, and we need to monitor you. How long has it been?"

My nails dug into my thighs, panic causing my breathing to turn shallow.

"W-w-what?"

The *voice*. The woman who used to haunt my dreams. I only mentioned her to Dr. Reed once, and it didn't seem as though she cared very much.

So why bring her up now? Had she been judging me for that this whole time?

And my past…

That had nothing to do with who I was now. She'd tried to talk about my foster homes before, but I'd always brushed her off. There was no reason to discuss it. It wouldn't change anything.

I didn't even know where to start.

Dr. Reed's frown softened. "First things first, I suppose. Let's discuss the voice from your dreams. Have you heard her lately?"

I didn't understand. Was she searching for a sign I was mentally unstable? I wasn't stupid. Hearing voices wasn't a good thing, but I had been too stupid to keep quiet. On top of everything else, of course they would use my imagination against me.

Besides, I'd been a child. I'd outgrown it already.

"No," I answered, slightly hesitant. "I haven't heard anything. It was just an imaginary friend. So it doesn't matter. Why do you care?"

She hummed but didn't address my question. "There's another thing I've been wondering about. Just how close are you with the boys?"

"T-t-the boys?" I'd been around a lot of boys lately, but I doubted she meant Bryce. Sure, I didn't loathe him anymore. Nor did I dream about making him disappear mysteriously into the night. Still, I hoped she, too, wouldn't fall under the spell of trying to make me be nice to him.

It would never happen.

"I am referring to Damen Abernathy, Julian Kohler, Miles Montrone, and Titus Ducharme," she responded, confirming my suspicions. "How long have you known them? How did you meet? What is your relationship like?"

Why should I tell her? She wasn't my friend. She wasn't even a good therapist.

"I stopped my medication two weeks ago," I told her, not really answering her question. "I met them about a week ago. They already told me everything."

Dr. Reed raised an eyebrow.

"How does Bryce know who my parents are?" I asked instead, recalling his words and their reaction. Did everyone think I was stupid? "How would they know who he is?"

She seemed about to respond, but a commotion from the hallway broke into the moment. Dr. Reed shot to her feet and was halfway to the door when it slammed opened.

Julian strode into the room without a word, his aura sharp and dangerous. His gaze instantly landed on me, and as our eyes met, the skies cleared. I could breathe again. I wasn't sure how he had found me, or even why he was here. But I was so grateful.

He would take care of everything.

A nurse stumbled into the room after Julian, reaching for him. But Julian dodged him easily and pushed past Dr. Reed. He was beside me in an instant.

"Bianca..." His voice was soft as his fingers trailed over my cheek. "I..."

The nurse cringed at Dr. Reed. "I'm sorry, I—"

"Don't bother." Dr. Reed waved her hand dismissively at the nurse, who, without another word, left the room. Her focus was entirely on the two of us, and I didn't miss the way her frown deepened as her gaze lingered on his hand. But even more surprising than that was the next exchange.

"What are you doing here, Julian?" Dr. Reed sounded as if she was forcing herself to be patient.

Julian stiffened beside me, turning to narrow his eyes at her. "The same could be asked of you, Mother."

Shock raced through me, and the stare down between them deepened—rife with tension. A long moment passed, and finally, I couldn't hold back my question any longer.

I looked at Julian—I could barely hear over the thundering in my ears. "M-m-mother?" Dr. Reed was his mother? I didn't understand. What was going on?

"Yes." His tone was regretful, and his attention returned to me. "I didn't realize until you gave us your medication… I'm sorry. Really, I had no idea. I would never—"

"Julian had no idea of your existence. I've still not heard how you met though." Dr. Reed sighed, returning to her chair. "And Julian, Bianca is my patient, and we are in a medical setting. You don't even have clearance to be in this room."

"You can't make me leave." His voice was low. "I have every right to stay with her, no matter what you think. She is my—"

"Unfortunately, the law doesn't take that into consideration." Dr. Reed leaned back in the chair. "And there are things that I need to discuss with Bianca. Private things regarding her health. Go wait for me in my office."

"N-n-no!" He couldn't leave! His presence was the only thing keeping me from the darkness.

I pulled his hand to my chest, and Julian turned to me in alarm. "I want him to stay! P-p-please, don't make him leave. I'll give my permission. I don't care if he's here."

"Bianca," Dr. Reed said, patience threaded throughout her voice, "we're going to discuss your medical history. Are you certain that you want him here?"

My heart skipped, realization buzzing through my awareness.

The fear of being alone was suffocating, especially with comfort so close at hand.

"Stay…" I tightened my hold on his hand, but he didn't complain. "Please."

Julian's expression morphed from a worried mask to professional in an instant. His focus shot back to his mother, and there was a tone of a command in his voice when he spoke. "What's going on? Let me help."

"Bianca has no right to make major treatment decisions, so keep that in mind." She straightened in her seat. "If you want any of your suggestions to count for something with her parents, you'll need to be present as more than a friend. They're wary of you."

Julian blinked at her. "Mother?"

"I know how you are," she said, determination setting into her expression. "And I know that you know who she is. You'll meddle, anyway, so why not use your enthusiasm for something? I'll take you on as my temporary intern. You *are* at that stage in your training. But there will be things in her records that you won't be able to access, at least not now. And if Bianca doesn't want to discuss something with you, then you are not to press it. In the end, she is my patient."

This was happening so fast, and now he was going to be my doctor? I hadn't agreed to this.

My grip on his hand loosened as the fear turned my blood to ice.

There were things Julian *couldn't* know about me. Things I never wanted anyone to know. What if he found out?

This was a terrible idea. I just didn't want to be alone.

But relief practically radiated from Julian—and how could I take that away? And did Dr. Reed seriously think he might be able to help with my parents?

I just had to talk to Dr. Reed privately—only for a moment. I needed to ask her to never reference certain things around Julian. It would ruin everything.

Darkness swam in the corners of my vision.

"I'm here now," Julian said, pulling my attention back to him. He touched his forehead to mine and pressed his hands against my cheeks gently. "It'll be all right. Just breathe with me."

We'd done this before—him coaching me through a panic attack.

Every cell in my body became electrified. Even though I'd been a second from fainting, it was impossible to ignore his words.

He wanted me to breathe—so I followed his guidance. A warmth began to spread from my chest, and my skin heated as I allowed him to lead me.

I'd felt this before. It was still alarming to give up control, but now I understood the desire. At least a little.

The dizziness passed, and the black dots in my vision faded. Nothing else existed, only Julian's soulful eyes.

What was this feeling?

"Are you okay now?" His voice seemed to flow over me, like a balm soothing the edges of my nerves.

I blinked slowly, trying to pull myself out of the lazy haze that had surrounded me. "Yes…"

A movement from the corner of my vision pulled my attention. Dr. Reed was writing furiously in her notes.

"I've never seen anything like that before," she explained, not even glancing up. "I knew our abilities can control physical responses to some extent. Obviously, we're most effective against Fire elementals, since we're their controllers. But Julian, I had no idea you could use your abilities like that."

Julian frowned, watching his mother. He seemed hesitant. But he must have seen something in her that I didn't, because a moment later, he replied, "It is a common misconception that our abilities are meant only to control, harm, or to manipulate." He sounded different than usual, almost older. "People believe that because we've made it seem that way. But Water is a nurturing element. You can manipulate it for harm, just as you can for good. You've calmed your patients before, I've seen it."

My breath hitched.

After my adoption, I could barely even speak. Dr. Reed would touch me, just a casual a brush of her fingers against my hand. After that, I would be able to respond without frustration.

She had been using her abilities against me?

Honestly, I wasn't even angry. In those days, those moments of calm meant everything. I just couldn't believe I'd never thought it was strange or even noticed at all…

"You aren't wrong." She glanced up, watching the two of us. "I do use my abilities to set my patients at ease. But you completely negated an anxiety attack before it had time to crest. I've never seen that before."

Julian shrugged. From the thin set of his mouth, I knew he wasn't going to elaborate anymore. His mother watched him a moment longer before she seemed to realize it, too.

Instead of arguing or pressing him further, she gave him a resigned look. Almost as if she knew that there were things that Julian would never tell her—even if she was his mother.

Was this normal? Was this what being a Xing meant? Were we the holders of secrets that we weren't even able to share with our families?

If that were the case, I didn't understand how I could be such a person. Every other medium knew far more about interacting with ghosts than me. Maybe there was a mistake?

"In any case"—he turned her attention back to me—"how long have you been off your medication?"

This again… She wasn't going to let up.

"Two weeks," I repeated. "I feel fine."

"Her abilities are growing stronger, but something is still holding her back." Julian squeezed my hand. "Is there something else? She summoned spirits and sent them away successfully, but she was drained from it."

Something else…?

Dr. Reed's brows furrowed. "No, there may still be side effects. She's been on the medicine for a long time. Bianca, I want to put you back on them, at least on a lower dosage. We can discuss taking you off later."

My throat closed. I couldn't believe what she was saying. But it was Julian who answered.

"Why does she need to do that?" His voice was ice. "She's already been off two weeks."

She shot Julian an almost-exasperated look. "Julian—"

"Why do you want to suppress her abilities?" he asked.

"That's confidential," she replied smoothly, not looking at all afraid at the cold glare from her son. "If you're going to be interning with me, then you need to learn to trust me. My patient is Bianca, not you. Now sit there quietly and let me talk to her."

Julian froze, and fury rolled off him in waves.

"Now, Bianca." She completely ignored her irate son. "How have things been? I see there's been some changes." She looked pointedly at our hands and the spot where Julian's leg touched mine. "That's a good thing. But as for others…" She paused, seemingly hesitant to speak, but pressed forward anyway. "Bianca, how has it been—seeing spirits?"

Julian jerked. Surprise cross his expression. He peered down at me, our eyes meeting, and I shrugged.

I didn't understand the reason for the question. Especially after the subject had been avoided for so long.

"Fine…" I answered slowly, unsure if there was a correct answer to this. It was strange to be discussing this with the doctor who'd told me everything was my imagination. "They're there…"

It wasn't a lie. The spirits were there. I didn't know what else she expected.

"You're not frightened of them?" she asked.

Well, it would be lying to say that I wasn't, but—

"They aren't all bad." I glanced at my leg. The mark on my ankle had disappeared. "One attacked me in a bathtub. Another one tried to strangle me. Then there was a wolf who wanted to eat me for dinner. And there's a sexist old man who keeps insulting me."

Her eyebrow had risen higher with each point. "And you're still… all right?" I shrugged in response, and she tilted her head. "Did you see anything that frightens you in particular?"

Not necessarily. They were all creepy and scary in their own way. However, the living were far scarier than anything in the spiritual realm. For example, Daniel Cole. And even myself…

I was worse than anything else out there.

Julian fidgeted before speaking, unable to hold himself back anymore. "What is the point of these questions? What does that have to do with any—"

"Bianca." Dr. Reed put her hand up, cutting off Julian's question. "Are you ready to talk about your first spirits?"

My musings halted, and a sense of numbness began to crawl out over my skin. "What?"

"The first spirits you encountered as a medium," she repeated, holding my gaze. She was looking for something, but what it was, I had no idea. "Everyone remembers their first. What was yours? Can you tell me what happened?"

This question *again*.

It was one of the worst questions they'd ever asked me. My ability to speak was suddenly lost. I was suffocating.

It was my fault. Everything was my fault.

Sound muted, and time faded from my awareness. All that existed was the cold dark night and the drowning rain. Kieran's face swam in my vision, his expression darker than usual. Worry and fear flashed across his silver eyes as he realized what I had done. He didn't have to say a word, I could already hear the lecturing in his deep voice. I'd replayed that conversation so many times.

I messed up. There was no way to make things right.

Gradually, color began to flash through the darkness. I wasn't there. That was a long time ago. A familiar voice whispered into my ear as safe arms held me. My eyes opened. I was looking up into Julian's panicked face.

"Bianca." He sounded a second away from crying. He'd pulled me into his lap, and his hand cupped my cheek. "Bianca, are you all right?"

Dr. Reed, who had been hovering in the background, slowly returned to her seat. "That's worse than before…"

"Before?" Julian turned to her. "This has happened before?"

Dr. Reed, instead of answering, watched me. "You still can't talk about the past; but you're not afraid of spirits anymore?"

I blinked at her confused, and Julian's hand fell away.

I had never been afraid of spirits, per say. It was only certain ones that pulled fear from me. Spirits—if you ignored them—would *generally* leave me alone.

Why in the world would she think this? "That's not what scares me. I've never been afraid of ghosts."

She visibly jerked, a look of complete astonishment passing over her expression. "But…" Her flipped through the pile of papers in her lap. "But…"

"Will you please explain to me what is going on?" Julian arm's stiffened around me as his patience reached an end. "You've put her on medication because you *thought* she was afraid of spirits?"

"Not entirely." Dr. Reed's lips pursed as she scanned her notes. "But it was one of the reasons."

Julian's eyes narrowed. "And what else?"

She closed the folder and stood. "I've got to look something up. Considering what you've told me, I don't think we should put you on a full dosage. But really, it all comes down to what your parents believe to be best."

"You can't let them medicate her against her will!" Julian held me closer to him. "What are you researching? Why are you even medicating her?" He asked the same questions that had been racing through my own mind.

Dr. Reed paused, studying him. For a moment, I thought she wouldn't answer.

"I might need you later, Julian. But first, there are a few things I need to follow up on." Her gaze traveled between the two of us. "Just stay the course."

And with that, she left the room, leaving Julian and me alone.

Julian held me to him, his expression severe. Slowly, dread began to fill the emptiness.

My parents had full control over my medical decisions. It didn't matter that I was eighteen. My life wasn't mine.

They could force me to take the medication again. They could force me to stay here.

And I still didn't even understand *why* I was here.

Dr. Reed seemed to be sympathetic. She'd found a way for me not to be alone, at least. But what if she couldn't stop them? Could they override her suggestions? I wasn't sure. I hadn't even known that my parents had *that* much control over me.

My entire life was spiraling, and I had no say in the matter. I couldn't make my own decisions.

"Bianca." Julian brushed his cheek against mine. "Are you all right, dearest?"

I wondered about the answer to his question myself. The truth was, I didn't know.

Everything was different. Not even a week ago, I knew nothing other than what Finn and my parents told me. And now, a whole new world existed.

A world that, from what I was beginning to suspect, didn't want me in it.

What other reason would this be happening to me? Damen said that the elders wouldn't accept me. And for some reason, my parents were working very hard to keep me unnoticed.

But why? Was I that terrible of a person?

I had killed people, so I was dangerous. But the others were allowed to live in peace.

What made me any different?

Chapter Two

Julian
Change

Three days had passed, and still I'd gotten no answers. At least I'd been able to visit Bianca. But the situation only made me anxious.

The part of her records I'd been able to access didn't tell me anything new.

Bianca suffered severe anxiety. It was a condition especially bad for empaths. It was imperative that, early in their lives, they learned to filter the emotions of others. Otherwise, they were prone to psychological disorders.

The rest of her records were off limits to me.

That's what concerned me most; what my mother wouldn't let me see in those files. I couldn't help Bianca without knowing.

The only thing Mother would tell me was when she had first met Bianca, she was in a crisis state. And that the damage had already been done.

That statement really didn't bode well.

The last three days had shown a decline in Bianca's condition. She was barely sleeping, and she wouldn't eat. If nothing changed, they'd force her to do that, too. And they'd already started her on her medication. A lower dosage, but still…

And now, while our emotions were reaching a breaking point, an emergency conference had been called. However, despite all attendees being present, the room remained silent.

Damen had given up the pretense of calm a long time ago and was now pacing near the head of the table.

Brayden was present. Anthony, too.

But what goaded at me the most was Finn.

He was so close—this would be the perfect time to get answers. I only needed to convince Damen to give me time alone with the little blond freckle. He would tell me things that my mother continued to hide. He had to know more than he'd let on.

However, Damen would never allow me to murder his brother.

Shame.

"So." Brayden rested his chin on his hand. "What's going on?"

I was surprised Brayden had spoken first. It was Bryce who'd called us here, after all.

Bryce, instead of opening, appeared to be deep in thought. He stared at a vase in the middle of the table, the strangest expression on his face. Almost as if he was finalizing the pieces of a complex puzzle and wasn't a fan of the result.

"You hardly know more than me," I pointed out, meeting Brayden's gaze. "Is there a point to this, or are we quite done? I have things to get back to, since you two were the ones who allowed her to be taken from the hospital."

Brayden frowned. "What was I supposed to do, lay in front of the ambulance?"

I knew my accusation was unfounded, but it was getting on my nerves that Bryce hadn't said anything yet.

"You weren't the only one there." I shrugged, hoping to goad Bryce into a response before Damen lost his temper. He hadn't even wanted to meet today, so Bryce's inaction wasn't helping.

Damen stopped pacing, grabbed one of the phones, and threw it at the vase. Everyone across the table jerked as it shattered.

I hoped he was being strategic, and not losing his temper. Damen's control kept Titus in check. Unfortunately, Damen wasn't known for his ability to handle strong emotions. There was really no way to know how long our luck would hold out.

No one knew what to expect with Titus—he had never been in this situation before.

He wouldn't talk to any of us. At the moment, he was in his dragon form, curled in a corner behind us.

Without Damen's control, Titus might destroy everything to get to Bianca. And he wouldn't be subtle about it. Mass murder tended to attract attention, which was the last thing Bianca needed.

When she embraced her role, she would have enough problems. The elders could not know about the mate bond.

Miles sat unmoved beside me—unaffected by Damen's display. His face remained buried under his arms, and I knew he was either sleeping or plotting. My money was on the latter, but since he hadn't slept much since she was taken, there was a possibility it was the former.

"Do you know who Bianca's parents are?" Bryce asked, frowning at the shattered vase.

His question caused Miles to shift, Damen's glare to darken, and Titus to focus his attention on him.

None of them were in any position to talk, so I did. "No one knows who her parents are—she's adopted."

Bryce rolled his eyes. "I *know* she's adopted. You think I haven't been able to figure that out? I'm talking about her adoptive parents. Do you know who they are?"

Finn—who'd been seated between Bryce and Brayden—shot the other man an almost panicked look. "Hey—"

Damen leaned over the table. "No," he said. "There's no record of her parents. We assumed that she took their name, especially since she was a foundling. There was so much going on with Aine's house that the research was secondary. We didn't even ask."

Bryce scowled at the broken glass. "Her adoptive parents are Jonathan and Abigail Geier."

Miles jerked up, his face a picture of shock. I didn't blame him. I knew that mine was as well. Even Damen expression had lost his anger, and Titus stirred.

"What did you say?" Miles's words were barely discernible through the tightness of his jaw. His eyes shot to Brayden, who stared at his brother in the same manner as the rest of us. Apparently, Bryce hadn't let his sibling know. "How did you not know this?"

Finn covered his face with his hand.

"I-I…" Brayden's gaze turned from Bryce to settle on Finn. "How?"

"Have you spoken to Hanah about what's going on?" Miles growled, his voice a bit scary. "Call her," he said, pointing to Brayden.

Brayden was still stunned, so it was Bryce who responded. "Why don't you call her? She's your Jiangjun; she'll listen to you."

"Don't start with me," Miles snapped. "I'm not an idiot. I know I *could* call her. But that was my phone that Damen broke."

Brayden, once more, glanced at his brother before pulling out his phone. "Okay…"

At least we wouldn't have to wait long for her to arrive. Hanah's shop, *The Ivy Garden*, was just down the street from Dean Abernathy's home.

While Brayden typed, Finn shifted beside him. My focus zeroed in on him. We already knew he had been hiding things from us, but he clearly had also known Hanah was involved.

Of course she was—it was *her* parents who had adopted Bianca.

This was worse than I imagined. "Who else knows?"

Finn froze, his gaze turning toward Damen. Damen was still beside me, his body tense and his breathing labored.

"Don't look at him," I snapped, annoyed that he was still trying to hide behind his brother. "Is there anyone else besides Hanah who knows about Bianca?"

Finn's mouth pressed in a line, and the tension in his frame was tangible. But still, I couldn't relent. My focus was intimidation. Damen was on his own; I had no remaining resources to control him. After a second, Finn looked away, responding. "Yes."

Damen slammed his hands against the table. "Who?"

Miles had gone silent, which was almost as frightening as Damen's fury. Because if he snapped, it would be a terrible thing. Only Bianca would be able to stop him.

And Titus… He hadn't moved since Finn's admission.

Finn continued speaking. "We were only following orders. There are a lot of reasons why it had to be this way—"

"I don't want to hear your excuses!" Damen snarled. "And you don't follow orders from anyone other than *me*. Who is involved? Is Norman?"

Finn grimaced. "No, not Norman. Just Kayla, Do Yun, Jiayi…"

My heart raced.

Both Kayla *and* Do Yun? That meant my only loyal officer was Anthony.

Even so, at least my situation was better than Damen's. His own brother was a traitor. His brother and his Tongjun. How did Jiayi come into the picture?

Titus was lucky to have escaped unscathed. But shifters always had a different sort of loyalty.

"This has been going on for ten years," I pointed out, noticing that Finn hadn't named anyone older than thirty. "Besides my mother, who was involved? Who gave you these orders?"

Finn's gaze traveled back to Damen, his tone wavering. "Mr. Sao, my mom…"

Damen stopped breathing, making me wonder if he seriously hadn't suspected. Or if he had, did he try to convince himself otherwise? The evidence had been present the whole time.

"How did it happen?" I pressed.

"Bianca was dying. She needed Kayla and Do Yun's help. Your mom tried, but it wasn't enough," Finn said, the haughtiness completely gone from his expression. "Don't be mad at them. They saved her life."

"Don't tell me who to be mad at." Anger swelled in my chest. "Why was Bianca dying? What happened? Why did no one get me, or even Anthony instead? We were always here. What about Jiayi?"

Finn grew paler with my every question, and by the end, he wouldn't even look at me. Anthony had noticed his avoidance and watched Finn in suspicion.

"What did you do?"

He flinched. "I didn't—"

A knock at the door interrupted him, and Hanah Geier walked into the room.

She must have been working. Her pixie-cut hair was in disarray, and there was a smudge of dirt across her cheek. More dirt covered the knees of her threadbare jeans, and the edge of her patchwork shirt was caked with mud. Most people would have tried to clean up first. But from her grave expression, Hanah was aware of the seriousness of the situation.

She sought out Miles at once. She didn't even greet Brayden as she crossed the room to stand beside him.

Miles's tone was deceptively calm. "Hello, Hanah."

"Miles." Hanah tapped her fingers together. "What's—"

Miles sliced his hand through the air. "Why didn't you ever mention you have a sister?"

Hanah's eyes widened. "Bianca?" Her voice squeaked. "You know that I haven't seen my parents in eight years. Did something happen to her?" She sounded genuinely concerned.

"Bianca was in the hospital. And while we were dealing with the council, your parents and Dr. Kohler committed her to an institution. We only know of your parents' involvement because Bryce was there. Otherwise we never would have found her. Finn wasn't being so forthcoming." Miles's delivery was factual and emotionless, his face carefully blank.

"She was in the hospital?" She looked at Finn. "Is she okay?"

I narrowed my eyes at the exchange—why would she look at Finn? He had done something before, I was certain of it. He'd almost killed people simply by failing to control his power.

Had he hurt Bianca? I would rip him apart.

"No, she's not okay!" Miles punched the table, finally losing his temper. "She was injured, and now they've taken her away. She told us what happened—you all told her she was crazy. We know about that medication. I want to know what the fuck is going on!"

Finn and Hanah were still looking at each other. It was Finn who finally responded. "Bianca cannot be the Xing."

I moved to stand up, wanting nothing more than to break his neck. "What are you—"

Damen held me back with his hand on my arm. Even now, he didn't want me to hurt his brother.

"She is," he said, his voice strained. "We've already seen her use her abilities. She has the mark."

"Hold on!" Hanah moved in between the two of us. "You're misunderstanding. Finn doesn't mean that she can't be Mu!"

"Then what is the problem?" My whole body quaked with the desire to hurt him. Finn had done something, I knew it. I only needed to figure out what. "What was so terrible that you couldn't tell the four of us that you'd found the missing link in our quintet?"

"Julian!" Hanah waved her hand in my face. "Bianca is adopted!"

My eyes snapped to her determined ones. "So what."

"You know before she was forced out, my mother worked for the FBI. You also know what she did. Her job broke her. Even after that, she'd still be asked to go back in the field for special missions. She was on a high-class assignment ten years ago." Her face grew more determined as she spoke. Each word chipped away at my fury. My entire being was focusing on this.

There was no way that she was insinuating…

"*Where* do you think my parents found her?" Hanah finished. "My mother is a disaster with children. She never even wanted me. Why do you think they adopted Bianca in the first place?"

My heart stopped. I understood what she was saying. But my mind screamed in denial. I couldn't accept this.

Everyone faded from around me, and I fell back into my seat. I couldn't look away from Hanah's eyes. This had to be a terrible joke.

"She was eight," I heard myself say, as if her age would change anything.

"Technically, she wasn't eight yet," Hanah said. "And before my parents found her, she had lived two other places. We don't know much. It's impossible to get her to talk about what happened."

Of course she wouldn't want to talk about it.

My heartbeat echoed in my ears. I was so stupid—I had known that something was wrong.

We felt an attachment toward her from the moment we'd met. It had been familiar, our normal. The feeling made sense after we knew who she was. And while she would allow us to hug her or hold her, she'd been uncomfortable with anything more.

Her reactions had been worrisome. Out of all of us, Mu was the most affectionate.

We'd known something was off. Damen and I had gone over this and assumed that her anxiety stemmed from abuse. Sexual trauma wasn't unheard of, of course, but we hoped that wasn't the case with Bianca. She did allow us to touch her, after all.

We'd hoped it meant she was spared that pain.

But we were wrong, and in the worst possible way. Because Abigail Geier's department specialized in child trafficking.

"Where did they find her?" Damen's voice sounded odd, detached almost, and he continued to lean over the table. His shoulders were tight with strain.

"It doesn't matter." Hanah sighed. "It was abandoned shortly after they left. They never found the culprit. They kept looking, but Bianca never said anything that would help officials locate him—"

"It wasn't her responsibility to tell the investigators how to do their job." Miles's tone was venomous. "They immediately questioned a seven-year-old victim? Did they even give her a chance to see a therapist?"

It couldn't be true. They couldn't be that cruel.

"My mother." This must be how she got involved. "Did Abigail take Bianca to see her? Is that why she's still her patient?"

"Yes…" Hanah's voice wavered. "Bianca was terrified of her abilities. Anytime she talked about spirits, she would panic. That's one of the reasons why Dr. Kohler put her on suppressants. The theory was that she'd learn to live normally, she'd learn to not be afraid. Then they would reintroduce the paranormal back into her life."

"You didn't agree?" Miles had also picked up on her sneer.

"No, I didn't agree. I never thought lying was right. They wanted her to be normal, but Bianca was *never* going to be normal. You can't fix what happened, you can only move past it." Hanah's voice was sharp. "I couldn't stand seeing it. Why do you think I left? And Finn—"

My eyes snapped to the blond man. His head rested in his hands, his elbows braced on the table.

Damen began to quiver—he was about to lose it, and Titus still hadn't moved. This did not bode well.

"Finn what?" I asked, almost not wanting the answer.

"He's overprotective," Hanah said. "None of us know how to act around her. She's not getting any better, mentally. She refuses to talk in therapy. When you force it, she shuts down. He worries he—"

Finn cut her off. "She's not ready to be out yet. The courts are a dangerous place, even for the most worldly of fae. And you never know what might trigger one of her attacks. Sometimes it's seeing an act of violence. Other times it's her *research*. You all know that the worst of the world is easily seen on the internet."

Hanah turned to Finn in shock. "You're still restricting her searches? You told Kayla you would stop!"

"You have no idea what it's like! She wouldn't talk for a day because she accidently came across werewolf erotica!" Finn narrowed his eyes. "What else am I supposed to do? Somehow, I missed that one. Thankfully, it was yaoi, so she wasn't traumatized."

"I think you're underestimating her." Hanah crossed her arms. "Did you even try to talk to her to see if she was upset? Or were you assuming again? Jiayi says she's quiet when she's imagining something."

"She's *always* imagining something." Finn waved his hand in the air. "She's paranoid. She jumps to the worst possible conclusion and thinks everything is trying to kill her. She makes herself sick with worry."

"Shielding her from reality doesn't solve anything." Hanah frowned. "You're only making it worse."

Damen's low voice cut through their conversation. "How is Jiayi involved?"

"Jiayi is Bianca's roommate," Finn said, his voice sullen. "Don't be angry at her. She's only been brought in recently. We needed someone to watch her on campus when I couldn't."

"Surely you knew we'd find out; or she would notice something. This is a school for those with paranormal abilities!" Damen said.

"Unless you were planning on keeping her on medication forever," I pointed out. "It's not like the paranormal is overly emphasized here. It could be explained away."

"No. We knew we were out of time." Finn glowered at the table. "Dr. Kohler wanted to lower Bianca's dosage after midterms. The plan was to give Bianca a chance to get used to college life and for Du Yun to have time with her. It wasn't supposed to happen suddenly. You don't teach any of her classes, so you wouldn't have noticed," Finn said, nodding toward Damen. "Bryce's presence threw things off. We knew he'd eventually be interested in her. Even with suppressants, it couldn't be helped. But it helps that she hates him. I never expected her to stop her medication."

"*That's* why Do Yun is here?" I'd wondered why my Tongjun had decided to transfer his practice to this college but figured it wasn't my business.

"Why didn't you come to us for help? Why wait?" Damen's voice was still in that dangerous state. "You had to know we'd take care of things. She's *ours.*"

Finn flinched slightly. "Well, Dr. Kohler wanted Julian to finish school. Then there's…" He hesitated briefly, before glancing at Damen. "It's *you.*"

Damen pulled back, surprise flickering across his tight expression. "*Me?*"

"You'll sleep with any woman who gives you the time of day," Finn grumbled. "You're grabby, pushy, and you don't understand boundaries. You have two moods: carefree or angry. Bianca can't handle the flirty side of you, and anger frightens her. You would scare her, and no one wanted that."

I leveled my attention toward Finn—he wasn't wrong. But since when was he insightful? But also, considering recent events, he was a bit hypocritical.

"Actually, we've been doing rather well. Bianca and I have an agreement, and we didn't even require your help to manipulate our bond. We've created something that works for us. Besides, it doesn't matter. I don't even think she realizes I'm flirting with her most of the time." Damen looked offended. "Besides, *you're* the one who hurt her! You're the one who lost control of your abilities. If I hadn't stopped it, she'd be in serious trouble."

A flash of something—almost like panic—crossed Finn's expression. "I didn't mean to. I really didn't…"

"How did she end up in a place like that?" Bryce spoke for the first time since this conversation had begun, his voice was rife with disbelief. "I don't understand."

I knew what would happen a second beforehand. Still, when Damen snapped, I couldn't hold him back.

"This is all your fault! I don't know how you did it yet, but I'll find out!" Damen had crossed the room in a second, grabbing Bryce by the front of his shirt and slamming him to the floor. Chairs were thrown to the side as everyone clamored to their feet.

Chaos erupted, and once Damen had lost it, Titus was no longer under his control.

One instant he was restrained in a corner. The next, he was free. Miles's wards alone weren't enough to hold him back.

But Damen didn't seem to hear the dragon roar. Nor did the onmyoji notice Titus shattering the windows as he escaped into the dusk.

"Shit!" Miles stopped in front of me, pausing in his movements. His focus shifted between the broken window and Damen. "What do we—"

I rushed past him, grabbing his arm. "Titus will keep for now. We need to stop Damen first."

Hopefully, he'd only go to his house and destroy his room. But it didn't matter. Without Damen, Miles and I had no hope of controlling Titus by ourselves.

"Damen, stop!" Brayden was trying to pull Damen off Bryce, as was Anthony, but they weren't succeeding. Damen was so far gone even Anthony's abilities couldn't touch him. Which meant it would take all my concentration to break through to him.

I couldn't focus on what we'd learned, nor could I think about Finn. Even though he was watching the scene with more emotion than he'd had in a long while. He stood to the side, not stopping his brother. Nor did he seem concerned that Bryce was being beaten to death.

In fact, he watched the scene with the same level of animosity that Damen was displaying.

"Anthony." I pulled my brother's arm and he glanced at me. No longer was there humor in his gaze. "Stop Finn before he does something stupid," I said.

Anthony didn't question my order and backed off Damen immediately.

It had been difficult to stop Damen from killing Garrett Cole, but this anger was on an entirely different level. Damen was a powerful man. He wasn't at his full strength yet, but what he lacked in magic he made up for in raw physical strength.

Bryce wasn't even fighting back, but Damen was too far gone to notice. And he probably wouldn't before the other man became an unrecognizable husk of beaten flesh on the ground.

Miles was trying to separate the two of them, but Brayden was in the way. Panicking. His actions were becoming more of a hindrance than help.

"Hanah!" I spotted her. Between the two of them, they should be able to physically restrain Brayden. "Do something."

"O-okay!" She stepped beside Miles, and they were able to clear the way.

I hadn't had to resort to using this level of power in this lifetime. Because of that, it initially felt odd to reach for this magic.

My blood turned cold, and a ripple washed over me. Old magic prickled under my skin. An echo of the person I was once, a manifestation of the power that remained buried beneath my current skin.

"*Stop.*" I grabbed Damen's arm, directing my focus to him. "That's enough."

His movements slowed as he was no longer able to act freely. As his fists fell, his stunned eyes lifted.

I held his gaze, unrelenting. "I know you're upset. But this is not the time. We have other priorities."

His gaze bore into mine, and I could feel his resistance. His body shook with it.

"It'll be okay," I lied. It might not ever be okay again.

There was blood, so much blood. Splattered across his features, covering his torso and arms. I didn't even need to look at his hands to know that they were red, too.

I wondered if Bryce was still alive, but I couldn't check.

Damen blinked, and all the fury that had been present in his gaze vanished. Instead, he looked lost and afraid. Completely unlike his usual cocky, annoying, arrogant self.

He'd broken, and it wasn't hard to guess why.

Huo's weakness had always been Mu. I controlled Fire through force. But Mu could get him to do anything with only a word. Mu inspired him.

Tu, our spiritual leader and Miles's incarnation, traveled for work. And Jin—Titus's first life—was a general. He spent half of his time on the battlefield, working to make Mu's plots a reality. Neither were particularly close to Huo.

I stayed in the palace, or rather, the dungeons. My responsibilities consisted of dealing with spies, or suspected spies. The traitors. They were all sent to me, and they knew that death was coming.

I could destroy a person from the inside out, and then get answers from their dead bodies. I had spent lifetimes perfecting my craft, and I reveled in the violence. Darkness and blood were my domain.

I did it for him.

Mu was always Seelie. He *could* kill. He was rather good it, actually. He was a logical person and detached himself from his emotions during stressful situations. But his heart had never been into it.

He was the optimist, he always tried to see the positive. And his instincts were frighteningly accurate. It was he and Tu who held the rest of us together. Huo, Jin, and I were simply too different.

But although we all carried aspects of our previous lives, Bianca wasn't Mu.

In some ways, she was the same. Her mind was always working, and the conclusions she came up with—the ones that I'd heard at least—weren't technically wrong.

Although they did border on the more dramatic side.

However, in this life, a darkness existed in the way she thought.

Bianca was naive, but that was because she was being fed incorrect information. Her strangest thoughts though might even be denial. Her way of thinking had lost its innocence.

We had seen signs but hadn't put the pieces together.

Bianca was terrified of being hurt, unless it was in a situation where she was defending others. People frightened her. And she was petrified of relationships and physical intimacy.

Now we understood why.

No wonder Damen looked so lost. I felt the same. We had been so obsessed with who she was, and the danger that she'd been in, that we hadn't been focused on her.

We were moving too fast. We were already failing.

But nothing good would come from wallowing in self-pity.

Damen fell back, subdued. With him out of the way, I focused on Bryce.

I wasn't sure how he was still conscious. But he was pushing away from the two of us, holding his face.

I reached for him, but he raised his arm in response. "No," he wheezed. "Forget about it."

Forget about it? His face was already swelling, and it looked like he had a broken nose. "Bryce—"

He staggered to his feet, then Brayden and Anthony were at his side, helping him stand. Bryce ignored them. "Don't bother," he told me, and avoiding eye contact, the three of them left the room.

Miles stepped beside me, looking equally guilty.

Bianca's top officers were our best bet at keeping her safe. And Bryce had been pummeled to a pulp. I should have done more to help him.

At the same time, I felt strangely detached about the situation. Now that I thought about it, Damen wasn't wrong. How had Bianca become the Xing to begin with? What about Bailey?

Bryce *had* done something, I was certain. Or he knew about it, at the very least. The only thing that had kept me from hurting him myself was the self-loathing in his eyes.

We would have to talk to the Dubois family. There was no way this was a coincidence.

"Julian?" Miles looked at me, devastation on his face. "What do we do? I can't even…"

My chest heaved under the weight of the added responsibility. Miles was supposed to be the level-headed one—but he was barely able to function.

It would have to be my responsibility, for now.

"First"—I faced the broken window—"we need to find Titus. Finn." The other man was moving toward the door. He paused mid-step, glancing at me. "You're staying with us."

Chapter Three

Bianca
Demand

The hallways had been unnaturally silent for a while, and I'd been left alone with my thoughts. I didn't know how long I'd been here, but it felt like forever.

Dr. Reed visited me frequently. So did Julian. But he hadn't come in a while.

I didn't know what she expected from our short sessions, but as time went by, she seemed to be happier. That seemed like a good thing. It probably meant I wasn't dying.

Just like before, I was treated differently than other patients. The aides didn't interact with me, only doing their jobs. They brought food, sometimes a change of clothes. They also brought me my medication.

I took it, because if I didn't, I knew they could force me to. That much had been made perfectly clear.

Unlike before, the staff was a tiny bit friendlier. I wasn't certain why they'd changed, but I suspected it had to do with Julian's presence.

I wasn't sure what to think about that.

Others had been afraid of him, too, and I couldn't imagine why. Was there something I hadn't noticed? Try as I might, I couldn't find a single reason for anyone to fear Julian.

It made no sense.

He was one of the kindest people I'd ever met. And out of all my friends, he and Miles were the easiest to talk to. Despite everything, I considered myself a pretty good judge of character.

It was obvious there was something I was missing, and that knowledge nagged at me.

And where was he?

The hours lagged by, and I reflected on the mystery of Julian's existence rather than the reality of what was happening.

A soft knock sounded through the room, breaking through my thoughts. My head snapped up in time to see Julian closing the door.

His eyes briefly met mine before his attention moved to the untouched tray at the foot of my bed. "Darling, you didn't eat again?"

"I'm not hungry," I said. Tasteless prison food held no appeal, and I didn't trust anyone to not try to kill me—even if they were afraid of Julian. Death by food would be a poetic way to die. It was becoming ever apparent I would have to take poisoning lessons from Bryce.

That was, if I would be allowed to leave.

Darn it, I was even starting to miss *him*. Glaring at Bryce had been such a fulfilling pastime. And things would be better between us now. He had submitted. I could order him around to my heart's content. It would be great.

I was losing my mind.

"Bianca." The bed dipped as Julian sat. A long moment later, the weight of his arm draped my frame and he pulled me to him. "I brought you something."

The familiar words, spoken by Titus not so long ago, caused a pang to shoot through my chest. With everything that had happened, I had forgotten to follow up on his mother's hairpin. Surely it was destroyed, and I had made such a scene over it. He had to know.

But why hadn't he said anything when I saw him in the hospital?

I missed them all so much.

I wanted to ask Julian about the others. Not knowing was driving me crazy. He was close, and it was impossible to not see the pain in his eyes. It was a look that caused my heart to ache. "What's wrong?"

He blinked, stunned at my question, but a moment later the emotion vanished. Completely replaced with a serenity that I knew, now, to be a lie.

"Julian?" Something had happened, I was certain.

Julian sighed, pulling out a small cloth bundle and handing it to me before he continued. "There's a lot going on right now, and it's stressful. Titus has destroyed his mansion, and—"

"Why did Titus destroy his home?" I asked. I no longer watched him, opening the handkerchief to find a small, yellow cake. "You brought me food? What is this?"

"It's a honey cake," Julian said, breaking off a piece and placing it in my mouth. "Miles made it for you. Titus was upset, but he's under control now. We'll figure it out."

My lips tingled where Julian's fingers touched me, and the sweet flavor of the cake spread through my mouth. I'd been ravenous, and this was one of the first things I'd eaten in a while. But how did Miles know my favorite food?

"Thank you." I licked my lips. "I didn't realize what it was. It looks different from the way Finn makes it. Honey cake is my favorite."

Julian's brows furrowed. "Finn made you cake?"

I nodded, holding my hands out in the shape of a small circle. "Every day he'd give me one like this. It was flat. I've never seen one look like a muffin before."

Julian pinched his nose. "Finn made you cake."

My heart jerked. I'd never thought anything of it, but what if this was a bad thing? What if everything was part of Finn's sinister plans? "Shouldn't he have?"

"It's a sign of affection." Julian sounded put out, his face still hidden beneath his hand. "It's tradition to leave offerings to the fae. Usually those offerings are in the form of small cakes, milk, chocolate, and fruits."

My face flushed. I wasn't sure what Julian was saying, but it wasn't like him to speak about Finn without death threats. "I thought you hated Finn."

"Oh, I still dislike him immensely, don't worry." Julian dropped his hand as his eyes met mine. "But I've also become aware there are some things that need reevaluation."

Reevaluation? What did that mean?

He watched me as he raised his hand, almost touching my face. He seemed almost afraid.

Before I could question it, his fingers grazed my cheek.

I could barely feel him, but the connection was stronger than anything we'd shared before. And as I watched him curiously, I couldn't stop myself from leaning into his touch.

Why wasn't he saying anything? Why was he acting so strange? "Julian?"

"You really don't mind when I touch you?" Julian asked, his gaze softening. There was a hint of disbelief in his voice.

My eyebrow raised in response. Didn't we already have this discussion? "I already told you I like it… I still have that word to use if I don't."

"But you don't like anyone other than us four touching you?" Julian seemed to be searching for something. I wasn't sure what, but his question caused a shiver to shoot down my spine.

"N-no," I answered, my breath thin. "I don't like when other people touch me."

Julian tilted his head, and the weight of his attention was almost suffocating. "Why?"

Why in the world was he talking about this now?

"I just don't!" My attention turned to the lapel of his shirt. This was a stupid conversation. "It makes me feel sick."

"Bianca." His soft voice urged me to face him. "When we first met, were you afraid of us?"

I narrowed my eyes. How quick he was to forget—

"Besides you thinking Titus was scary," Julian clarified, a smile touching his expression before it vanished. "Were you ever afraid of the way we touched you? We were strangers. I held your hand…"

My breath caught. This was the strangest line of questioning ever. But their actions had stood out to me. I knew it was odd that, instead of making me feel sick, being with them had felt right.

I had never let anyone get that close to me before, not even Finn.

Sure, sometimes I'd hold Finn's hand. That hadn't been horrible, and there was something that drew me to him. But it had taken getting used to and

Finn was never affectionate, so it was rare for that to happen.

Then there was my ill-thought-out plan to marry him... How awful. But that was because I knew nothing else, no one else. I couldn't imagine anything different. I would get over it.

But when I met the boys... It had been different than anything I'd experienced before. I thought it was strange to feel as if this was familiar, but I never questioned it either.

It felt weird to admit this to Julian, but he looked so concerned. I had to tell him.

"Even from the beginning, I wasn't afraid your touch." I glanced away, biting my lip. "Not even Titus..."

Julian's hooked his finger under my chin, tilting my head toward his, and it was his turn to raise his eyebrow. "But you maced him, kicked him in the balls, and ran away. You were clearly afraid."

My voice squeaked. "Because he was scary. He was *stalking* me. He *felt* scary." I couldn't believe we were talking about this. "But when he *held* me, I wasn't scared. I only worried that he might drag me into the Mafia underworld and murder me."

"Titus isn't part of the 'Mafia.' That's such an outdated term." He still watched me, concerned. "And he would never have hurt you. Are you sure you weren't scared?"

What in the *world* did that mean? I wanted to ask for more Mafia clarification, but Julian's expression indicated he was still stuck on this touching topic. Why he was suddenly so obsessed with this, I didn't know.

So I tried to reflect honestly. Titus had held me a lot, and there had even been a time where I had only worn a towel. But...

I shook my head. I hadn't been afraid. I wasn't sure how to describe how it made me feel, but it wasn't normal. "I wasn't scared. Is that weird?"

Was that relief swimming in his eyes? But why would he care?

"You aren't strange," Julian said, tapping my nose. "Not if you consider our past bonds. Whatever happened to make you have this fear in this life, you've had lifetimes of memories with us. Even if you don't recollect that connection, your subconscious does."

The pressure against my chest seemed to lift. Of course there was a logical explanation for my behavior.

And now, on to more important things.

"If Titus isn't Mafia, then what is he?"

"Not Mafia," Julian responded as he broke off another piece of cake and lifted it to my lips. "It's more like a collaborative."

A *collaborative*. That explained nothing.

But I couldn't ask. I could only watch Julian with suspicion as he kept shoving food in my mouth. He was avoiding the subject, and after three more pieces, I held back his hand. "What collaborative?"

Julian sighed, clearly uncomfortable. "It's shifter business. We stay out of each other's work. You'll need to ask Titus."

Oh, I would.

Collaborative shifter business that was not Mafia, but was probably the same thing. I freaking knew it.

What in the world did Titus do all day? "Does he kill people?"

"Maybe?" Julian shrugged. "I don't know. I've never asked."

He totally killed people.

Even if Julian had never asked, he obviously suspected. Visions of Titus slaughtering his enemies while covered in their blood danced through my mind.

Did he wear a suit while doing his 'shifter business'? Or maybe that's what the plaid was for.

It didn't matter, either scenario made my skin warm.

"Darling." Julian touched my face. "Titus wouldn't hurt you."

I glanced at him in confusion. He was bringing this up *again*? "I know that."

"Oh." Julian face morphed in confusion. "Then what…"

"Never mind." It was suddenly difficult to meet his eyes. I wasn't even sure what had come over me. "I'm tired," I said, leaning back into his chest.

"Go to sleep then," Julian replied, patting down my hair. "I'll be here."

Despite being tired, I couldn't sleep. So we laid in silence as I soaked in Julian's presence.

But, eventually, Julian was asked to leave. There was a sense of loneliness in the wake of his exit. This was a strange feeling, almost as if I was growing to depend on his presence.

Honestly? I didn't like it.

I'd grown to depend on people once before, and look at what had happened.

I went from struggling to survive, to not having a say in my own life. My adoptive parents decided everything for me: where I was to go to school, what I wore, and even what I ate. As I got older, my mother tried to control what I read. And Father—even though it was never an issue—decided I wouldn't be allowed to date. I went along without complaint because I was so grateful to have a family. I tried to pretend things were normal, although, in my heart I knew they weren't.

Then there was Finn.

Somehow, he'd wormed his way past my defenses. I could have fought it harder, but I wanted a friend. But still, it had taken me so long to become attached. Once we were friends, I was afraid to disappoint him. It felt strange to recall that only a few short weeks ago, I believed I was in love with him. The thought, now, was horrifying.

What if I was projecting my need for acceptance onto Julian and the others?

Julian kept talking about a bond and how everything between us was normal.

What if they were only nice to me because of who I used to be. I didn't know anything about that person, and I had no memory of any past lives. I wasn't even sure I fully believed in it.

But—if it was true—there was no way we were the same person.

The boys were leaders. People looked up to them, and they seemed to know what they were talking about. They were also able to defend themselves and weren't scared of anything.

This person who was supposed to be me—he had to be like that, right?

If that were the case, something must be wrong with me. I wasn't strong. I couldn't function, I was messed up.

This must be why everyone wanted to keep me secret. The realization hurt. At the same time, it was a reality check.

I wasn't stupid. If I wanted things to change, I would have to start with myself. I was going to have to prove everyone wrong.

But it was going to be so, *so* hard.

The short meadow grass tickled my bare feet, and gray clouded the sky, making it difficult to tell the time. The air was heavy and stale, and only my immediate surroundings held any color. Outside of that, a blank canvas that stretched in every direction.

I was lonely, so lonely. The ache of it was a painful pressure against my chest.

"Mu." A voice drifted to me. It was a feminine, husky sound, and so familiar. Yet recognition remained just out of grasp. "You're finally waking up."

Her words were different, not English. The meaning translated to me regardless.

"We had an agreement," she said, her tone a strange mixture between alarm and annoyance. "They're trying to stop us, and you must wake up. Tu is already becoming suspicious, and the others will soon follow."

A strangeness settled over my body. I no longer felt like myself.

I responded, even though the words weren't my own. "Did I not make you a promise? You need to trust me."

The world moved and color began to break through, swirling through the air. Black and red, and so much green, but nothing further than that.

The voice that was mine continued, "Is it still love?"

After my question, the colors stilled, and the scene snapped into focus.

A woman stood in front of me. She looked tall, but for once, I didn't feel short in comparison. She was thin, with black hair that reached the ground. It fell around her like a silk blanket. She wore an elegant gown that showed no skin but her neck and head, and the redness of it matched her painted lips.

Her mouth pointed down as she looked at me, and her golden eyes flashed with annoyance.

"I don't know. Human emotions are so strange," she said, glancing to the side. "But I thought out of everyone, you would understand, considering."

My attention turned to our surroundings.

We were in a forest, and the trees arched over us. The space was secluded, and no one could find us unless I willed it so. And that wouldn't happen. Not even the others could know.

This meeting had to remain secret. They weren't ready.

But why?

"Where am I?" This time when I spoke, it was under my direction. But the sound still wasn't mine; though the voice was light, the tenor was too deep. Male.

The woman glanced back at me, and amusement flickered in her eyes. "Where are you now?" she asked, tilting her head. "Are you here, or are you sleeping?"

What a strange question. I was here, wasn't I?

But I also didn't know where here was… "I don't know."

I didn't know, although the scenery was inherently comforting. This place was old, and it was mine. I knew this, just as I knew her. At the thought, my heart began to race, because slowly, trickling into my awareness, was reality.

I'd heard this woman before. This was the voice that haunted my nightmares. "You?"

I watched her as I pressed my hands over my pounding heart. Shadowed recollections flashed through my mind. And suddenly, this woman's presence turned into a threat. Although I was unable to pinpoint exactly why.

"You called me your imaginary friend." Her smile was almost sad. "And here I thought our connection was so much more than that."

Why was she here? I thought I'd outgrown this. "Why—"

Once again, the air moved. Without warning the scene faded around me, leaving me with a sense of emptiness and longing.

"Don't wait so long in between visits, Mu." Her voice circled the air. "We've much to catch up on."

Her words still echoed in my ears as I sat up. My hands shook, and I clutched at the sheets, bringing them to my chin, as though they could be a shield between me and my racing thoughts.

It was *her*, the voice that Dr. Reed had asked me about. There was no way this was a coincidence. Even so, I couldn't tell her it was back. Who knew what kind of things they'd do to me? And Julian, he was already so worried. If he really knew how messed up I was…

Well, there was no way they'd be all right with that.

This was something I would need to figure out on my own.

A loud thump drew my attention to the door, and I pulled the sheets tighter around me, barely able to see through the darkness of my tiny cell. "W-w-who's there?"

The door opened, and one of the younger nurses popped in her head. "She's awake." She glanced back behind her, tucking her curly brown hair behind her ear. "Might as well get it over with, then you can go on break."

"Fine," came a deep male's voice in response.

My heart was beating furiously now as trepidation filled me. With my every breath, the room grew more and more out of focus.

Brightness filled the room, causing spots to fill my vision, and they stepped into the room—two female nurses and a dark-haired male—pushing a cart between them. It was covered with a white towel, and there was no way to tell what was on it.

My body and thoughts had become sluggish with the continuation of my medication, but I still had enough clarity to press myself against the corner of the bed. The bronze of the barred headboard felt cold under my bare arms.

But even after they'd entered the room, locking the door behind them, the three of them never even glanced in my direction as they surrounded the cart—blocking it from my view.

"W-w-what are you d-d-doing?" I didn't really expect them to answer—they never did. But I couldn't help myself in asking anyway.

To my surprise, the redhead with a pixie cut peeked at me. She was the only nurse I'd seen in days who seemed to regard me with anything close to compassion. "It's time to change your bandages."

Really? That might not be so bad. But wasn't it in the middle of the night?

It was hard to keep track. "W-w-what time is i-i-it?"

"Don't *talk* to her," the brunette snapped. "Didn't you get the memo, Tiffany? She's dangerous. Fae cannot be trusted, especially this one."

I blinked, stunned by the strange remark. I'd known they thought I was bad—but there'd been a memo sent out? I hadn't done anything wrong.

"W-w-what?"

No one answered, and during my brief moment of distraction, the large male nurse had closed in on me. He grabbed my ankle, jerking me down the bed. My broken yelp echoed throughout the room, and before I could regain my bearings, my wrists had already been restrained.

Adrenaline was burning through me, and I kicked out as confusion and fear clouded my thoughts. "W-w-what—"

But then a cloth was roughly shoved into my mouth, cutting off my question. Darkness swam in the corner of my vision, and it had nothing to do with the fluorescent lights blindingly shining down on me.

"I can't believe we got stuck with this," the woman's sharp tones cut through the room. "Cover her eyes already, Jayden. The Fae can steal your soul with just a glance."

"She seems pretty harmless," Tiffany responded, her voice soft.

"That's what they want you to think," the first nurse said. "Bryce Dubois is pretty to look at too. But those who've been bewitched by him feel differently. Don't let your guard down, their type wouldn't even hesitate to rip out your guts."

My throat closed as the male nurse—Jayden—dropped a cloth over my face. Panic filled my senses—now I couldn't see *or* talk. I tried to scream, but the sound was muffled. The only thing I could feel was the cloth bindings cutting into my wrists, and a large hand pressing down on my knees.

I was going to be sick.

"If you're so afraid, why did you take this job?" Jayden asked, there was a hint of humor in his question.

"Well, we never expected *her* kind to come here now, did we?" she snapped in response. "Usually they keep to their own facilities. Now shut up and move over, I need to do my job."

Cold hands loosened the neck of my gown, and my blood turned to ice as the bindings around my neck were removed.

Logically, I knew it would be less painful to just let them do what they wanted. But my common sense had fled with the remains of my calm. When her touch turned painful, I couldn't hold back my outward display of panic.

Something—a bottle perhaps—crashed to the floor, and the hand that had been pushing against my neck moved to my wounded shoulder instead.

"Stop squirming!" she growled, a hint of panic in her tone. "You're making it worse."

It hurt, and I howled into the gag, shaking.

"Maybe she's in pain?" Tiffany sounded farther away than the others. "Is it time for her medication?"

"It can't make it worse. Give me half," the nurse said, sighing. "And throw in a sedative. She's making this impossible. We don't have all night."

I jerked at my bindings. The movement caused fire to flare down my arm, but I didn't care.

"Are you—" Tiffany began, sounding unsure.

"Just do it," the brunette interrupted. "Who is the senior nurse here, you or me?"

The other woman sighed, and a moment later a needle was jabbed into the skin between my neck and shoulder.

Tears filled my eyes as the last semblance of control stripped from me. Numbness fell into place of my panic. My skin crawled, but I couldn't make sense of it.

I was so tired.

I needed to breathe, but it was so hard.

Voices drifted around me, but nothing made sense. My ears buzzed as my thoughts drifted.

This wasn't so bad.

But then I gagged. The cloth covering my face was wet, and I choked as the damp weight threatened to pull me under.

"Be careful!" The not-so-bad nurse said somewhere in the background.

"I tripped," said the male. "It happens. These bowls suck."

It felt as though my heart might burst, and as another wave washed over me, I gave in to the darkness.

Chapter Four

Titus
Regret

Sunlight peeked through the blinds, illuminating the room. Like the daybreak bringing light into the dark, rationality was beginning to cut through the chaos of my thoughts.

The world was beginning to clear.

Regaining control over my beast was a slow process. When my dragon was closer to the surface, everything was sharper, more focused. Instincts, emotions, the drive to protect.

I was the barrier between the world and my quintet. And it was my job, *specifically*, to protect Bianca. I controlled Mu in nature, and that had always given the fae a sense of fragility in my eyes.

When Bianca had stepped into our group, it hadn't taken long for my instincts to take over. Mu had always complimented me, too. His logical—but wild—strategies inspired me, and between us, we'd secured countless victories.

Every life, I had been born first for the sole purpose of making sure he was safe.

And this time, I'd failed.

There was plenty of evidence of my failure, stacked in neat piles on my desk. I glared at the folders that were filled with painful words I had spent the night pouring over. On the other side of my desk were two small digital drives—interviews I'd yet to watch.

After I escaped Damen, I hadn't been certain where to go. But my rage required an outlet.

What I *wanted* was to take her away from everything. I could have made it work. It was possible to disappear, to make it so even the council would never have been able to find us.

We'd been reborn countless times, and into countless cultures throughout the world. As such, I'd been able to prepare little by little, with each life. There were no limits to my safe homes and allies.

I always prepared for the worst-case scenario. Warfare had grown deadlier with every generation, and the dark side of human nature was more evident in the battlefield than anywhere else. I'd worked in law enforcement, and on the other side. Both were equally corrupt.

The others weren't completely naive about the cruelty of the world. But they hadn't been witnesses to mass bloodshed year after year.

Nor had they ever seen crimes like human trafficking up close…

They knew what it *meant*. And I was sure they could imagine the horrors that Bianca must have suffered. But they'd never seen it.

I had.

My company subcontracted out to law enforcement agencies. I also owned satellite companies, straddling the gray areas of the law. Shifters were generally stronger, healed faster, and had senses the normal population didn't. In many cases, it was our shifter abilities that stood between taking down a criminal or letting them go free.

So, yes, I'd witnessed the aftermath of many raids. Usually, victims were caught in the crossfire. And I'd seen too many mangled bodies in filthy rooms. The sight haunted my nights.

Humanity never seemed to outgrow their cruel nature. Despite knowing this, such depravity always managed to surprise me.

And now, every time I closed my eyes, I imagined Bianca as one of those children.

When I left the others, I returned home.

I returned because there wasn't a second longer to waste. Hanah said her tormentor had vanished, and that was unacceptable. It meant the likelihood was high he roamed free to this day. It was a rare and difficult thing to bring down a trafficking network.

Until I learned otherwise, I would assume he was still out there.

I couldn't talk to Bianca about this, not yet. But I would need to soon.

She was vindictive, and brave—even if she was damaged. I could see it in her eyes. When we first met, she had been scared. But she still struck out against me. And she instinctively fought for Damen.

She believed she was weak, but she was far stronger than she knew.

It was too soon to force her to confront this now. That didn't mean that I couldn't prepare in the meantime.

I only hoped I could handle it.

The door clicked open, and Damen entered my office. His presence dragged my attention from the small pile of recordings on my desk.

"You found a video interview?" he asked, noting where my attention had been. He loosened his tie, slumping into the chair across my desk. It looked like he hadn't slept last night either.

"Maria brought them a little while ago." I glanced back at my desk, thankful for my cousin.

Sometime between my rampage and returning to my office, she had been told. The instant I arrived, touching down on the roof, she was there for me. There had been no pity in her gaze. She didn't question my actions. She only asked what my next steps were.

I needed information on Abigail Grier's investigations.

Shortly thereafter, the others arrived. Supposedly, it was shocking that I was 'functioning.' Which was absurd. Who did they think dealt with the most amount of pressure? Did they not understand how wars were won?

Even so, once I explained my research, Damen remained with me, demanding to help. I was certain he thought he was helping me control the dragon, although it was unnecessary. But it didn't matter, I'd rather have him where I could see him anyway.

Miles was in and out of my office. He'd started looking for ways to extricate Bianca from the current situation. She was over eighteen, but had been declared medically incompetent. We had the option to fight that, but it would result in a messy legal battle.

Going to court would draw the council's attention. That was something we needed to avoid at all costs.

Julian was able to see her, at least. But from his worn expression, I wasn't sure if it was something to be jealous about. He was worried, which caused Miles to worry even more. Julian said she hadn't been eating and she looked sick.

Julian's words spurred Miles to work harder. Once Julian left, Miles also vanished and hadn't returned the rest of the night. From what I understood, he was doing research at the school and contacting his mentors.

It was best to let him be. He came up with his best ideas when alone.

"Have you been up all night?" Damen was alert. He leaned over my desk, his eyes seeking mine. "Did you watch them yet?"

"Not yet," I said, my voice scratchy. "I'm bracing myself."

Damen frowned, his expression knowing. "You should have let me know. I was awake anyway. You didn't have to sit in here glaring at them all alone."

"It wasn't just the videos." I nodded pointedly at the manila folders. Damen raised an eyebrow and reached for them, but I didn't want him to expect to find anything helpful. "They're useless."

Damen shot me a look of alarm. "Useless?" He picked up the top folder anyway and opened it, turning his attention to the pages. "What—"

"Almost everything helpful has been redacted," I summarized. "When Bianca was adopted, it was done swiftly and with little legal involvement. Outside of that, any instance of entering her further into our system was avoided. That's probably why her name had never been changed. When she was declared medically unfit, it was granted under Dr. Kohler's suggestion. Bianca's never even been to court."

Damen lowered the papers slightly, glancing at me. "But didn't Hanah imply that Bianca had been questioned? She'd had to have been to court, or have at least seen a lawyer?"

I shook my head. "Everything went through Dr. Kohler. They never even released Bianca's name alongside Abigail's work. Unless they knew Abigail adopted the child they wanted to question, investigators wouldn't have any indication she was the same person. In most cases, after a child is rescued from that kind of situation, they are put into shelters—homes equipped to deal with their psychological needs before returning to society. A victim wouldn't have been moved in with a family right away. I'm certain it was done to hide her. When Dr. Kohler speaks of Bianca, she only identities her as 'The Victim.' She answers all questions on Bianca's behalf."

"And no one was suspicious? Especially with that kind of timing…" Damen was thumbing through the files. "I find that hard to believe."

"I'm sure people were," I replied. "I would have been. But nothing could be done about it. She had guardians at that point, and they refused to allow her to be questioned. As did her personal doctor. They would have to make a strong case to forcibly bring her in."

"Not that it would have been good to question her…" Damen muttered, frowning down at the empty papers. "I'm grateful they didn't. But I'm only saying…"

He hadn't realized it yet, so I added, "If she was put into a shelter or questioned, the elders would have found out who she was."

Damen let go of the paper, and his head shot up. "I didn't even consider that." He dropped the folder closed and pinched the bridge of his nose. "I don't know if I should kill them or thank them. So much should have gone differently. They lied about her whole life. And there is a lot we don't know, but…"

"If they hadn't done it this way, she'd be dead." It was painful to admit the truth, but until I was able to use my abilities fully it would have been impossible for me to protect her. In fact, once the elders learned about her, it was going to be next to impossible *now*.

The council was established to keep the balance in between our rebirth cycles. When we were here, they were supposed act as a counterbalance to our authority. And while we created the council, it wouldn't be good to retract our own declarations.

It was the council who would have a problem with Bianca being born a female. They were prejudiced, and all because of a prophecy even Damen hadn't been able to confirm.

And as far as I was concerned, if Damen hadn't predicted it, it was of no consequence.

Damen covered his face, so his voice was muffled. "You're right. You know, once she gets out, we need a reason for her to be with us. Something that they won't suspect…"

The last part of his statement remained unsaid, but I knew what he meant.

We needed to keep them off our backs. We might have rushed into this, but we couldn't survive without her now. I couldn't send her away either. There were only a few people we trusted, and who knew what might happen without us. I refused to risk it.

Especially after what she'd already been through.

My attention returned to the recordings. Disgust caused the hair on my arms to raise. I wanted to shift, to destroy something. Reading the files, even with most information blacked out, was enough to stir my anger once again.

The files, the recordings. It had made everything real. This wasn't just a story. It was something that had actually happened.

Before I could catch myself, I snarled. Damen's head snapped up.

"Titus." He frowned, touching the edge of my desk. "You can't. We have work to do!"

"I know that." It was becoming harder to keep control, even with Damen's presence. It had to be this mate business, because I'd never come this close before.

"Let's just watch it," I snapped. "Putting it off isn't going to change anything."

"Can you handle it?" Damen's cautious gaze bore into me. His presence a reminder that, if necessary, he had the power to subdue me.

But I didn't want him to interfere. I needed to feel angry. It made every detail clearer, and put my instincts on full alert.

"I'll be fine." I set up my computer, forcing myself to touch one of the small drives.

Damen sucked in his breath, and I swiveled the screen to where we both could see. A moment later, the video flickered to life, displaying the familiar sight of an interview room.

Sitting at the table was Abigail, younger and not as angry.

The interview began. Within moments, it became obvious this wouldn't be helpful.

It was only a preliminary disclosure. Abigail was asked to accept the mission despite her retirement. Her employers knew almost nothing about their target. They had an address, which branded itself on my subconsciousness. They also had a general overview of what to expect, from conjecture.

The majority of their suspicions lay in sketchy school reports, and a claim that the location, which claimed to be a center for troubled foster children, had a far more sinister background.

But outside of that, there was nothing. Not even a name.

Damen was rubbing his forehead by the end, and I frowned at the screen. If the second file was as useless as this one, I wouldn't be happy.

Hoping we'd get a lead, or anything at all, I switched out the drives.

The screen flickered to life, and this time it was Dr. Kohler seated at the table.

Her hands were folded in front of her, and she was giving a disapproving look at the interviewer. The camera angled toward the back of his head. It was only possible to see that he was of medium build and had black hair.

The way he held himself seemed familiar, but I couldn't place him. Which was odd, because normally my recollection for people was perfect.

Before I had a chance to think on it, the interview began.

"Can you state your name for the record?" he asked, his voice an emotionless droll. And again, something about the man triggered memories I couldn't grasp.

"Dr. Trinity Reed," she said, still frowning at the man. "And as I've already told you, I'm not telling you who she is. I have an obligation to my patients."

"No one is telling you to disclose your patient's identity," the man said. "But you will provide us with *some* information. You're not breaking any confidentiality agreements."

If Dr. Kohler could have shot flames from her eyes, the interviewer would have been a scorched spot on the floor.

"Or would you also like a lawyer to be present?" he asked. "I'm certain that we could request a continuance, go before a judge, and—"

"No," she interrupted, still glaring daggers at the man. "I don't want to drag anyone else into this. What do you want?"

"How cooperative." The man sounded pleased as he shuffled some papers on the desk. "Four months ago, we sent an investigator to scope out a potential trafficking hub. She reported that it was run by a man known as Eric Richards. Shortly thereafter, that same investigator adopted a young girl named Bianca Brosnan. We've been made aware that around the same time, you'd taken on a high-risk patient who was removed from Eric Richards's custody."

"I'm not certain how you've heard that, but it is a coincidence. Everything else sounds above of my paygrade." Dr. Kohler was frowning at the man. "I'm not sure what you're asking."

"Eric Richards is a pseudonym," he replied. "We've raided his base, and everything was abandoned. There is also no information on an Eric

Richards anywhere. We are certain that, if we could speak to her, then—"

Dr. Kohler laughed. "You're asking me to allow you to question my patient—a child—who was living in a highly abusive environment?"

"Yes," the man said coolly. "I know how it seems, but she wasn't the only one there. Other children are at risk. We wouldn't be asking if this wasn't our last resort. We need her to talk to us."

"She's not going to talk to you." Dr. Kohler watched the man warily. "She's in no condition to do so, and no judge can force that. Attempting to do this would be detrimental to her mental wellbeing, and I will not allow it." She paused, and her mouth dipped before she continued. "But, if you wanted to know if she knew Eric Richards to have any other name, the answer is no."

The man's fingers twitched. "How do you know?" She gave him a pointed look, and he sat up straighter in his seat. "You've read her?"

Dr. Kohler was quiet a moment before she responded, and her tight expression fell slightly. "Sometimes transference can't be helped, especially in highly emotional situations. The fear she has when she speaks about him… You won't be able to get her to talk about it, but I doubt she knows him as anyone else. You won't get anywhere continuing in this direction."

He was silent, tapping his pen over his paper before he spoke again. This time there was a thread of hesitance in his question. "Your patient… In what manner of imprisonment was she…" his voice trailed off at the look on Dr. Kohler's face.

"What?" her voice was like ice.

"We know there's trafficking involved, but we don't know the magnitude of the matter." He waved his hand in the air, frantic for the first time. "We've never been able to pinpoint what exactly he was up to. If I can report with how dangerous this man is, then maybe we'd have more resources allocated to—"

"She was prey," Dr. Kohler cut in, her tone just as cold as before. "She was sexually abused, but she suffered other injuries as well. It's obvious she had been hunted for sport. You're looking for a shifter."

Chapter Five

Bianca

Limits

"You look upset." Dr. Reed's voice cut through my thoughts and I glanced at her. "Did something happen?"

She and Julian had been conversing on the other side of the room for the past five minutes. I was taking advantage of quiet, still shivering from a feeling I couldn't quite place.

When I woke up, everything seemed normal. I was dry, in my bed, and the morning nurses seemed the same as always. Had I imagined the night before?

It was possible. I had also had that very weird dream right before. I might even be going crazy.

I couldn't tell Dr. Reed though, it would make everything worse. I had to get better, or she would get suspicious. I hadn't even realized they were paying attention to me.

We were in an office, as Dr. Reed had decided to move my therapy sessions somewhere other than my room.

Julian had arrived a few minutes late today, but his presence seemed to curtail Dr. Reed's questions about disembodied voices—a topic she didn't want to let up on. However, she seemed to avoid discussing the topic further in front of Julian, for which I was thankful.

Did I hear voices? Did it feel like I was losing control of my abilities?

There was no way to admit to something like that. Besides, how was I supposed to judge anything about my abilities?

"I'm fine," I said, referencing her constant questions about my abilities. "I can't feel them as easily"—I glanced toward the door, outside of which a spirit lingered. The asylum was filled with them—"but they're still here."

"Bianca." Her voice urged for my attention. "Finn mentioned something that concerns me."

Of course he did, the traitor.

"He claims you told him your medication never worked." She sounded odd, and, if I wasn't wrong, appeared to be fearful. It didn't escape my attention that Julian was now watching her in interest as well. "Is this true? Why did you never say anything?"

It was no use lying now, since we all had abilities here.

That knowledge was strange, to say the least.

I pushed back on the settee, wrapping my arms around my knees as I watched the two of them. Right now, Julian was my doctor, not my friend. This distinction was glaringly obvious in where we sat. It also hadn't escaped my notice that when Dr. Reed touched his arm as he moved to come to me, he had stopped.

The look in his eyes made my soul ache.

With difficulty, my focus tore from his and returned to hers. "I don't want to talk about this."

Dr. Reed sighed. "If you don't discuss this, no one will know the correct dosage to give to you. We could over-medicate you. Even if you don't want to talk about anything else, please don't lie about your medication. Why didn't you tell me the truth?"

I watched my feet. This wasn't fair. Nothing she was saying explained why I needed medication to begin with. No one could answer that, apparently.

"Bianca—"

"I didn't want them to send me back." I hated this, but if I didn't respond, she was only going to keep asking. "If I was normal, they wouldn't have to."

"Send you back where?" she asked. "Mr. Richards?"

The echo of her words permeated through the air, poisoning the space. I hadn't heard that name in so long, and I'd worked hard to forget.

My skin turned to ice, and I was a child again. Everything, even Julian, faded from the room. "Y-y-yes."

"*Bianca.*" Her voice was strife with disbelief, and it startled me out of my panic. My heart pounded as our eyes met.

She looked angry. What did I do?

But she didn't even get me a chance to ask. "Are you saying that all this time you believed you were going to be sent back to him? Did your parents say anything to indicate that they would, or—"

"No." I didn't know how to explain without sounding stupid. I pulled my knees closer to my chest, trying to get warm. "I didn't want them to be unhappy with me. They wanted me to be normal. I couldn't go back. It was an accident that they adopted me to begin with. I wasn't supposed to be seen. If I went back after that…"

"You weren't supposed to be seen?" Dr. Reed's voice had softened.

"You've never spoken about this before. What happened the day you were adopted?"

"I ran away a few days before." My body buzzed and I scratched the edge of my gown, trying not to pick at my arm. "He didn't like it when I ran away. Not when he didn't want me to."

"You ran away?" her voice was gentle. "Did you do that often? Where did you go, and for how long? What made you go back?"

"I had to go b-b-back." The feeling was growing stronger—I wanted to crawl out of my skin. "I had a hideout, in the woods. No one could ever find me there. I couldn't stay too long, there wasn't much to eat. I was gone for a week that time. I missed the announcement. When people came to look at the foster kids, the rest of us had to hide. I was supposed to, but… I didn't know. That's how my p-p-parents saw me."

There was a short pause, and the air in the room grew heavy. It was hard to breathe.

Then Dr. Reed spoke again, and despite her sympathetic tone, it didn't stop the terror from racing through me. "You weren't a foster child?"

My eyes shot up, and Julian's tight, pale expression barely registered through my panic. Only Dr. Reed was important right now. "Don't tell them! They can't know."

"First of all." Dr. Reed's face was calm, and she projected such sincerity that my racing heart began to slow. "At your age, even *if* your parents gave up guardianship, you wouldn't go back to him. You'd simply be left to your own devices."

She tilted her head, still studying me. "Secondly, they *knew* who Eric Richards was. They were helping an investigation when they found you. They knew what was going on. Even if you had said something, they wouldn't have taken you back. And while we might not have agreed on methodology, they do care. They only wanted you to focus on recovery.

That's why they wanted you to not think about the paranormal."

"Recovery…" What was I recovering from, exactly? "I don't understand."

She continued speaking in that same tone. "Would you like to talk about what happened in your foster homes?"

"No." The fake calm receded, and my heartbeat echoed in my ears. There was no way this was happening.

If they knew…

Was this why my parents wanted me to stay locked away? Why I wasn't allowed to decide on my own treatment? Because they thought something was wrong with me?

Were they ashamed?

"I'm fine." My voice shook despite my effort to prevent it. "I don't need to talk about it."

"Are you sure?" she asked. "It's okay to be angry—"

"I said no."

I opened my eyes, my back pressed against the wall. I was farther from them before. And this time, Julian ignored his mother and came to me before I even had time to suck in a breath.

"Darling, it's all right." He pulled me into his warm arms. I couldn't stop my shaking. "There's no need to talk about it right now. Only when you are ready."

I clung to him, his fresh scent washing away the raw edges of my nerves. "No."

What was everyone going on about? There was absolutely nothing to discuss. Whatever had happened was in the past, and I'd lived through it.

Nothing good ever came from revisiting that sort of thing.

They had no idea what they were doing.

"Bianca…" Julian sounded torn, but I knew that he would never press me. He obviously didn't like to see me uncomfortable. I hated using that against him, but I really, *really* didn't want to stay on this topic.

"I don't want to talk anymore." I pressed my face deeper into his chest. "Please stop."

I could hear his pounding heart, feel the tenseness of his arms. The longer I was held by him, the more the fight pulled from me. My body relaxed despite myself, and a comforting heaviness fell over me.

"That's interesting," Dr. Reed said, her voice sounding near. Julian shifted, pushing himself against the wall and turning as he continued to hold me against him.

She was sitting on the seat that I had abandoned, her mouth thin. "What are you doing, Julian?"

"I'm not doing anything," he replied, his arms tightening. "I'm only holding her."

"Really?" Her eyebrow raised, and I probably should have been offended at the look on her face. But I was more relaxed than I'd been since arriving at this place. I didn't want to do anything to have that comfort taken away.

"It looks like her abilities are still fairly strong," she continued. "She blinked."

"She's blinked before," Julian said, his voice even. "It's what she does when she's under stress and needs to escape."

"She never did as a child," Dr. Reed said. "And she's on medication."

"She's the Xing," Julian didn't miss a beat. "You know that even the officers don't blink until they are older. And, quite frankly, I'm shocked this medication works at all. We aren't normal humans."

That seemed to surprise her, and her eyes moved to me once again. "Bianca, about your medicine—"

I didn't care anymore. "It never worked. It was harder to see and feel them, but there was always an awareness. The medicine made it easier to pretend."

She didn't seem to be happy about my admission. "But what about…" Her gaze drifted toward Julian, and her voice trailed off. "You've always had your abilities?"

I shrugged, hiding my face into the crook of Julian's neck.

But she saw the movement. "And you've never noticed anything else odd?"

Julian's frame stiffened, and his voice was tight when he cut in. "What do you mean by that? What else would she have noticed?"

She ignored Julian. "I noticed you have old bruising. Do you bruise often? How did that happen?"

It was Julian who responded. "That wasn't natural, Finn did something to her. Damen says it was a curse or Finn losing control of his abilities. He also did something to stop it from spreading."

"Finn did it?" Julian's explanation didn't comfort his mother at all. In fact, she only sounded more concerned. "Between *that* and you being off your medication, Bianca, are you sure you haven't heard—"

"No." My heart leaping into my throat. She couldn't bring up the woman in front of Julian. Every instinct inside of me screamed that would be a terrible idea. "There's nothing abnormal going on at all."

Julian's heart pounded, and he shifted, pushing me back in order to meet my eyes. I longed to look away, but this time he held my chin between his thumb and pointer finger, trapping my gaze to his. He was as serious as he'd ever been toward me. "What is my mother talking about? Had you heard *what*? Is there something going on we don't know?"

"No," I lied—and from his expression, he knew it. But caution crept over his expression, and he hesitated to push further. Guilt racked at me; I knew he worried.

I didn't want him to worry…

But I couldn't ignore my instincts, and they screamed at me to not say anything.

"Everything is fine." I touched his cheek, trying to make up for my dishonesty. It felt terrible to hide things, but he was better off not knowing everything.

I was the worst person in the world.

The room was dark. But when the lights flickered on, it illuminated the shadowy figure that had been stalking Finn. The figure was familiar to me now, it had been something stalking my thoughts since it'd first appeared.

I'd had this dream a thousand times. I was in the classroom where my speech lessons had been held. It was a strange feeling, to know that you're asleep during your dreams.

The figure should go away soon. It always did.

But this time, it didn't.

Instead, it grew closer to me, and the smoke-like figure spoke.

"You wish for me to leave him alone?" It was female, speaking with an aloof and almost mocking tone. It sounded as though she was continuing a conversation, the first half of which had been missed. "What payment are you willing to give me for your request?"

Words jumbled together, hers and mine, but everything remained stubbornly out of reach. It didn't matter, I knew what was being said. Fear washed over me, and the only sound I could focus on was that of my own heart.

Then, the agreement was made. She was pleased. Her golden eyes watched mine, and she reached a limb-like appendage out toward me. "You must agree."

I was that child again, and the terror had almost petrified me. The last thing in the world I wanted to do was to touch this thing. I knew it was a memory, but everything felt so real.

I wanted to run away. I wanted to say no.

But I couldn't. If I didn't do this, Finn would die.

I had had no choice. "Y-y-yes."

And then there was pain. Fire spreading through my every nerve. I was being burned alive.

For the second time in two days, I jerked awake. Even though it hadn't been real and I wasn't there, the echoes of pain echoed through me. The memory of that day still caused me pain.

"What's wrong?" Damen's voice, thick with sleep, pulled my attention from the remnants of my dream. The pain vanished as my attention shot toward the corner of the room.

Damen was pushy and annoying, and he made my heart race. I should have been happy to see him. But the sight of him lounging between two chairs caused a surge of annoyance to shoot through me.

Out of *everyone*, why did it have to be him?

The surge of emotion faded quickly, guilt immediately taking its place. Why was I annoyed he was here? This was a good thing, right?

But how was he here?

Goose bumps broke out over my skin. "D-D-Damen? What are you doing here?"

He rubbed his eyes, shaking his head. An instant later, the sleep wiped from his face, he was on his feet rushing to me.

"Bianca." This time when he said my name, his voice was strange. He sat on the bed, facing me. Close, but not touching. "What happened?"

What did he mean? I still had no idea how he had even gotten in here. "What are you—"

"Dr. Stephens pulled some strings for me. I'm now a temporary employee!" he explained, an almost proud look on his face. "He's claiming it's a part of my internship."

Oh Lord.

Why did he look so proud, as if he'd solved world hunger? There were so many issues with this plan I couldn't even begin. Starting with, "Didn't you say, repeatedly and very loudly, that you have no interest in clinical psychology? You're a forensic psychologist. They aren't the same thing." How in the world did these boys make it so far in life without my wisdom?

"I know that." Damen frowned, appearing slightly put out. "But the undergraduate degree is the same."

I rubbed my temples, a migraine beginning to form. "I thought you wanted to be discreet. This isn't discreet at all," I muttered, wondering how long it would take for rumors to spread. It was one thing to have Julian be my doctor, but people were bound to notice Damen was suddenly hanging around a clinic.

He wasn't even dressed for the part!

"You're not wearing scrubs," I pointed out, noting his rumpled shirt and jeans. "You're not even trying."

"You're not happy to see me?" Damen leaned closer, lowering his head to meet my gaze. We were close, but the intensity between us seemed different. I couldn't put my finger on how. "Am I making you uncomfortable? Do you want me to leave?"

He moved closer, and I couldn't stop the heat rushing through my blood. The room was getting too hot, and it was harder to breathe. "N-n-no…"

"Perfect," he said, standing up and walking to the door. I watched, confused, as he opened it and whispered something to someone on the other side. Then he returned to his previous position in front of me.

"How do you feel?" he asked.

I frowned at him. Why was he acting weird?

It wasn't his words. It was the way that his gray eyes flickered over my frame. Gone was the usual hilarious expression he adopted when he tried to flirt. Now there was something else there, something that I didn't like at all.

Why wasn't he acting ridiculous? I could see the desire there, lurking under the surface. But for some reason, he was trying to be someone he wasn't.

This new Damen made me feel weak.

"Why do you look like that?" The words burst from me before I could second-guess myself. "Why aren't you hitting on me?"

Damen blinked, shock crossing his expression. It passed, and a second later, something else began to settle in its place. And this time when he gave me a once over, I felt the heat continue to rise under my skin. The way he looked at me, it was as if he thought that I was the most beautiful thing in the world. Which was ridiculous. I hadn't had a decent bath in an eternity and was wearing a shapeless, white gown.

But it didn't seem to matter.

He leaned forward, trapping me between the headboard of my bed and his arms. My heart raced, because this was it. I was so excited. He was going to say something stupid and cheesy. Then everything would be normal again!

"You like it when I flirt with you?" he whispered, his breath brushing over my ear.

My pulse raced, and I was melting. "W-w-we have an agreement!"

Damen froze, pulling back slightly. The hesitance began to creep back into his expression. "That's not what I asked."

My blood turned to ice as he began to pull away. Why was he running? I didn't know what he was doing, but if he planned on playing mind games, why did he come here in the first place?

Then I saw it in his eyes—the self-loathing.

For some reason, he was holding himself back. I had no idea why, but I was sure it had to do with his stupid question. Did he think I was angry at him? I had told him to leave me alone at the hospital.

He was wrong, I hadn't been angry. Not at him, at least. Dear God, I had forgotten how sensitive he was. He even looked as though he hadn't slept in days.

I was a terrible person. The poor guy was wallowing in guilt at my callous words.

I had to rescue his fragile self-esteem, and the only way to do that was honesty. I gripped the sleeve of his shirt, my face growing warm. "I like it when you flirt. We've talked about this already! I like when you pay attention to me."

Damen froze, his eyes meeting mine once again. "Really?" His confidence grew with every second, and a smile began to touch at the corners of his mouth. I couldn't imagine why he would smile at my admission.

Then he continued to speak, his hand covering my own. "You like it when I 'pay attention to you', baby girl?"

The purr was back in this voice, causing my pulse to soar and my ears to warm. I couldn't even respond, because the look in his eyes had me trapped. His focus moved to my mouth, and the temperature of the room continued to rise.

I wasn't sure what he saw, but his grin grew wider. "You do!"

He leaned in, pushing me closer to the head of the bed. Only our hands separated our chests, and I had to crane my neck to look at him. My mouth went dry under the pressure of his gaze.

"You're not scared of me at all," he said.

Scared?

I wasn't so certain about that. When he did these ridiculous things, my heart raced and it became harder to breathe. God only knew why I wanted him to flirt with me. His antics were something I both loved and hated. But when his eyes held mine—when he was paying attention to me and only me—I couldn't deny it thrilled me.

"You're incredibly brave," Damen continued. "That's good. You need to be brave to play with fire."

I wasn't sure what bravery had to do with anything. It probably had a lot more to do with potential brain damage. I was about to tell him so, when there was a knock at the door.

Instantly, his scorching expression vanished and he pulled away. I hid my inflamed face in my knees as I listened to Damen talk while I took a moment to steady my shaking breath.

Then the scent of food drifted toward me.

I peeked up to see Damen seated at the foot of the bed. A covered tray rested on a small cart beside me. I had been so flustered I hadn't even heard him wheel it into the room.

I frowned at the tray. "What's this?"

"Breakfast," Damen said, his expression guarded—a stark difference from a moment ago. "I know you haven't been eating."

That explained how long I'd been asleep, there was no good way to tell time here. It was just my luck the one time Damen tried to feed me, it would be prison food.

"I'm not hungry."

Damen's lips thinned as he studied me over his glasses. There was an appraising glint to his eyes. "You need to eat, you've got to be hungry. I know you like food, and I'm not like Julian—sneaking you in snacks. You need real food, he's been coddling you too much."

"Who doesn't like food?" I retorted, hoping my face wasn't as red as it felt. "That's not the problem! And don't say that, Julian doesn't coddle me."

"There's a difference between coddling and encouraging. He's blurring that line." Damen was frowning, his steel eyes seeing right through me. "He's afraid to push you right now, but don't get used to it. He won't always be like this. He knows he's wrong, and he has his limits. Meanwhile, someone with some sense needed to come in here and make you eat."

I gasped. Who did Damen think he was? He was so wrong. "You can't make me eat! You don't know what the people are doing to it. I'd rather die than eat poison!"

The words were barely spoken before Damen was in front of me. He grabbed my wrists, pulling me closer to him. Gone was the calculating look in his eyes, panic in its place.

"Don't joke about that." His words were jilted, completely unlike his usual, smooth tenor.

"I'm not joking." I tried to pull my wrists away, but his grip didn't let up. It should have scared me, but instead his pushiness made me angrier. "Let me go. It's not any of your business if I die or not. You're not the one with people forcing medication and treatment on you. *You* can't make me do anything I don't want to do."

The banked fury in Damen's eyes flared to life, and he released my hands only to grab my shoulders instead. "It's not my business?" There was something powerful in his voice I'd never heard before. But instead of scaring me, the sound caused my toes to curl.

"It is my business," he continued. "You're the most important person in my world. You always have been. And if something happened to you, I would be destroyed. You need to take care of yourself."

I knew there was something there, but the deeper meaning behind his words escaped me. All I could focus on was his hands—large and hot against my skin. I had the sudden urge to do something about it, but I had no idea what. Frustration pooled in my stomach.

I didn't care who was mad at me anymore. I was tired. Tired of everyone taking away my choices. Tired of everyone telling me what to do. And I was *so* tired of people lying to me.

I didn't care if they had "reasons."

I might be curious to hear about those reasons one day, when everything calmed down. But right now, none of that mattered.

I was angry at the boys, even though they had helped me and had taken me in. Even though they had done so much for me.

Julian's subtle pushing was annoying, even though he was trying so hard. And now Damen was trying to boss me around too. I had no idea what Titus and Miles were doing. But if Titus had destroyed his house, it was probably nothing good.

I was so mad, and so worried about them.

And I was angry at myself, because I was just as bad. They'd told me about their world, and I promised to talk to them about my past. Yet, because I was a coward, I hadn't been able to do that.

I'd run away instead.

Plus, I should tell them about the woman in my dreams. Every second where I didn't tell them made me even more of a hypocrite.

But I couldn't, there was something undeniable screaming at me to keep it secret.

I didn't understand what the heck was going on anymore.

"Don't tell me what to do." My breathing grew heavy and stars crossed my vision.

I had to do something. I needed to touch him. Without another thought, I grabbed the front of his shirt in my fists, bunching the fabric. Damen's furious expression fell, and the tension in arms lessoned, but it was too late. I didn't care anymore.

And before I could talk myself out of it, I took advantage of his surprise to jerk him to me.

I'd never been kissed before, and I wasn't even sure if one could classify my attack as a real kiss anyway.

When I pulled him to me, I was desperate for something just out of reach. Even the feeling of his hard chest under my fingers hadn't been enough to satisfy these urges. The only solution had been to kiss the poor man.

Obviously.

The instant his soft lips met mine, my own actions shocked me into immobility. Because it couldn't be denied that in my anger, I had molested Damen. This was the worst.

But it was also the best feeling ever.

Kissing was both strange and exciting. An awkward second passed, and then another, and there was no response from my partner. But just as I was about to pull away and apologize profusely, Damen sprang to life.

His scent surrounded me, and the world faded as he pressed forward. His mouth moved over mine as he gained control and turned it against me.

The feel of his response rekindled my desire to touch him. This time I didn't hesitate, and when Damen pushed me to the mattress, not breaking his mouth from mine, I was lost.

A burning spread where our mouths touched and despite being pinned to the bed and feeling the heavy weight of his hips over mine, I wasn't scared at all. Instead, the contact made me yearn for more, and I pressed my hips into his. My fingers seemed to move on their own, unbuttoning his shirt as

I sought out bare skin. A pulse raced through me as my palm brushed over the mark that was so much like mine.

I wasn't the only one who lost control. His presence was everywhere. One hand pressed my hair away from my face and cupped the back of my head, and the fingers of his other entwined in my own.

And his kisses caused my toes to curl.

For the first time it occurred to me that he had been holding back, even when he'd been so pushy in the past.

I was breathless by the time he pulled back, but hardly had time to do more than inhale before his mouth trailed over my jaw. He grazed his teeth over my neck, while whispering words I couldn't understand under his breath.

It was too much.

"What's that?" I asked, surprised at how shaky my voice came out. "What are you saying?"

He froze, his mouth pressed over the corner of my jaw, before he pushed up. He held himself up with one arm. He continued touching me with his other hand, running his thumb over the hollow dip near my eye. "What's wrong?"

"You were saying something," I said. I didn't want to break this moment, but at the same time, the blush that grew over Damen's face intrigued me. "What was it?"

"Nothing," Damen said, looking to the side.

Now I really needed to know. "What language was that?"

"None." Damen continued to avoid my gaze.

He was wrong. It had sounded like how they spoke when using their abilities. "I'm pretty sure that was Chinese. Did you take Chinese?"

Damen's gaze drifted back to me, to my mouth, but I put my finger to his lips before he could distract me. "Tell me."

He groaned but didn't move away as he responded. "We've been reincarnated into almost every culture. But in our first lives, we were born into what is now known as China. You must have realized this."

"I have…" I was waiting for the real explanation. This explanation was obvious. Titus's dragon form, the language, the way that the abilities were classified. "You've learned Chinese to honor that, or…"

"Even though we are reincarnations, it does not change who we are. I am Damen, you are Bianca." Damen moved his hand from my face to hold himself with both arms over me. "But eventually, you'll have memories from past lives. Some more than others, as some were less eventful. But the most prevalent life is our first, where I was Huo and you were Mu. That's what laid the foundation for everything. Those are the first memories you'll recollect, and which will influence you the most. And," he said, holding up his finger now, cutting off the beginning of my interruption before it began, "certain things, such as language and mannerisms, carry over from those memories."

"So." This could be extremely favorable. If I ever made it back to school, my life in academia might not be lost. "I'm going to start knowing Chinese?"

"Yes." Damen raised his eyebrow. I attempted to ignore his judgy look.

This was excellent. So much less studying would be required. "Don't they have Chinese at our school?"

"You are not switching your foreign language elective to Chinese," Damen drawled, the judgmental expression remaining. "That's cheating."

Yeah, he totally couldn't stop me, it wasn't like he had any authority at the college, nor of my person. But still… "You're no fun." I frowned at him.

"My father wouldn't let me," Damen said. "He said I'd be using an unfair advantage for—"

"That sounds like it's your problem," I interrupted, even more annoyed now. Because if his father had to refuse, it meant he'd tried. And now he was lecturing me? "No one can stop me from doing it, you're not my dad."

Damen's mouth thinned and his gaze flicked to the side. When he looked back to me, it seemed that within that instant he had made up his mind about something. "You need to eat."

This again. "You can't make me."

I expected him to argue, but instead, he kissed me again. This time the feeling of his mouth over mine was far more aggressive. And the passion that had been fading fanned into an inferno.

I was still annoyed at him for continuously trying to boss me around, but my reason was soon lost. The only thing that mattered was his weight pressing me into the mattress, and the way his hands moved over me. His kisses stirred feelings that were both wonderful and strange.

But then his hand moved down, and his fingers brushed over the fabric protecting my stomach. At first, it felt nice. The warmth of his hand against me was comforting. And the small movement caused my muscles to twitch under his touch.

Then, without warning or reason, the feeling vanished, and a familiar terror rose up instead. My blood turned to ice.

This was no longer enjoyable in any way, and I was suffocating.

"No." My heart stuttered dangerously as my mouth tore from his. Blackness crept into the edges of my vision. It wasn't Damen over me anymore. Instead, it was *him*. I couldn't see from fear and pain, and my arms and legs felt heavy.

In some part of my mind, I knew it was Damen. But nothing made sense.

I was going to be sick.

He'd frozen in response to my word. He was saying something. But everything felt distant and unreal. My thoughts raced, and I tried to grasp on to anything that might keep me safe.

Then I remembered Julian and what he had said.

"Pineapple." I was so grateful for his brilliant thinking. "Pineapple, pineapple, pineapple!"

The weight vanished, and Damen was gone.

Yet, even with the pressure gone, it felt like an eternity before my heart stopped thundering in my ears. The darkness took longer to fall away from my eyes, and when the panic had subsided, a hollow feeling was left in its place.

The room slowly returned to focus: the bright white ceiling, the plain walls. I was on the bed, alone, and my limbs felt weak as I finally moved to wipe my eyes with my shaking arms. My face and neck were wet, and I hadn't even realized I'd been crying.

Then I remembered Damen, and his quietness caused me to forget about myself. I pulled myself up, searching.

He was on the other side of the room, his face in his hands as he sat in one of the chairs there. I'd never seen him so still. The line of strain radiating from him was almost palpable. There seemed to be a dark energy radiating from his general direction.

He was mad at me.

My pulse thrummed, because the last thing I wanted was to make him angry. And we had an agreement... "D-D-Damen?"

His head snapped up and his face was dark and unreadable as his gaze met mine. The expression faded, turning into concern. "Bianca."

He was kneeling beside the bed within an instant. He started to reach for me but paused, his hand in midair. "Are you all right?" He seemed to regret his words the second he asked, and followed up with, "That's a stupid question, of course…"

I wasn't sure what to say.

Anything was bound to make me seem crazy. There was no rational explanation for my sudden freak-out, or at least, not something he'd understand. My stomach twisted as I wondered what might happen next.

There was no way I hadn't ruined everything. Only moments before, he'd been furious.

But as he held my gaze, I realized he wasn't expecting me to say anything at all. For once, he wasn't going to press me. I wasn't sure why, but I was beginning to suspect he didn't think any less of me either.

"Do you mind if…" he began, glancing over my face. There was a slight hesitation to his voice as he continued. "Do you mind if I touch you right now, or hold you? Or would you rather be alone?"

I wasn't sure what possessed me to do it, but I'd raised my arms before he'd even finished his sentence. Then he was on the bed, pulling me into his lap.

"Oh, baby." He held me against him so tightly I might break. He roughly stroked my arm. "I'm so, so sorry." His voice rumbled under my cheek.

Now that he was close to me, I could feel his shaking. It caused my chest to tighten. Even more than my own pain, I couldn't stand hurting him. "I-i-it's not your fault." My voice wavered, and his hold grew even tighter. "I'll be okay." I fought to make my words stronger.

"You *will* be okay." There was not an ounce of doubt in his voice. "Because you're the strongest person I know."

I was shivering against him—cold despite the heat from his body. And my face was still wet from tears. So I wasn't certain why he'd say something so strange.

But I had no energy left to argue, these episodes always left me feeling weak. It took everything I had to rest my face against his chest and focus on his breathing.

He was wrong, but it was nice of him to say. It made me feel a little less pathetic, in any case.

Chapter Six

Miles

Plans

Professor Aine Hamway hadn't returned to teaching yet. When we'd been brought to the council about the Cole case and our actions, she had been called back from her trip. But instead of testifying why she failed to report suspicious events in her home, she'd vanished.

Being fae herself—even though she was of a lower class—there was no way she didn't know something was going on. She had set Bianca up, of that we were certain. But the question was, why?

But because of her absence, Bryce had come back to campus today. There was still a school to be run, and he couldn't stay away. Since he didn't have his doctorate, he couldn't become a tenured professor. However, he was still qualified to teach the lower level classes until Aine was found.

The glimpse I had of him earlier in the day was the first since Damen had beat the shit out of him. His face was a mess. His nose was still swollen, and one of his eyes was a blackened mess. One side of his face was heavily bruised.

I usually would have felt bad for him. Or even offered a salve—although Jin probably already had. My Er Bashou wouldn't allow someone in his quintet to be in pain and not do anything about it.

But after learning about Bianca, I wasn't feeling kindly toward Bryce. Damen might have overreacted and targeted Bryce in his anger, but he wasn't wrong in his accusations.

Bailey wasn't who we'd thought. The others had to suspect this, but no one verbalized anything yet.

I didn't have the connection that the others did to Bailey. Outside Bianca, I was the youngest. So when Bailey was born, I hadn't been old enough to be involved. And, later, when the Abernathy family lent their services to the Dubois family, I didn't witness the falling out between Damen and Bryce. I had been in France at the time.

By then, Bianca was thirteen. She'd already been adopted and only had Finn to help her.

This rubbed me the wrong way. Maybe because it was our job to be there for her—as we were for each other. But she had been basically alone.

I wasn't jealous… Or maybe I was a little. But at the same time, I was almost grateful for him. As horribly awkward as Finn was, he had *tried* to be a companion. And it was clear from his face when we spoke about her that he held feelings for her.

Not that *that* was allowed.

But that was the least worrying thing at the moment. The only thing I could focus on was the implications of Hanah's words. This was partially my fault. I was supposed to know about my officer's lives.

I had missed something this big.

Guilt ate at me, and my pen ripped through the top layer of my notebook.

"Oh my God, did you see Professor Dubois this morning?" A loud whisper drifted from a nearby group.

I glanced up, over my pile of books, and spotted her. She was an underclassman, still in the process of settling down with her friends. She was with a small group—three including her—and in front of them was a collection of science textbooks.

Bryce's students.

Another girl was watching her with wide eyes, her expression pained. "Stop it, babe. I can't talk about his face. I'm so upset."

They *did* look upset. For some reason, students tended to lust after him. Seeing him this way was sure to be shocking. People were bound to notice he looked like a monster.

"I bet it's *her* fault," the sad girl continued, pouting down at her notebook. Though her word were accusatory, her tone wasn't.

Who was 'her'?

She continued, sighing. "Sara saw her leaving campus with him. He's sent her to his office before, too. Haven't you noticed the way he watches her? I bet you, *he* must have found out and threatened to ruin their romance, that's what usually happens. Professor Dubois won, of course. No one can beat him."

"Professor Dubois is not the only one in love." The first girl leaned forward, waving her hand in the air eagerly. "She watches him too. It's almost cute—a forbidden romance between professor and student. It's been a few days since she's been last seen with Finn Abernathy. She obviously made her choice."

At this point I was choking. They couldn't mean—

"What was her name?" the eager girl continued, crossing her arms on the table. "It was Bianca, right? I bet they've already gotten married in secret. You can watch them and feel their chemistry. It's electrical. The sex must be phenomenal."

Chemistry?

I felt like passing out. The blood left my head as this ridiculous conversation echoed through my mind. I stared at the girls, stunned, and was thankful they hadn't noticed me yet.

This was the rumor going around campus?

Were people really that idiotic? The only thing *electrical* about the way they watched each other was the visible animosity. Bianca was clearly plotting to murder him while Bryce was just... being Bryce.

Before I knew what was happening, I was standing beside the girls' table.

Their gossip silenced and they stared at me in alarm. I could have probably done this without scaring them, but there was no time for niceties. I was onto something now.

Their stupidity was giving me an idea.

"Pardon me." I tried to sound as friendly as possible, considering. "I couldn't help but overhear, but what you're saying... Are you saying there's a rumor about Bryce Dubois and Bianca Brosnan?"

The girl who had originally made the announcement was watching me in slight terror. "Mr. Montrone! I didn't mean to offend you. We know gossip is against the rules, we'll never do it again—"

"I'm not upset." I waved my hand, stopping the gaggle of apologizes before they began. "Just tell me, what else is the rumor saying?"

The third girl, a short-haired redhead who hadn't spoken up before now, responded. "I'm Mary Graham, and I'm actually in the Biology 101 class. I've seen it firsthand. I've also seen Bianca around—though no one knew her name until recently. She keeps to herself, you see..."

"And?" I pressed.

"Well." She seemed hesitant, but at my urging look, continued. "She's been spotted around campus with you and Professor Abernathy. It made people curious about her. Plus, she knows Finn Abernathy. Then there's the fact that Jiayi Chou is her roommate, and she's weirdly protective over her. We'd been wondering how she knew all of you, since you're all... you. Then she and Professor Dubois began to make their affection more obvious. They spend forever staring at each other in the middle of class. Rumors started, especially when they were seen together outside of class. We know it's against the rules for a professor to date a student. But that doesn't stop it from happening."

I wasn't certain what my face looked like, but a strange sound echoed in my ears. Despite my horror, the plan continued to form in my mind. It was a terrible plan, but at the same time, it might work.

The problems this could solve...

"There's also..." Mary wavered as she glanced at the others. "The rumors state if she's with him, it makes sense that she knows your circle. She can't be with *you*," she said boldly. "You're not like that. And she can't with Professor Abernathy. She's been seen with him too many times."

I was desperately fighting the urge to hold my face.

"So," I ventured, needing to make sure that I had this perfectly straight, "people are saying that Bianca and Bryce are together? What's this part about a fight?"

"Finn got jealous." The original girl who caught my attention spoke up. "He tried to jump Bryce when he found out, but Bryce won."

First of all, Finn would never lose to Bryce. Why people thought this was astounding.

How in the world did people come up with this crap? Did everyone have nothing better to do than to gossip and make up stories about our lives?

But... this was helpful.

I hadn't considered this option, but it might work. After all, when it came to medical decisions, a spouse's rights would override a parent's claim. Ideally, Bianca would be established as able to make her own decisions, but that would take a while. We needed to get her out of there first and deal with the legal matters later.

Bianca was going to kill me.

Or maybe she wouldn't. Last time I saw, she didn't seem to hate him nearly as much. Besides, if my theory was correct, it wasn't like this would be legally binding anyway.

But nobody had to know that part yet.

"Um…" Mary's voice broke through my thoughts, and my focus snapped back to the present. The three girls watched me warily, and I realized that I'd been glaring this entire time.

"Sorry." I stepped back, my mind already working through the logistics. We'd need help, of course, from people who could make the paperwork official. But it would work.

"Thank you for telling me." I nodded. Their wide eyes followed my progress. "I'm sorry for disturbing your work. Have a nice evening."

With that, I gathered my bags and rushed from the room. But I didn't move fast enough to miss their excited whispering.

"Have you lost your mind?" Bryce placed his hands on his desk, his shock so evident that his eyebrows had nearly risen to his hairline. "What kind of idiocy is this? I can't marry her!"

Finn scowled, leaning back in his seat as he looked between the two of us. It was obvious from his posture he took personal offense to this suggestion. "If you're going this route, why can't I marry her?"

Besides the fact that he didn't deserve her?

"There are two problems with that suggestion. First, she loathes you more than Bryce right now. And second, the marriage would be legally binding if it's you," I snapped, barely taking the time to throw a glare in his direction. "This is temporary, and we'll need this to be as painless as possible. Besides, she might not even agree."

"So why are you asking me?" Bryce put his hand to his chest. The look of offense on his face was almost comical when combined with the swelling and bruises. "How is this any less horrible?"

"Don't be stupid." I crossed my arms. I was suspicious, but now I had to get him to admit it. "It'll be easy if it's you. There are already rumors about the two of you. We'll play into that, and once people learn you are siblings, the marriage will be annulled anyway."

Bryce's face lost all color, and he fell back into his seat. His shocked gaze stayed steady on mine. "What are you talking about?"

Glancing at Finn, I noticed he was watching the two of us, his expression blank. But he didn't appear to be surprised. His hatred for Bryce was beginning to make a lot more sense.

Damen's was different. Though, from his recent reaction—the way he blamed Bryce in his father's conference room—he clearly suspected.

However, having a suspicion was different than knowing. And now I was certain—the confirmation was written all over Bryce's face. Newfound horror flooded my emotions.

But not toward Bryce.

"You were five. There is no way this was your plan. Why didn't you *say* anything?" I asked, holding his gaze even as his face twisted. "Who put you up to this? What happened? I thought your family wanted that child. So why would she be sent away? Because of that, she—"

"You don't need to repeat what she's been through," Bryce hissed, his fists were clenched on the desk. "I was there when Hanah told us. And as for your questions, I don't have the clearance to divulge that information."

"Don't have the clearance?" I couldn't believe the stupid words coming out of his mouth. Even Finn, who had begun leaning forward, watched Bryce in suspicion. "You're an Er Bashou, you have almost all of the clearances that a person *can* have."

"I don't have clearances for everything," Bryce said, his gaze unwavering.

Alarm clouded my thoughts. It was too soon for the council to know about Bianca. I thought we'd have more time.

But someone on the council had known about Bianca all along?

She was in even more danger than we suspected. And no fake marriage would throw them off.

"The council knows?" Finn asked, his voice alarmed. He was pale, and his face filled with horror. "They know about her? But—"

"No, the council doesn't know." Bryce rested his chin on his hand. "Only one previous council member knows about this, and they wouldn't say anything."

A previous councilmember...

People didn't generally leave the council. In fact, there had only been two instances of that happening in recent history.

It couldn't have been Gloria Protean. She wasn't at the Dubois residence when Bianca was born. But Gregory Stephens had been.

"Gregory?" I asked, although the answer was obvious. He'd shown no indication that he recognized Bianca. However, sometimes he wasn't the most observant. "Do you think he knows who she is?"

"I don't think so." Bryce frowned. "He's mentioned her once, but he only finds her amusing and thinks she is a powerful medium. He's never said anything about Bianca being… *her*. I'm actually surprised—he was there when I named her."

"Then you did know her! Who is Bailey then?" I was still confused, even though some of the anxiety had ebbed away. The council wasn't going to come after us, at least not yet. Bianca was still safe. "Where does Bailey come into play?"

Bryce's mouth pressed in a line and his shoulders stiffened. He wouldn't divulge anything more. "The point is, they don't know. Yet."

"If you're actually worried about it, then you should be more than happy to help with this plan." I said. "You said it yourself, we need to think this through. She needs a reason to stay around all of us. Being 'married' to you solves that."

Bryce rubbed his forehead. "I'm her brother."

"But no one who would call us out knows that," I pointed out. "The marriage would only be on paper, just until we can have her legally emancipated from her adoptive parents. And Bryce, if you don't do it, *he* is still an option." I pointed at Finn.

It wouldn't happen—Julian would murder him first. But Bryce obviously needed incentive.

Finn straightened, hardly containing the eagerness in his expression. "Like I said, I could—"

"No." Bryce glowered in his direction. "I'm grateful you took care of her when we couldn't, but she's not getting married to you. Your feelings are fairly obvious and this needs to be a façade."

"A Xing can't get married anyway," Finn pointed out. "It would still be fake."

"That's not entirely true. *Legally*, we can get married," I said.

Some of us had been married—and had children—in past lives. But the resulting complications was what caused these rules to be enacted to begin with.

"The consequences of us marrying would be severe," I said. "And we agreed to follow these rules. Considering that, if she's actually married when everything comes out, it would be even worse for her."

Bryce sighed, defeat already weighing heavy on his face. "This is still stupid. She hates me. She's not going to say yes."

I shrugged. "We can always ask Brayden. He knows who she is, right?"

"Don't ask Brayden." Bryce rolled his eyes. "And of course he knows who she is. But Brayden doesn't know how to be subtle. He hides behind sarcasm and humor, but he's about ready to snap. He's been holding back the urge to fight the lot of you off every time you come near her."

"He's better at being subtle than you are with being sensitive," Finn said. "Remember, if you do this, she's been through a lot. You cannot be a horrible person. You can't be *yourself*."

"Why does it sound like you're reciting a line? Someone must have told you this recently, I presume." Bryce shot a glare at Finn. "Besides, didn't you already lose control around her? Didn't you curse her, or some sort like that? What did you do anyway? I've never been able to get a straight answer."

"I didn't mean to do it. We can talk about it later." Finn's expression closed—he was hiding something. "First we need to get Bianca home. Then we can deal with everything else."

I watched Finn in suspicion. "Wasn't it a part of your plot to keep her locked away, and *on* that medication? Why are you suddenly being so helpful?"

Finn crossed his arms, looking at the floor. "I didn't think she was ready. I still don't think she is. But there's nothing to be done about it now. I always knew she'd hate me afterward."

I frowned, resisting the urge to point out that it was his own fault she hated him.

"I'd hoped for more time," Finn said. "But that's passed. The only thing I've left to lose *is* her, even if she won't talk to me. I just want her to stay alive. So, yes, I'll help you, but I have a request." He looked at Bryce. "Can you *please* convince her to stay on her medication? She has to be monitored before she can stop it."

Bryce scowled, distrust flashing through his eyes. "Why?" When Finn didn't answer, he pressed. "What are you watching her for, exactly? It's unnecessary to control her empathic abilities. Brayden can help her. We are prepared to deal with her background and how it might affect that aspect of her powers. But I get the impression that's not where your concerns lay. Or at least not all of them."

I glanced between the two of them, my senses on high alert. Bryce was right, Finn wasn't telling us something. This entire discussion rubbed me the wrong way.

"Finn." I waited until his eyes met mine. "Where's your shikigami?"

A muscle in his jaw jerked at my question. "Why?"

"That's a good question," Bryce said. "In fact, why don't you summon her? It's been a while since I've seen Kiania."

Finn's pale face grew even whiter. "I don't *want* to summon her. We don't get along. Why do you want to see her anyway? What, exactly, are you accusing me of?"

I'd always distrusted Finn because he was odd and secretive. He was socially awkward, and rude. And I disliked like how he lied to Bianca and how he'd spoken to her.

But right now, I wasn't getting malicious vibe from him. In fact, he seemed to be one second from bursting into tears.

This was not the look of an evil man. He did know something, but he didn't do whatever thing he was hiding. At least not on purpose.

He almost seemed afraid for his life.

"I don't think *you* did anything." I watched him shift in his seat. "But you're not always the problem. Kiania lost Damen's trust a long time ago. That's why he wasn't happy you contracted with her. Did *she* do something?"

"You might not blame me, but Julian and Damen are different. Can we talk about this later, please?" Finn glared between the two of us. "Like when Bianca isn't stuck in a hospital?"

"Damen takes your side with everything." My pulse picked up. Why would he be afraid of his brother? "You're one of his least regulated Er Bashous. He might react badly at first—he does have a temper. But almost nothing you could do he wouldn't defend once he calmed down."

Finn glanced to the side. "You think that, huh?"

Something wasn't adding up, but Finn was right. In the grand scheme of things, we had other priorities. We had to get Bianca home.

"All right, but this conversation isn't over," I said finally, turning my attention back to Bryce. "As for the plan, you're agreeable?"

Bryce sighed, looking defeated as he rested his forearms back on the desk. "I've no other choice. Are you going to tell her who I am before you ask?"

Like I would make it that easy for him.

"I'm not doing your job for you. We'll get you in there, but you're the one who needs to tell her who you are, and ask her about the plan," I replied, watching him evenly. "I'll start on the paperwork. If she agrees, you can act on it right away."

"She'll never agree. She'll hate me even more." Bryce covered his face. "It's our fault she wasn't home."

I paused, recalling past conversations. When we spoke of our families, Bianca had looked so sad.

"I don't think so," I mused. "Bianca wants a family, and you *are* her family. She's a logical person. Be honest and see what happens."

Chapter Seven

Bianca
Choices

Damen held me for what felt like hours, only letting go when it was time for my therapy.

Once again, it was only Julian, Dr. Reed, and myself.

After I'd entered the room, Julian ignored his mother's orders and rushed to my side, begging me to explain what was bothering me.

But there was nothing I could say. How could I tell him what happened with Damen?

I'd had anxiety attacks often, but those were different. I hadn't felt that way in a long time—not being able to breathe, helplessness surrounding me, the desire to rip off my own skin.

It was far worse than any anxiety or ghostly attack.

I would *never* be able to fulfill any of the boys' physical needs.

"Bianca." Julian traced over the edge of my jaw before he nudged my face upward. His gaze pulled me out of my thoughts, but even his presence couldn't soothe the raw edges of my emotions.

His blue eyes shimmered in worry. He had noticed his usual processes weren't working.

"Darling, what's wrong? Isn't Damen in your room? We thought seeing him might make you happy, but—"

I shook my head. "T-t-that's not i-i-it." I struggled to speak. I couldn't control it.

"We need to get her out of here." Julian shifted to see his mother. "She's getting worse."

"I'm doing my best, Julian." Dr. Reed sighed. "But her parents believe that this hospital is the safest place for her. The council knows her name now, and they are panicking. They know she is not mentally ready to face scrutiny."

"She *was* getting better when she was with us," Julian accused. His arm tightened around me, and anger leaked into his voice. "You can't keep her locked inside a room forever!"

"Abigail is worried—"

"Don't tell me how worried she is." Julian's voice was a snarl. "She hasn't come to visit her even once."

I was barely paying any attention to their conversation. My thoughts continuously replayed what had happened with Damen. Every misstep remained branded in my memories.

"I-I-I used the word!" I wailed, squeezing my eyes shut. The confession spilled from my mouth before I could stop myself. "I ruined e-e-everything!"

The room went silent, and Julian's frame had become statue-like. Dr. Reed finally broke the silence. "What word?" Dr. Reed watched us curiously. "What are you talking about?"

"Mother, can you please leave?" Julian's voice was tense, completely lacking the gentleness to which I'd become accustomed.

"What?" Her eyebrow rose as she studied her son. "I'm not going to leave, I'm her doctor."

"*Please*," Julian repeated. Even though he'd asked, his tone left no room for argument. Dr. Reed studied him for a second longer before she nodded and left the room.

The instant the door shut, Julian was on his knees in front of me. He pulled my hands into his own, and, through my watery vision, I noticed his expression was deadly.

"What happened?" he asked. "What did he do?"

"I a-a-attacked him!" I still couldn't believe it. My breath caught in horror at the recollection of my actions. "He was trying to make me eat and I was so mad!"

Julian blinked, his murderous expression morphing into confusion. "What?"

Anger was beginning to burn inside once again. "Everyone keeps telling me what to do and giving me no choice, and he wouldn't stop bossing me around! I wanted to hit him, or something."

Julian's expression was close to bewilderment now. But I wasn't finished. "I don't know how it happened, but then I kissed him instead."

His surprise morphed to shock. His mouth opened, and for a brief moment nothing escaped. Finally, his stilted words reached me. "*You* kissed *him*?"

I know, it was terrible of me.

"He was being really annoying," I explained. "He said you coddle me. Then he was all flirty and bossy. I couldn't stop myself."

Julian's eyebrow raised, and his gaze turned contemplative. "Coddle?"

I ignored his question, "So when he wouldn't shut up, I grabbed his shirt and attacked him. I'm sorry."

"Why are you apologizing?" Julian asked, tugging at my hands and lowering his face to mine. "There's no need to apologize. Didn't we agree to let this happen naturally? There's no room for jealousy between us. We're not normal, and what we've always had was non-conventional. Don't worry. If you want to kiss Damen, then kiss him."

"But I shouldn't have done it." My breath hitched, a sob stuck in my throat. "He taunted me with food, then kissed me again. It was nice at first… But then I freaked out."

"Did he force you to do anything?" Julian's tone was wary.

I shook my head. "He didn't do anything bad. I just… freaked out."

"That's normal, Bianca." Julian's gaze had softened. "The important thing is that he respected your boundaries. Do you know what triggered you?"

"He touched my stomach." My heart pounded, shame rushing through me. I was the stupidest person in the world. "It was over my clothes, but I couldn't…" I trailed off, breaking eye contact, because there was no way to explain.

"I couldn't breathe anymore," I offered, my voice small.

Julian rubbed his hands over my arms, and when he spoke, his voice was a measured calm. "Darling, do you know *why* that triggered you?"

My breath hitched as my heart jerked wildly. I nodded.

He watched me, his touch feather light against my skin. It was as if he thought I'd break. "Would it make you feel better to talk about it?"

I shook my head, moving back from him. My panic faded, my defenses slamming into place around me.

There was no need to continue this conversation, everything was fine.

I just needed to avoid everything, forever. Now that I knew another of my limits, it would be easier.

"No." I crossed my arms, trying to get warm again. "Isn't this session almost over?" My insides crawled with anxiety, and I was desperate for some peace. Even the air felt disgusting. "It needs to be almost over."

"It can be over." Julian stood up, holding his hand out for me. "Let's go back to your room. I'd like to see Damen before I leave."

I followed Julian as he led me past the door. He somehow evaded his mother's questions, and she didn't stop Julian from kidnapping me.

Julian didn't let go of my hand even once. The farther away from the office, the more the buzzing faded from my ears. Slowly, Julian's presence started filling the emptiness inside with a sensation of peace and belonging. By the time we reached my room, I was calm, collected, and feeling much better about the entire situation.

Then Julian opened the door, and I saw Bryce Dubois, sitting on my bed.

I knew I should have used my hours of solitude for more productive affairs. But instead of plotting for the future, I'd been wallowing in self-pity.

What had I been thinking?

All that wasted time. I hadn't even decided what to call him yet, and now here he was before me. I was totally unprepared.

So instead of being witty and suave, my reaction to finding Bryce lounging on my bed was to point at him as I made an embarrassing sound of horror.

Damen's chuckle echoed through the room. The sound of it pulled my attention away from Bryce's frowning face.

Damen sat in one of the chairs, balancing himself on the back two legs. He smirked at Bryce. "I love her reactions when she sees you," he said. Bryce glared at him. "Nothing brings me greater joy."

Julian walked past me and smacked Damen on the back of the head. "Be nice. Bryce, what are you doing here?"

My attention returned to Bryce, and I frowned as a pang of sympathy twisted in my chest.

"What in the world happened to your face?" I asked. I didn't like the man, but by God. He looked like he had been mauled by a wild boar. What kind of monster could inflict such damage on another person?

Damen continued to snicker, and Bryce frowned but didn't answer. Instead, he reached behind him. "I'm here to see you, Bianca. And I brought you something."

Julian froze and Damen's chair slammed down onto all fours. But neither made any effort to intervene.

"Food?" Could it be? I'd been wondering about that smell.

Bryce paused, mid-motion of pulling out a brown bag, and shot me an impressed look.

"Actually, yes," he said, finishing his previous action. The movement had made the aroma even stronger. "I picked this up. I figured you might want something to eat."

"I thought you brought it for yourself." Damen rolled his eyes. "Don't bother, she won't—"

"Thanks." I closed the distance between us, sitting down on the bed next to Bryce, and unpacked my offering. Perhaps he wasn't so bad after all. "You've read my mind, good job."

I unwrapped a McDouble and took a large bite, uncaring about etiquette.

"No one else understands." Bryce nodded. "We're a misunderstood lot."

"What the fuck?" Damen's exclamation broke into our bonding moment, and my eyes shot to him. He—and Julian, too—stared at us as if we'd lost our minds. "Why are you eating for him?"

I took another bite, thoughtfully chewing before I replied. There wasn't an easy way to explain… "He brought it here, from the *outside*."

Damen frowned. "So what?"

"Do you not have a single shred of survival instinct, or has she always been saving your butt since the beginning? *Obviously*, outside food—especially fast food—is less likely to be poisoned. You must always be cautious in times of war." Bryce held up his finger. "Especially if you're trapped in hostile territory. Never trust your enemy. I wouldn't be surprised if they've tampered with her food in some way. It's obvious they hate fae."

Damen rubbed his temples, so it was Julian who answered as he glanced doubtfully at my hamburger. "I really don't think—"

"You don't *think*," Bryce interrupted, shrugging his shoulders. "Bianca *exists* to subjugate those who work in this establishment. She's a threat just by being near. These are not officials used to being around power. They are going to fear her. Do you honestly believe she's been treated like any other patient? I'm sure they're on their best behavior in front of you, and maybe Dr. Kohler. But what do you think happens behind closed doors?"

Julian's mouth was still open, his expression stunned. Meanwhile, Damen's hands dropped as his head snapped up.

"What?" His eyes sought out mine. "What happened?"

I finished my cheeseburger, no longer excited about eating the second. Not with Damen and Julian watching me as if they'd come to a horrible realization. "I told you before that the nurses are mean…"

I had told them, at least of what I was sure was real. I told everyone. But no one believed me.

It was interesting to watch Julian and Damen's expressions become similarly murderous.

Damen's eyebrow twitched as he leaned forward, but Julian spoke first. "What have they been doing?"

"When you leave, they shut off the lights. I'm supposed to have a light on…" I glanced toward the barred door. "Dr. Reed ordered someone stay with me, so I'm not bored or lonely. But when she's not here, no one talks to me. She told them to give me books. You brought my textbooks." I looked at Julian. "But they won't let me have them… They won't give me anything to do.

"I feel like I'm being punished. It's not so bad, this time. Because you're here. That's the only way I know time is passing. When they bring me food, it's always seems random. They're not really nice when they change my bandages. And, when I try to sleep, they'll stand outside my room and talk about me."

"What do they say?" Julian asked, his voice calm despite the murder written on his face.

"They're scared of me. I've done bad things," I said, trying to remain detached. "I've hurt people, and I'm dangerous."

"I'll show them dangerous." Damen jumped to his feet. But he was stopped by Julian's hand on his arm. "What?"

"You can't handle this." Julian's expression had closed off, and his eyes darkened as he responded, "This needs to go to Miles."

"Why Miles?" I tilted my head. The fact they were angry made me feel a little less crazy.

"Most of the employees here are his," Julian said. "Earth types tend to be drawn to nurturing professions. But true professionals don't allow prejudices and fears affect their care. They've broken rules Miles has been upholding for centuries. They've abused and neglected a patient and need to be held responsible."

Damen fell back into his seat, covering his eyes. "We're still not listening."

My appetite returned. I slowly took another bite of my dinner, watching the two of them. I had no idea what Damen was talking about. However, it hadn't taken me long to learn that if no one else was talking, he'd keep giving out information anyway.

Julian didn't respond to Damen's statement. "We need to get her out of here."

"I'm trying," Damen replied. "Miles said he had an idea, but I haven't heard anything."

Bryce, who had been silent until now, cleared his throat. "Speaking of," he began. Wariness washed over me at the look in his eyes, and I doubted his next words would make me happy. "We should let everyone know we're married."

My food suddenly tasted like ash, and I stared at him, dumbfounded. "What?"

Before Bryce could explain his sudden delusion, there was a choked sound from the other side of the room. Julian interjected, his voice strained. "Pardon me?"

Damen still stared at Bryce, his face slowly turning scarlet.

"It was Miles's idea." Bryce shrugged, his tone factual. "A spouse could override Mr. and Mrs. Geier's claims. He's started the paperwork already. Supposedly, we've fallen in love and got married after classes began. If you want to leave, just tell them that you're with me. I'll get you out."

My heart thundered as the cheeseburger dropped to my lap.

It was a brilliant idea. But this was *Bryce*. What were his motives?

"Is that why you brought me food?" I turned my narrowed eyes to him. "You're using a cheeseburger to bribe me into marriage? What kind of engagement gift is this?"

"Actually, no. I've more class than that. The food is extra." Bryce shrugged. "I'm getting you a ring."

Damen jumped to his feet, pulling me behind him. He didn't seem to care about the mess he made with my meal as it fell to the floor in the movement.

"Absolutely not," he seethed. Before I could even process what was happening, Julian had also moved between us. I couldn't see Bryce anymore.

"You must be joking." Julian's voice was tight. "Or Miles has lost his mind. What would possess him to come up with such a plan? You know she's not allowed to get married. Once it comes out who she is, the council will be dangerous enough to navigate."

"Hey…" I tugged at Julian's shirt. "What do you mean?"

The boys had mentioned this before. They couldn't have relationships and children. But for some reason, it never registered as something that applied to me. I wasn't even interested in a relationship like that, but that was my own weirdness. It kept me safe.

But being *forbidden* from doing it was something entirely different.

Julian glanced at me. "Why are they dangerous? Because the council is made up of a bunch of superstitious, old—"

"I'm not talking about that." I pulled his sleeve again. "I can't get married?"

The furious expression faded from Julian's face in an instant, and Damen tensed.

"Darling, no," he said, his tone a mixture of horrified and apologetic. "I didn't realize that you didn't understand… It's one of the rules that we've agreed to follow and—"

I technically knew that, but having it confirmed…

My breath caught as another aspect of my own bodily autonomy was suddenly ripped away.

"Why not?" My voice sounded so strange. I had never thought to press this subject before, but now it felt urgent.

Damen answered. He turned, placing his hands over my shoulders. "It was originally a suggestion presented to the council, but we all agreed. The council turned it into actual law around three hundred years ago."

"A *suggestion*?" My voice squeaked. "What kind of idiot would come up with this? What business of theirs is it that—"

"Darling." Julian pressed his finger to my lip, silencing me. "This was your idea."

Surprise pushed away my shock, and I blinked at him. "What?"

"*You're* the one who went to the council," Julian said. "You helped write the law. There are a number of arguments for it, all of which are very sound. At the time it made sense, and the council agreed. In those days, we had issues with our direct descendants. Then there was a prophecy that came up, too, which had the council concerned."

"We've always planned on revisiting it after the paranoia died and our bloodlines thinned," Damen said. "We needed to come up with something more permanent. But part of the law is that only you can change it."

"And a certain number of votes must be for the change." Julian glanced at Damen. "But that's not going to happen now."

Damen rolled his eyes. "There's no merit to that bogus prophecy. I've already done countless decades of research into it."

"What prophecy?" I looked toward Damen. Because he really didn't seem the type. "You do fortunetelling?"

"It is one of my skills," he said, letting go of my shoulder to touch his glasses. "But I've never seen—"

"What's the prophecy?" My eyes drifted back to Julian, noting the hesitance in his expression. "What is it?"

Julian sighed, leading me to the bed where Bryce remained. The other man didn't seem overly interested in the conversation, so I assumed he knew what this was about already.

Julian sat at my other side, holding my hand, and our gazes locked and he spoke. "Titus was the only one of us who never had children. In fact, he…" Julian paused, glancing at Damen.

Damen pulled up one of the chairs, answering as he sat back down. "He's a virgin," he stated, completely unfazed.

My face heated at his words. Titus? Once I got over them not being monks, I had assumed…

And *Titus*, the one who most closely resembled a living sex god?

Titus with his long, flowing hair and Adonis physique?

"How?" I asked. "He said that *Forbes*—"

"He's had many admirers throughout all his lives." Julian shot Damen a disapproving look. "That includes this life. But he's a dragon—he's focused and possessive. He's not interested in anything less than full commitment. A mate."

"He's never had a mate. A shifter can only have that bond with someone of equal strength," Damen broke in, a curious expression on his face. "No one has ever been at his level."

I blinked at him, unsure if I understood. "But—"

"Shifter forms are inherited through the father. *Our* children were powerful, but they were still human. Shifters are not entirely human, and are much harder to kill," Julian continued, touching my shoulder. "Any of Titus's children would be terrifyingly strong."

"One of the divination masters had a vision. The council wanted to do anything they could to make sure Titus wouldn't procreate," Julian said.

The way his voice had deepened caused my heart to race rapidly.

"The prophecy states Titus will have a mate, and the union will be the beginning of the first dragon hive," he said. "The very thought of it continues to worry the council, and people outside of that circle as well."

"But…" I glanced between the two of them. "You said no one has been able to reach Titus's level. So it won't happen."

"We're the only five who have comparable strength," Julian said slowly. "None of us has ever been born a female before. When the law was made, the possibility wasn't even considered. The council thought a talented Er Bashou might qualify—so the rule would apply to that."

"But you're on his level. The council will do *anything* to make sure Titus doesn't have children. And he is untouchable—it is almost impossible to kill a dragon," Bryce grumbled. "But you? You were targeted the moment you were born. The only way to keep you safe was to send you away."

His tone turned my blood to ice. My attention turned to Bryce. He looked nervous, and even slightly apologetic.

"You must be joking. We don't even look alike!"

Bryce frowned, blinking slowly, before he pointed at his own eyes, his widow's peak, and last, his wavy, brown hair. All features I also possessed.

"Two of those are dominant traits!" I snapped. "Lots of people have widow peaks and brown hair! That proves nothing."

"And our eyes?" Bryce raised an eyebrow. "What about our pigmentation? We must return you to class, there are some foundational elements missing from your education—"

"Shut up!" I pointed at him. "I understand genetics perfectly fine! I just can't believe that you... *you*... Who is Bailey? Why did you..."

My question trailed off. No, it was just an excuse. They really thought their only option was to abandon me? I couldn't believe my parents would agree to this. It seemed too easy and convenient. He was wrong.

And why did Bryce suddenly care now?

"You proposed to me! You can't be my brother!"

"That's exactly why," Bryce replied, his tone even. "As Miles pointed out to me earlier, this marriage would only be on paper. So long as you're not hurting yourself, I have no interest in controlling you. I'd let you make your own medical decisions, including checking yourself out of here. Meanwhile, Miles is beginning work on restoring your rights."

"But, we *can't* be married," I said.

"No," Bryce agreed. "It wouldn't *actually* be legal. But the only people who know won't want to draw the council's attention, so they won't speak up. From what I've seen, they've been working too hard for too long to risk that. This also provides a cover for your... closeness to the rest of your quintet. After all, Damen and I were best friends once." His gaze drifted over my shoulder, and he continued, "It will work, but only if Damen is willing to bring his A-game."

"*I loathe you.*" Damen's voice was dark, commanding. Instinctively, I turned my attention to him.

He was an imposing figure, his frame rigid and menacing. His hands were clenched over his knees, and the focus of his molten gaze was entirely on Bryce.

"She won't be able to live on campus as a married woman," he said. "And she's not living alone with you."

"That's up to Bianca," Julian cut in, wrapping his arm over my shoulders. "And she hasn't even made a decision." His eyes sought out mine, and I could see his question. "Darling?"

This was happening so fast. My thoughts were in overdrive.

Bryce was my brother. The crazy law that the boys hated was my fault. And there was that prophecy, which held implications I couldn't digest at the moment.

And now I was supposed to be married?

My mind kept going back to one thing: my family. This could be my chance to find out who they were. I might even meet my birth parents.

But did I want to?

My focus returned to Bryce. It was strange to see him as anyone other than my challenger. But he *was* family… and he was trying to help me. But I hardly knew him, and the thought of being alone with anyone other than the boys filled my heart with dread.

What was I supposed to say? "I-I-I—"

Then a brunette nurse stood at the door, a faux apology written in her expression as she glanced between Julian and Damen. It didn't escape my notice that she didn't look at Bryce or me at all. And from the sudden tenseness in Julian's arm, he picked up on it this time as well.

"Sorry, sirs." Her voice was deceptively cheery.

Dread rushed through me at her tone—tonight would be especially bad with the gossip. This time, I'd had three men in my room.

"Visiting hours are over," she said. "Miss Brosnan needs her rest. If you could just—"

"You've made a mistake. My name isn't Bianca Brosnan." My skin felt strange, the world hazy. But I forced myself to my feet, and brushed my gown with shaking hands. "My name is Bianca Dubois." I barely spared a glance at Bryce, but it was enough to notice him jerk upright at my words. "My husband was delayed. But now that he is here, you'll see that he wants me released from this establishment immediately."

Chapter Eight

Bianca

Rain

The nurse finally looked at me, shock written across her face. "Excuse me?"

Despite the thundering of my heart, I tried to fake my confidence.

"I'm leaving." I crossed my arms. "Bring me my discharge paperwork."

Her gaze drifted to Bryce, who had moved to stand behind me. "What?"

"You heard what she said," Bryce said, his voice calm. "And make it quick. We'd like to make it home before it gets too late."

She appeared to be stunned, and her gaze shot to the others. But when no one else interjected, she glanced at us again.

"I don't know," she squeaked, backing out of the room slowly. "Give me a moment." And with that, she scurried off.

I turned to Bryce. "Do you think it worked?"

"She's gone to get someone higher up, I imagine," Julian said, stepping to my other side and wrapping his arm over my shoulders. "I'm proud of you." He pulled me from Bryce, leading me back to the bed. "Now sit before you collapse."

"I was so nervous." I admitted, obeying.

"They're going to ask where you're being discharged to," Julian stated, handing me the last hamburger from Bryce's offering.

"She doesn't have to answer." Damen said, moving to my other side. "It's not any of their business."

"But if she has nothing to hide, she will." Julian said.

"We're going to my condo, of course." Bryce hovered near, arms crossed as he watched the three of us curiously. "Where else would she go?"

I glanced at him, a chill running down my spine. We were going to live together, alone? Could I do this?

"You live an hour from the college. The commute must be exhausting for you." Damen's voice was tight. "Why don't you move in with me, I have plenty of room."

"Move into that run-down shack?" Bryce said, incredulous. "Why in the world would I—" His statement ended in a yelp as Damen kicked him. "You!"

Before another word was said, Dr. Reed hurried into the room. "What in the world is going on here?"

"Hello, Mother. We're ready to leave, if you could…" Julian said.

"If I could *what*?" She shuffled a stack of papers against her chest, glancing between the group of us. Finally, her eyes settled on me. "Bianca, what is this I hear that—"

"I want to be with my wife," Bryce interjected. "I've come to take her with me."

The look she shot him was a strange mixture of alarm and exasperation. Then, slowly, she pinched the bridge of her nose. "This is a nightmare. I knew you were difficult, but Bryce, are you really—"

"Is there a problem?" Bryce didn't seem intimidated by the older woman in the least. "I have medical jurisdiction since my wife has, apparently, been deemed incapable. Surely you aren't going to fight the *law*?"

Dr. Reed opened her eyes slowly. "And just where do you think you'll be taking your wife? What does your father think about this insanity?"

I watched the two of them, entranced. My pulse picked up.

His father...

I didn't think this through. He would be my father, too! What *would* he think about this plan? I had literally no idea what he was like. What if he was just like Bryce?

That would be terrible.

Julian's pulled me closer as Damen covered my hand with his own.

"It's okay," Julian whispered. "We can talk about it later."

"You'll find that Father is more than welcoming," Bryce said, waving off Dr. Reed's concern. "And in the spirit of agreeableness, since my wife is in a delicate state, I'll even let you know we've decided to move in with my best mate, Damen Abernathy." Damen's hand twitched, but Bryce continued, "He's never had a keen eye for landscaping, you see. He kills everything he touches—strangles the life out of it. Therefore, he's requested my expertise. It's his only hope."

"So he plans on entering gardening competitions?" Dr. Reed narrowed her eyes at Bryce before turning her attention to Damen. "Is it true, you're friends again?"

"Oh, *absolutely*." Damen's voice was strange. "It's my pleasure to have a live-in groundskeeper. You can never have too many servants."

Julian covered his face with his hand, while his mother sighed.

"Right..." She focused on me. "Bianca, are you sure?"

"Of course." I breathed, hoping she'd get on with it. I didn't want to stay in this building another second. "Why wouldn't I want to be with my husband?"

She turned her eyes heavenward before she glanced pointedly at the three of us. "There's the matter of this ménage. And while your husband is standing only three feet away. That's bound to raise some eyebrows."

Damen's hand pulled away from mine. Julian gasped. "We're offering her emotional support!" His cheeks darkened. "We're best friends!" He protested, using one of my lines. Which, for some reason, caused me to blush.

It really did sound ridiculous.

"Yes, son," Dr. Reed said, forced patience lining her voice. She snatched a pen from her hair. "I'm sure that's *exactly* what it is. Be sure to keep it in check. You've always been a horrendous actor."

"I'll get your discharge paperwork," Dr. Reed said as she wrote, not looking up. "But I am recommending you stay on your medication. *And* that you stop to see Dr. Nam three times a week once you return to campus. He is practicing at your university. We will begin to lower your dosage again after your first visit."

I frowned at her. "I don't want to see Dr. Nam."

She glanced at me. "Why not? Has he done something?"

"No. All he does is make tea," I explained. "And it tastes awful. He won't even let me use sugar! He doesn't say anything, he just watches me drinking it for an hour! It's boring and useless. He could at least let me bring a coffee."

Dr. Reed rolled her eyes. "I'll talk to him. Now, as for your script, I'll send it to the pharmacy."

But I didn't want this. I didn't want to take anything. "I don't—"

"Honey-bee." Bryce stepped forward, holding out his hand. "We can discuss the details when we're back home. But first let's leave, all right?"

Honey-bee?

The awful nickname overshadowed the conversation we were *certain* to be having later. Julian's hand lowered to his mouth, and he watched Bryce with an unreadable expression.

Meanwhile, Damen's eyebrow began to twitch. He remained next to me, barely touching me since Dr. Reed had pointed out his closeness, but I could feel his leg bobbing.

"Yes…" I still had no idea what to call him, but it was time. I had to think of something fast. If we were married, there was no longer an excuse to avoid addressing him anymore. "Daddy."

Bryce's hand lowered, and the look he shot me was close to panic.

"No," he hissed, his eyes flickering to Damen. "Don't call me that. Anything but that."

"Why not, *Daddy*?" I fake-pouted in response. I loved this. His reaction was bringing me great enjoyment during tenebrous times. I didn't understand why he was complaining. From what I understood, it seemed a common thing to address your significant other as such.

I thought it might be embarrassing—and weird—but the fact it horrified Bryce was everything.

"We'll talk about it later." Bryce reached for my hand. "And stop saying it!"

"Daddy!" I began to pull my hand out of his reach. "Why—"

Damen snatched my hand, cutting off my question. He basically elbowed Bryce as he pulled me to my feet, and I was dragged behind him as he faced Dr. Reed.

She was watching us with a bemused expression.

"Can we leave?" he asked, his hand hot over mine.

She smirked, the first time I'd ever seen her wear such an expression.

"Yes, Damen." She handed him a paper. "But make sure she goes to see Do Yun on Monday."

That brought up a good question. "What day is it?"

She turned back to me, her smile fading. "It's Thursday. You've been here almost a week."

A *week*? I had no idea! Would I even be able to go back to class? "What—"

Before I could ask if it was hopeless, Damen stalked forward, pulling me along behind him. He didn't stop to greet the nurses who smiled at him, nor did he acknowledge the guard at the door. He moved with a singular purpose until we reached the parking lot.

It was raining again—a cold autumn downpour. It drenched us instantly, and I shivered.

Still, Damen didn't pause.

We didn't make it ten feet past the sliding glass doors before Julian caught up to us. He jerked on Damen's arm, dragging us to a halt.

"What the hell do you think you're doing?" He was furious. Without even waiting for an answer he released Damen, turning toward me. "Here." His voice gentled as he draped a coat over me and pulled the hood over my head.

It was large—the bottom hem reached my knees—and warm. My hair was already stuck to my cheeks. He bent toward me, uncaring about the rain, and pushed some wayward strands away from my face. "Better?"

I stared at him, unsure how to respond. Julian had cursed, *and* he was angry.

Damen spun around, his eyes wide. He had lost the force of his fury. "I—"

"I don't want to hear it," Julian snapped before focusing on me once again. "Bianca." He voice was soft. "Are you warm enough? You don't have shoes on, can I carry you? Let's get you out of the rain."

Didn't he care his own shirt was plastered against his skin. Wasn't *he* cold? I shook my head. "I'm okay."

I wanted to redo this last hour. I wasn't sure what I'd done, but between Damen's growing look of dread, and Julian's obscured rage, it felt like I was drowning.

"Okay." Julian held my hand. "Let's go, now that you're not forced to walk in the rain in only a thin, white hospital gown," he said accusingly. He glanced at my feet. "Are you sure…"

I shook my head. I couldn't let anyone see me being carried out.

"I'm stopping home to pick up some items." Bryce was suddenly behind me, holding an umbrella over us. "Are you sure you'll have room for us? Doesn't Titus live there now?"

"Titus always lived at my house." Damen's posture was subdued. "He used his house to store some of his collections."

"Oh." Bryce sounded confused. "Well, I'll be there later tonight. Bianca"— he touched my shoulder, and my heart jerked—"do you want me to stop by your room and pick up anything? You room with Jiayi, right?"

His question cut through the stone in my stomach, and I forced my attention on that instead of the weight of his hand. I was too tired to care much about how he knew my roommate. But knowing him, he probably stalked my student records.

"No." I pulled the jacket around me, trying to hide my shaking. "No, I don't want anything they bought for me. I want to throw it all away." My voice was firmer toward the end, my anger overshadowing my fear.

I didn't need *anything*.

Bryce didn't respond, and Damen and Julian only glanced at each other. But as my brother moved past me, I couldn't stop myself. My resolve had only lasted ten seconds.

"Wait." I grabbed his shirt, hoping he wouldn't make fun of me.

He faced me, and I pulled him with me, away from the others. But he was still too tall, and I tugged on his arm until he bent down.

"I need my rabbit," I whispered in his ear.

Bryce's skin turned pale, and his eyes met mine. "What?"

"I have a pink rabbit…" I was pathetic for wanting it, but I was too weak to give it up. "Can you please get it? Jiayi knows where it is."

Bryce's expression was strife with dread, and it made me worse for asking. But I couldn't lie and say it didn't matter.

After a moment, he groaned. "*Fine.*"

"Thank you." I was near tears, and I hated myself. "I don't want anything else."

"It's okay," he said, pet my shoulder, and left for real this time.

I returned to Julian and Damen, who were conversing in low tones under another umbrella Bryce had given them. They stopped when they saw me, and Julian reached for my hand once again. "Is everything okay? What did you ask him to get?"

I couldn't tell them, they'd make fun of me. "Nothing..."

Julian paused, but then carried on. "That's fine, are you ready to go?" At my nod, he fell into step beside me as we followed Damen. "We're taking Damen's car."

"The Jaguar?" I asked, spotting aforementioned vehicle.

Damen pulled out his key fob and the engine turned over.

"We're all wet," I tried to warn him. Didn't he realize? "We'll mess it up."

"It'll dry." Damen's voice was still strange. "Don't worry about it."

Julian frowned at him again but didn't say anything as we approached the vehicle. Once Julian opened the passenger door, waiting for me, I hesitated. I glanced at Julian, and then to Damen, who watched the two of us from the other side of the car. What were they waiting for? Julian's legs were much longer than mine. "I'll sit in the back."

"Don't be ridiculous, Bianca." Julian touched my back. "Of course you can sit—"

"Just let her sit wherever she wants," Damen said. "It's my car."

I glanced between the two of them, this tension, again, making me feel sick. Perhaps I had made a mistake after all.

"I want to sit in the back." I stared hard at the ground. "I want to lie down…"

Julian sighed. "Darling, you need to wear your seat-belt—"

"She can lay down if she wants!" Damen smacked the top of his car. "Why don't you stop telling her what to do?"

"Why don't *you* stop acting like an ass?" Julian glared at him. "I know you agree, so why are you arguing? You're going to scare her."

Damen's eyes zeroed in on me, and I almost flinched from the burning intensity in his gaze. He was angry again. But I had no idea what he was upset about now.

That wasn't true, actually. I did know what his problem was.

Because of me, he'd been forced to allow Bryce into his home. But didn't he understand? Once again, he was missing the bigger picture. Bryce would be completely at our mercy.

Once he cooled down, I'd help him see the light.

Plus, there was the other matter of what had happened…

Of course after having time to reflect on it, he was upset.

I turned from them, and before Julian had a chance to move, I was in the back and settled. Damen and Julian both peeked their heads through their doors, but I didn't want to see them. Not if they were fighting.

I pulled the hood over my face, blocking them from my sight. "I'm going to take a nap."

There was a moment of silence, then some shuffling before both doors closed. A second later, the vehicle began to move.

The quiet remained for what felt like an eternity. My eyes were heavy, and I was on the edge of losing my consciousness when they spoke.

"What is your problem?" Julian's voice was almost indiscernible. "You were better at this before today."

"It's partially his fault," Damen grumbled. "I don't want him near her."

"He did the best he could. You can't blame him," Julian replied, the venom slightly gone from his tone. "And you can't deny he's trying now."

Another long moment passed, and I thought they were finished. Their strange conversation about Bryce, finally over. But then Damen spoke again. "She was afraid. Earlier."

I knew instantly what he was talking about. It took all my control to hold back my sound of alarm.

"I heard," Julian said. "She told me."

"She *told* you?" Damen asked, disbelief threaded through his voice.

"Yes," Julian said mildly. "She thought you might be upset with her."

"Why in the world would I be upset with her?" Damen's tone was incredulous. "That was the last thing on my mind."

"And you're also not upset with her because of Bryce, the whole marriage fiasco, or having him live in your home?" Julian asked, an edge to his voice. "Despite your actions, you're a rather private person."

"That is not what I'm upset about either," Damen said. "Although he is overstepping. You have no idea how much I'm looking forward to this."

Julian paused again before pressing. "Then what's wrong?"

"I keep messing up," Damen said. "I want to take care of her, but I can't help her. I don't want to scare her and I don't want her to be angry at me… But I also don't know what to do to make her not afraid."

"How interesting," Julian said mildly. "This low-confidence look isn't you at all, and it's especially pathetic considering your major. Darling, are you scared of Damen?"

My heart, which had been going a mile a minute throughout the entire conversation, jerked in my throat. I peeked out of my hood to see Julian looking at me.

"Bianca, are you scared of, or angry at, Damen?" he asked again.

"No…" I glanced toward Damen, and I could see the tightness of his shoulders.

"Why did you think he was angry when you used the word?" Julian prodded.

My vision remained locked on Damen's form. "Because he looked angry…"

His voice was tight as he responded. "I wasn't angry at *you*—"

"He already told you he wasn't angry at you," Julian interrupted. "We discussed it *in detail* earlier. So why would you still believe that?"

"Because people don't stop when you ask!" My breath came out in a rush and my face heated. "It worked like you said it would, but I don't understand why. Once he had time to think about it, he might change his mind. Why wouldn't he be angry?"

It took me a minute to realize that we had parked. Damen and Julian were both turned in their seats, staring at me.

"W-what?" My voice shook. Their dismayed faces were outlined by a faint light from the outside. Their expression compounded my panic.

"The reason you believe that is because no one has ever respected your boundaries," Damen said in a gruff voice. "But when you're with people who care about you, who respect you, they will not get angry at you for saying no."

"I was one-hundred percent sincere when I said you could use that word with no repercussions," Julian added.

"Then…" I still didn't get it. Then what was Damen so upset about? "Then why did you get angry in the first place? Why have you been mad all night?"

The air grew heavy, and I sat up. My focus remained on them, but now that I could see outside, I realized we'd arrived at Damen's house.

We should have gone inside, but this was more important. I needed to know. Otherwise, I would never understand what I'd done wrong.

"What were you angry about?" I almost pleaded for the answer, my mind going over their conversation. "What do you blame Bryce for?" They looked as though they had been caught doing something wrong, and I couldn't help but feel it had to do with me. My pulse spiked. "What is it? What did I do?"

Julian sucked in a breath, causing a ripple of movement from the front seat. "No, you didn't do anything."

"We should talk about this inside." Damen was already reaching for his door.

"No." I was tired of games. "I'm not going inside until you tell me the truth."

"Bianca..." Julian began, distress lacing his tone. "We really should go inside and talk about this with Miles and Titus. They are just—"

I wasn't ready to hear any more excuses. "Tell me now." I needed to know what I'd done, so that I could never do it again.

"Bianca." Damen gave up trying to leave. "We talked to Finn."

"Okay...?" Confusion overshadowed my fear. What did it matter if they spoke to Finn? The worst he'd do now was tell embarrassing stories about me, or talk about my childhood bullies.

But none of that explained why they'd be angry. "You're upset because people picked on me in school? Because he did beat them up quite a few times. He even got suspended for it once."

"What?" Damen growled and his jaw clenched again. "No, he didn't say that. I'm talking about..." His voice trailed off, and his eyes scanned my face. "You didn't talk to Finn about your adoption *at all?*"

Dread began to pull at my awareness, and I hadn't forgotten that Julian had access to my medical records. I thought Dr. Reed had kept that aspect private.

And what was this about Finn?

"Why would I talk to him about my adoption?" I said slowly. "He knows nothing about my past. It's none of his business." Julian watched me in trepidation. "What are you talking about?"

"Finn… and Hanah told us about Eric Richards," Julian replied, his voice soft. "We know—"

"Hanah?" My voice cracked. With every passing second, the car began to feel smaller. The sound of the rain became distant as my focus zeroed in on the boys. "You know my sister? And what exactly do you all *think* you know?"

"Hanah is a witch. She's Miles's second, actually. Like Brayden's relationship to you," Julian said. "We didn't realize who she was until Bryce saw your adoptive parents in the hospital…"

I didn't care. I didn't care about anything other than this. "*What do you know?*"

"We know who Eric Richards was, and what he did," Damen said, his gaze holding mine. There was an anger there, deep but not directed toward me. This time, I didn't doubt it. "Titus already started investigating. We'll find him. We know he's a scumbag who tortured and sold little girls. He doesn't deserve—"

My hand had been hovering over the door handle since the beginning of this conversation and as soon as it became obvious what was happening, I escaped.

I hadn't made it ten feet before the doors slammed open behind me. Damen's alarmed yell reached my ears.

"No," I shouted, spinning to face them in time to see them freeze their advance. My hand shook as I pointed at them. "This is none of your business."

"But Bianca"—Julian reached for me—"we're here to help you. We are supposed to work together. You don't need to go through this alone."

"*Alone?*" My voice was slightly hysterical now, but I didn't care. Titus and Miles had rushed onto the porch, and my next statement was directed to them as well. "You can't just come into my life and try to make everything better. It's too late. I've been dealing with this since I was *five*, when the first parents I'd ever known were murdered in front of me. And I survived, *alone*, until I was adopted. If Finn knew this whole time, if everyone knew…"

I was shaking, fury making me lose control of rational thought. "I'd never mentioned those things to *anyone*. If *everyone* knew… Is that why they're lying to me? Does everyone think I'm a fucking damsel? I-I-I—"

Julian stepped toward me, and I turned my wrath on him. "Don't come near me!"

He stopped instantly. I couldn't let the hurt on his face waver my resolve.

"I will handle things *my* way. I don't want your pity!"

"Baby," Damen said cautiously, and the familiar all-knowing expression was etched into his face. "I know you're independent by nature and this is very hard. Especially since you're very trusting to those you let in. But it's all right to be scared."

His words cut like a knife. Panic and fury warred for dominance.

I didn't want to deal with this right now. Hadn't I been through enough?

The words exploded from me. They were laced with the frustration of the last week and all my fear and anger. "Leave me alone!"

And with that, my wish was granted.

I stood under a covering of trees. Damen's house was close by. I could see the lights from here. But still, a small distance away.

My heart was still racing in a dizzying rhythm.

I stood for a second, wondering if I might have gone too far. Done something that couldn't be undone. But it was too late to back out now.

So I ran.

Chapter Nine

Damen
Passion

She had blinked. I couldn't believe she used her abilities to escape from us.

"Leave her be." Julian stopped Titus as the dragon—still in his human form—stepped past us. "She's in the woods," he said. "She'll be fine for a little while."

He guided Titus toward the house, and I automatically followed the two of them.

Her words raced through my thoughts. Her heartbreaking expression frozen in my mind.

Why couldn't I have shut up? I'd seen how upset she was getting.

But I didn't understand what she was doing. This wasn't like her. She'd never been one to avoid problems in her past lives, and Mu had always been a master of his emotions.

It was becoming glaringly obvious things were different.

It was understandable though. *She'd* never been in a situation like this before. Archetypes—the Xing—were protected from the time we were born. Security had gotten lax in this lifetime. Colette—Miles's sister—had been good at hiding things. And even though Julian's father had been abusive to his mother, the council turned a blind eye. They said that since Julian hadn't been abused, they couldn't intervene. Only when Julian almost killed the man himself did they do something.

But this… It was far beyond what we'd suffered. If she'd been with us, this never would have happened. But if she'd been with us, she'd probably be dead.

The fireplace was already roaring, and the room was warm. I stalked through the living room, the fury I'd been suppressing leaving a bitter taste in my mouth. My focus zeroed in on the one thing that could help me think.

"Damen…" Miles hurried after me but didn't prevent me from snatching my mezcal and taking a swig. But apparently the amount was too much for his discretion, and his hand gripped mine, pulling the glass down. "Damen, no. You cannot have liquor right now."

Why did he have to look like he understood? He seemed to have his shit together.

Why was I the only person close to losing it?

It pissed me off.

"*Fuck.*" My vision turned red, and I threw the bottle against the wall, where it shattered. "Fuck!" The destruction wasn't making me feel any better, even though it'd worked in the past.

She'd panicked from a touch to her stomach. No matter how many more lives I lived, I would never be able to forget the look on her face. Her whimpers still rang through my ears.

I kicked at the cart, causing the drinks and dishware to crash to the floor.

I shouted—not even sure what, at this point—reaching for whatever was in reach. How dare things be so orderly. Not when I was *this* close to losing my sanity. It was unacceptable.

How dare that man still be at large.

I had to call in Kasai. It was time to act. The vows we'd made were for times of peace, but this was war. I would gladly unleash the fires of hell to get vengeance.

The thought excited me.

Then something tugged at my awareness, pulling me from the seductive call of destruction. I tried to hold on to it, but the addicting sensation of fire and victory faded. A cold sense of reality settled in its place.

"No." I gasped when awareness slammed into me.

I was pinned under Julian. His now solid black eyes peered down at me. He'd reached into the deepest part of himself in order to restrain me. His power continued to wash over mine, stripping away the familiar hum of my abilities.

The longer his hand pressed against the mark on my chest, the weaker I became.

"Stop," I grumbled. "I'm fine now."

But Julian gave no indication that he'd heard me. Instead, his eyes remained steady on mine.

"I'm fine now!" I pulled from Miles, who'd been holding back my arms, and he released me at once. Only to—before I could do it myself—place his own hand on Julian's shoulder.

"Julian." He watched the other man warily. "You can stop."

The darkness scattered, and Julian ripped his hand away a second later, pushing back to his knees. "Good."

Shame washed over me. The others silently watched me, disappointment heavy in their gazes as I pulled myself to sitting.

The air was thick with judgement. I'd really screwed up this time.

"Whoa!" A familiar voice suddenly broke through the room. "What the hell happened in here?"

Brayden Dubois stood in my double doors. There was a suitcase on the ground next to him, and he was looking around my living room as if he was witnessing a train wreck.

"What are you doing here?" My voice sounded rough. I tried to ignore the broken dishware, the spilled liquid, and the broken wooden cart. "How did you get inside?"

"Your front door was open." Brayden shrugged, stepping into the room and making toward one of my chairs. "So, which room is mine? Where's Bianca?"

I opened my mouth, but Julian touched my arm.

"Bianca is taking a moment," he said calmly. "I wasn't aware you were—"

"I'm moving in!" Brayden flopped in the chair and crossed his legs at the ankle. "Bryce already told me what's going on. I came right over. We've so many years to make up for. There are so many things we can do to Bryce together. It hasn't been enjoyable to prank him on my own. I have a feeling she'll be all for it."

Julian was frowning, disapproval etched into his face. "This isn't a game. Bianca is in a delicate—"

"I know," Brayden interrupted. He leaned forward, bracing his elbows on his knees. His tone grew somber, and his expression menacing. "There's also that." For the first time in my recollection, he resembled the warrior he was supposed to be. "I'll need you lot to stay away from her."

Julian groaned, hiding his face. I was stunned in silence, and Titus continued to scowl at Brayden.

So it was Miles who replied, watching him incredulously. "What?"

"You can't be surprised." Brayden's fierce gaze was unwavering. "After all, look at what I've arrived in time to witness—another one of Damen's famous tantrums." He waved his hand in the air, gesturing around the room.

My heart was beating wildly, shame burning at me. He was right. Seeing this would have terrified Bianca. It would have broken everything we'd only just begun to build between us.

"She's not here…" This time I was lucky.

I *never* had to control myself around Mu. This was entirely new territory.

Mu's temper rivaled mine, and he was persistent and forceful. His anger took on a different direction though. It had always depended on the person, and why his anger was triggered. But no matter what, he almost always held a grudge—even long after the events in question. He could grow obsessed with plotting revenge.

In comparison, I was generally calm expressing myself, but I needed an outlet. If that wasn't possible, Mu and Shui were able to pull me out of my fury.

But Bianca wouldn't be able to do that. I would terrify her.

I felt helpless and stupid. I'd been avoiding it for too long. For the first time in all my lives, I was going to have control *myself*. Bianca couldn't see this, and I couldn't always rely on Julian.

It was such a basic skill, but I'd never had to do it before.

I'd never been more disappointed in myself.

"You're lucky she's not here right now," Brayden said, unaware of my tumultuous thoughts. "Because I would have killed you if you scared her. I don't care who you are. She doesn't need you fucking up her life because no one has ever held you accountable."

He was right. I stared at the broken glass across the room. "I know."

"And she also doesn't need…" Brayden began, but then his voice trailed off. "What?"

I met his stunned stare.

"I'm going to change," I told them, and the weight of my resolve settled over me. "I'm going to work on my temper."

"You?" Julian let out a short laugh. "*You're* going to work on your temper? You've been volatile and selfish since the *beginning*. Why do you think I can't stand you?"

I thought we'd gotten past that.

"I'll do better," I promised. There were ways, it shouldn't be hard. I had a degree in psychology for goodness sake. I could figure it out. "It's your fault, too."

Julian's eyebrows raised in unison. "What?"

"You're enabling me," I pointed out. "Instead of letting me deal with my own emotions, you always subdue me."

"You were about to open the gates of the underworld!" Julian gritted his teeth, death written on his face. "What else was I supposed to do?"

"Well, you need to hold me accountable." I waved my hand, nodding. The solution was so obvious. Tomorrow morning, I'd start yoga. Studies had stated that deep breathing techniques were amazing for teaching self-control.

"Hold you accountable by allowing you to infest Earth with demons?" Julian's voice was still tight. "You almost killed Garrett Cole in your father's conference room. You almost killed Bryce!"

That was true, but would the last one really have been a loss? It could be counted as a learning experience. Sacrifices must be made for the sake of progress.

I pulled myself to my feet, already planning my new routine. "Are you leaving any time soon? I'm surprised you've waited this long. No one is stopping you anymore," I said to Titus, ignoring the stunned looks of the others.

Titus blinked at me. "Going where?"

I fought the urge to roll my eyes. "Are you going to get Bianca?" I gestured to the door. "You're in the best position to convince her to come back."

"What do you mean, 'come back'?" Brayden straightened. "Where did she go?"

I ignored Brayden, watching Titus as he got to his feet.

He seemed eager, but slightly afraid. "Do you think it's been long enough? She was pretty upset."

I nodded. "She's been outside for a while. She's probably cooled off. See if you can get her to go to bed, take her to your room tonight. I haven't set up any guest rooms yet."

"Outside?" Brayden shot to his feet. "Why in the world is she outside?"

Titus left without responding. Meanwhile, I moved toward the dust cabinet, pushing past Brayden. "All right everyone, we need to clean up before she gets back—"

"You clean up after yourself." Julian stood up, not taking the broom I offered him. "I'm going to my room."

"Julian...." But why? We had to take turns. It was part of the code.

"I'm holding you *accountable*," Julian snapped, heading for the door. "You can clean up after your own mistakes."

Then he was gone, leaving Miles, Brayden, and I looking at the empty doorway.

"Well..." I wasn't sure how to respond, but since he'd left, it was too late anyway. I was getting the impression that he was upset, though.

He'd always said I should learn to control myself, so I wasn't sure why he had an attitude. He should be happy about this.

"Hey." Brayden pulled at my sleeve. "Why is Bianca outside?"

"Don't worry about it, Little B." I went to the mess. "Titus is getting her now. Why don't you sit down and wait?"

"Don't call me that!" Brayden sputtered. "Now tell me why—"

Miles, who had been quietly observing through all of this, stepped forward. "While you do this, why don't I show Brayden to a room? I can also get Bryce's room ready for you. Where do you want them to stay?"

I paused in sweeping the broken glass and considered.

Where *should* Bryce Dubois sleep?

The possibilities were endless.

Chapter Ten

Bianca
Secrets

The rain had cleared not long ago, but the cold air pressed in around me. My small shelter—a hideaway at the base of a large oak—hadn't done much to protect me from the elements. I was completely soaked, shoeless, and shivering, but I didn't dare go back.

I had never been more embarrassed in all my life.

They knew.

I couldn't hide it anymore, it was obvious they knew now. I was so ashamed I wanted to die.

The night sounds gradually quieted, which was the first hint of his presence. But I just knew he was here. I pulled my face from my knees, already knowing what I'd see.

There was no way to avoid him forever.

Titus sat a short distance away. Close enough where he could reach me, but not touching. He'd been watching me, and when our gazes met, he didn't look away.

"Y-y-you're stalking me again," I pointed out. My voice shook, but I wasn't afraid.

I'd almost expected he'd be the one to come after me. However, unlike the other times I'd hidden from him, my pulse didn't spike in fear.

I couldn't place my finger on it, but there was something different in his demeanor.

"I'm not stalking you," Titus replied, his expression unchanged. "And I'm definitely not *hunting* you either. But you already know that."

My breath hitched. I hadn't accused him of hunting me, even though, when we first met, I'd been afraid for that very reason. "Then how did you find me? I don't want to go back."

He tapped his nose, and his mouth thinned. "And I didn't come here with the intention of bringing you back against your will. I'm only here to observe."

I blinked at him. "What are you observing?"

"What difference *intent* can make," Titus said. "I messed up, in the beginning."

I was too tired for this. I had no idea what he was talking about. "What do you mean?"

"I'm a shifter. We play games," he said. "I knew you were scared, but you fought back and tried to hide it. Because of that, I thought it was okay. It wasn't until you mentioned it while we were setting up in the basement that I realized I was coming on too strong."

I frowned. "What?"

"I'm a predator and you're prey. I didn't consider that with my approach." Titus's voice was a smooth tenor. "We know how to change how we're perceived."

My heartbeat echoed in my ears, and I wasn't sure I understood. This sudden admission from Titus was strange. "*What* are you talking about?"

"I *was* chasing you. This had never happened to me before, so I followed my instincts." His face was dark. "I thought it would be fun. The way you brushed me off was endearing, and it was even more impressive when you got me with the pepper spray. I *knew* you were scared, but I thought you were playing, too. I didn't realize there was an underlying cause for your fear. I—"

Before he could continue this confusing monologue, I'd moved to my knees, pressing forward until I was able to silence him with a finger to his lips. "What is your point? I told you I'm not scared of you anymore."

He pulled back slightly. "But you *did* say you were afraid of being eaten before. I knew that hunts existed, with fae being their prime game. I should have made the connection."

My arm began to shake.

The boys had done *all* their research. This was more than I'd ever wanted anyone to know. "I didn't know they were s-s-shifters…"

Titus raised an eyebrow.

"It's obvious *now*. I tried not to think about it. No one ever changed in front of me. I thought they were wild dogs. Which, if you think about it, is scarier. I thought I was going to die."

My teeth were chattering, and then Titus's arms were around me. "It won't happen again."

"How do you know?" How could he make such an impossible promise? "Are you going to toss me in one of your secret treasure caves so no one can find me?"

Titus's chest rumbled beneath my cheek. "Which one?"

I knew he had a cave! I tried to look at him, but his arms held me firmly against him. "Titus!"

"I have many homes around the world," Titus said, sounding somewhat amused. "The others don't know the extent of my connections. But no, I'm not going to take you anywhere unless you ask. There's no reason to; that's no kind of life."

He didn't sound scared. But considering what Julian and Damen had told me, shouldn't he be worried? "I know about the prophecy."

Titus's heart thudded and his arms stiffened. But when he spoke, his voice was the same as ever. "Is that so?"

"It can't be true, can it?" I asked.

Titus responded, wariness lacing his tone. "Damen hasn't confirmed it, so in my opinion, it's not valid."

I let out a breath. "Of course not, there's no way—"

"But you *are* my mate," Titus said, and for the first time his voice had lost that smooth confidence.

The denial burst from me. "You're wrong. It can't be me!"

Titus grip tightened, and when he pulled back, one arm remained wrapped around my shoulder. His other hand, however, held on to my chin as he forced my eyes to meet his.

His green eyes had transformed to a dark sage, his irises only a shade away from being swallowed up in black. The expression on his face was heartbreaking. "You're rejecting—"

"No." My breath came out in a rush. The last thing I wanted was to hurt him. "I'm not rejecting you. That's not it." I'd never been so flattered in my life, but... "What you're saying, the mate stuff. It *can't* be me."

He searched my face before the grief faded from his expression. He tilted his head, and a nervous sweat broke out over my skin.

There was no way to avoid the inevitable question.

And sure enough, after a second, there it was. "Why do you think that?"

I couldn't lie, this was his future too, and he was being so honest. He deserved to know.

I forced myself to focus. If only for a little while longer. I could give in to my panic later.

"The prophecy says you'll have children," I whispered. "I can't do that."

A family was something I'd always wanted. I dreamed about it my whole life. It was the same dream that Damen had told me not long ago. But in my dream, I would adopt.

Biological children weren't in my future.

Titus didn't show much of a reaction to my admission—he only raised his eyebrows.

My heart was breaking. Did he not understand? "Titus…"

"I don't care," he said, his expression calculating. "I only care about how I feel. It's you. It's always *been* you, in different ways. In different lives. For you to have been born into this form leaves no question."

Titus had never looked so intense before, and it was suffocating. The weight of responsibility pressed against my chest, making it hard to breathe. "But the prophecy…"

"I told you I don't believe in that nonsense," Titus said, rubbing his thumb over my cheek. "All I care about is what you want, and if you don't want—"

"That's not what I'm saying! I *do* want children!" I didn't want him to get the wrong idea. "I don't think I *can* have them." It was very important that he understand this. Although the fact we were discussing this topic at all was beyond horrifying.

In order to have children, you'd need to have sex, and, well…

"You don't *think*?" Titus frowned, confusion glittering in his eyes.

My face burned, and I gripped his shirt, twisting the fabric. My world was falling apart around me. "I've never been… normal. And lots of things happened. I never…"

My admission seemed to confound him further, and his frown deepened. "Dr. Kohler told you this?"

I swallowed—my mouth was so dry.

"I never told her." I spoke in almost a whisper. "And I might have lied to her during my physicals. So she never checked." The look he gave me made me feel guilty. "I'm sorry…"

"Don't lie about your health," Titus said, his gaze narrowing on mine. "Not anymore."

My throat closed. "But everyone tries to make me do things I don't want—"

Titus cut off my protest, pressing his thumb against my mouth. "They won't. Not anymore." He sounded so certain. "Bryce won't let them, and he is a formidable opponent. But if he doesn't do anything, I'll stop it *and* rip his head off."

But I didn't want Bryce's head to be ripped off! He needed to teach me how to defeat poison. Then maybe we could bond as siblings or something. "But what if—"

"And if people still disrespect your wishes, I'll take you somewhere no one can bother you," he said, his thumb slid over my lip before he cupped my cheek. "Hiding from the council is a last resort. It would be a life of secrecy. But you wouldn't be alone. Now that I've found you, no one will be taking you away again."

I wasn't sure what to say about that, but it sounded almost romantic. Distantly, my mind kept going back to the central point of this conversation. "I'm your mate…"

Titus blinked, pressing his forehead against mine. "Yes."

Then there was something I needed to know. "You're not going to bite me, are you?"

His face jerked back, and he gazed at me in surprise. "What?"

"Am I going to be maimed? Or do I get a mate tattoo?" I tried to recall my shifter romance stories. "How does marking, or claiming, or whatever work?"

"It's not like that at all." Titus's expression cleared, and there was a hint of a smile on his lips. "Would you like to see?"

I pressed my hand against his face as he lowered it toward me.

"No, not right now." There was a question in his eyes. "I don't understand, how does this work with…" I wasn't sure how to explain. Calling it 'the arrangement' was becoming embarrassing. "The others," I finished lamely, biting my lip. "I feel… connected with all of you. I can't—"

There was a wetness in the center of my palm, and I pulled my hand away back, looking at it in disgust. "Did you just lick me?"

"I don't like it," Titus replied without pause. "They've all had their families, their relationships. They had their chances at life. I don't like the idea of sharing mine."

My heart thundered at the sudden dark look on his face. "Titus…"

"But it's *you*," he said, his expression unwavering even as his voice grew softer. "You've always been close to all of us, and I can't make you choose. I'm not the only one who has always felt this way."

My heart pounded—what did he mean? "Titus?"

"Just don't forget about me." He pulled me close. His hand pressed against my head, and I could hear the wild beating of his heart. "Every lifetime, I'm always the furthest away."

"Why would you be the furthest away?" I gripped his shirt again. "You're right here."

Titus sighed, pressing his face into my neck. "I always will be, if you let me."

It probably wasn't the best timing, but my anxiety wouldn't let me avoid the question anymore. "Are you disappointed?" His mouth had pressed against my skin, but he paused at my question. "That I'm not a virgin, too?"

Titus was silent for a moment—unmoving—before he pushed back. This time he looked confused, and almost angry. There was a hint of red swirling within the depths of his eyes, as if he couldn't decide which emotion to focus on. His lips pursed, before he finally responded. "Too?"

I thought it was obvious. My pulse raced; I would have to explain.

"I'm not a virgin..." My voice wavered. "And Damen and Julian said you've never..." My words trailed off at the expression on his face.

He seemed genuinely offended.

"There are many incorrect assumptions in your first statement. I'll address those when you're in a better state. You don't seem like you're ready for that discussion," he said finally. "But as for the second. I've never had sex in *this* life"—his cheeks dusted over in pink—"but that doesn't mean I've never—"

"You've been married and had children?" My spine stiffened. But the others had said…

Titus frowned. "No."

"But you've had sex before," I said. "Doesn't that mean that there might be little dragon babies—"

He didn't even hesitate. "There is absolutely no chance."

"But you've had sex with a woman…" My words trailed off as realization washed over me. Scenes from my secret stash of comics flashed through my mind.

Titus stared at a point over my head. His face was darkening with every passing second.

It was all the confirmation I needed. "You've had sex with men? Titus, are you gay?"

"What?" Titus's eyes snapped back to mine. "I'm not gay. I'm not *any* label. I've only ever been interested in one person, *always*. I guess it doesn't matter which form they are born into."

My mind screamed in embarrassment, because how could I not remember?

And that manga, all those romantic X-rated moments. Usually such things frightened me, but I hadn't been able to look away. No wonder they were so interesting. Men were different, and I was having flashbacks! They had been strangely fascinating.

Reincarnation worked in mysterious ways.

"What are you thinking?" Titus asked, touching my cheek. His eyes met mine, and a second later, a smile touched his lips. Suddenly, he seemed very proud of himself. "Are you imagining it?"

"No!" I pushed against his chest, trying to put some distance between us.

Between this and everything else today, I was not in the right frame of mind for this conversation. "I'm so not." My voice shook.

"It's late." Titus's mood shifted in an instant, and he looked over me. And this time, I realized he'd been trying to distract me from the inevitable. "Are you ready to head back now?"

My heart sank, and I pulled away, hugging my knees back to my chest. "I can't," I told him. "I yelled at everyone and ran away. It was rude."

Titus let out a sound that suspiciously sounded like a laugh, and I peeked at him.

"Rude? How many times have you injured one of us already?" he asked. "And you've run away before."

I opened my mouth to respond, but he'd already touched my forehead. "Besides, you yelling at someone isn't uncommon. I can't wait for you to scream at Miles."

"What?" I gasped. Sweet, darling Miles? I would never.

"But I think there's another reason you're avoiding going back."

"Yes," I mumbled into my knees, my eyes drifting to the ground. "It's not the same."

"What's not the same?" Titus said, unmoved.

"You know what," I said, embarrassment racing through me. "You all know about it now. Everyone is going to be imagining it. Damen will keep asking questions. Julian will still try to help. I don't even know how Miles will react. No one understands."

The silence that followed was almost deafening. And when I thought he'd say nothing at all, his voice broke through my tumbling thoughts. "I might not be able to relate, but I *have* seen it before."

I glanced at him, but he was no longer looking at me. His focus remained at a point off to my side. "My work is client-based, and I've worked both sides of the law. I have been on teams hired to intervene in trafficking rings. I've seen what happens."

My breath caught, and the sound of my heartbeat echoed in my ears. I would almost prefer the speculation. But… at the same time, if he knew, then it meant that he might be able to relate. At least a little.

I wouldn't have to go over it again—I didn't need to relive it.

"I won't let them push you." His arms surrounded me. "They have good intentions, but…"

"I don't want to think about it." I was trembling. "I can't. For ten years, all anyone's tried to do was ask about it."

"They are trying to help. They want justice. I'm not going to push you, but… The reason you're hesitating…" His words trailed off as his breath brushed against my ear. His fingers tangled in the hair at the base of my neck, and shiver shot down my spine. "Are you still scared of him?"

I clung to him. He was solid around me, an impenetrable force of mass and muscle. I knew without a doubt that if anything were to happen, Titus would defend me without hesitation.

But that didn't stop the terror from racing through me.

"Bianca?" His thumb moved over the back of my head, and his voice soothed my fear.

"I'm scared." I pressed my face further into his chest, his musky scent washing over me. "He's gotten away before. He used to talk about it all the time. What if he found me? If he knew I'd told anyone…" Titus's hand continued to caress my neck, and I tried to steady my shaking. "I know it's stupid."

Titus was silent while I shivered against him. Only when my shaking subsided did he respond. "I'm going to find him." His reply was so direct that my vision wavered with unshed tears.

He was staring at a hard point over my head, his face a devastating statue of retribution. There was dark stubble over his chin, and that, combined with the faint red reflection in his eyes, made him look deadly.

"I'm going to find him," he repeated, the calm growl of his voice laced with the fury banked in his expression. "He won't be able to get to you, I can promise you that. But," his tone turned darker, "I'm also going to promise you'll have no more doubts about your safety once I bring you his spine."

A chill passed over me, and I didn't doubt the truth in his words. "I might not want to see it," I whispered. "Can't you just tell me, in detail, how you kill him? Can you make it hurt?"

His eyes were deep recesses that pulled me in, and the world hummed in the back of my awareness. Everything, my worries and fears, faded away as his presence cloaked me.

"Oh, princess." His voice didn't hold an ounce of hesitation. "Between me and Julian, we'll make him wish he'd never been born."

Chapter Eleven

Bianca

New

I woke up surrounded by Titus's scent, but was alone in the room. I vaguely recalled him bringing me here last night. It was very late when we'd come back to this house. I'd been too tired to function, too exhausted to face the others.

But it ended up being a non-issue. Once we arrived, no one was around anyway.

The place had been silent and felt abandoned, even though a fire had still been burning low in the hearth.

Titus didn't seem to care. He took me to his room, tucking the two of us into his bed.

I'd fallen asleep almost instantly.

But now I was awake and Titus was gone. In the daylight, it was easier to take in the space around me.

Damen's home was Victorian-style. But he seemed to have no decorative rules with the private bedrooms.

Titus's room was twice the size of the bedroom I'd grown up in, and my adoptive parents had been well-off. My room had consisted of a fireplace, sitting area, walk-in closet, along with a queen-sized bed. But it was small compared to this space.

Two large windows and light gray walls decorated with abstract artwork surrounded me. Across the large bed hung a television, and there was a metal desk with three monitors on top.

Titus had no blinds on his windows, only airy, elegant curtains folded over to the sides. And that was the reason why the sun was blinding me now.

I couldn't even focus on the rest of the room—my day was already ruined.

"No…" I groaned.

This was hell. I already felt like crap, my head still foggy from the night before. And now there was light.

Someone better have made coffee, or everyone would die. I wouldn't argue with an offering of bacon, either.

I covered my eyes and stepped away from the bed, only to fall onto the darker-gray carpet. It happened so fast I hadn't had time to shout.

Spotting the cause of my clumsiness, I glared at the small pile of clothing.

Titus must have laid something out for me. Which was nice. Although, why he put them on the floor and not on one of the many plush chairs that decorated his room, I had no idea.

These boys…

Still, the fact that he had been thoughtful brushed away my annoyance. Pushing myself to my knees, I pulled the clothing to me, curious about his choices.

My face warmed. *Hello Kitty* boxers and a plain white V-neck tee. I had no idea they even made *San-x* in this size.

Then, before I could even lower the underwear, Miles walked into the room.

"Oh." He stopped. Surprise flashed across his face. "You're awake!"

"The sun." My voice was scratchy, and I nodded toward the windows. "Make it go away!"

Miles's lips quirked, and he closed the door before stepping toward a panel on the wall.

"I would do almost anything for you, mon rêve," he said, typing. The room darkened as heavy blinds lowered over the glass. "But this is as far as I can go to stop the sun from shining."

I could see again!

I looked back to Miles, and my breath caught. Despite his playful words, his face was serious. Now he stood, bracing himself against the wall, his expression cautious.

I hadn't forgotten last night. I'd yelled at Damen and Julian—and by extension, him. Titus and I had already spoken, but was Miles angry?

I hid my face behind the red-bowed kitten. I was still so embarrassed.

"Don't hide from me." He had moved closer. "And especially not behind those." He jerked the boxers out of my hand and tossed them to the side.

I tracked their path, and the undershirt that followed an instant later.

"I would rather not see Titus's undergarments between us. Are you going to talk to me?" he asked.

I turned back to him.

He crouched in front of me. He seemed wary, but his expression was different than the others. He seemed almost afraid.

"Talk to you about what?" I said. "What's wrong?"

"About Bryce." His mouth thinned. "It was my idea. And I know how much you dislike—"

"I'm not angry about Bryce," I interrupted, meaning it. "It was actually a brilliant plan. Thank you, Miles." My stomach was twisting painfully, and I found it difficult to believe his biggest worry was Bryce.

Why wasn't he looking at me with pity or asking questions?

He blinked, his cheeks darkening. "Are you sure? Because I'd rather you yell at me now—"

I touched his mouth, cutting off his statement. "I'm sure. I'm not going to yell at you."

Relief entered his expression, and his tense shoulders relaxed.

"Besides, I don't usually shout," I said. "I'm not sure why you think so little of me. I'm always a calm and rational person."

Miles's eyebrow rose, amusement dancing in his eyes. "You're so self-aware."

"I know. It's a mark of maturity." I nodded, moving to my feet, reaching for Titus's clothes. "It's a talent that takes time to cultivate. Last night was a rare exception. Besides, I don't get angry."

No, there was no point to getting angry. Uncivilized ruffians would let their anger control them. I was different. I got even.

It wasn't the same.

Like my eventual showdown with Finn. After I pushed him through a wall and crushed him under my heel, we would be even. Then I could move on with my life.

Maybe we might be friends again one day. He hadn't been terrible when we were imprisoned by Daniel Cole.

My insides twisted with conflict, because now I owed him a debt. I didn't like owing people.

Speaking of owing people… I needed access to my funds.

"Miles, how do I…" My voice trailed off at the incredulous look on his face. "What?"

"Just now!" He moved to his feet, pointing at me. "As you turned away, you had a look on your face. Then you went tense. What were you thinking about?"

I pursed my lips. "What look?" Was he delusional?

"It's the one that says you're going to do something terrible." Miles stepped back. "You weren't thinking about me, were you?"

I fought the urge to roll my eyes. Why was he so paranoid? "I wasn't thinking about *you*. If you *must* know, I was contemplating Finn's punishment."

"Oh." His arm dropped back to his side, curiosity replacing the fear. "You're still going to punish Finn? What is it this time? Are you still going to kill him?"

I frowned, looking at Miles disapprovingly.

I couldn't believe he would consider such dramatic extremes. "I'm going to stomp on him. Perhaps I might push him, too. Why would I kill him?"

Now Miles seemed confused. "But you *said* you were going to kill him. You said you were going to kick him in the balls. What happened to that plan?"

Oh, *that*.

I waved my hand in the air. How simpleminded he was. "Plans can change depending on the circumstance. Punishments must always reflect the nature of the crime. And right now, he deserves a good slap."

"You *just* said you were going to stomp on him," Miles said. "And within the span of thirty seconds you changed it again."

"But I can't hit him on the face…" I muttered, touching my chin. I was a fair individual, and he was attractive. It was bad enough Bryce had been ripped apart by a demon. I didn't like to see so much pain and suffering.

I should probably wait until after Bryce was better.

"Where's my money anyway?" I glanced back to Miles. "Damen said Bryce had my money. Where is Bryce? Is he at the school?"

Miles eyebrow rose slowly. He studied me as if he'd never seen me before. "Now you're looking for Bryce? He's cancelled classes today."

I nodded, pulling my hospital gown away from my body and glancing at it disdainfully. The smell made me gag. Why in the world hadn't Titus insisted I bathe last night? "I need to take a shower. Where is there a shower? I need to go shopping."

"You're making all sorts of plans." Miles sounded amused. "What about your classes?"

"They can wait until Monday. I need to go to the registrar's office, too." Miles suddenly looked way too innocent. I narrowed my eyes at him. Didn't *he* have classes today? "Why aren't you in school?"

His skin flushed. "I wanted to see that you were okay. I missed you," he said, shyly.

And with that, I melted. I couldn't think of a single response.

I'd missed him, too. It should have been simple to say, but my lips wouldn't form the words. It was easy to joke with him, but had we ever discussed his feelings? I'd talked to Damen, Julian, and now Titus about their strange expectations.

However, Miles never expressed much of an opinion on the topic. He was an enigma. And I had no idea what he was thinking. About me—or this whole plan.

"Oh, come here." His voice was gruff. He grabbed my smock and pulled me into him. The top of my head fit perfectly under his chin, and his arms held me to him. I could feel the pounding of his heart and hear the shuddering intake of his breath.

"I missed you," he said again. "I skipped classes every day."

The heat fled from my face, and disappointment replaced my nervousness.

"Miles!" I tried to push back, but his hold was solid. "Miles, you'll fail!"

"Oh please." Miles sounded amused. "I have the top grades in my year."

His words did little to reassure me. "Did you really skip classes every day?" It was bad enough I had missed my classes, and I was no valedictorian.

"I'll tell you if you take a shower," Miles said, releasing me and turning me to face another door. He pushed through the entrance and turned on the lights.

Unlike the bedroom, the bathroom retained the style of the house. Stone and marble covered the space, and a claw-footed tub with a shower was nestled in the far corner of the room. Behind it, a stained-glass window reflected squares of red and orange onto the floor.

I raised my eyebrow, glancing at Miles.

Before I had to explain, Miles picked up on my question. So, apparently, this had come up in conversation before.

"Damen doesn't care what we do to our bedrooms, except for changes to the framework. But he says he doesn't want to compromise the integrity of the ancient plumbing…" Miles paused, rubbing his forehead. "Or something stupid. He's slowly trying to repurpose the interior. He's freaky about art and antiques."

That gave me hope. "Is he planning on doing something about the outside?"

Miles sighed. "He doesn't care what it looks like. I think he does it to keep the property taxes down, and he's gotten no permits for remodeling. He won't let anyone come inside. He's been trying to scare people off. Sometimes he and Titus go into the woods and shoot their guns to make sure that the value of the area doesn't go up."

What in the world?

I stared at him, surprised, as Miles turned on the water and proceeded to pull fluffy towels out from under the sink. He set the towels aside. "It's not that weird," he argued.

No, it definitely was very strange. The guy owned a Jaguar.

"Don't misunderstand. Damen isn't cheap." Miles correctly read my expression. "He's actually the worst with money management. He does this because he doesn't want neighbors moving in nearby or unwelcome visitors. Despite how he acts, Damen is an *extremely* private person. When you first showed up, he was probably panicking. No student knows where he lives. If he ended up not liking you, he might have killed Gregory."

"But…" Damen hadn't looked upset. He'd been all charm and smiles. "He was flirting with me."

"Damen flirts to cover his nervousness." Miles leaned against the sink, studying me with darkened eyes. "He does it to redirect people from his true intentions. You could spend lifetimes attempting to figure out the source of his passion, never to realize you were looking at the wrong place the whole time. He must be terrified right now. He's never had such an obvious weakness."

His words almost sounded like a warning. I swallowed. "What do you mean?"

"I don't want to talk about Damen anymore." Miles changed the subject. "I'm wondering, what would you do if I became angry?"

A trickle of confusion passed through me. "You get angry?"

Miles frowned, almost looking offended. "You saw me fighting my teammates at practice… or did you leave before that?"

"Oh…" I bit my lip, glancing away.

That was true, I did see him bodyslam a teammate into the dirt. But how could I tell him… "I did see that."

"Oh no." Miles expression changed into concern, and he rubbed his hands down my arms. "I scared you with that? I'm so sorry."

"No, you didn't scare me." Perhaps I should mention it? He seemed so upset; his eyes searched my face in trepidation. "Your form is wrong. And the way you tossed the other guy through the air could be improved."

"What?" Miles dropped his hands, his eyes widening.

I nodded, a plan already beginning to form. Someone had to tell him, and I guess the person chosen for that task would be me.

"Maria wants to go to a WWE match," I told him. "You should come. You lack passion when you fight. It'll be educational to watch a professional."

"Wait." He frowned at me. "You *want* me to fight?"

"Not particularly." I touched my chin, studying him. Miles had a bodybuilder's physique, so he looked formidable. Yet, he lacked the sincerity in wanting to murder his opponent. If I didn't toughen him up, he'd be a target for the rest of his life.

He was so sweet, so kind.

I would bet anything that people took advantage of him. They either took advantage of his kindness, or they flat out bullied him. This was how stalkers targeted sincere men. I hadn't forgotten about the women picking on him during his soccer practice.

I would have to save him before something terrible happened. Before I needed to hurt someone again.

It was my job to help him.

"You should hang out with me while we're at school. It's safer that way." I tapped my chin. "Then we can begin your training."

"What training?" Miles didn't sound amused, or happy, anymore. "And didn't we already establish that you're escorting me to my classes?"

I wasn't sure what training yet. Maria might have some ideas; she was tough.

"We'll see…" I noted his wary expression. "You'll like it. Let's do our homework together later, okay?"

Miles frowned, stubbornness bleeding into his face.

"I don't want…" he began, but then his words trailed off. The stubbornness gave way to contemplation. "You want to do homework together?"

Something in his voice caused my heart to skip.

"You'll have French!" he sounded so happy. "We can email your professor to get your assignments."

Crap on a cracker!

My breathing had caught in my throat. How was I supposed to tell Miles I was dropping French for Chinese? This was horrible. The only way to avoid hurting his feelings was to pretend to take French forever.

But there was a problem with that plan—I wasn't getting out of doing any work this way.

"Okay…" I whispered, putting off the inevitable. One day, I might have to break the news to Miles. But his face was glowing in a way that caused my pulse to spike.

There was no way I could do it right now.

Chapter Twelve

Bianca
Law

"Good morning." Brayden jumped to his feet as Miles led me into Damen's kitchen. He and Bryce were in a sunny breakfast nook, seemingly deep in a discussion before we arrived.

They wore their pajamas still, which made me feel less self-conscious about being in Titus's oversized clothing. But the sight of Bryce in navy cotton bottoms was very strange.

They watched me a second too long, studying me in a way I didn't recognize. All pretenses had gone, and I wondered how long they'd known who I was.

Brayden raised his eyebrow, disapproval darkening his previously relaxed expression. He pushed his sleep-tossed curls from his face, rubbing his eyes. And when his hands lowered, the look had vanished. "What's wrong, Bianca? Those aren't yours, right?" he asked, stepping forward and grabbing my hand. "Do you need to go shopping?"

His words caused my stomach to tighten, the feeling distracting me from the sensation of his skin against mine. This was the first time Brayden—the better brother—had ever touched me. And like with Bryce, the feeling made my skin itch.

"Yes..." I allowed him to guide me to the table between him and Bryce and pulled my hand into my lap the second he released me. I studied the empty placemat. "I didn't want anything they gave me. It's okay though. I have money."

"You have money?" Brayden sounded surprised. I glanced at him, and he held his hands into the air. "You said you were a 'poor college student'."

Miles, who had wandered off, returned. He placed a mug of coffee in front of me and ruffled my hair before turning back to the stove. I wasn't sure what he was making, but it smelled like bacon was involved. As Brayden glanced after him, I responded, "Yes, Bryce is going to give me my money."

Bryce, who had been sipping his own coffee, choked and began to cough. It took a moment for him to compose himself, but when he did, he shot me an alarmed look. "What?"

Playing stupid, was he? I pursed my lips. "Titus and Damen told me that since you're my Er Bashou, you've been in charge of my funds. I'd like to access that money."

"Oh." He pushed his coffee away and crossed his arms. He sounded slightly regretful. "I can't give you that money."

"Why not?" Did he spend *my* money on something stupid? Titus said he had enemies. Perhaps he dabbled in illegal things and that was why his luck was so terrible.

"Because no one can know you're the Xing," Miles replied from the kitchen, nonchalantly. "Bryce can't give you access to those funds. He can't take anything out either."

My heart dropped. My plans were ruined. How was I supposed to get clothing and everything now? Without my money, I had nothing.

Miles leaned over the island, studying me. His expression was sympathetic. "You know we have no problem paying for—"

"No." It wouldn't be right. I already owed them enough.

"You know—" Brayden linked his hands under his chin, watching me. Nervousness surrounded him, and his eyes searched mine. "—our family is—"

"No." My voice came out harsher than intended. "I am not taking money from them."

Brayden frowned, lowering his hands. "But it's your money, too. They are your family. Father has always set aside allowance and inheritance for three—"

"I don't want it." I pushed back my chair, digging my nails into the table. My stomach churned painfully. "I don't want anything to do with it."

"But why?" Brayden sounded genuinely distraught, and it made guilt rush through me.

"It's obvious." My heart was racing, my earlier fears flooding back into me. The prophecy changed nothing. I used to think knowing why I'd been abandoned would help, but now it was worse.

My life had been in danger, and my *parents* had left me. Did they know the kind of world they were sending me into? I couldn't blame Bryce for this.

If they really wanted to keep me, they would have found a way. But they hadn't.

They must have really hated me.

"Bianca," Brayden began. "What are you—"

"Don't imagine it's worse than it is. Father was a bit distracted when you were born," Bryce cut in, voice as smooth as ever. "He wasn't thinking clearly." My knuckles were turning white, but Bryce continued before I could speak. "But we are married. Use my account, and we'll transfer the funds back once you access your savings."

Bryce still had that refined look to him despite his beaten face. There was no shame radiating from him, and he returned to sipping his coffee.

"This is so weird," Brayden said, laying his head over his arms. The tension fled from his frame, and he latched on to the new topic. "Did Dad say anything about you marrying her?"

Bryce shrugged. "He understands. Though"—he glanced at me—"there's the matter of your Biology class. I've cancelled everything for today. This afternoon, I need to go before the administration to pretend to plead with Mr. Abernathy for my job—"

"Hold on." I held up my hand. "Damen?"

"Dean." Bryce's brows furrowed. "Finn still hasn't told you? His father is the primary shareholder for our college. The Abernathy family owns a number of educational establishments. And they have massive political influence. Dean knows who you are, of course. Damen told him last week."

I gaped at Bryce, uncertain at how to process this information. Finn had never even hinted…

"Finn's dad owns the college?" I repeated, recalling past events. "Is this how Finn was able to close off portions of the library? Or manipulate the teacher's schedules?"

"Partially." Bryce frowned. "I've spent some time with him this last week. He's admitted to having some skill in hacking these days. Which makes sense. Although it was a bit surprising, considering his interests don't lie in that direction."

"How does that make sense?" My voice rose an octave. How could Bryce say something like this so nonchalantly? "It doesn't make sense to me!"

"Finn's mother, Rhea Abernathy, is the founder and CEO of a global internet conglomerate. She's a genius in software engineering," Bryce said. "But neither Finn nor Damen had any interest in their parents' businesses.

Damen was always terrible with technology, and Finn followed his brother around everywhere. When Damen decided he wanted to go into criminal justice, Finn wanted to be with him. But when Finn contracted with his shikigami, everything changed."

"What…" I listened to Bryce, shocked. I had known that Finn once wanted to be the chief of police. But I'd never known why. I also knew Damen and Finn used to be close. When we first met, Finn gushed about him.

"What does his shikigami have to do with anything?"

"Kiania was one of Huo's most frequently contracted shikigami," Miles said, sliding some plates onto the table and slipping into the seat opposite mine. "She's almost as old as we are and is one of his most powerful shikigami. No one outside of Huo has been able to sustain a connection with her, although many onmyoji have died trying. She expected to be contracted in this life—it's been a while since she's been in service—but Damen contracted with Kasai instead. She wasn't happy about being passed over. When Finn did his ceremony the summer he turned eight, she intercepted. The ceremony is a private affair, so Damen had no idea what happened until it was too late. Once a contract is established, only the shikigami or onmyoji can change the terms."

"Finn refused to break the contract." Bryce cut in as he spooned scrambled eggs onto my plate, and I wolfed them down as Bryce continued to speak. "He wanted to be strong enough to help Damen. But everyone was afraid he was going to die. His health declined, and his parents fought over it. Dean couldn't convince Finn to change his mind, to talk to Kiania. Rhea is a divination master, but she only knew things would eventually work. Over summer break, Mr. and Mrs. Abernathy divorced because they argued about the approach. Damen changed schools and lived with his father. Finn continued to attend one of the sister schools while living with his mother."

"He did poorly for a while." Miles pushed the bacon toward Bryce. "But Finn ended up pulling through and can now maintain Kiania's contract. But he wouldn't associate with anyone after that. Damen has never gotten over it. He blames Kiania for everything. That's why Damen allows Finn to do what he does."

Bryce was stacking bacon on my plate. My dish was full in front of me, but there was no way I'd be able to eat any more. My stomach twisted, nausea threatening to overpower me as their words pulled at my memories. Pieces that had been missing throughout most of my life seemed to fall into place.

"I met Finn when I was eight…" I whispered. "I transferred into his class right after summer break."

Bryce's arm froze midair, and three sets of eyes focused on me.

My lips felt numb. "The first time I saw him, I thought he was dying. There was a shadow always following him around. I thought it was a demon. It sucked away at his life, like Kasai does with Damen."

"Bianca," Miles said softly, "Kasai isn't—"

"I talked to it." I shook, recalling my latest dream. "I'm not supposed to tell you this…"

It took everything to not to lie, especially when my instincts were screaming for it.

Why couldn't I shake this feeling? Did I mess everything up? But if I did, they needed to know.

"Bianca." Miles reached across the table, grasping my hand.

"I don't remember all the details," I admitted. "But I talked to it… *her*. I didn't know what she was though."

Miles's lips thinned and he tilted his head. "Do you remember what you talked about?"

"I told her to leave him alone. She told me he was dying." Goose bumps broke out over my arms.

Finn was my first friend, and I couldn't let him die. Not if there was something I could do to help. No matter what it cost me, I wasn't able to allow it to happen.

"She said she would change the nature of their contract. That it would save his life."

Miles's grip tightened over my own, and his next words were wary. "She wanted to change his contract?"

I nodded. "She called me Mu. I didn't know what it meant. She said it would work." Why did I feel so guilty telling them this?

Bryce and Brayden were still beside me, but it was Miles who broke the heavy silence. His voice sounded like a dream. Or maybe that was the ringing in my ears. "Let me guess. She asked you to become her energy source, and you said yes." There wasn't even a question in his tone.

"I didn't want him to die," I whispered. "He was my first friend."

The deafening atmosphere lasted a moment longer, then Brayden's panicked tones broke through the air. My eyes shot to him—he was pale, and his hands were shaking. And he was looking at Miles. "What should we do?"

"What happened after that?" Bryce hooked his finger under my chin and turned my focus to him. "This is important."

"I passed out and woke up in the hospital…" I glanced between him and Miles, who seemed to be deep in thought. "That's when I met Dr. Reed."

"That's when you *met* her?" Miles interjected this time, his tone incredulous. The blank expression was slowly giving way to anger. "You never met her before that?"

"No. There was another lady there, too, but I don't know who she was." I frowned, pulling my hand away from his. I touched my fingers together in my lap. I didn't understand, everything had turned out fine. "I didn't remember what happened. They told me I had a heart attack. Dr. Reed was angry at my parents for not bringing me in earlier, but I'm not sure…"

Miles expression grew darker, and I could no longer ignore it.

"What's wrong?" I asked. "Did I break some kind of rule?"

"The bond between a shikigami and an onmyoji is meant to be between the two of them *only*," Miles said. There was something ancient about the way he held himself suddenly. "It was one of Huo's first laws and is the most strictly enforced. Technically, a shikigami can remain on Earth by surviving on anyone's energy. But that would expand the bond into a three, or more, way connection. It is dangerous and unethical to practice, and in every case has always caused the energy source to die. It is practiced when power-hungry onmyoji contract with a shikigami they cannot control. The relationship between a shikigami and onmyoji must be balanced. In most cases, the onmyoji can sustain the connection with his own life-force. There is no need for another energy source."

My pulse pounded in my ears. It was true. I had done something terrible.

"Anyone who breaks that law is punished, then put to death," Miles continued, his eyes holding mine. "Huo would eventually destroy the shikigami, but only after decades of torture and isolation. Shui acts on behalf of the victim and punishes the onmyoji. It's his responsibility to control Fire elementals."

"Julian and Damen would?" It was hard to breathe. "But that's not fair. Finn didn't know what was happening. I did it on my own!"

Miles raised his eyebrow. "I got that impression. Where was he?"

"I stayed behind for my speech lessons. Finn went home." My hands were shaking again, and I clasped them in my lap. "When she talked to me, she said he'd be unhappy." I glanced at him. "Why would the newly bonded person die?"

Miles's lips thinned. "Shikigami exist in another realm. It is different there, and only those of the Fire element are compatible with that kind of connection. To anyone else, the energy required to forge the bond would feel like fire. Depending on how strong that person was, it could last minutes to hours while their energy is being used. But it always ends in death."

"I'm not dead," I pointed out, trying to think optimistically. "And I've felt it before… Maybe that's not what happened this time?"

"No, it makes sense." Damen's voice suddenly cut through the space, causing the three men around me to jump. His voice was colder than anything I'd heard from him before, and I spun in my seat toward him. "We've never had someone survive long enough to know what long-term effect there might be. But now that we know the cause, it's fairly obvious."

My throat closed. Julian and Damen stood across the room next to an entrance I hadn't even noticed. Their expressions were murderous, and focused entirely on me.

Chapter Thirteen

Bianca

Questions

Brayden broke the silence. "What long-term effects? It won't stop with the initial bond?"

Neither boy looked away from me, even as Damen responded. "The connection between the three of them won't just go away." Damen pulled out his phone. "One moment…"

Bryce shot Damen a started look, and his expression morphed into wariness. "Are you calling Finn here *now*? Should we contact Maria and Jin? If you're doing something, the whole group should be present—"

"No." My heart raced with panic. Their faces filled me with dread, and before I realized it, I stood in front of them. I'd raised my hands, my gaze remained locked on their surprised expressions.

"Don't be mad at Finn," I pleaded. This one hadn't been his fault. "It really wasn't—"

Julian's gaze softened slightly, and he touched my face. His eyes were distant. It felt as though I was losing him. "You're too kind for your own good sometimes. You had to know, on some level, agreeing with her wasn't a good idea."

What else was I supposed to do?

"I couldn't let him die…" My voice sounded so small and my excuse pathetic. They couldn't have expected me to—

Julian sucked in a breath, but before he could respond I had been pulled from him.

Then I was pressed against Damen's chest. My hands were trapped by my face, and his arms engulfed my shoulders and head. He was shaking, and the world surrounding me was dark. All I could feel was Damen, warm against me. "Damen?"

"The medication?" Damen's voice grumbled, and I wasn't sure what he was asking.

But it was Julian who responded. "It has to be related. That's what my mother and Du Yun are watching for, I'm sure. They probably thought that by suppressing her abilities, they were weakening the bond."

"Bianca." Damen squeezed once more before loosening his grip. Then his hands moved to my shoulders, holding me from him. The force of his presence almost overwhelmed me. "Can I see how the marks on your arm and back are healing?"

I blinked at him, unsure of how this related. "You mean the curse?"

"It might not have actually been a curse." Damen was frowning now, barely disguised concerned flickering in his eyes. "You're back on the medication. If it's what I think, the marks should be nearly gone."

Julian grasped the edge of my sleeve. Titus's shirt was way too big on me, the bottom of the fabric brushed low against my elbows. I hadn't considered the loose neck, and Julian was able to see down my back.

"They look better than they were even two days ago." Julian's finger tugged at my shirt. "They started healing faster once the medication resumed."

My heart raced at the unexpected touch. I turned, ripping away from his hold, and put my back to the door. "You don't need to look at them!"

Julian's hand was still raised in the air, his face a picture of surprise. Damen, too, seemed stunned. It was better than the furious looks they had earlier, but my racing pulse didn't steady in relief.

In fact, it only worsened. My fear blossoming as more connections were made. Past events I'd thought were unrelated. Another time when Finn, in his anger, had caused me to bruise in a similar way, rose to the forefront of my mind.

I was scared. They were looking for evidence against Finn. But I wouldn't let them use me. It was one thing to hate him because he was a liar and a jerk. Or because he did, in fact, slam me against a wall and twist my arm.

He did deserve a beating, and I would help.

But it was another thing to *kill* him over something *I* did.

I would never be able to live with myself. I wasn't sure what was going to happen, but I refused to let them use me to bring him down.

"Bianca!" Julian's voice caused my stomach to clench. "Bianca, there is no need to worry yourself over this," he said. "But you cannot hide. I still need to check up on you. You're not recovered. The pain medication has to be almost out of your system. You were shot, and your neck cut. And I need to reapply your bandages."

"Stay away from me." My heart was beating wildly, and my breathing shallow. "You're trying to use me to hurt Finn."

Julian's expression grew fierce, and his gaze seemed to darken. "He broke the law. You could have died. I am not giving him a free pass."

"No!" I pressed against the door. I should never have said anything. "If it is anyone's fault, it's mine! I was the one who met with her."

"This never would have happened if he wasn't stubborn." Julian's jaw tightened. "He should have had more control over her—she never should have been able to meet with you alone. Now you won't be able to use your abilities as you should. With that bond still active, you won't be able to support Damen."

My protests died, my thoughts slamming to a halt. My attention shifted to Damen—waiting for him to disagree. But his eyes were guarded now. His mouth thinned as our gazes met. "That's a theory. You're bonded outside of your quintet, and even you aren't strong enough to sustain both of us."

He nodded toward Bryce, who—along with Brayden and Miles—had gotten to their feet. "It's *Bryce's* job to support Finn. It's *Finn's* job to bond with his shikigami."

"I already support him." Bryce crossed his arms. But although his words were argumentative, his tone was filled with contemplation. "Since Kiania has never affected me, I was assumed Finn was strong enough to handle it. Without Bianca carrying the burden, how much worse would it be?"

"Bryce won't be able to support Finn on his own," Julian said, narrowing his eyes at Damen. "Kiania is too strong. That's why she's never been contracted with anyone besides you. I told you it was suspicious, but everyone ignored me. You need to break the bond."

I wasn't sure what Julian meant. But from the torn look on Damen's face, and the horrified expressions of the others, it wasn't anything good.

I couldn't breathe. "I can do both! Leave him alone!"

Damen glanced at me, poised to speak. But the door behind me opened suddenly, cutting off his words.

A familiar presence draped over my shoulders, and Titus pulled me back against him.

I couldn't see him, so I couldn't tell his mood from his expression, but his voice was eerily calm when he spoke. "What is going on? I leave for five minutes, and she's upset."

"Titus, thank God you're here." Julian shifted his attention to the taller man. "I know you'll agree with me. I can already tell from Miles's face he doesn't. And in this instance, Damen doesn't count."

Damen frowned at Julian. Miles stepped closer, affronted. "Hey—"

"What am I supposed to agree with?" Titus replied coolly. "The fact that you're disregarding Bianca's wishes? Or you're latching on to the first opportunity you've gotten to get to Finn? We all know how long you've been waiting for this."

Julian's expression darkened further. I glimpsed why people might be so scared of him.

He wasn't angry—at least in the way that most people would be. His fury was something that remained barely contained under his calm exterior. There was a determination churning in his bright blue eyes that filled me with dread.

There was nothing Julian couldn't do once he put his mind to it. He was probably scarier than all the others.

"It could kill her!" He pointed at me. "It *is* killing her."

"It's not going to kill her within the next few days," Miles broke in, holding out his hands. "She's been bonded to them for ten years already."

"She is not supposed to be bonded to them," Julian seethed. His attention returned to Damen, who was watching him with a particular expression. "This is *your* rule. Why aren't you doing anything? You're the one most affected by this!"

Damen's mouth thinned. "I'm not saying we're not doing anything. But we should wait—"

"You only want to wait because he's your brother!" Julian was angrier than I'd ever seen him before. "You'd have killed anyone else already. You two and your entitlements are driving me crazy. You should have let me do something about him three years ago! He was wrong then, and his actions are criminal now."

Julian's words broke through my attention. My fingers dug into Titus's arm.

This was the missing piece—the reason Julian hated Finn.

From his tone, it sounded bad. But there was nothing from three years ago that stood out as significant. Finn had always acted the same around me.

What happened?

"Julian." Miles closed the distance between them, clasping his hand over Julian's elbow. "You need to calm down. If you promise to let it drop for now, to listen to the whole story, maybe Bianca will still let you help her. But acting like this, you're not getting anywhere."

At the mention of my name, Julian's posture drooped.

"Julian…" He was a tiny bit calmer now, but still scary. But I wasn't scared for me.

He ran his fingers through his hair. My heart twisted guiltily; I hated that it was because of me, that he was struggling with his emotions. "Bianca, I—"

Whatever it was he was about to say was interrupted when Finn strode into the room, Anthony on his heels. Both looked confused. But once Finn spotted me, the expression wiped from his face, indifference replacing it.

It made me feel even worse.

"What do you want?" He turned to Damen. "I was only just able to spike Anthony's coffee with NyQuil when you texted. As you can see, it hasn't worked yet, and he's still following me. You're ruining what could have turned into an otherwise peaceful day."

"It's not like I have a choice," Anthony protested, frowning down into his paper travel cup. He tossed it in the sink, then gestured at Julian. "He told me to."

"And for good reason!" Julian's temper was beginning to bubble over once again. "Why do you keep medicating people? Did you really put something into his drink?"

"Finn!" Without a second thought, I'd pushed away from Titus, crossing the room until Finn and I stood toe to toe. I was so nervous, and I wrung my hands in front of me as my mind raced to figure out how to make things right.

But I was lacking any brilliant ideas. "Finn, I didn't know…"

"You didn't know what?" Finn's voice was detached, a defense mechanism he adopted when trying to act brave.

Jaiyi had been right! I might not have known about the truth of Finn's life, but I did recognize his mannerisms.

Not *everything* was a lie.

"What do you *want?*" he asked again.

Damen had moved to the counter, crossing his arms as he rested his hip against the edge. He scowled at Finn.

I held my breath, because Damen hadn't said *how* he felt. Outside of his initial reaction, it had been impossible to tell if he was angry, or something else. But when he'd held me, thanking me, I hoped it was because he was grateful.

"I'm going to ask you this only once." His voice was calm, but his gaze steady as he watched his brother. "Why didn't you come to me *immediately* after your contract with Kiania changed?"

Finn stiffened; his breath locked as his gaze remained steady on Damen's. I was right in front of him, but I had no idea how to warn him. I was the worst ex-best friend ever.

"I'm sorry..." I couldn't think of anything else to say. "I'm sorry, I'm sorry..."

His focus shot to me. The dread had left his expression, replaced with surprise. "Why are you sorry?"

My heart lurched. Didn't he realize? "I told them what happened. I didn't know..."

"Oh please." Finn rolled his eyes. "Like anyone is going to blame you. It's not *your* fault she was waiting for you. You're so naive."

I stared at him, not feeling any better with him acting like a jerk. How was it possible to feel so guilty, yet also want to punch him in the face?

Why was he so infuriating?

"Finn!" Damen's voice was commanding, and Finn's attention shifted back. "Stop acting like an idiot and answer my question. Why didn't you come to me?"

"I don't know!" Finn threw his hands in the air. "I didn't know what to do! Everyone was trying to figure out what happened and how to deal with it. Plus, if we went to you, you'd have found out who Bianca was, which they didn't want."

This seemed to mollify Damen. His severity melted into contemplation, and he paced. "This has never been successful before... You never cursed her, did you?"

"Of course not!" Finn sounded genuinely offended. "I was angry! My emotions affect the bond. When she's on her medication, it seems to control it better."

When he was emotional?

"When we were in school…" My pulse picked up, fragments of memories flashing through my mind. "Was that what happened when you beat up Cory?"

His voice was curt. "Yes."

I touched my mouth. I couldn't believe how stupid I'd been. This had happened before, but I never made the connection. "I thought it was just a bruise."

"It wouldn't have happened if you hadn't jumped in." Finn frowned, his eyes flashing. "You have no business getting into my fights."

A loud bang echoed through the room, cutting off my response.

Damen still rested his hand on the counter, his expression severe.

"Everyone into the living room." Damen pointed to the door. "We are not having this discussion standing around the kitchen, but we're getting to the bottom of this right now."

Chapter Fourteen

Bianca
Secret

Finn, surprisingly, made himself right at home and headed toward an armchair. I started to follow him, but Titus snatched my arm, pulling me to the couch to sit between him and Miles.

Bryce and Brayden, still silently observing, had claimed two other armchairs. Anthony, on the other hand, stood next to Finn.

Everyone's attention was on Julian and Damen. Julian was leaning against the wall next to the empty hearth. Damen continued his pacing as he muttered angrily under his breath.

I wasn't sure what he was saying, but, slowly, the annoyed expression he'd worn since the kitchen began to fade. When he looked at Finn again, he was calmer.

"Who is Cory?" he asked. "What are you talking about?"

My face heated in embarrassment. I would much rather be discussing anything else.

Weren't we supposed to be talking about my impending death?

Finn frowned, leaning into his seat. "Cory was our classmate. He kept targeting Bianca, and she wouldn't fight back. Once, after Kiania changed our contract, he and his friends hurt her. So I beat the shit out of them."

I hid my face behind my hands. This was so humiliating; I couldn't even bring myself to protest. Did he really have to go into this much detail? I sounded like such a loser.

"That's when Bianca jumped into the fight. I grabbed her arm to pull her out of it," Finn continued.

How dare he say it like that! "I was trying to stop you! I didn't want you to get into trouble," I said. I had saved him from being expelled. He should be grateful.

Finn waved his hand in the air, ignoring me. "She had a mark where I touched her. It looked like a bruise. Dr. Kohler didn't know it was because of our bond or if she injured easily. She couldn't find any research on it. But it wouldn't heal."

"There's not going to be any research." Julian stroked his chin. "So the medication does suppress the bond?"

"They weren't sure it would work," Finn said. "But the marks were starting to spread. It was hurting her. Then there was the fact Bianca was afraid of her abilities. So they decided to try the medication to see if it could help. It was luck that it ended up working."

I blinked at Finn, just a bit lost. But everyone was nodding, as if his words made perfect sense.

This was the second time this had come up.

"Um…" I tentatively interjected, and eight gazes shot to me. My pulse picked up, but I continued, nonetheless. "I don't know why you all seem to think I'm scared of my abilities. But that's not true."

Finn frowned, watching me in confusion. "When you bring up the paranormal, you're shaking and terrified. And you always seem to think you are going to die."

I narrowed my eyes at him. "I'm not upset because I can see ghosts."

Finn's frown deepened.

"Most of the time," I added. He did have a point about being fearful of being killed.

That was, after all, a highly ranked concern of mine.

At Finn's look of disbelief, I pressed forward. "I was nervous because I wanted you to believe me. This is stupid, you're the worst best friend ever!"

Finn's brow furrowed. "What?"

"Why didn't you ask me *why* I was afraid?" He was such an idiot. "For the record, in general, I'm *not* scared of ghosts. There are many things out there more terrifying than the paranormal."

"What…?" Finn still seemed confused.

"The only ghosts that concern me are the ones who are actively trying to *kill me*." I pointed at him. "Such as the one in Professor Hamway's house. The one I *told* you about!"

Everyone looked between the two of us, disbelief radiating through the room.

It was Bryce who finally spoke. "Finn, you need to work on your communication skills."

Finn turned his burning gaze on him. "I don't want to hear that from *you*," he growled. "Besides, that's not the only reason." His vision snapped back to mine. "If you're not scared, why won't you talk about your first experience? Every medium likes to brag about it. You've *always* freaked out."

My mouth opened in protest, my heart pounding at his accusation.

This was why he thought I was afraid?

But I wasn't afraid. He was wrong. I could talk about her.

I was just like everyone else.

There was a buzzing echoed in my ears, but no one else seemed to hear it. Instead, they all watched me. My vision tunneled, and Finn's face remained at the center. His expression turned from anger to regret in the span of a second, but as he moved, that too faded.

"Darling, it's okay." Julian's hands were on my face, and his blue eyes filled my shimmering vision.

"I-i-it's not." My voice shook. Even though he'd pulled me back from the abyss, nothing was okay. I felt so stupid.

I could feel everyone's attention on me—they had to be curious, and there was no way they weren't judging me. Titus and Miles held my hands, and I sensed Damen nearby.

"What happened?" Anthony asked, his voice laced with concern. The fact that he, Bryce and Brayden had witnessed this made it even worse. "I've never seen—"

"Don't worry about it," Julian cut him off, his gaze still caught with mine. "We have other things to focus on."

"Do you see what I mean?" Finn cut in from somewhere behind Julian, and the sound of his voice caused Julian's eyes to harden. "How was I supposed to know?"

"You still shouldn't have assumed," Damen said, his tone cool. "But that's beside the point. Julian's got her now. But this discussion is not over."

Julian shifted, motioned for Miles to move and took his vacated spot. I didn't even have time to start shivering. An afghan was wrapped around me, and I was pulled into Julian's lap while my feet rested on Titus's thighs.

Despite my better judgement, I glanced at Brayden and Bryce. Were they ready to run yet?

I was a terrible leader.

Bryce frowned deeply, watching Damen. The other man had begun to pace again, and thankfully commanded most of the attention with his movements.

But Brayden was looking at me, making no secret of that fact.

I glanced at my lap, unable to deal with him right now. I'd wanted so badly to impress them. But because Finn had brought up *that*, I had failed miserably.

"Bianca." Julian's fingers traced over my shoulders, bringing my attention back to the conversation. His hand drifted over the loose blanket to the too-large neck hole of Titus's shirt. He tugged it down slightly, his eyes not leaving mine. "We got off topic. Can we see the marks again please?"

My heartbeat was echoing in my ears, and I could feel the weight of expectation in the air.

"Don't hurt him…" Julian held my gaze as I whispered. He hadn't promised yet.

His expression darkened again slightly, but it was Damen who responded. "It might actually help." He sounded so far away. "If we knew how it was actually affecting you, it might give us some answers."

It could help.

But I felt like breaking into a thousand pieces. Everyone's attention was on me. There were too many people, and I didn't care who they were.

Yet, I couldn't say no—it was selfish. I still didn't want Finn to get into trouble.

What if it helped?

I tore my eyes from Julian, glancing at my ankles. Titus's hands rested over my feet, and I focused on them. "Sure…"

There was a movement nearby. Miles. But it was Titus who cut in first. "No."

Julian's breath hitched, and his hand froze. "Titus?" He sounded shocked that Titus had spoken at all.

I glanced up, but Titus wasn't looking at me. He was watching Damen. "I don't want anyone else looking at her. I might lose control and eat everyone here. Especially that lot." He nodded toward Finn, Bryce, Brayden, and Anthony—all of whom bristled at his attention. "I'm hungry, and I haven't tasted blood in a few days."

I blinked at him even as everyone else blanched at his words.

A few *days*? Just how often did Titus kill people?

"Titus," Julian said slowly, forced patience lining his voice. "We don't have time for this right now. She's going to have to see medical professionals at some point."

"No, never." Titus's response didn't hold an ounce of hesitation, and his gaze shifted to Julian. "I guess you'll have to hurry and finish your medical degree as fast as you can."

Miles was giving Titus a curious look, and Damen raised his eyebrow. Julian pinched his nose. "Titus…"

"I can only stand the three of you being here," Titus interrupted, his hand squeezed my ankle. "Everyone else can get lost."

Julian opened his eyes, and he glared at Titus. The two of them were quiet a moment, communicating silently, before Julian studied my face.

I didn't know what he saw there, but whatever it was caused his expression to morph into self-loathing.

"Get out." His voice was a low hiss.

I couldn't breathe, his icy gaze was still locked on mine. I never thought he'd say such a thing to me.

But a moment later, it was Bryce who responded. "Why? I have every right to be here. Her health is my concern, too."

"*Now.*" Julian narrowed his eyes at Bryce. He'd had gotten to his feet, stalking toward us. However, before Titus could even twitch, Damen had already intercepted my brother.

"Get out," Damen repeated Julian's earlier statement, the tension thick in his voice.

But Bryce, instead of listening, narrowed his eyes. "No. I want to see—"

"Bryce." Brayden grabbed Bryce's arm, cutting him off. "Come on, I need to talk to you."

Bryce glanced at Brayden. "Why do you need to talk to me? I talk to you every day."

"It's a secret." Brayden pulled at him, glancing nervously at Finn and Anthony, who also got to their feet. "You'll like it."

"What secret?" Bryce frowned. "You don't have secrets. Circumstances notwithstanding, you're awful with secrets."

"I know!" Brayden jerked Bryce's arm, finally making Bryce stumble forward. "That's why, if you come with me, I'll tell you what it is."

The group moved toward the exit, Bryce complaining under his breath, when Damen spoke. "Finn, you stay here. Is that okay?" he asked me.

My heart pounded with sudden fury. I wanted to throw a vase at Damen's head at the suggestion. However, Anthony might kill Finn on Julian's behalf when I wasn't watching. He seemed to enjoy picking on the blond.

Sighing, I nodded.

Julian and Damen stepped close to the hearth, conversing with each other in low voices. Finn frowned, returning to his previous seat.

The room felt larger with the others gone. And I felt bad about being relieved, especially considering who they were, but…

I hardly knew Anthony. And even though Bryce and Brayden were family—and my subordinates—I couldn't stand them seeing me so vulnerable.

"Titus…" I pulled on his sleeve, waiting for his attention to turn to me. "Would you really have eaten them?"

He didn't answer, but the corner of his mouth curled up. His grin caused my heart to race. But from fear or something else, I didn't know. He looked almost predatory, yet even more attractive, at that moment. "Titus?"

In response, he winked.

What had happened to the chatty Titus from last night? Why wasn't he answering me with words?

Why was my face growing warm?

"Stop doing that." Miles stepped forward. "It's bad enough watching Damen's awkward attempts at flirting. Don't you start, too."

"There's the difference." Titus shrugged at Miles, frowning. "I'm a natural."

Miles chuckled darkly. "Oh? You think so?"

"Enough." Julian strode forward, Damen trailing behind. He didn't stop until he'd reached me. "I can't believe I didn't notice..." His words trailed off, and he swallowed. He paused for a moment longer, but then continued, "Is this better, Bianca?"

Shame burned through me, and I looked at my fingers.

Titus had been faking! And Julian—and possibly the others—knew it, too. I hadn't been able to hide my discomfort at all.

But still, I was grateful.

"Yeah..." I said. I hated that they knew. I hated that my every action was going to be under scrutiny.

"Bianca..." Julian sounded unsure, but I buried my face against Titus's chest.

"Didn't you two want to check something?" Titus asked.

When Julian responded, he was more composed. "Yes. I need to rebandage her, and she'll need her medication. Then I want to check the marks from the bond."

I could feel his presence beside me, but I still couldn't look.

"Why would the bond cause a mark anyway?" Miles interjected, and I was so thankful. I just needed a moment to gather my composure. "That's what I don't understand."

"Onmyoji are Fire elementals, so bonding with a creature of the underworld doesn't injure us physically. Finn's issue with the bond is a spiritual symptom of overextension," Damen explained. "But when someone who is *not* immune to the physical affects—like a Wood elemental—is added to the bond, it puts them at risk. There's the energy needed to create the bond—to sustain it. But it's passive and requires barely any effort. But there's a different sort the shikigami draws on to perform spells. When I call a shikigami, I'm actively using my abilities."

"Okay...?" Miles tilted his head. "So how does that work with Finn's curse."

"I didn't curse her!" Finn protested.

"I *believe* the medication suppresses Bianca's abilities enough to prevent Kiania from drawing on her. Kiania would have to use Finn as her active energy source," Damen said.

"That's right," Finn said. "Kiania draws only enough from Bianca to stabilize our bond. She doesn't want to hurt her."

"That's why you don't like summoning Kiania," Miles mused.

"I can do it for short periods of time," Finn said. "Most onmyoji bring their shikigami out for practice at least once a week. I'll bring Kiania out every few months or in emergencies."

"So the bruises?" Miles pressed.

"When Bianca is stronger, it's difficult to control the flow of energy." Finn sighed. "Just like any of you, an onmyoji will draw on our abilities when we're emotional. If she's not on her medication, and I lose control of my emotions, Bianca's energy is drawn to me simply because it's *there*. It's not on purpose. That's when it would hurt her, because her body is not compatible with Fire. She has a physical reaction—usually triggered by my touch. But if she's suppressed, and I lose control, there's only a void. You can't draw on something that's not there. Usually, the feeling passes. If it doesn't go away, I see Kayla."

"But Bianca could *always* see spirits," Miles said. "And feel them."

"Yes..." I spoke up, my voice wavering. I didn't understand half of this, but it seemed to not bode well. "But stopping the medication did make it easier."

"So…" Julian seemed deep in thought, he glanced at me. "It helped, but only slightly. I would never expect the medication to completely suppress you, considering who you are."

"Bryce has been helping too," Finn said. "Although he hasn't realized. We have our quintet bond. It's made me able to control things a bit."

"That's grand, but this is not sustainable." Julian spoke again, fury touching his voice once again. "There's only one of two ways this ends. You'd have to suppress her abilities her entire life. But you've said already that wasn't the plan. The other option would for Bianca to be strong enough to withstand the bond."

"We were going to watch out for any adverse reactions, to test the limits." Finn sounded hopeful. "Then, we thought once she joined with you she might be able to—"

"That's not going to matter!" Julian bellowed, slicing his hand through the air. "Even *with* my help. Damen can only do so much, and he's missing out on the link that *he* needs. We can't risk that. Why aren't you angry?" He glared at Damen. "You should be angry about this."

"I'm thinking." Damen glowered at Julian in turn. "Something you aren't doing right now. Stop being so hard up that you lose sight of what's important."

"I *am* thinking. I'm more convinced than ever now, actually," Julian replied. "You've all lost your minds. I'm the only one looking at the whole picture. We've seen how this ended before. This is nature. We *need* to end the bond."

"No, we need more information. Stop overreacting." Damen crossed his arms, his expression unreadable. "I am angry, but I'm not comfortable making a decision right now."

Julian made a frustrated noise, but before he could say another word, Miles interjected. "Julian, knock it off!" He squared his shoulders, stepping between Finn and the other man. "If you make me warn you again, I'm just going to resort to murder."

"And how's that not an overreaction?" Julian protested.

"You are making this about *Finn*!" Miles's voice suddenly turned dark, and a ripple moved through the air. He wasn't yelling, nor did he touch Julian at all. But the other man flinched back.

Miles gestured at me. "This is about *Bianca*. Get your head out of your ass, because we need you to be focusing on what's important. We have no idea what is going to happen."

"Fine." Julian's tone turned subdued. "I'll let it be. But if anything happens to her in the meantime, I'm holding all of you responsible. I can't…" Whatever he was going to say was lost as his voice trailed off, and his attention drifted toward the floor.

In that moment, Julian's furious expression faded.

He looked a person who'd just been told someone they loved was going to die.

I was shivering in the aftermath of their argument. The room had turned to ice throughout their heated discussion, and a damp aura lay heavy in the air.

Julian was basically radiating sorrow; the suffocating sensation seemed to come from him.

How powerful were these men?

Worry still pounded away at me.

"You won't hurt him?" My words sounded strange, breaking through the silence. "You won't hurt Finn?"

Surprise flashed across Finn's face. But Julian's expression captured my attention.

As he met my eyes, there was defeat and devastation in his gaze. But then a new kind of determination washed over him. He seemed different.

He stepped forward, lowering to his knees as he touched my face.

"I'm sorry," he said, his voice returning to its normal gentle caress. "I've reacted so badly about so many things lately. And I need to thank Miles for reminding me."

"I'm right here." Miles frowned at his back. "You could thank me right now."

"But it doesn't excuse anything," Julian continued. Our gazes locked, and I was entranced. "I almost reached my limit. But I'm fine now," he said. "Can I check everything?"

I nodded, my fears assuaged. His calm was contagious, and he now seemed a different person. I only wished I understood what Miles had done.

But outside of that, my shoulder hurt again. And my neck burned.

Julian frowned, as if reading my thoughts. "Miles." When he spoke, his voice was authoritative. "Can you bring my bag and her medication?"

"Right." Miles rushed from the room. As soon as he left, Damen leaned against the back of Finn's chair.

"So what are you doing first?" Damen's tone was somewhat wary.

Finn jumped at the sound of his brother's voice, glancing at the other man in surprise.

"I mean," Damen cleared his throat. "What medication?"

"She needs morphine." Julian frowned, touching the skin under my eyes. "After that, I'll rebandage the other wounds. Then we can see what happens after she takes a suppressant."

I opened my mouth to protest, out of habit mostly. I had been listening, so I knew this was probably for the best.

But still, I rebelled at the thought. I didn't want to do anything that would make me weak.

"Please, Bianca," Julian interrupted. "Only for now? I want to make sure it's safe."

It was completely logical, but tears of frustration welled in my eyes.

I was useless to Damen. And now it was going to be harder to help with anything.

It wasn't fair. I wanted to strangle Kiania with my own two hands. I would make it a painful death. And after she was dead, I wanted Damen to punish her for eternity.

Perhaps he'd toss her in a bottomless pit. I only hoped she couldn't fly.

"*That's rather unkind,*" a familiar melodious voice echoed through my mind. "*Especially given our history together.*"

My eyes dried instantly, before Julian could even react, and my breath stopped.

It was her! The woman in my dreams. She was that horrible shikigami!

No one told me shikigami had human forms, but somehow it made sense.

And she could talk to me in my head. Just lovely.

"Bianca?" Julian's brows were furrowed in worry. "What's wrong?"

"In a second." I would tell him about her. But first I had to figure out, morally, if it counted to curse someone in your mind. Would it make me foul-mouthed and rude?

But she kind of deserved it.

I wondered if she could read *all* my thoughts.

She really should know that bright red lipstick didn't look good on her. Plus, she desperately needed a haircut. Also, I bet her shikigami form was something stupid, like a badger.

"Bianca?" Julian's frown deepened, and Titus moved slightly. But both were interrupted when Miles walked back into the room, Julian's bag and a glass of water in his hands.

Julian's attention was redirected. I'd dutifully swallowed the pill, and he wasted no time in changing the bandages on my neck and shoulder.

There was no pain as Julian's deft hands prodding at my injuries. But that was probably more the morphine and less about his skill. A warm haze spread over me.

This was nice. This feeling was nicer when I wasn't stuck in an institution. It made sense though, I was safe here.

I giggled. That was strange. Why would I feel safe while being possessed by a demon? All this time, I'd been worried about Damen.

I wondered what Kiania thought about *that*?

"What the hell?" Titus sounded alarmed. "How much did you give her?"

"It's a small dose." Julian didn't seem concerned, and he continued to move expertly over my injuries. "It's less than what she got at the hospital. She's less anxious than before, and she's weak. It might affect her more. I'll do a lower dosage next time."

"I suppose that's fine…" Miles sounded doubtful. "She's not high, is she?"

Julian opened his mouth, but I interrupted, narrowing my eyes at the witch. "Nooo…" His lack of faith in me grated on my nerves, yet was amusing. I was so confused. "I'm not high! I'm just trying to figure out what to say to the lady in my head."

Miles's mouth thinned, and Julian froze. Titus didn't even have a chance to respond before Damen stepped forward, blocking my view of Finn.

A glimpse of his authority leaked from his expression. "Excuse me? What lady—"

"She's in my head." I pointed at my head, trying to explain. This was serious. "She talks to me sometimes. But not so much anymore. She came back though."

Damen's eyes flared with fury, and he glanced at Finn.

Finn, on the other hand, was watching me in shock—his pale features even more pronounced now.

"You didn't mention that she could talk to Bianca," Damen said accusingly.

"I asked her!" Finn's eyes tore from me. "She said she couldn't! And Bianca never mentioned it to me before!"

"Yeah…" I rolled my eyes. How had they made it through life without common sense? "Like I'm going to admit I hear voices in my head. Besides, I'm not supposed to tell you. It's a secret. She said I can't tell anyone. It's really important."

Damen's face morphed into a roaring inferno, and his eyes remained fixated on Finn. "Summon her!"

"Hold on!" Julian protested. "He can't summon her right now."

Confusion, then realization, crossed Damen's expression before he sighed, pinching his nose.

"Right…" He sounded so tired.

"No, he should totally summon her!" I argued, struggling to escape from Titus's unrelenting arms. He might not have been contributing to this conversation, but he seemed to not want me to leave him either. "I want to meet the badger!"

Everyone settled into a shocked silence, before Miles stepped forward, looking both horrified and amused.

"I can't decide how to feel." He glanced toward the others. "It's almost funny, but mostly sad."

"I didn't do it on purpose!" Julian snapped, rubbing his temples. "They must not have been giving her the correct dosage. Now, she's not used to it."

Damen's almost-amused expression vanished, and his mouth thinned. "That wouldn't surprise me. They were kind of terrible."

"What does that mean?" Titus chose this moment to finally participate.

"Yes," Miles said, suddenly serious. "What *does* that mean?"

Julian and Damen exchanged a glance before Damen refocused his attention on the others.

"Later." He nodded toward me. "We have something else to take care of first."

"Who cares about those stupid mean nurses." I pushed at Titus's arms, even as he continued to ignore my efforts to escape. They'd brought it up though, and I was half-tempted to tell Titus about them. Maybe he'd go have a snack. He did have a people-eating quota to fill.

But first…

I really wanted to see this. "I want to meet her!"

Finn watched me cautiously before he glanced at his brother. "I've already summoned Kiania recently. She was off her medication already," he admitted, his voice subdued. "It didn't seem to do anything to her then."

Damen jaw tightened. "What?"

"I had no choice!" Finn pointed at Miles, who jumped at being singled out. "He wasn't paying attention, and she was left alone with Mr. Dungworth. I sent Kiania to intervene."

I stopped struggling against Titus, my attention captured by the two of them.

I knew what Finn was saying, but I didn't believe it.

There was no way the friendly tiger who didn't eat my hands was Kiania.

"I also sent her to scout Aine's house when Bianca first mentioned a spirit," Finn continued. "Nothing happened. It only seems triggered by my emotions."

Damen shared a brief glance with Julian before Damen spoke again. "Then do it," he told Finn. "Bring her here. Julian will watch and intervene if he needs to."

Chapter Fifteen

Bianca

Leverage

"But…" Finn hesitated.

"Oh stop." Damen shot his brother a disapproving look. "You are far beyond the point of stage fright."

Finn's face turned red, and he glared up at Damen. "I don't have stage fright!" His voice was low, embarrassed. "Just shut up. I'll do it."

I was about to ask how one summons a shikigami but didn't have a chance. Finn put his fingers to his mouth, and an ear-splitting whistle rang through the room. Julian grasped my hand, holding tight as the air in the room warmed.

Along with the heat, came a thick denseness. Smoke covered the floor, and I couldn't help but notice it hadn't taken Damen nearly as long to summon Kasai from the time I'd heard his whistle.

Julian was watching me. "What—" I started.

He pressed his finger to my lips. "Just watch."

He seemed to be waiting for something to happen. I watched Finn, my chest tight with anticipation.

If I hadn't been watching the cloud grow thick between us, I might have missed the change.

A shape formed from the mass. And an instant later, it solidified, confirming my fears.

It *was* the same tiger.

I glanced at her before turning my attention to Finn. "That took almost a minute. Damen summons Kasai in like, five seconds." I so wasn't impressed.

Finn flushed and crossed his arms. "Well, I'm not Damen, okay?"

"Finn's time is actually quick for an onmyoji," Damen said even as his focus remained on the tiger. Who, for all the world, seemed rather chill about being here today. "Kiania, you've some explaining to do."

'*Hello, my lord*,' she purred. Her voice made my pulse race. She sat leisurely, her tail curling behind her as she cleaned it. '*Have you missed me?*'

"That's not how I'd describe it." Damen narrowed his eyes. "Quite the opposite, in fact."

"What did she say?" Julian asked, his grip almost painful over mine.

"She said—"

"You can't hear her?" I pulled on Julian's hand; both to get his attention and to try to escape.

Damen focused on me, his expression becoming even more severe. "And you *can*."

"Kiania." Finn moved to stand beside his brother. "Why didn't you tell me you could talk to her?"

'*The relationship between Mu and me is our own*,' Kiania said, not opening her mouth. Instead, she licked the bottom of her paw. *'And what we have predates you, little boy. Mind your business.'*

"See." Finn faced Damen, gesturing in her direction. "No other shikigami would argue like this. She doesn't listen!"

"Actually, that's not true. It depends on their personality." Damen didn't even look at Finn, he was still frowning at Kiania. "Kiania has always had a mind of her own and does what she wants. That is why if you were having trouble dealing with her, you should have come to me."

Finn's shoulders slumped. "I—"

"What do you want, Kiania?" Damen interrupted Finn. "Why did you come back? You had to know that would prolong your sentence."

She paused, her tongue still out, and when she opened her golden eyes, they flickered toward Damen. *'I still do not understand human emotions.'*

"That's not what I asked," Damen cut back. "Why are you here? You had to know what would happen if you were caught targeting Mu again. Give me one reason why I shouldn't end your existence right now? Finn can always get another shikigami."

'You can try, but you'll destroy her in the process.' Her voice was calm. *'The three of us are successfully bonded, this isn't like your other cases. Haven't you realized what'll happen by removing one of us from the equation? It's not so very different than a regular contract, in theory.'*

Both Finn and Damen paled, but I wasn't certain what this meant. I supposed the drama was lost on me, but I was sure it probably ended in my death. Everything else seemed to.

"What did she say?" Julian asked again, urgency lacing his tone.

"I can't kill her... *yet*." Damen's voice shook. "She and Finn have been splitting the physical effects of their connection with Bianca."

"So it is similar to a basic bond." Julian frowned, and he nodded to Finn. "What about him?"

I wasn't sure what Julian was implying, although I suspected. And Kiania's next words confirmed my thoughts. *'The energy works the same way, so I don't think you'll like the result.'*

Damen paled further, and Finn waved his hand in Kiania's direction. "See what I mean?"

"Without him, Bianca would be left bonded with Kiania, alone," Damen translated. The foreboding in his expression slowly bled into something furious.

"Why does anyone have to die? Can't you change the contract?" Miles piqued, his voice almost hopeful. "You've already done it once."

'We could, but myself and the majority of parties involved have to consent. Why would I do something so stupid?' Kiania replied lazily. *'This arrangement works out well for all of us. Removing Mu will kill Finn. Taking him away, will kill her.'*

"You're just protecting yourself," Damen growled.

'Perhaps,' Kiania said, not seeming very threatened.

"She will die if you keep drawing from her," Damen seethed. "That won't help you in the end."

Kiania shrugged, a strange movement for a cat. *'We all die one day, but I've a job to do first.'*

"No." Damen's expression filled with determination. "I can handle another shikigami. If you are so keen to be stuck on earth, come back into my service. Release Bianca. I'll help Finn."

She laughed—low and mocking. *'You must think I'm a fool.'*

"Why?" Damen raised his eyebrow. "I wouldn't be able to do anything to you while you're contracted to me."

'Because I don't want to be with you anymore.' Her voice was petulant. *'Why must you always interfere? I'm staying with Mu. Your jealousy is going to be your downfall.'*

The heat flared through the room as Damen's anger became a palpable thing. He stepped toward Kiania, his jaw tight and his fists clenched at his sides. "Why you little—"

My vision flashed red as agony shot through me, breaking through my happy haze. I was being burned alive, the flames fanning up from my feet. My head pounded, and I thought my heart might explode. And—despite the drama—I couldn't stop the pained noise that escaped.

Time stilled, a growing darkness began to cover my vision, and the room was silent. My body grew impossibly warm as an uncontrollable shaking seemed to take over me.

Titus roared, his arms tightening. Julian yelled something, then shouted at Titus to let me go. And Damen…

He sounded so very far away, but so angry. Then, everything faded into silence.

When I came to, my body ached—the effects of the morphine long forgotten. I was on a bed. In the distance, I could hear arguing. Male voices, loud and angry.

Two bodies pressed to either side of me, the sensation jarring. For an instant, my heart jerked even as my body remained still.

I was simply too exhausted to do anything other than accept it.

But then I heard Julian, his whispering a gentle caress against my ear. His presence caused my panic to flee.

There was nothing to worry about. It was only Miles and Julian, holding me between them as if they wanted to shield me from the world.

Yet it wasn't me that Julian was talking to, but was, apparently, Damen.

"Why did she lash out in the first place?" Julian's voice was soft whisper.

"She was using Bianca." Damen sounded farther away. "It was a warning to not cross her again." His voice was low. "I wasn't thinking. I never expected her to—"

"She knows your weakness," Titus spoke. "The problem is, she's always known. But she's never been bold enough to use it against you before. She can read our energy; she knows who we are by sight. It must have been a dream come true for her to find Bianca alone."

"Daniel Cole planned on using her to hurt you, too." Miles's breath brushed over my head, and his chest moved against my nose. "You've gotten worse at picking your enemies."

"I can't stay away anymore." Damen sounded sad.

"You're selfish." Titus's voice was stern. "Even if this thing with Bryce works, it will need to end eventually. What are you going to do when people *know* who she is? She's always been a target because of you."

"I don't care if it's selfish. That's who I am. Besides, you're one to talk," Damen retorted, his tone slightly sharper than before. "You're even worse than me in this case."

When Titus didn't respond, Julian said, "What are you implying, Titus?"

"I was only checking," Titus said smoothly. "You can't blame me for trying."

Julian's hand, which had been lightly drifting down my arm, froze. "Trying what?"

"To see if everyone would be willing to back off." Titus's tone was casual, even if his words carried a veil threat.

Damen scoffed.

"You must be joking?" Julian said.

"It couldn't hurt to ask," Titus replied. "I need to mentally prepare, in either case. What about you, munchkin? You've been quiet."

Miles took in a shuddering breath. "What do you want me to do?"

"It's not about what we want," Titus said. "Don't avoid the question. Are you in this or not?"

"We've been over this before," Miles said calmly, even though I heard his racing heartbeat. "Or have you forgotten?"

"Things aren't the same in this life," Julian said, a warning underlying his tone. "Everything is going to be different. She's not even remotely ready for this."

"It is always, eventually, the same. I don't care what it takes, or how long I need to wait," Miles said. "Are you shutting them up any time soon? They are giving me a headache."

For a second, I had forgotten about the yelling. I'd been so focused on the conversation that everything else had faded.

"I'll tell them to knock it off." Titus sighed, moving farther away. "If that doesn't work, I'll make them live in the shed."

Damen gasped as the door closed. "I cannot believe I didn't think of that!"

"You can't do that," Julian said. "You've already given them their rooms."

"I'll figure out a way. I can demote him." Damen sounded so certain and so full of hatred. "Somehow."

"Bianca is the only one who can demote Bryce." Julian didn't miss a beat, humor entering his voice. "And I don't think she'll do it."

Damen sounded venomous in his response. "Oh, I think she'll do it."

This pretending-to-sleep business was fascinating. I was learning all sorts of new things.

Like the fact that Bryce's fate rested entirely in my hands.

"You're awake." Miles's chest moved, and his fingers brushed over my forehead. "You've got an evil look on your face again."

I opened my eyes, meeting Miles's expectant expression. That wasn't even fair! I hadn't even planned to do anything yet. "I do not have an evil look."

"Leave Bryce alone," he said, his expression serious. "He's a great asset, and he's blindly loyal. You can't crush that because of your rivalry."

Confusion, and a tiny bit of self-consciousness, creeped up inside. "What are you—"

"You were right to distrust Bryce. He *was* challenging you. He had no idea who you were and was protecting his position," Julian said, his hand moving over my arm again. "But, if you've noticed, he's stopped."

I glanced at Julian, who had repositioned so I could see him. "What?"

"He's accepted who you are. But he's having trouble adjusting," Julian continued, his gaze slightly sympathetic. "I suggest you give him a break. He's always been overbearing and protective. But he's shy and doesn't know how to channel his emotions. Keep in mind, Bryce has been trying to take on your responsibilities on his own. Besides, that family…" Julian's words trailed off, and his face twisted as if he couldn't decide how to phrase the next part.

That family? My family? My heart was thundering.

"Although they are highly respected in their community, the Dubois line has suffered a lot. So has the Stephens's family, which is your mother's maiden home." Miles's words pulled my attention. "Some say they are both cursed."

Cursed? My brows furrowed, and concern settled in my stomach. Somehow, I couldn't help but feel this was my fault.

"I think you and Bryce have a lot in common." Miles ran his thumb over the crease in my forehead, soothing it out. "Try to bond with him."

Lies.

Julian moved and touched my arm, pulling me onto my back. "How do you feel?"

Come to think of it, I was groggy. And somewhat stiff.

Julian gently squeezed my arm. "You've been asleep for almost a day. Which is better than before, I suppose. Finn said you were in the hospital a week the first time this happened."

He helped me sit up. Miles stacked some pillows behind me, but my mind was too occupied to even thank him. "I've been asleep for a day? What happened?"

"Kiania's upset and took it out on you. But don't worry, it won't happen again." Damen crossed his arms, meeting my eyes. His expression was softer than I expected, considering the raw anger in his voice. But he seemed certain of his declaration.

In fact, he seemed to be too confident of this. Why did he look a tiny bit guilty, too?

Meanwhile, Julian and Miles weren't even looking in my direction, and their frames had gone tense. Their actions further confirmed my suspicions. Damen had done something.

"Damen?"

"Finn was right," Julian said, tucking a wayward lock of my hair behind my ear. "Kiania doesn't want to kill you."

I studied him, unsure. Because it had certainly felt like it.

"We were wrong. It doesn't matter if you're on medication or not, she can pull from you regardless," Julian explained. "What she did earlier was to get back at Damen. To show that she had the upper hand."

My blood turned to ice. "Why does she want to do that? Why does she hate Damen?"

Julian didn't reply. Titus re-entered the room. He clearly heard what we were discussing, because he opened with, "Why don't you just show her?"

Julian twitched, an undistinguishable emotion crossing his face. He responded, his tone soft and wary. "It's not my memory to—"

"No, it's not yours," Miles said, moving to the foot of the bed. "It's her memory."

I glanced between them, frowning. "What do you mean?"

"You know Shui can pull memories." Damen was watching Julian. "It's one reason he excels at information gathering."

"Don't sugarcoat it," Julian snapped, glaring at Damen. "What I did was torture, and you know it." My heart pounded at the furious look on his face, but Julian wasn't even paying attention to me. "My abilities were twisted into something evil."

"We all have a darker side to our powers," Miles said, his wary gaze on

Julian. "Don't lose sight of the reason why it was necessary. If you hadn't, you would have regretted it."

"Don't misunderstand." Julian turned toward Miles. "I don't regret doing it. My issue is using it on her."

Titus frowned, resting his hip against the closed door. "But you use your abilities on Bianca all the time."

Julian glared at him, and Titus waved his hand and said, "You help her with her anxiety and when she can't relax."

"That's different!" Julian flushed. "You've all come to me. You never cared what I saw. But Mu and I had an agreement. I have never, ever pulled memories from him in any life."

The faces of the others turned from curiosity to shock. I probably should have been intrigued at their surprise. Yet, alarm flashed foremost through my mind instead.

My heart raced. Inside, I was screaming—he could never, *ever* touch my memories.

He said before he couldn't entirely control what he saw. And even though they knew about parts of my past, it was different than him seeing it.

"How does it work?" My voice was quiet.

Julian glanced at me, the fierceness in his expression fading. "How does what work?"

"The memories. The 'pulling' stuff you were talking about?" I asked.

"It's called psychometry," he said. "You'll hear of individuals who see glimpses of thoughts, emotions, and memories by touching a person or object. But its purest form is stronger than that."

"Remember what we did with Lily?" Julian asked. When I nodded, he continued, "It's a similar ritual. The target—you, in this case—would be forced to relive your memories. The practitioner would be there, viewing—as we were with Lily. I try to guide a target toward certain memories, if they seem relevant. But it's a lot of guesswork. The target can subconsciously change which memories are recalled. Usually that happens with unresolved trauma. They can be stuck on those events instead. Their mind won't be able to move past it, and I can't control it."

As he finished his statement, he turned his attention toward Titus. "And *that*'s another reason why I refuse to do it on her now."

"Of course not." Titus's brows were drawn together, and his mouth thin. "But you've never mentioned that before."

"Because none of you needed to know," Julian snapped in response. "It's not something that's come up often in my work."

Damen's expression was guarded. "When did it happen before?"

"That's none of your business." Julian crossed his arms over his chest. "Titus, I don't ask you how many people you've eaten. Or about Damen's deal with the devil. Then there's Miles's not-so-secret dallying in dark magic."

Miles flushed, glancing at me. "I have no idea what he's talking about."

"The point is," Julian cut Miles off, "we've always respected each other's work. Mu made this request lifetimes ago. There are only two ways I would break that promise. First, if Bianca's life is endangered and she cannot consent. Or second, if Bianca asks me to do it."

"I'm not asking!" I interjected, holding the sheets against my chest. "Why can't you tell me instead?"

"We don't know the details," Titus admitted.

"Kiania is one of my top three shikigami." Damen stepped forward. "There's also Enemi and Ming. Out of them all, you once considered her a friend. They resemble humans in their true forms, but they lack emotions. In *this* realm, they usually appear as animals. Kiania has always chosen to be a tiger. But, when interacting with you, she'll take on her human form."

"Why?" I wasn't certain how this was relevant. However, it was good to have my suspicions about their human appearance confirmed.

"She's never told me why." Damen shrugged. "Then, after you died in one of our lives, she's refused her human form since."

I blinked. "And why was that?"

Damen crossed his arms and widened his stance. "We're not sure. We were hoping you could tell us. I thought talking about it might help trigger a memory."

"No…" Outside of my dreams, I had no recollections of any previous lives. But perhaps, "How did I die?"

"We're born in the order of our creation. Jin is first, followed by Huo." Julian tilted his head toward them. "Metal includes the foundational elements in which life is rooted. The chemical necessary. And Fire is the energy that sparks transformation. Then, since life cannot exist without Water, I come after them in the cycle. Then Tu arrives as a grounding force for life to thrive. Then last, there's you—Mu. You're always the last born, and when we die naturally, you're the first to leave the world as well."

I titled my head. "I have to be born last?"

"You are always the youngest," Titus confirmed.

Julian touched my chin. "But in answer to your question, you've always been with us throughout all your lives, but you have your secrets. We have no idea how you died. Although the conditions were suspicious. It happened around eight hundred years ago. Then, three hundred years ago, Huo contracted with Kiania again. For the entire duration, she completely abandoned her human form. And, for the most part, avoided you. When you were together, she would try to fight with you. From the little we overheard, she seemed to hate you."

My concern grew, and I couldn't help but wonder—despite how strange it felt to phrase. "Why didn't you ask me what happened? Did I never remember?"

"We did ask," Damen interjected, his voice curt. "And you remembered. But you refused to tell us."

The disapproval in his expression put me on edge, and my heart raced. He was annoyed.

My past still affected me in ways I didn't fully understand.

Who was Mu? The nurses who hated me, was it because of him? Even when I was a child, they knew. Comments that used to make no sense were now perfectly clear.

I was evil. I had hurt people.

It wasn't fair. People were constantly judging me for something I had no control over. Reincarnation did not define the person I was now.

I held Damen's gaze—he couldn't be allowed to think it was acceptable to have an attitude over something someone else did. "*I* didn't do anything."

The tight look faded from his expression and slowly, he blinked. "Bianca?"

I jerked from Miles and glared at each of them in turn. "It's one thing to try to figure out what happened, but don't be angry at *me* over something *he* did."

Damen's mouth thinned and his eyebrow shot up. "You're misunderstanding the cause of my frustration."

"Oh yeah?" I crossed my arms, narrowing my eyes at him. "And what's that?"

"You've always been the most vulnerable of us." Damen stalked across the room until he stood a breath away from the edge of the bed. "If we don't do our jobs, you'll suffer. And you're the easiest target to use to get to one of us."

What was he saying? I could feel my stomach churn, embarrassment and anger mixed together. "So, I'm the weakest link?"

"No!" Damen pulled at his hair. "That's not what I'm saying!"

"Because, technically, it seems like you're doing perfectly fine without me," I said, the logical part of my mind taking over. "Who cares if my secrets hurt me. It's not like it affects you—"

Julian slapped his hand over my mouth, pulling me to him as Damen glowered at us.

"It's that!" Damen waved his hand at the two of us. "*That's* what frustrates me!"

I stared at him over Julian's hand. He was frustrated because Julian was touching me?

I must not have hidden my confusion very well because Damen rolled his eyes. "I'm frustrated because you always have that same exact mindset. You're always trying to protect the rest of us. And you're always sacrificing yourself for some other purpose. And it's not *him*, it's *you*. Or have you forgotten about the hyenas?"

Julian shifted, moving his hand from my face. "Don't yell at her."

"I'm not yelling!" Damen's gaze moved to Julian. "I might be angry, but I am completely rational. Besides, you feel the same way."

"You're angry?" I had forgotten he'd been upset earlier, and that he had been up to something nefarious. Probably.

"I am *livid*." Damen's voice was low, furious. "I've had it with you protecting me all the time. I refuse to let it happen again."

He did do something bad! "What did you do?"

When Damen's only response was the thinning of his mouth, Miles cut in.

"Kiania wouldn't break your bond. But—to keep the effect of the bond off you—he managed to convince her to change it slightly. Now he has two shikigami: Kasai, and he shares Kiania with Finn."

Chapter Sixteen

Bianca
Gray

I allowed Miles's words to wash over me. Heavy expectation weighed on me. But what reaction everyone was expecting, I wasn't sure.

"Hold on." My mind caught up, connecting the things I did understand. "You have *two*... Isn't she super strong? Can you handle two shikigami?"

Damen's impassive expression was all the answer I needed.

"Damen!" My breath caught. Kasai was already mooching off him, and now he had made it worse. He was so stupid! "What if you die?"

A shadow crossed his features. "I'm not going to die."

"Oh, so you've done this before?" I quipped, holding his gaze. "You know this? You don't even know how the bond works!"

"I'm not going to die," he repeated, frowning. But his refusal to answer spoke volumes.

I crossed my arms, mentally daring him to lie. After everything I'd done for him, he'd better not.

Finally, he sighed. "Kiania isn't going to kill anyone. She wants to stay in this realm. We need to think long-term. I need you, and Finn needs to be able to do his job. I offered a compromise: I would give her what she needs, and she'll use me instead of you. She accepted."

"But—"

"In return, Kiania agreed not to take her frustrations out on you," Damen continued. "But she refuses to consider severing your connection. For now, I have no choice but to trust her."

And from his expression, he was extremely begrudging about this entire situation. I didn't imagine for a second that he trusted Kiania. "But—"

"It's your job to not worry about it." Damen leaned over Julian and touched his finger to my forehead. "What are you supposed to be focusing on right now?"

My brows furrowed in confusion, because I had no idea what the heck he was talking about. It wasn't my fault that Damen had terrible communication skills.

"You have classes and a life to get back to." Damen changed the subject, his voice suddenly light. "And when you feel up to it, you need to go shopping. Bryce has not shut up about it. What do you want me to tell him?"

He looked hopeful, most likely assuming I'd say no. But now I was mad at him.

"*Absolutely*. I'm thrilled at the idea of shopping with Bryce." Besides Bryce still owed me a ring. I couldn't pretend to be a lawfully wedded woman without one.

Damen's expression dropped slightly, and his mouth dipped. "Well, okay then."

But still, although my muscles were tight from disuse—and I needed another shower—there was something else missing.

My arm still hurt, and my neck was tender. But the bodily aches from my bruises had faded.

I sat up in Julian's lap, pulling up the loose sleeve of Titus's shirt. Miles and Julian had said I'd been asleep for only a day. That shouldn't have been long enough for the marks to fade.

Yet all traces of those bruises were gone.

"What happened?" I asked, touching my side.

"Damen," Julian said, caressing my back. "Since the bond has spread to him, the last of the physical effects were removed from you."

The thought of Damen putting himself at risk made my throat close and my stomach twist. He focused on the wall across the room, the frown still etched into his expression.

"Damen…" I wasn't sure what to say that hadn't already been said.

"You don't need to take your medication anymore." Julian's words cut through my thoughts. He wore a knowing look. "I thought you might be interested. With Damen's presence in the bond, it should be safe for you to stop them."

"Really?"

"You should explore your abilities. Use Bryce and Brayden," Julian said, twirling a lock of my hair around his finger. "They're your best resources. Brayden, in particular, can show you how to block negativity."

Was that what they were arguing about? I'd recognized their voices, as well as Finn's. "What about Xavier? Should he teach me anything?"

Julian's mouth dipped. "I'd forgotten you met him."

The room had grown tense at the mention of my Tongjun.

"You should avoid him," Titus interjected. "Focus on Bryce and Brayden."

"Why?" I glanced at him. "Everyone seems to have different specialties, so what do they do?"

"Brayden is an empath and a medium," Damen said. "Bryce is a medium and can compel others. But they are members of the Seelie court. While they *could* delve into the darker side of your abilities, they won't."

Julian cut in, answering my unspoken question. "No, we don't know everything about that side of your power."

"Xavier does. He's Unseelie, and his moral compass is set differently," Damen continued. "Because of his position—and the fact that he's in a different court—he's able to get away with things that Bryce and Brayden aren't."

"Like what?" I was not liking the direction of this conversation. But if there was depravity going on, it needed to stop. "What things?"

"Dark magic…" Damen began, his voice trailing off as he glanced at the others. I suspected he might have been plotting to not tell me. But then he sighed. "He's a sadist, Bianca. They use their powers in questionable ways."

A sadist? I knew what the word meant, but… "You mean he…"

"Fae are sexual creatures, and the Unseelie court is riddled with perversion. It's a male dominated culture." Damen's words made my pulse race in my ears. "Without a Xing to stop them, it's gotten out of control. One day, you'll be expected to bring order to the two courts. But as it is right now, do you really think you're ready to handle something like that?"

My throat closed. "But he called me Mistress. He was really nice."

"You're his better, and he knows it," Julian interjected. "Xavier wants to keep his position, so he will defer to you. But, honestly, is that something you think you can handle?"

"She's going to have to handle it one day." Miles spoke, his voice close behind me. "And she can't avoid Xavier forever, he's her third."

"She doesn't have to avoid him," Julian said, glancing over his shoulder. "He's not the concern. But he'll have to be warned to avoid the courts."

"That's what they were arguing about," Titus interjected, nodding toward the door. "Xavier wants to take Bianca on a tour posed as a nymph."

Julian's hand jerked. "Has he *lost* his mind? What did Bryce say?"

"Bryce said he would rip out his heart first," Titus answered, shrugging. "And I offered to help. Xavier understands, but still insists she visit soon."

"I'm not so certain about that," Julian replied. "But knowing him, he'll try to manipulate Bianca into going along with it. A nymph is the 'safest' disguise, considering. But still"—his focus had returned to me—"don't let him trick you into it."

I bit my lip. Their reaction didn't bode well for this plan. "What is it?"

Julian flinched slightly but answered regardless. "A nymph is a sexual slave shared among high-ranking officials. Being with Xavier would make you untouchable by most people, but I still don't trust it."

Just the implication of his words made me nauseated. "Oh…"

I looked away. I could feel their eyes on me. They wanted to ask me something, and I had a suspicion of what it might be.

"T-t-that's probably not a good idea."

The silence that followed was heavy—almost as if no one knew how to break the mood. But then Miles, thankfully, changed the topic.

"You'll need to take some medicine and have a shower." He tugged a lock of my hair.

I tried to look at him, but it was impossible. I was sitting in Julian's lap.

But was he implying that I smelled?

"Miles has a point." Damen stepped back, glancing at Titus. "And we have plans to make."

Damen crossed to the door, then paused, turning back to me.

"This is your room." He waved his hand in the air. "Julian and mine are on either side, and Titus and Miles are one level above us. You have your own bathroom through that door." He pointed at a doorway off to the side. "We can decorate however you'd like, but just don't—"

"Change the bathroom," I finished.

Yes, I remembered. Damen had a freaky antique fetish and integrity was important, or something. I didn't even know with him anymore. But honestly, none of this hard work was going to pay off unless he renovated the exterior of the house.

His gaze narrowed on mine. "How do you know that?"

I resisted the urge to look at Miles. From Damen's reaction, I suspected this might be a sensitive topic. "I know everything."

"Real convincing." Damen frowned, turning his attention to the others in turn. "Someone's been talking." But when no one offered to take the blame or deny their wrong-doing, Damen sighed. "No matter, we have rules. If you want to hire a decorator to come in and redo the space, then feel free. You can put it on the house account."

I pursed my lips, glancing around the room. Now that the space was *mine*, my surroundings took on new meanings. The canopy bed was my style, but the gray and white fabrics weren't so much.

But this wasn't exactly the most opportune moment to be redecorating. "It's fine. Thanks."

"Are you sure?" Damen raised his eyebrow. "You don't want green everywhere or something?"

I frowned at him. "Unlike the rest of you, I am not a stereotype. Green is an accent color. If you do too much, you ruin it."

"Then what color would you choose?" There was a thread of hope in Damen's voice. But for what reason, I couldn't imagine.

Besides, wasn't it obvious?

"Pink, different shades of it." I pointed at the windows. "And maybe some cream. Crystal chandeliers, a white vanity over there." I waved toward an empty corner. "Lots of sheer fabrics and tiny lights…" My voice trailed off—Damen's expression had turned into something disturbing. "What?"

"I have things to do." Damen turned abruptly and left the room. Titus, with a wink to me, followed him.

"What things?" I asked once the door had shut behind them.

"No idea," Miles said. "It could be one of two things. The first is not something I want to think about. And the second is something else entirely. In that case, I'd rather not spoil it."

This time I leaned back, glancing around Julian's arm toward Miles. "What are you talking about?"

"It doesn't matter," Julian interjected as he patted my thigh to encourage me to get off his lap. "Now it's time for you to take a shower. Then medicine and fresh bandages."

"Fine…" I'd figure it out eventually. Damen couldn't keep anything to himself anyway. Knowing him, he'd be making an obnoxious, bold declaration soon.

"What about clothes?" As I stood, I glanced down at my shirt and *Hello Kitty* boxers.

"No one has wanted to go out to buy anything without your approval. You would probably yell at everyone for spending money, and it's scary. And you have your own style." Julian frowned, touching his chin.

That wasn't true at all. I had money these days—my marital funds.

Besides, "I don't mind suggestions…" I muttered.

Just so long as they weren't ugly suggestions.

Miles walked across the room, grabbing a small pile of folded clothes from the window seat.

"Here," Miles said, returning to me. "This is Julian's, wear this for now."

I glanced at Julian—unsure if I should accept this offering—but he only shrugged. He was touching his forehead, something else apparently on his mind.

His distracted expression seemed to drag the whole room down.

"Besides, he's the scrawniest." Miles pressed the pile into my arms, his lips turning up into a grin. "They'll fit you."

Julian frowned, snapping to attention at Miles's words. The distant look left his face. "You're shorter than me."

"Yeah." Miles nodded. "But not by much. Everyone knows you're the least intimidating."

Julian's brows furrowed. "Are you trying to annoy me?"

Miles pressed his hand to his heart, his tone light. "I have no idea what you're talking about. These are the simple words of someone still awaiting their 'thank you'."

Julian didn't miss a beat in his reply. "That moment has passed. Now stop being obnoxious and fetch my bag."

"You fetch it," Miles replied, the humor dropping from his expression. He crossed his arms, scowling. "Your chicken legs could use some building up."

Julian's frown deepened, "I—"

I'd been following the banter silently but felt obligated to interject. Bullying wasn't nice, and Miles was definitely being unkind. "I like Julian's legs."

The following silence was almost embarrassing. I'd suddenly become the center of attention as Miles and Julian stared at me, unabashed. Their amused—and slightly horrified—expressions left me scrambling, and I hugged the clothes against my chest.

"I thought he might be a model…" I tried to explain, hiding my warming face behind the clothes.

Julian's face turned from bewilderment to contemplation and he stroked his chin thoughtfully. "You did mention that before."

"She said that?" Miles turned to Julian, gasping. "Why didn't you tell me?"

"It's between me and Bianca!" Julian cheeks darkened.

I glanced between them, not sure why Miles seemed so happy. I was simply stating a truth, so I wasn't sure why I was embarrassed to begin with. "It's a compliment."

Julian sighed, getting to his feet, and put his hands on my shoulders, turning me toward the bathroom door. "Go take a shower, Bianca."

"But…" I started to protest, but quieted as he opened the door and ushered me inside, shutting the door behind me. My questions faded as I glanced around the space.

The bathroom followed the bedroom's theme. The walls were lined with subway tile, and the floor was a gray damask. A deep tub was nestled under a rose-patterned stained-glass window.

This would do. This would do nicely.

Julian and Miles talked while I bathed. But the tile magnified the sound of the water, and I couldn't make out their words.

They'd given me black sweats and a navy shirt, and the fabric felt cool against my skin. But even though Julian was the thinnest of the guys, he still towered over me. Which, of course, meant that his clothes were too big.

I frowned at my reflection. I looked ridiculous, with the hem of my pants folded twice over. My sleeves hung below my elbows, but at least the neck was more modest than Titus's shirt.

It was a sad sight, but at least I was clean again. And until I owned my stuff again, I had no choice but to make the best of it. My hair reached my hips when wet and was generally a hassle. It would take too long to dry it now, so I grabbed a towel before stepping back into the bedroom.

"You're finally done!" Miles flounced toward me, startling me as he tugged me to the bed. "We've been waiting for you."

"Don't scare her." Julian sat cross-legged on my comforter. And he didn't even glance up from the laid-out medication as he chastised Miles.

Miles made a quick motion back at him but turned back to me. "Sorry." The smile had faded from his lips. "Did I scare you?"

I'd been startled, and my heart was still slowing. But Miles could never scare me.

"No," I whispered. "You're too cuddly. It's impossible to be scared of you."

"*Cuddly?*" Miles released me, touching his stomach. "What's that supposed to mean?"

I blinked at him before glancing at Julian, who was now watching us warily.

What did I *mean*? Was he looking for some sort of validation? Was he feeling left out because I complimented Julian's legs?

"You're cute…" My face warmed at the admission. But I had to help Miles be the best version of himself… apparently. Gentle encouragement and affection were desperately needed. "You're soft and gentle. It's adorable."

"I'm *soft?*" Miles sounded horrified, lifting his shirt. He poked at his six-pack, frowning deeply. "But—"

"I can't watch this anymore!" Julian moved elegantly to his feet. He stopped in front of Miles, snatching the edge of his shirt and pulled it back down over his stomach. "She's not calling you fat. She's talking about your personality."

"That doesn't make it any better!" Miles's cheeks turned pink, and he seemed unable to meet my eyes. "I'm tough!"

"You're *nurturing*," Julian corrected, giving me a pointed look. I nodded.

My heart was pounding now, and my stomach churned with sick. I'd hurt Miles's feelings, which was the last thing I'd intended.

How was I supposed to know this was a sensitive topic?

"I think you're really strong." My thoughts scattered as I tried to make this better. "You're insanely hot, too. I just meant that you're also sweet. So I could never be scared of you."

The redness had completely covered Miles's face, and he stared at the floor.

"Thanks…"

Thanks?

That's all he was going to say? I had poured out my most horrifying inner thoughts and everything. Where did his response even leave me? It wasn't like I could say, *You're welcome.*

"Um…" I touched my fingers together, turning to Julian as I silently pleaded for help.

I was terrible at human interaction.

Julian rolled his eyes at Miles, turning back to me. "All right, it's time to get you fixed up. There's no shopping today. I want you to rest and we can go tomorrow. Miles will bring you food."

But I felt perfectly fine!

I prepared to argue, but my body betrayed me, and I swayed.

Miles jumped forward, wrapping his arm around my waist as he led me to the bed.

Julian tsked, his demeanor turning clinical. His touch over my shoulder was light, then he moved to my neck. His face darkened.

"What's wrong?" Miles slid beside me. "Is it not healing properly? Do you need me to do anything? Does she need to see a *real* doctor?"

Julian shot Miles an even look.

"It's fine," he said. "Relax. I'm only wondering if we should bandage it tomorrow when she goes out in public."

My breath caught and I raised my hand to my neck.

I'd checked in the bathroom, out of curiosity. The initial wound hadn't been too terribly deep, and it was healing fine.

But it was still rather jarring.

"I look like a massacre victim," I whispered, glancing at the two of them. There was no way I could go out like this. People would stop and stare.

"You do not," Julian replied. "Let it be today, and tomorrow I'll cover it. People will just assume you're wearing a choker."

"Will they?" Was he lying to make me feel better? If he was, it was working. My breathing had begun to slow and the room stopped spinning. I smoothed my hands over the seat of my pants, trying to gain confidence from his words. "Will they assume that?"

Miles scoffed, but Julian nodded. "Of course they will. I'll go with you, if you want."

"You will?" I clasped his hands in my own. "Do you promise?"

I felt so much better at the idea of him coming with me. His serene presence would offset Bryce's annoying one. But then, could I bother him with that?

Miles made another sound, and I noticed him watching Julian with a raised brow. "You're as predictable as always," he said.

Julian pulled back briefly, returning to his ministrations. His fingers were gentle as he continued to clean my wounds. But his tone was inscrutable as he responded. "I haven't a clue what you're talking about."

Chapter Seventeen

Bianca
Wear

By the next day, I was so ready to get out of Damen's house.

I'd spent the rest of the day—and the night—with Julian lounging on a chair in my room, while Miles flitted about, criticizing the books in my library. Which wasn't even fair, because I had nothing to do with the current selection.

Eventually—in between times he'd brought me food—he'd stalked off to his own room to bring back a velvet hardcover with elegant gold lettering.

I had no idea what it was, and when I asked, he turned even more secretive. He brought me *The Hobbit* instead, and then took up residence in my window seat.

It was suspicious, but at the same time I really couldn't be bothered. Despite having had slept an entire day, I was still tired.

So when I wasn't reading, I slept.

And the next time I woke up, it was morning.

They were still there, and the two of them gave me a similar outfit to yesterday. Which kind of sucked, because it was glaringly obvious Julian's pants just wouldn't work for me.

Which brought us to shopping with Bryce.

"You really don't need to go with him," Miles said, leading me to the living room. "No one is going to care."

"Except Bryce," Julian pointed out.

"Well, yes." Miles nodded. "But I don't think Bianca cares."

Why did they have to say it like that? I wasn't a terrible person. It wasn't my life's goal to hurt Bryce's feelings.

But I'd only said yes to annoy Damen. And now I was obligated. Besides, I owed him. He was helping me by pretending to be my husband. How could I deny him a measly shopping trip?

Darn it.

"No, I have given my word," I said, somberly. "I must see it through to the end."

"You don't need to sound like you're going to die." Julian raised his eyebrow. "And I'll be with you. Miles has things to do here."

Bryce, Finn, and Brayden were sitting around Damen's coffee table talking to Damen and Titus in low voices. But at our entrance, conversation stopped.

Damen's mouth pressed together as his eyes traced over me. I hadn't seen him at all since the day before, and he was still wearing the same clothes from yesterday. "You still look sick, baby girl," he said. "Are you sure you're up to go—"

"I'm perfectly fine." There was no way he could talk me out of this. I was still very angry at him. "I've been looking forward to this *all night*."

Bryce perked, but I ignored him. I dared Damen to fight me.

Damen sighed, glancing at Julian and nodding toward the mantle. The gesture meant something to Miles and Julian, and Julian leaned down, muttering in my ear. "Go sit with Brayden for a minute. I'll be right back. Eat something."

Then the two of them joined Damen and Titus on the other side of the room.

I was still hungry, and there was a plate of pastries on the table between Finn and Brayden. It was tempting to go over there, but my ex-best friend was watching me in a way that made me want to puke. Then there was Brayden. He trained his gaze on me eagerly.

The last I'd seen Brayden was after my freak-out.

Even with the promise of food, I wasn't sure how to handle them.

So, instead of joining them at the couch, I retreated to an empty corner of the room. It was colder here away from the fireplace, but I didn't care. Hopefully they'd get the hint and would allow me to fade into obscurity.

Of course, luck was not on my side. And at my weakest moment, Bryce struck. He stepped beside me, hands in his pockets as he nonchalantly leaned against the wall. His presence caused the hair on the back of my neck to stand up. What did he want?

He wasn't talking, nor did he seem inclined to do so. And he hadn't even brought a pastry with him!

He sure had a lot of nerve. "Can I help you?"

"I got the thing." Bryce lowered his frame toward mine slightly, his pose serious and intimidating. His low voice was barely discernible through the chatter in the room.

I glanced at him, fighting back a shiver. I had no idea what he was talking about.

Then, as he raised his eyebrow, I recalled his mission. Relief raced through me as warmth flooded my veins once again. The air in the room seemed to grow light, and I grabbed the sleeve of his white shirt, meeting his gaze. I was so grateful.

"Thank you." He might not be so terrible after all. This might just work.

"It's not a problem," Bryce said gruffly, not moving from my grasp. "Though I'm not certain why you'd need it anymore, considering the arm-candy at your beck and call these days."

The warm feeling vanished, and my hand dropped back to my side. "What do you mean?"

"I can't imagine you sleep with it." Bryce's words were strange, but his expression was genuinely bewildered. He rubbed the back of his neck. "You're not a child. If you find yourself needing comfort, there are other alternatives."

Heat—a different sort now—washed over me, and my jaw locked. It took everything in me to not stomp on his feet. Only the knowledge it wouldn't hurt him—since I had no shoes on, and he did—stopped me. "What I sleep with is none of your business."

"What are you two talking about?" Titus materialized by my side—his body still warm from the fire—and I covered my face in preparation for my shame. This was exactly what I'd been trying to avoid. There was no way for my day to get worse.

Titus moved closer, but his focus remained on Bryce.

"What is Bianca taking to bed?" he asked. His question seemingly echoed through the room.

Silence followed, and everyone's attention turned on us.

Now I really wanted to die.

"Bryce!" I hissed, glaring between my fingers at him. This was all his fault!

"I only asked you a question. You never told me what you wanted me to do with it!" Bryce frowned as he crossed his arms. He would no longer meet my eyes. "That pink monstrosity cannot stay in my room. It's giving people the wrong idea. Brayden saw it on my bed and made fun of me this morning."

How dare he blame his inability to be discreet on me! It wasn't my fault he sucked at covert operations. "I never said you had to keep it on your bed! You're the one who put it there, so maybe you secretly want it."

"That thing is yours?" Brayden choked as his face paled. "Now I feel bad."

"All right, just stop." Miles stepped between us, shielding me from Bryce's disdain. "Before the rest of us have heart attacks, can someone please explain what you're talking about?"

I fought back a groan. Shame prickled at me, replacing my annoyance at Bryce. When I responded to Miles, I couldn't even look at him. Instead, I studied my chewed fingernails. "I'm talking about my rabbit. I asked Bryce to get it for me from my dorm. It's the only thing I wanted."

There was a moment of silence before Bryce cleared his throat. "It just occurred to me, but it's not quite how it sounds. I, too, was confused at first."

I peeked up at Bryce as he spoke to the others.

"Confused about what?" I asked.

He ignored me. "She's referring to a stuffed rabbit toy. It's filthy and worn, and she should not be sleeping with it."

"Don't make fun of me!" Indignation hit me, and I glowered at him. "And don't say it's filthy. I wash it all the time. And just so you're aware, I don't even keep it in my bed! You know what? I regret asking for your help."

"What is it?" Damen's eyebrows were raised in question. "Why is that the only thing you sent Bryce to get from all of your possessions?"

I covered my hot face again. But, thankfully, I was saved from answering. Julian had pushed his way to my side and wrapped his arm around my shoulders. "Does it matter why she wanted it?"

"No." I could almost hear the frown in Damen's voice. "I was just wondering."

"Besides, that brings up a good point." Julian's hand squeezed my arm. "We should be headed out soon."

"You're ready to go shopping?" Bryce sighed, lowering his crossed arms. "I suppose I have no choice but to—"

"Julian." I pulled at his shirt, interrupting Bryce. This was the perfect revenge. "Julian, when we go shopping, will you pay for me?"

His brow furrowed. "But I thought that—"

"Please?" This was going against my every instinct, but I persevered. "I'll pay you back."

"Of course," Julian replied, rubbing his thumb in circles over my arm. "And you don't need to pay me back."

"*I'm paying you back,*" I said.

"Yes, dear." Patience laced his voice. "We can leave now, while Damen sorts out things here."

"It doesn't matter." Bryce made his move, shrugging. "She can be as stubborn as she wants, but you can't stop me from coming. But you're overlooking something rather important." I frowned at him, but he continued, "She needs shoes."

"You didn't even grab shoes?" Damen lectured. "How neglectful."

Bryce crossed his arms. "She said she only wanted the one thing."

"Why are you so literal?" Damen said in a scathing voice.

Finn suddenly stood, shoving his hands in his pockets as he looked at me. "You left a pair of shoes in my car."

My breath caught, and, for a moment, I forgot to hate him.

His words gave me hope, although I had no idea which pair he might be referring to. "Which ones?"

"How am I supposed to know?" Finn shrugged. "They're blue. They're fancy. And they have buttons."

"My Tory Burch flats?" I covered my mouth. How could I have forgotten? I'd changed out of them the day we purchased my Tamara Mellon wedges. Not all hope was lost.

"You were wearing Burberrys the other day, too." Bryce was giving me a curious look. "Do you have a shoe fetish?"

"I do not have a fetish!" My happiness faded into embarrassment within a second, and I glared at Bryce. "I just like to take care of my feet."

"Are they all luxury brands?" Bryce ignored my denial as he stroked his chin, seemingly in deep thought. "That's surprising. Abigail is extremely frugal. But even if you managed to convince her, they cost hundreds of dollars each. Considering your issues with gifts, I'm shocked you would accept them."

"Well, they weren't gifts and they're not from *her* either." I wanted to wipe that contemplative look right off his face. Besides, how did Bryce know anything about women's shoes?

"He got them for me." I pointed toward Finn. "And I earned them."

"You earned them?" Damen glanced at his brother. Suspicion laced his tone now. "How exactly do you earn shoes?"

"I took care of him." I shrugged, not sure why they cared. "He likes things done a certain way."

Finn was hiding his face, and the temperature seemed to fall twenty degrees.

"Bianca." Julian turned my face toward his with a touch. "What do you mean? Like…" His next words were stilted. "In the bedroom?"

Why did this upset him?

"Um…" I glanced to Finn for help, but he wasn't even looking at me. My gaze returned to Julian's. "Yes? Then there was the kitchen and living room, and—"

He seemed about to shatter, but he had asked…

"The bathroom too," I finished, waving my hand. "He's really weird about stuff in there."

"You bastard!" Julian lunged in Finn's direction.

Finn's eyes snapped open, seemingly feeling the threat to his life. He jumped back, barely missing Julian's swinging fist. His words flew out in a rush. "She was cleaning!" He dodged another grab. "Do you really think that little of me?"

Damen and Bryce, who'd also had started to move in Finn's direction, halted. And the air in the room shrank while Titus stumbled to a halt and Miles's deadly expression cleared.

"Cleaning?" Brayden sounded scandalized. "But you have servants!"

"That's not the problem," Damen replied, straightening from his lunge and crossing his arms. "Why—"

"I had to think of something for her to do to *earn* stuff! She's always refused gifts!" Finn waved his hand in my direction. "She'll only accept things if it's a necessity, like clothing. Sometimes she'll resist even that. But I noticed she looked at different brands online—"

"You stalked her searches in order to discover what she likes?" Miles asked dryly.

Finn's jaw clenched. "She picked them all out herself." His attention returned to me. "Do you want the ones in my car or not?"

My chest tightened. I'd been following the conversation, of course. But the torrent of conflicting emotions made it difficult to decide how to feel. I felt violated. But it wasn't news to me that he'd been monitoring my phone. It hurt, but…

I'd worked so darn hard for those shoes.

The smell of Finn's laundry would forever be etched into my senses. The mental scars would stay with me the rest of my life. What kind of person would sit and eat cookies while their friend scrubbed their marble floors?

He always got crumbs over everything.

Besides, they were mine. And if I didn't take them, no one—besides maybe Bryce—would appreciate them the way they deserved.

I would have to punish Finn accordingly, but there was no need to waste perfectly good flats. We were civilized people.

"I want them." I stepped forward, holding out my hand for his keys. "Give them back."

Bryce trailed along as Julian and I moved through the mall. It wasn't crowded, and Julian would occasionally point to a window display, offering me glimpses into his preferences.

It was often variations of skinny jeans and short skirts with thigh-high boots. Everything with dark colors, I'd noticed. But nothing remotely like his sky-blue eyes.

"I thought your favorite color was blue?" I asked after he pointed out yet another strappy dress. "What's with the black?"

Julian's finger was still raised, and he paused as his face darkened slightly.

"This has nothing to do with my favorite color." His words came out in a rush, and the lie was thick in his voice. "I only thought they might look good on you."

"The color representing Water is a darkish blue, but usually black." Bryce strode past us, his hands linked behind his head. He didn't even glance as he continued toward the game store. "Julian's favorite color is Prussian blue. Just thought you should know."

Wow, Bryce really knew his colors. I was so impressed.

Julian's face grew darker, and he glared after Bryce.

"I thought we had an understanding," he muttered under his breath as Bryce stepped into the store. "But this might be war."

War? Because Bryce embarrassed him? "Julian? What's wrong?"

"Nothing." Julian's attention turned back to me, but the warmth of his smile didn't quite match his eyes. "Bryce is in a petty mood today. He's probably annoyed I'm here. I think he wanted to spend time alone with you."

"Why though?" My eyes shot to the store, suspicion growing with every beat of my heart. He wasn't plotting against me already, was he?

"Nothing like you're imagining, I'm sure." Julian entwined his fingers in mine. This time when he spoke, the calm matched his expression. "Bryce is a generous person. You *should* let him buy you something. Ask him to spoil you. It'll make him happy."

My eyes flickered back to the glass door, not understanding this logic. How would that make anyone happy? When I had my money, it was *my money*. I didn't buy things for people, and I would kill anyone trying to steal it. "But why?"

"Some people like to give gifts for no reason," Julian said. "We would like to buy you stuff without you getting upset, but you don't seem to welcome that."

He couldn't be right. That wasn't how life worked.

"Nothing is ever free." Gifts always came with a price, even if the price was kindness and loyalty. "I don't understand."

"It's a way of showing affection," he said, as if oblivious to my inner turmoil.

"There are other ways of showing affection. I don't have a problem with presents. If you care about someone, it's better to make something. I like food. I like heirlooms. I like things that people make with their own hands." I wasn't entirely unreasonable. "Someone who is really invested in your relationship will actually take the time to make something. It's insincere to gift things you can just purchase with money, and those people are usually the worst with wanting payback."

"I know it's not what you like, but this is the way society is today." Julian shrugged. "And Bryce was raised in this world. If you want to try to understand how he thinks, let him spoil you."

That was stupid. Why should I need to understand *him*? He should be the one kissing up to *me*.

But then again, Bryce did have control of my money. It was probably prudent to figure out how his mind worked. See the kind of steward he was.

I narrowed my eyes at the bright game store sign. "If he wants to give me something, he can buy me another pair of Burberrys."

Julian lightly pushed me toward the store. "Let him buy you something, or don't. But just go see what he's doing. I need to do something."

My attention returned to Julian. He was pointedly not looking at me anymore. "What are you doing? Are you trying to get rid of me?"

"I'm doing *something*," Julian repeated, his mouth lifting in the corners. "And *you're* the one who will never be rid of *me*, so don't worry about that."

"What—" I began, but Julian slipped away.

Grumbling under my breath, I stomped into the store, spotting Bryce instantly. He was in front of a colorful shelf, game in hand as he studied it with intense concentration.

I watched him—something was off about this picture. He looked unhappy.

He was supposed to be partaking in a joyous hobby, so why did he look so solemn?

Why did I suddenly care about his happiness? This was an odd feeling. I didn't like it. Gosh darn it, Julian was right. I was going to need to let the man purchase something for me.

"What are you doing?" I stepped beside him, and he jumped. I buried my glee at the realization that I'd scared him and pressed forward. "I want a game."

Bryce lowered the case and turned critical eyes to me.

"Okay?" His gaze left mine, glancing behind me. "Where's Julian?"

"I don't know." I shrugged. "He said I should let you buy it."

"Oh, did he?" Bryce frowned, narrowing his eyes toward the doorway. "What do you like?"

"I don't know." I cocked my head. That was such a loaded question. What did anyone like about video games? Was it possible to claim honest affection toward something that only existed in a box? Perhaps so, but I had never contemplated this before. "I've never thought about…"

My words faded, a colorful poster of adorable characters on the wall besides Bryce captured my attention. "What is *that*?"

"That?" Bryce followed my gaze. "Oh, *that*." He spotted the advertisement. "You wouldn't be interested in that. It's for children—"

"I want it." I pushed past Bryce, grabbing a case from the display.

"You don't even know what it is!" Bryce followed me, forced patience lining his voice. He narrowed his eyes at my arms. "Why in the world do you want it?"

My face was already burning, but as I hugged the game to my chest, I knew I had no choice but to answer. He tapped his foot, impatience leaking from his features.

He'd never let me get it without a reason.

"It looks cute…" I admitted.

Bryce blinked, and for a moment he seemed dumbfounded. His voice was cautious when he finally responded. "That's not a reason."

He was wrong. It was *the* reason.

"I need it." If Bryce wouldn't get it, I would tell Titus. Titus would understand. It was our special bond.

"Have you ever played a video game before? What systems have you used?" Bryce rubbed his head. "And besides, this is stupid. You wouldn't like—"

"Don't judge me." Why was he arguing with me about this? He was supposed to heed my every word. This was highly unprofessional. "It's better than your shooting game."

His brows drew together, and he glanced at his hand. "There's nothing wrong with this game. It takes practice and skill to master."

"I could beat you." I couldn't seem to stop. Victory was close at hand. "If you buy me this game, I'll fight you on *that*. If I lose, you can bring my game back and I won't hold it against you."

"You don't even play video games. How in the world do you expect to beat me?" Bryce asked, incredulous. "What if I make you cry?"

My pulse was pounding, and excitement raced through my veins. I won, and he had no idea. I'd teach him to make assumptions. "I won't cry. You'll be the one crying."

"What?" Bryce pressed his hand to his chest and glanced around us, as if to make sure we weren't overheard. And when he responded, his voice lowered. "You're not going to be able to make me cry! I don't cry."

Why didn't I believe him? His face was totally the face of a crier. "I—"

"How about this, honey-bee?" Bryce interrupted, the confidence leaking back into his tone. "I'll get you this game, *and* a new system with *all* the extras. Because if you're picking stuff like this, I'm assuming you'd want the console that comes with it. When I win, I'll let you keep it. But you'll have to obey me for a month. If a miracle happens and you win, I'll listen to you instead."

I narrowed my eyes at him. Just who did he think he was? He had to obey me anyway!

That was no reward, considering he already had to obey my every whim. But I couldn't pass this up. With this negotiation, I didn't even owe him a thing! It was brilliant.

"It's a deal." I ignored his smug smirk and glanced past him. "Where is it?"

The smile dropped from his face, "Where is what?"

"The console, *Daddy*." I didn't see it anywhere. He better not be lying to me. "I want everything."

"I told you not to call me that." He grimaced. "And it's not out here. We'll need to ask at the register. Follow me."

Chapter Eighteen

Julian
Glass

With Bianca gone to bond with Bryce, my good deed of the day was now completed.

I shoved my hands in my pockets, trudging toward the jewelry store. I could hurt him later, but the clueless man needed all the help he could get. He'd never make the first move in forming a relationship with his sister, and Bianca was just as awkward.

Watching the two of them was almost painful.

But whether she would admit to it or not, she already saw him as a big brother. It was time for Bryce to step up.

However, playing babysitter wasn't exactly how I'd planned on spending my day. Nor was this next part. But since Bianca had asked me to come… I couldn't not stop by.

After all, it would be rude not to say 'hello' to family.

Besides, my cousin and I had a score to settle.

As I stepped through the doors, I spotted the tall, dark-haired woman. She was bent over the display, deep in conversation with Hanah Geier.

I didn't even wait for my cousin to notice me, otherwise she might run away. "Kayla!"

She jerked upright. "Julian!"

I'd crossed the room in an instant. "Why have you not returned my messages?"

"Because you weren't being nice." Kayla frowned. She was already on the defensive, hiding her fear behind snark, but I knew her well enough to tell the difference. "You need to respect your elders. And why are you visiting me at work? You hate the mall."

"I'm here with Bianca." I waved off her attempt at redirection. "*She's* what I need to talk to you about."

"Bianca is here?" Hanah stood, her eyes searching past me. "Where is she?"

"She's with Bryce. Are you looking for her, or looking to run away?" I asked, noting the way her skin paled. "You knew who she was the whole time. Is that why you wouldn't come outside when we visited *The Ivy Garden?*"

"I'm not hiding from *her* any more than Kayla is running from *you*," Hanah replied. "Stop your posturing; *you* don't scare me."

I frowned at her because she was right. The only people in the world besides my quintet and my own brother who didn't fear me were Hanah and Jin. Even Catalina—Miles's third officer—tended to steer clear.

It was a bit refreshing. Usually officers were still wary. So I always wondered, "Why not?"

"You pretend you don't care that people are scared of you, but you do. You hate it. You like to take care of people. That's why you're in medical school. You want people to see you helping others and not just the scary bits."

I frowned at her. "Maybe I'm in medical school because I want to learn how to kill people more effectively."

She laughed. "Sure, Julian. Whatever you say."

"I'm pretty sure it's true." Kayla raised her eyebrows as she studied me.

"Which?" Hanah asked.

"Both of you knock it off." I ignored their teasing and studied my cousin. "That's not why I'm here. Why don't you confess?"

She pulled at one of her black curls. "Confess what?" she asked, even though from the guilty expression on her face she knew exactly *what*.

"I don't know," I said, unperturbed by her aversion. "How about the depths of your actual involvement with Bianca? Finn mentioned you've been helping contain him."

"Who cares?" She continued to avoid my eyes. "Finn and I have an understanding. You don't know him like I do."

The way her cheeks darkened and her continual refusal to look in my direction caused alarm to rush though me.

"Don't tell me that you have feelings for him?" Even though I asked, I already knew. "Kayla, how could you?"

"It's really none of your business, Julian," Kayla said, her tone somewhat snarky. "You don't own me."

"Kayla, he's violent, unpredictable, and already put one man into a coma. Then when his victim was on the verge of recovery, he broke into the hospital and paralyzed him. There was *no* reason for that." I couldn't believe her stupidity. I would have thought after seeing my father she'd know no matter how charming a man is, you couldn't trust one who was evil at the core. And Finn was one of those people.

Instead of helping her understand, my words caused her expression to turn fierce. "You're one to talk, you hypocrite." Her eyes glittered with anger.

"Kayla?" For the first time in my life, I found myself wary of my cousin.

"You may be my superior, and you may be infinitely more powerful than me. But that's no excuse." Her eyes flashed, and her finger pressed into my chest. "You don't control my life, nor what I do in my free time."

"What?" My heart thundered. That was no excuse for lying to me.

They'd kept Bianca a secret.

The entire situation made me sick. The recollection made me want to kill again for the first time in a long time, and it was taking everything in me to bury that feeling.

It wasn't just that Bianca's existence had been kept secret. It was more.

The bond between Mu and myself was unique, and it was my job to be there for her always. No matter what our lives, or the situation. And now she'd grown up basically alone.

All because no one could trust me.

That's what pissed me off the most. I screwed up, and my selfishness impacted her. Because of my actions, no one thought I could handle the added responsibility.

If Kayla wanted to be stupid with Finn, that was her business. I just needed to know, was it really because of me?

"It was after *him*, wasn't it?" I asked. "That's why no one said anything. They thought I wasn't able to handle it. Everything else is just an excuse."

The snark left her expression in an instant. "Julian…"

It was all the confirmation I needed.

"Finn claimed they wanted me to finish medical school." I was sinking.

"But she didn't want to say anything because they thought I'd lose it."

Kayla was silent a moment. Her expression was all the answer I needed, but she verbalized it anyway. "You were a very angry person back then. She wanted you to focus on getting past what happened with your father."

My heart sank as my deepest fears were confirmed. "It was my fault…"

"Not only you," Hanah interjected, her gaze travelling between the two of us. "Damen was too immature. Miles was having attacks all the time. Then after Kiania, no one knew if she would live. She was afraid of people—of everything. Mom worried that any exposure to the paranormal would trigger her. Or bring her to the council's attention. You were all growing up still. Then there's the fact she's scared of men. We didn't know how she'd react."

Honestly, after knowing everything, I was surprised she was doing as well as she was.

But she hadn't been afraid of me—she'd said it herself. I was so thankful the companionship we shared in past lives was enough to bind her to us without fear.

The echo of Hanah's words ran through my mind. And something else she said, earlier when she'd broken Bianca's story to us, now stood out. "But you never agreed." She'd been angry at the mention of her parents. "That was why you wouldn't go home."

"That's true." Hanah crossed her arms. "I don't think lying is ever justified, no matter what happened in her past."

I agreed, and was just about to say so, when she continued. "We still don't know *how* she ended up in the system. Or how she ended up where she was."

I tapped my chin. "She was a foundling. She was left at a hospital at birth."

Kayla raised an eyebrow at the sudden turn of the conversation, and

Hanah's frown turned into confusion. "Yes, that's what Eric Richards told my mother."

"But…" Something wasn't adding up. "How did she get to the hospital? She was born at Whisperwind. Bryce won't say how he did it. Who took Bianca, and where did they go?"

Hanah's frown deepened. "I don't know," she said finally. "But she does have proper foundling paperwork."

I ignored her musings, continuing with my own. "And who were her first foster parents?"

Kayla was watching me, her expression devoid of answers. And I knew I'd stumbled onto something which no one—outside of one person—held the answers.

"Bianca says her 'first parents' were killed in front of her," I explained. "But Titus pulled up her records. She lived two places before Abigail adopted her. She was briefly with an older couple before Eric Richards. They are now dead. Before that, there are no names."

"She admits to having *three* previous homes. But she won't talk about it," Hanah muttered. "Do you think *you* could find out who the first couple was?"

If it was anyone other than Bianca, then yes.

However, everything inside me warred at that thought of forcing her to disclose anything she didn't want. Unless she came to us, we might not ever know.

Her severe aversion to addressing anything that had happened to her, even ten years later, made me feel that getting an answer from her was going to be next to impossible.

"I don't know," I admitted, rubbing my temples. "I can offer suggestions for her to sleep or calm. But she knows I'm doing it. I won't force her to recollect memories that clearly cause her distress."

Hanah seemed hesitant. "Why won't you just look? Will she let you? It has to be easier."

"I made a promise." And that was all she needed to know. Even if it meant we'd never have answers, I would never betray her trust. Doing so would destroy everything that ever existed between us.

Hanah's lips pursed, and she cocked her head, but before she could speak, another sound echoed through the space.

"Hanah?" Bianca sounded unsure at first, but then she'd crossed the distance between us. She held on to my arm as she stared at her sister. "What are you doing here?"

Chapter Nineteen

Bianca
World

My breath caught, and nervousness ran through me, causing a shiver to shoot down my spine. I hadn't been sure, but her reaction had been confirmation.

She looked different.

Hanah used to have waist-length, straight brown hair, and, to my adoptive mother's annoyance, wore her skirts in dark colors with holes in the knees of her tights. She always had the appearance of someone who couldn't quite scrub the dirt from her skin or from under her nails, and there was a soft feminine beauty within the sharp angles of her face.

But when her deep chocolate eyes snapped to mine, I was certain it was her.

Julian had said they knew my sister, but still. It was a surprise to see her here, talking so casually with Julian.

It had been eight years. I hadn't seen her since the day she and our mother fought. She was upset about something, and she stormed out of the house, slamming the door behind her.

In all my life, she was the closest thing to a sibling I'd ever had. Bryce didn't count, and Brayden and I were still learning about each other, though it could be said that I knew more about Brayden than Hanah.

But it *felt* like I knew her despite her absence. Our mother would always talk about her.

I shook my head, catching myself before my thoughts rambled away from the topic at hand.

Hanah sighed, her shoulders slumping as her hands ran through her pixie cut. "Hello, Bianca."

"Hi…" I said again.

And the moment of silence that followed seemed to stretch on for an eternity.

"Well this is awkward," Bryce said, stepping up beside me. "I wonder how we could diffuse the tension. If only we had a source of comedic relief."

The pretty, dark-skinned woman narrowed her eyes at Bryce. Her mouth opened, but then slowly closed before she shook her head. After a long moment, she spoke. "I can't. It's too easy."

Her voice sounded familiar, but I couldn't place it off the top of my head. "Do I know you?"

Julian stiffened and she blinked, looking at him first. But then her attention returned to me.

"You *may* have seen me before," she said cautiously, shifting on her feet. There was a melodic ring to her voice that pulled at me. "We went to the same high school."

"Bianca, this is Kayla Taylor." Julian gestured to the woman before he pulled me to his side. "She's my cousin, and my Jiangjun."

"Jiangjun…" I glanced at him. "Like Matheus, Brayden, and…" Hanah was shifting nervously, and I recalled the Damen's fleeting statement about my sister. "Hanah? How long…?"

Had Hanah known who I was the whole time?

"Officers are sorted into their eventual quintets when they are thirteen, but quintets aren't sealed until everyone is of age," Bryce said, misreading my expression. "Hanah is the oldest on the Jiangjun level."

This only solidified my suspicions.

"You left when you were eighteen…" I said, attempting to keep the accusation from my tone. At that point, Hanah knew her place in this world. She had known Miles. She bit her lip, averting her gaze.

I would have to ask. "Did you know who I was? What about—"

"They thought they were protecting you," she interrupted, correctly guessing at my question. "Mother isn't the best at handling sensitive situations. But this isn't the best venue to be having this discussion." Hanah gestured around the shop.

To my surprise, the movement of her arm ended with her hand outstretched toward mine. "Your phone?" she asked. "They can't really keep me away anymore. Let me give you my number and we'll talk. That would just *burn* them."

"Are you being vindictive?" Bryce asked, raising an eyebrow. "This is unlike you."

"I have no idea what you're talking about," she said, not moving her gaze from mine as I slowly gave her my phone.

"You talk more now," Kayla noted, tilting her head. "You always used to hide behind Finn, letting him speak for you."

Julian's arm went rigid and his breath hitched, but I ignored him. We all knew about his loathing of Finn.

"It wasn't that much…" I protested, even though it was. In fact, I was surprising myself by even continuing this conversation. However, with Julian's presence surrounding me, it was difficult to feel the anxiety that would normally leave me speechless. He was probably doing something, but I'd confront him about it later.

This was more important. I didn't understand why this girl felt familiar, or why I couldn't get her voice of out my head. "Were you stalking me? Why don't I remember seeing you?"

Her mouth twisted, but it was Bryce who responded. "Kayla doesn't *stalk* anyone. She's too proper." He watched her with something akin to respect.

"She doesn't," Julian agreed. "Instead, she *lurks* and lies by omission."

"Lurks?" A flicker of annoyance crossed her expression, and Kayla turned her narrowed gaze on Julian. "What do you—"

"This isn't over," Julian interrupted, holding me to him tighter. "Before the next week is out, I'll be meeting with you, Anthony, and Du Yun. I fear you've been given a bit too much leeway."

Kayla blanched, Hanah shot the other woman a sympathetic look, and Bryce only made a tsking sound under his breath.

"But in the meantime, I have plans today," Julian continued. "And I'm not going to let you lot upstage them."

Yes, shopping. Shouldn't we be nearly finished at this point? I'd already changed into one of my new outfits, purchased on loan from the man beside me. And Julian and Bryce both had some bags on the floor by our feet now.

None of that included the items that Julian had *sent* to Damen's house. As if people of the world existed to do his—or our—bidding.

And again, I was reminded of how out-of-touch I was with this world.

Then I was pulled out of my spiraling spiel of self-pity, noticing Bryce frowning down at a ring display.

Which reminded me of another slight I'd suffered.

"Bryce, *stay*." I pointed at him. He glanced at me, the frown deepening as his eyebrow rose. How dare he look confused. "You can catch up to us later. I want to be alone with Julian." Besides, this would be the perfect opportunity for him to perform his husbandly duties. Lord only knew that he'd been terrible at them thus far. "I wear a size five."

"You want to be alone with me?" Julian asked, the corner of his mouth lifting slightly.

I grabbed the front of his shirt, pulling the fabric until he lowered his face near mine. "*I want my ring.*"

"Ah." Julian blinked in understanding, the grin fading slightly. "*Jewelry*. And shoes. So you do have weaknesses."

"This has nothing to do with weaknesses. Bryce and I have an agreement. That's how marriages work!" I growled. "This isn't complicated. I'm a simple creature with simple needs."

"Does he even know what you're expecting?" Julian asked, raising his eyes to my fake-husband. Bryce might not be able to hear us, but clearly he knew we were discussing him. In response to our attention turning to him, he bristled slightly, trying to look innocent.

Lies, all of it. "It's *obvious*." Bryce was smarter than he looked. I, begrudgingly, would admit to that.

Julian nodded, his lips pursed.

"Maria wasn't kidding. And Julian, you're no help. You can't agree with her all the time." Kayla stepped from behind the counter, gliding gracefully to the two of us. She held out her hand toward Hanah. "Give me her phone."

"Kidding about what?" My face heated—had I done something to Maria? I thought we were friends.

"Despite my vow to stay out of the way, I cannot help myself. You need some girl-time in your life," she said, snatching it from Hanah's hands. "Don't worry. I'll steer you in the right direction. We can't let Maria have free-reign. If it were up to her, she'd get you drunk just for laughs."

"Why would it be funny?" Her words had taken on a sense of foreboding. I'd known public drunkenness was a rite of passage, but still… There was nothing humorous about throwing up on a bender.

She was typing now and responded without pause. "It wouldn't be. But someone has got to protect you."

"That's not nice." Hanah frowned. "Maria isn't all that bad."

"*You'd* say that. You're a bit biased," Kayla said, holding my phone back to me. "But you haven't heard about her *plans*."

"What plans?" Bryce's voice wavered.

"Girl stuff." Kayla shoved the phone at me after I'd made no move to grab it. "Don't worry about it. Now didn't you say you had stuff to do?" She glanced toward Julian, who watched her with barely concealed surprise. "I'm actually working here. Leave me be."

Julian's surprise turned to contemplation, then resignation. "Having you around with *her* would make me feel better."

"Now you owe *me*." She returned to her previous location.

Julian nodded in response. "Thanks…"

"It's not like I had ample opportunity." She sighed, sitting on a stool and crossing her arms on the glass. "Just don't be too hard on him?" she asked, glancing at Julian.

Julian's arm stiffened slightly before, after a breath, he relaxed. "I'll think about it."

And without another word, he led me from the store, leaving Bryce behind to talk to the two women. But even though I couldn't see them anymore, I could feel Kayla and Hanah's gazes burning into my back.

"Do you think they like me?" I asked, peeking up from my phone. Kayla had texted herself from my number. Did this mean she was going to message me first?

Hanah, on the other hand, had put herself in as a contact.

There was only sincerity in his gaze as he looked at me. "Darling, I'm still mad as hell at them, but I won't lie. They adore you."

I bit my lip, returning my attention to the screen. Their names blurred together. "What makes you think that?"

We were away from the jewelry store now, and he steered me down an abandoned hallway. But he didn't speak again, not until we'd stopped and he set the bags he was holding on the floor. My back was against the wall, and he turned toward me before gently touching my cheek. "I don't think that, I know it."

I opened my mouth, but he pressed his finger to my lips. "Kayla lied to *me* in order to protect you. She's extremely justice-minded. She wouldn't have done that without a reason, no matter who asked her." The confusion must have shown in my gaze. "Besides that, there are those of us whom everyone knows to never cross. For example, while Miles is formidable, he allows his subjects a lot of leeway. In comparison, Titus and myself are far more unforgiving. Out of everyone in the world, Hanah, Jin, and Miles are the most likely to stand against me. But never Kayla. And"—he sighed—"as much as I loathe to admit it, not Finn either."

"Are you saying that you think Finn actually *likes* me?" I couldn't keep the disdain from my voice. "After everything he did?"

"I *think* Finn is an idiot." Julian pinched the bridge of his nose with his other hand. "But even the path to Hell is paved with good intentions. I don't think he's coming from a place of malice. However, his stubbornness is affecting *you*, and that's what I can't forgive. That, and the fact his feelings have ventured into places he's not allowed."

"What do you mean?" I tilted my head, the movement causing a lock of my hair to fall over my eyes.

Julian's mouth dipped as he moved it from my face, tucking my hair behind my ear instead. He studied the place where his hand touched, and a flash of darkness passed over his expression.

"Julian?" Why was he looking at me like that, and why did he seem upset?

The sound of his name seemed to pull him from his reverie, and he shook his head. "Never mind. Let's go home. Damen should be ready by now."

"Ready?" I asked as he picked up the bags with one hand and placed the other lightly on my waist. "What did Damen do?"

'*Ready*' apparently referenced Damen's attempt to redo my room.

And an attempt it was only because when Julian and I returned, most of the furniture had been removed but nothing else was done. The walls were only half-painted a light, pink color.

"What is this?" I stepped into the room.

Damen, who had been standing on a small ladder as he trimmed out a corner, made a surprised sound and almost fell to the floor.

"You're back?" he asked, turning toward me as he caught his balance. "Already?"

What did he mean *already*? I glanced at my phone and pursed my lips. "It's been *hours*."

This didn't seem to mean anything to Damen. "That's my point."

Well, I wasn't sure how long it took *him* to purchase clothes, but sensible people didn't need to shop all day. Then again, considering how vain he was, I could only imagine him trying on every item imaginable while admiring himself in the dressing room mirror.

That was the curse one must suffer when you were insanely attractive and nothing in the world looked bad on you. Shopping must be a nightmare—how did one know what to purchase when nothing made you look ugly?

"Baby girl, are you thinking something disparaging about me?" Damen was in front of me now. "Have I mentioned that sometimes when you look at me, I feel emasculated."

"I only think positive things." I waved my hand, stepping out of Julian's way as he followed me into the room. "What else would there be?"

Damen frowned at Julian, who put his hands in the pockets of his jeans as he surveyed the room. "Julian, I think she makes fun of us in her thoughts."

"Don't be ridiculous. Bianca doesn't know how to be mean. You're just being self-conscious." Julian didn't sound concerned. "I thought you'd be further than this."

Damen's mouth dipped. "I had to order furniture."

"It really was fine before." I frowned at the dust scattered throughout the space. "This isn't going to be one of those renovations where I'm going to be stuck living in sawdust and paint pieces for the next few years?"

I blinked, and Damen's scent surrounded me. He'd draped his arm wrapped around my back, and his spicy scent washed over me.

It would have been nice, if he also wasn't entirely filthy. Standing this close to him, I could easily see the dark, coarse stubble coating his jaw. And there was a thin sheen of dark dust covering his skin as well.

Which really didn't bode well for his painting project. Now dust was just going to get all over everything.

"What?" I asked, trying to pull away from his male-grossness.

His grin was too pleased. "Are you planning on staying long-term then?"

I smacked his arm away. "Maybe if you finish your little project. Get away from me. You're dirty."

"You don't like dirt?" he asked, lowering his arm as he tilted his head.

"I like to be clean. Where am I going to sleep now?" I brushed at my skirts, no longer looking at him. It was a little thing and probably sounded girly and dumb, but how could I explain that squalor brought back bad memories. I tried not to be spoiled and to be grateful for what I had. But there was a line that had to be drawn somewhere.

I hadn't slept on hardwood floors in bare rooms since childhood, and that wasn't a time I recalled with fondness. In those days, there was nowhere to hide, nowhere to escape.

"You could sleep with me." Damen sounded hopeful.

I would think not. He needed some initiative to finish this project. And Julian, he was still a medical student. He needed his rest. As for Titus? If he didn't go back to work soon, Maria would murder him.

And that left only one.

"Where is Miles's room again?" I asked. Didn't Miles usually stay closer to campus anyway? It wasn't like I had to sleep with him or anything. I was just borrowing his bed.

"My feelings are hurt." Damen's voice was barely discernable and a bit pouty.

"It's all very logical," I argued, glancing up. Julian stood to the side, a bemused expression on his face as he watched us. Meanwhile, Damen stood back, his hand pressed to his chest.

He quirked his eyebrow, frowning. "Are you going to explain your logic?"

"No." I didn't need to explain myself. Damen had already proven that his judgment was better left untrusted. Besides, it was obvious.

"So you're sleeping in Miles's room?" Julian stepped to my side, wrapping his arm around my shoulders.

My heartbeat suddenly echoed through my ears—that had been rather assuming of me. "Do you think he'll mind?" What if he wanted his bed tonight?

"Of course not," Julian said. "In fact, he'll probably be insufferable about the fact that you chose him."

"Come to think of it, I really should ask him first," I muttered, touching my bottom lip. "But what if he says 'no'?"

"He won't." Julian pulled my hand away from my mouth. "But there's a way to approach him. Would you like to know what it is?"

"What do you mean?" Why did Julian suddenly seem amused? I thought Miles was the direct, confrontational, type.

"Julian..." Damen's voice had taken on a warning tone.

"Relax." Julian frowned at the man, then returned his attention to me. "Miles likes to pick on *everyone*. He's had it coming, you'd be the only one who could get one up on him."

So… Was he helping me or not? I was so confused. And why, with every word out of his mouth, did it seem as though my initial conclusion about Miles not sleeping here tonight was incorrect? "What are you talking about? I don't want to pick on Miles."

"Don't worry," Julian replied. "Miles likes someone who can keep up with him."

Then Julian laid out his plan, and my mouth went dry. Why would I ever want to put poor Miles on the spot like that? I had been wrong—and it was too late to back out of the plan. And even more importantly, why was I suddenly nervous about the prospect of sleeping in the same bed as Miles? But this was much more than my accidental and sleep-deprived sleeping arrangements of the past.

As the night drew on, it was difficult to school my features into indifference. Even as I curled under an afghan on the couch in Damen's living room and read the same page of *The Hobbit* a thousand times, my focus wasn't able to remain on the book.

Guilt twisted in me, a twinge of anxiety. But under it, was something else.

Julian had said that attention from me would make Miles feel *special*. Was it true?

I glanced at the clock, noting the time. I couldn't put off the inevitable much longer before it became too late to get a decent night's sleep. I got to my feet and brushed my hands over the long skirts of my white nightgown.

My heart raced in anticipation—Julian had said this was the best way, but my nerves still pulled at me.

I would have to trust him.

Bryce and Damen were playing chess by the fireplace, but neither seemed to be enjoying the game. In fact, they spent more time narrowing their eyes at each other than moving their pieces. I wasn't sure I approved of all the glaring. It was a strange strategy.

Or maybe they acted this way as a defense mechanism, because neither seemed to be good at chess at all. It was painful to see, and I'd been trying not to watch the whole evening.

If Julian or Titus had been around, I might have challenged one of them. I had the feeling that both men knew what they were doing.

But alas, Julian had a night shift and Titus was… *somewhere*.

I could have, technically, played with Finn. He was a semi-decent player. But I had avoided talking to him, and he leisurely sat in the corner of the room, fiddling on his laptop. Brayden and Miles, on the other hand, were watching sports on Damen's flat screen.

And what the crap was that about? I had no idea Finn was staying here, too. Why had no one warned me?

No, I was not pleased with Damen Abernathy at all. Besides ripping up my room, he had also betrayed me. Just because I didn't want Finn to *die* didn't mean he had to be hovering about.

"Bianca?" It was Brayden who noticed me first. "What's wrong?"

"It's time for bed." I nodded toward the stairs, trying to ignore my pounding heart and sweaty palms.

"Right." Damen swiped his arm over the chessboard, ending his game in a dramatic tantrum. Then he ignored Bryce's protest and stood, touching the neck of his crew shirt. He seemed nervous. "I promise your room will be ready by Sunday. If you want, you can—"

"Come on." I turned to Miles, who'd been sipping on his tea as he watched us. I wasn't sure what Damen was going on about, but he knew the plan. Was this a last-ditch effort to get on my good side? "We're going to bed."

The witch choked and violently coughed before Brayden, after a short pause, began to beat him on the back.

"What are you talking about?" Brayden asked.

"Damen ruined my bedroom, so now I can't sleep there." I glared at the man who started this. He didn't even have the decency to look ashamed. "Julian said I could sleep in Miles's bed."

Miles's face turned redder and his coughing continued.

"Why don't you sleep in a guest room?" Brayden asked. "Lord knows there's enough of them. You don't need to sleep *with* someone."

I'd raised my finger in the air to protest before I realized he was right. Why hadn't I thought of this?

"Well, of course she's sleeping in a guest room!" Bryce crossed his arms, leaning back in his seat. "There's an empty one near me. Besides, it'll make me feel better if she's close."

"Who cares how you feel?" Damen frowned. Finn was also glanced up from work, shooting the other man a wary look. "You sound like a creeper," Damen continued. "What do you think is going to get to her in my home?"

Bryce narrowed his eyes, giving the man a pointed look. "It's not a *what*. It's *who*. *Who* present in this room is likely to act on impulsive, improper behaviors?"

"You had better not be referring to me," Damen growled. "I'm not the only impulsive one."

Finn also glared at Damen.

They were all stupid. But in this instance, I agreed with Damen. Rooming near Bryce wouldn't work. I'd rather snuggle on a bed of nails and slowly bleed to death.

Besides, who was he to tell me what to do?

"I don't think so," I said. "I don't need a guest room. I'm sleeping with Miles." Miles hadn't responded. Instead, he continued to stare at me, red-faced. It was the look of staunch horror on his expression that caused my anxiety to fade completely.

He was scared of me.

Mentally rolling my eyes, I crossed the room, grabbing his arm. "Let's go."

"You're serious?" Miles squeaked. "But *why*?"

"Because I'm tired," I said, tugging him to his feet. "Let's go."

Chapter Twenty

Bianca
Proposal

I shouldn't have worried about sleeping with Miles. Outside of not having an aggressive bone in his body, there was no doubt he was trying to disgust me.

To put it nicely, Miles was the worst roommate I'd ever had.

Yes, the way he flustered about his room, trying to kick dirty clothes under his bed, had been adorable—at first. But trying to sleep while knowing there had to be four full loads of laundry stuffed under the box spring had made my skin itch.

He played sports. So much sweat had soaked into those clothes. I knew there was research out there stating that male pheromones were meant to appeal to a woman's amorous state.

But it didn't work.

By the time morning came around, snuggling was the furthest thing from my mind. And it would have been impossible to curl up next to him, even if I wanted. Miles had pressed himself to the other side of the bed, against the wall, and didn't even so much as allow his feet to touch me the whole night.

It was offensive, actually.

What was his deal? Not long ago, he'd been dragging me around by the front of the jacket he'd lent me. Now he seemed to think I had cooties.

Men.

However, his intentions were of no consequence. And outside of a quiet breakfast, he hadn't been around the entire day. Nor had anyone else.

Because of them, I'd been forced to spend my time all alone in Damen's living room as I read *The Hobbit*. How was that for welcoming?

Well, Finn was here, too. He was clicking away on his computer, clearly watching me from time to time. But he didn't count as decent companionship.

"Are you thinking something mean about me?" he asked, pausing his movements over the keys.

"No." How the heck did he know what I was thinking?

He sighed. "You're going to have to talk to me sometime."

Since he wasn't in danger of being put to death, at least not any time soon, my sympathies toward him had vanished. "No, I don't."

"Bianca." Brayden peeked into the room with a slight smile. "Sorry, I had some things to take care of. But I'm ready for you now."

"Huh?" I blinked at the curly-haired man. What was he talking about?

"Finn was supposed to tell you. I'll be going over some of your abilities with you today." Brayden's gaze flickered to Finn, who didn't even have the decency to look ashamed. "Did he not mention it?"

"No." I frowned at Finn. How could he do this to me? He knew I hated surprises. "What lesson?"

Finn smoothly returned his attention to his laptop. "This is your own doing. If you were talking to me, I could have told you."

I growled under my breath, my fingernails digging into my palms.

If I didn't know better, I'd assume that Finn was *trying* to annoy me. He knew how important this was to me. He'd gone out of his way to put me on the spot, making me look unprepared and tarnishing my reputation with one of my older brothers.

If this was anyone else, I'd say this was deliberate. He was getting under my skin so I wouldn't forget about him. Hate was, after all, a powerful emotion.

But that was impossible. Finn lacked any emotional depth, and he cared about no one.

He was just a jerk.

"Okay." I got to my feet and brushed off my skirt. Although I was barely at the point of being comfortable alone with Brayden, it was certainly better than suffering under the weight of Finn's suddenly very heavy stare. "What are we doing?"

"Who taught you how to block emotions?" Brayden suddenly asked, breaking the monotonous nature of the lecture that had escaped my attention. He crossed his arms on the table and leaned forward, looking at me expectantly.

I blinked, pulled out of my perusal of the room he'd dragged us to. I should have been paying attention from the beginning, but seriously, I'd been surprised.

We were in a greenhouse that was *almost* intact enough to use. Considering that we were in *Damen's* home, this was basically the last thing I'd expected to see.

"Pardon?" I asked.

"You're no expert, but you're semi-decent at blocking emotions without trying. If you weren't, you'd have been driven completely mad already," Brayden said. "However, I've noticed that you struggle the most when your focus is divided. It'll become even more complicated when you counter in your quintet."

I tilted my head. "What *are* you talking about?"

Now it was Brayden's turn to look confused. He raised his eyebrow. "You can't tell when you're fighting the influence of a spirit?"

"Well, no. I just do what feels natural," I said. "When I feel overwhelmed, I focus on my breathing. But it's sometimes hard to distinguish between my emotions and spirits. Titus had to help me at Professor Hamway's house. I didn't even know, until recently, that mediumship and emphatic abilities weren't the same. But what does my quintet have to do with anything?"

"You don't know?" Brayden sounded unsure, and I pursed my lips. After all, if I knew what he was talking about, this conversation would be going very differently.

He correctly interpreted my expression. "Empaths aren't limited to feeling only the emotions of spirits. When we've accepted our roles, we can also pick up on the emotions of our quintets members."

That was ludicrous. Surely the boys would have said something.

I had my finger in the air, poised to argue. Then recent events came to mind.

I'd kissed Damen in a moment of passion. Knowing this, everything made much more sense.

It wasn't my fault. Although I'd attacked him, he'd seduced me just by *existing*. He had probably been thinking lusty things. No wonder my heart always raced and my skin felt warm when he was nearby. I was being influenced by outside forces beyond my control.

I had been foolish, with my guard lowered. I always believed it was only the emotions of the dead which affected me.

What in the world was happening to me?

"The emotions of your quintet are different than a spirit's. But if you've accepted your role, you are sure to feel both. Also, if your concentration is torn, it's more difficult to control." Brayden's voice sounded so far away. "You can learn how to compartmentalize these emotions though. I originally worried you were untrained, but I've been watching. You only lack confidence. Empaths need to be a master of their own emotions before they can resonate well with others. Who taught you before this?"

It was suddenly hard to breathe, and my focus turned toward the double-door entry. "I'm self-taught."

Brayden sucked in a breath, but before he could speak, the door slammed open. Bryce strolled into the room. He was wearing a suit—although it was Saturday—and as he crossed the space between us, he loosened his tie as he grumbled under his breath.

I'd never been so happy to see him, and a twinge of concern even touched me at his appearance. At this moment, he was far from the annoying man I'd come to know.

"What in the world is wrong with you?" Brayden dropped our previous discussion.

"It's Abernathy." He slumped into the seat beside me.

"Damen?" Brayden asked. "I thought he was painting."

Bryce shook his head. "No, not *that* one. I just came from a meeting with the dean."

"Of the college?" Guilt twisted at me. Why did I have the feeling this was my fault? "Is it because of…" Bryce turned toward me, and I waved my hand in the air between us. "Us?"

"Is it regarding our marriage?" Bryce raised his eyebrow. "In a manner of speaking."

"Are you going to be able to keep your job?" Brayden asked.

My breath caught. I hadn't considered this. But relationships between students and professors were forbidden. "What's going to happen?"

What about the plan? Would all of this be annulled, and I sent *back*?

Besides that, while I hated Bryce, and firmly believed he didn't deserve to be our teacher, I didn't want anyone to get into trouble on my account.

"That's not the problem. Aine Hamway is on suspension, there's questions about how she was able to purchase the Cole's family property in the first place. The elders don't believe in coincidence," Bryce said. "I'm in charge of her class until the investigation is completed. So long as someone else grades your work, Dean Abernathy doesn't care that you are my student. Though, we might have to be aware of rumors. People are going to be curious about you and might approach you. Dean is worried about campus security."

My heartbeat was thundering in my ears. "People will look at me?"

"People watch you anyway." Bryce frowned. "Haven't you noticed?"

I glanced at Brayden, and he nodded. "It's a part of your appeal. Anyone with an inkling of power is going to be drawn to you."

My stomach clenched. No. I had *not* noticed. But now that he'd mentioned it, I was certain to see gazes following me. My entire day would be filled with paranoia and fear… Well, even more than usual.

Thanks, Bryce.

"It's not a bad thing," Brayden offered, covering my hand with his.

"Shut up." I tugged my hand away, pressing it against my mouth. "This is a disaster."

"You don't like being the center of attention?" Bryce finished loosening his tie and ran his fingers through his hair. "Well, you're going to have to suck it up. This is your life now, honey-bee. Just wait until you're introduced to the courts."

I pushed my hands into my lap, glaring at him.

But he cut me off before I could say a word. "This is our mother's engagement ring." He held his fist out to me. His cheeks turned dark, but his voice remained oddly formal. "It would be my honor if you accept my proposal."

"*This* is why you're interrupting our lesson?" Brayden covered his face. "You don't need to actually ask her! I only said she needs to have something on her finger, not that you should make a whole dramatic production. You're already married."

"Shut up." Bryce glowered at the curly-haired man. "We have traditions to uphold."

"That's gross." Brayden shuddered.

My hand shook as I held my palm up. My silent acquiescence wasn't from the fact I approved of the manner of his proposal or that this wasn't disgusting. Because it was.

I was expecting a ring. But I thought he'd purchased it at the mall.

Not *this*.

My throat closed. The annoyance in Bryce's eyes had trickled away, and for a moment we were connected. All my negative feelings toward him scattered in the face of this new development.

Bryce was trying. I could see it in his gaze. He wanted to mend the rift in our relationship. To do that, he was giving me something that belonged to my biological mother.

How could I say no to that?

Physical evidence of her existence was so close to me. My breath was shaky and loud in my ears, and I couldn't hold back the breathy squeak of my voice. "Can I see?"

"The ring?" Bryce's eyebrow slowly rose. "Of course, it's yours." He opened his fist, and the antique gold band fell into my hand.

Brayden scoffed. "That's real romantic. I thought you were going for tradition."

"Keep your comments to yourself," Bryce retorted.

I could scarcely breathe. My vision wavered as my blurry gaze took in the gold band, I couldn't even make out any details yet. But it felt heavy. Surely it didn't weigh so much.

"But what about her?" My voice echoed in my ears. "Won't she miss it?"

The following silence was so heavy that, for a moment, it took precedence. My attention turned to them.

Bryce was staring at me, his jaw slack and expression pained. And Brayden… He'd gone so pale that I thought he might faint.

"What?" I asked.

"Oh, Bianca." Brayden was the first to snap out of his stunned state. He leaned forward, closing his hand around my fist. "I didn't realize you didn't know."

"Mother is dead." Bryce gazed at the dusty glass walls. "She's been gone for nineteen years."

Chapter Twenty-One

Bianca

Chasm

Dead?

The warm room turned suffocatingly warm even as goose bumps broke out over my arms. The light drifting in from the glass ceilings darkened, and Bryce's wary figure was the only thing I could focus on.

I couldn't breathe.

It was stupid that I'd be surprised. I'd always known my parents might not be alive. Growing up, I imagined a tragic accident had befallen them, which had given authorities no choice but to leave me in the care of the state.

The alternative was harder to accept.

But then, after learning that my family was alive… I had siblings, and they had mentioned my biological father. I didn't know why *exactly* they'd given me up. But I was an idiot for assuming *she* was there, too.

I should have known better. I'd expected this possibility.

So why did I feel lightheaded?

"How did she die?" I asked, although the answer was obvious. It had been nineteen years. It didn't take a genius to put two and two together—after all, I was nineteen. My birthday had just passed while being institutionalized. "What happened?"

Bryce and Brayden glanced at each other for a moment, expressions unreadable, before Brayden returned his focus to me.

"Why don't we talk about this later?" he said. "You should lie down."

I jerked from him, holding my fists against my chest. "I can handle this! Tell me."

Brayden was still reaching for me, and he blinked. "I'm not…" He glanced at Bryce again, almost pleadingly.

Bryce sighed. "She died when you were born," he said, confirming my earlier suspicion. "But we never learned how…"

"How is it not obvious?" I snapped. "Women can die in childbirth."

"She didn't die giving birth to you," Bryce replied. "The circumstances surrounding her death were strange, and Father suspected foul play."

"What?"

"It happened so fast…" Bryce's gaze returned to the glass walls. "When a Xing is born, the family is the first to see them. After that, your quintet members visit."

"But because of everything, Father didn't even get a chance to hold you." Brayden leaned forward again. "Despite what you believe, he cares about you. He's been searching for you your whole life."

"It was only supposed to be temporary." Bryce nodded.

My pulse raced. I was going to be sick. "*What* was supposed to be temporary?"

"You were born at home. Immediately after, Mother went into cardiac arrest and Father was occupied," Bryce said. "Brayden and I were a few rooms down, in the family waiting room. A nurse brought you to us. She left to help. She was supposed to be right back."

"She was hardly gone before the first attempt on your life was made," Brayden interjected. "But the assassin barely made it into the room before Kieran killed him."

The name washed over me, and bile gathered at the base of my throat. "K-K-Kieran?" Considering recent events, I wasn't naive enough to assume they were different people.

"He was Mother's personal bodyguard," Brayden said, his tone wary. He seemed almost relieved at my reaction, but I couldn't imagine why.

"Brayden..." Bryce's voice was low—a warning to watch his words.

"How do you know him?" he asked. "I don't have the same loyalty toward him that Bryce and Uncle Gregory do. But if he—"

"I've told you before, Kieran wouldn't have hurt her!" Bryce's harsh words caused my anxiety to spike further. "He would have died first."

"Well *someone* put her in Eric Richards's path," Brayden said, narrowing his gaze. The uplifting tenor of his voice had faded—now it was lined with something dark and frightening.

The insinuation that Kieran had done *anything* caused my stomach to twist. I never wanted to discuss my past, I never wanted anyone to know.

But I couldn't let this stand.

"I knew him." It was a miracle my voice didn't shake. Everything felt numb. I couldn't feel my fingers anymore, nor my lips. "Kieran was there as far back as I remember. He had nothing to do with... everything. He was gone before that happened."

"He's gone? You mean, he died?" Bryce's question cut through me like an accusation.

Did Bryce and Brayden know that I'd admitted my first parents were killed in front of me? Would the boys have told them?

I still remembered it.

Sorcha haunted my nightmares. I saw her stomach being ripped open with my own two eyes. She'd held me to her as she died, and I watched the life leave her expression.

I saw her spirit when she came back.

But Kieran?

There were spaces where conjecture had been made. I'd only been able to see bits and pieces. But I was certain he was dead. The signs had been there.

I'd never forget the suffocating dampness of the small, dark cellar where he'd locked me. He told me he would come back. And above my prison, I'd heard the fight.

I felt the warm blood dripping through the cracks in the floorboards.

He never came back, and I almost starved to death waiting.

He'd promised. He never broke his promises.

"He's dead." My words barely discernible. "I'm pretty sure. But I never saw his body."

By the time I'd been dragged out, there'd been no bodies left.

There was a heavy silence in the air, and I glanced between Bryce and Brayden. But my brothers were only watching each other.

Bryce suddenly leaned forward, and my heart pounded at the barely concealed glint of determination in his eyes.

He wanted answers. The problem was, I didn't know if I could provide them.

Sure enough, the questions continued. "Who was he to you?"

"My first foster father…" I nervously twisted my fingers over the edge of my sweater as I stared at my knees. The air was pressing in around me, and my throat threatened to close.

But I could handle it, for now.

"He told me I was a foundling. We lived in the mountains and didn't have close neighbors. He knew I could see ghosts, but I was never, ever supposed to talk about my abilities. Everything was fine, until one day it wasn't."

"That cryptic summary leaves so many questions. And Kieran was a lower-level medium. He wouldn't have known how to deal with a child with emphatic abilities." Brayden's voice was pensive. "How did he raise you, a single father? Where did you live?"

"I don't…" My heartbeat was echoing in my ears. "I don't want to talk about it."

"I don't care." Bryce touched my chin, nudging my gaze toward his.

In his eyes was a barely contained storm, and normally I would fight the command of his suggestion. But I was tired. Either he was taking advantage of my weakness, or he was so far gone in his anger that he didn't notice.

I'd known that Bryce was scary, but this was the first time he'd ever directed his anger at me.

"What happened exactly?" His tone cut into me like a knife, and my breath hitched. "How the hell did you go from being with Kieran, to being sold into a human trafficking ring? What else did they *do* to you?"

"Now that's just too far!" Brayden had gotten to his feet, grabbing at his brother. "Can't you see that she's upset?"

"Of course she's upset." Bryce let go of me and brushed Brayden's hand away. "And I want to know why so we can fix it."

But what was the point of rehashing the past? I wasn't in that situation any longer; I'd moved on the best way that I could.

I was trying not to be a victim.

So why couldn't everyone let it go?

Brayden continued to express concern, and Bryce refused to budge. It didn't matter who would win this argument though, because I couldn't answer anyway. There was simply no way.

I stared at them as the last threads of my composure stretched to a breaking point.

Titus had once told me that Bryce would stop at nothing to bring down his enemies. From the deathly expression currently on his face, I believed it. And even though Brayden was arguing with him, he also radiated murderous intent.

He wouldn't push me. But he held just as much anger as his brother.

The two of them hid their ferocity behind masks of indifference and joviality. And when the facade had fallen and their patience worn thin, the result was terrifying.

But, at the same time, my heart began to pound for another reason.

They were angry *for me*. Their bloodlust was thick in the air, making it hard to breathe.

That feeling was present on my behalf.

I wasn't sure what to think about this development.

Their emotional investment was almost as heartwarming, but way less disgusting, than Titus's offer to bring me Mr. Richards's spine.

I mean, what kind of offering was that? What would it accomplish?

It was much more practical to trap your enemies into soul-contracts where they had no choice but to do your bidding. Where vengeance would be eternal.

Still, it had been sweet of Titus to offer.

"What's going on in here?" As if I'd summoned him with my thoughts, Titus barged into the greenhouse. The door had slammed open with a crash that shook the tinted windows and threatened to break the glass.

His hair was tied into a knot at the base of his skull, and his glower was only accentuated by the thick line of grease across his unshaven jaw. His eyes sought out mine, and before Bryce or Brayden could even fully turn to face him, Titus had already crossed the room, pulling me from my seat and to his side.

"What's wrong?" He ran his warm hands down my arms, and the chill that had been lingering on my skin faded. "Did they do something stupid?" His voice ended in a growl, and his eyes flashed dangerously as his focus moved over the room.

Bryce made a sound, but I shifted, clutching the ring tightly against my chest, which drew the dragon's attention back to me.

"It's okay," I managed. "But I think they're going to kill people."

The air was thick with tension, but I wasn't afraid anymore. In fact, my skin grew even warmer as a strange, giddy sensation electrified my nerves.

The anger dropped from Titus's expression, curiosity leaking into its place. Even so, he continued to run his hands down my arms as his gaze remained locked on the two brothers.

"And that makes you happy?" he asked.

His question snapped my attention back to the present, and the feeling vanished.

"No!" What kind of question was that? I wasn't a monster. "Of course not! I don't want to see anyone killed!"

"Oh." Titus almost looked disappointed, and rubbed the back of his neck. He suddenly seemed nervous and out of place. "I could have sworn…" he started, but his words trailed off. "What were you happy about then?"

I glanced back at Bryce and Brayden. The two of them had finished their argument, and were now looking at us. My skin heated and I turned back toward Titus, burying my face in his chest.

It was too embarrassing to say.

"It doesn't matter," Titus grumbled under his breath. I could hear his heart racing and his presence seemed to seep into my pores. My anxiety continued to fade. "I heard arguing. Are you sure everything is okay? What were you talking about?"

My breath caught, and I swayed slightly.

I'd completely forgotten that we'd been discussing *Kieran*.

It was such a small reaction, but of course he'd notice. He drew closer, holding me against him. With my face pressed against his chest, I could hear his pounding heartbeat, and when he spoke next, his tone had become menacing. "What did you do?"

"It's okay," I said, interrupting Bryce and Brayden before they could respond. "They were just asking questions… about Kieran."

Titus stiffened, and the world shifted in a flurry of movement as he pulled from me. As his hands gripped my forearms, his face lowered toward mine. Within the depths of his green eyes, there was a hint of panic. "You know

Kieran?"

I nodded, words escaping me. Why did he seem stunned?

"It's such a coincidence. Kieran raised her, until his death, apparently," Bryce interjected. "He seems to have told her she was a foundling."

There was a note of hesitance at the end of his statement, and Titus narrowed his eyes at the other man. "But…?"

"Well, I suppose he had to have told her something about her origins." Bryce shrugged. "Did you know he escaped from Whisperwind after Bianca was born? Who would have thought he'd have taken her?"

Titus growled.

"It couldn't be helped. Things were chaotic in those days." Bryce waved his hand in the air.

"I would have protected her," Titus protested.

"At seven years old?" Bryce rolled his eyes. "You had barely grown into your dragon."

"Why are you opening up now?" Titus moved, putting his own body between mine and my brothers. "You refused to talk about it before."

"We swore an oath to never bring it up," Bryce said. "But we're not breaking any rules. Besides, we're *only* talking about Kieran."

"Technically." Brayden nodded.

"Whisperwind was dangerous for Keiran, as a mixed breed," Bryce continued. "He was safer away from the fae."

"Also technically true," Brayden interjected again. "As an Unseelie living in the Seelie court and trained in war by shifters, Kieran never quite fit in with his people. Outside of the prophecy, you have bad blood between the courts to contend with. Anyone born of mixed blood was at risk."

"Stop acting like this conversation is about Kieran," Titus snapped. "We already know about your family's heritage."

"It's the same for Kieran," Bryce pointed out.

"Mixed blood?" I tugged on Titus's shirt.

"Our mother was a Stephens," Bryce answered, acting as though that explained everything.

I glowered at Bryce. That statement had meant absolutely nothing to me.

Brayden rolled his eyes at his brother. "Our great-grandfather is Unseelie. He married into the Seelie court. Both our grandfather and Uncle Gregory, who is technically our great-uncle, are half-bloods."

"What about Mr. Weaver?" Their exclusion of the other man was obvious. But wasn't he Dr. Stephen's brother?

"Uncle Caleb has a different mother. He's one hundred percent Unseelie," Brayden said. "Fae are very strange about blood purity. And the Xing has always been Seelie. There are those who would be... very upset the Xing might be born with Unseelie blood. They'd say it's a curse."

"Why?" I wondered.

"We're *supposedly* more bloodthirsty than the usual Seelie." Bryce shrugged. "They say we have violent tendencies, frightening imaginations, and tempestuous tempers. But I can't imagine where they'd get that idea."

"Well..." Yeah, that was a stupid thing to be afraid of. I wasn't like that at all.

"It does explain quite a bit," Titus mused. "Though some of it might be a personality thing. You always did straddle the lines between the courts."

"Hey!" I pushed my hand against Titus's chest, glaring up at him. "What's that supposed to mean?"

"Nothing." Titus stroked my hair, and for an instant, time stopped. The adoring look in his eyes caused my heart to race and cheeks to heat. "You're perfect the way you are. You understand me."

"Oh, gag." Brayden crossed his arms and stomped past us. "It's bad enough when it's Damen, but we can laugh at his expense. But this is nauseating. You're not supposed to know how to flirt."

"How did Kieran die?" Bryce asked, returning to the original topic.

The question cut through the air, and Brayden paused mid-step, turning to glare at the other man. "She already said she didn't know," Brayden snapped. "Do you not understand *anything* about sensitivity?"

"She said she didn't see his body," Bryce said. "That's entirely different. But, *fine*, I'll drop it." He glanced at me, his eyes lingering on my closed fist. "In the meantime, put that on," he said, referring the ring. "When you return to campus, it'll be *something* to discourage the masses."

My attention turned to the ring, and I held it in front of me. "Why would this discourage anyone?"

There was a pregnant pause, and I glanced up. Titus was eyeing Bryce.

"It works," Bryce argued, shrugging. "Unless you have a better idea."

Titus narrowed his eyes and glanced at me, his expression softened slightly. "No," he said finally, raising his hand to touch my cheek. "It's better than nothing. I dislike the idea of her going on campus in general."

"You don't want me to go to school?" This was surprising. He had been most insistent about my attending classes.

"But this will work. Miles's idea is actually brilliant. The more visible you make your 'marriage', the safer she'll be." He turned to me, his mouth curling in the corner. "No one at that school is going to risk angering Bryce. I do *want* you to go to school. This is a good solution, and things are going to get worse before they get better. I just don't like the idea of you being anywhere I can't protect you."

"It is going to be pain in the ass," Brayden agreed. "No matter what."

Despite his words, Titus's eyes still held conflict. The look made my heart twist guiltily. I was making him worry.

What was I doing?

There was, of course, a solution that would resolve his fears about school. But should I suggest it?

I wasn't sure.

All I knew was if I went that route, I would have to rethink everything I'd planned for my life. But considering the changes that had taken place in my life lately, would that really be the end of the world?

Chapter Twenty-Two

Bianca
Shadow

Miles was in a deep sleep by the time I'd gathered the courage to leave the bed.

Damen still wasn't finished with my room—one more day, he promised—and while I enjoyed being around the boys, I needed a moment to myself.

I couldn't leave through the door—lights from the hallway trickled in under the door. At least one of the others was still awake, and Julian was due home at some point. I may run into him while trying to escape.

I liked him, but right now I wanted to be alone.

Which meant there was only one more way to leave the room.

The window creaked, but Miles didn't stir. Still, it was heavy. And I grumbled under my breath while my thoughts drifted over the many ways to kill Damen.

Structural integrity my butt. There was no thought behind this disrepair. I knew the method behind his madness—he was too lazy to update his home. Hopefully, though, the roof was sturdier than it appeared. With my luck, it would cave under me and I would land directly on top of someone's head.

The tiles were rough under my bare feet, and I inched myself the rest of the way out of the window. The waning moon gave just enough light for me to see my immediate surroundings, but nothing too far. I tentatively began to move across the surface until I'd reached the ledge.

Damen's bedroom light was on, and I tried to give him his privacy. Really I did. But while hidden in the shadows, I was close enough to see him. He stood in front of a floor length mirror, apparently having a passionate argument with himself. I could see his expression thanks to the reflection. And the look there gave me pause.

Fury blazed in his eyes, and there was something distinctly demonic surrounding him as well. The strong angles of his face seemed sharper, and the shadows that had been under his eyes these last few days had grown darker.

And unless I was mistaken, he was talking to his reflection.

My brows furrowed, concern lacing through me. Although no one else cared, I still remembered. I still didn't trust Kasai, and it seemed as though this possession was becoming a rather serious thing. Unbeknownst to the others, Damen had begun conversing with the Lords of the Underworld.

I was going to have to do something soon. This was turning into a serious issue.

But first, it was time for my moment of self-reflection. Then I could worry about Damen.

With that thought in mind, I pressed from the roof, trusting the branches below me to break my fall. My aim was true, and without injury, I scurried away from the house.

I already knew where to go.

The first time I was here, I'd sensed it—a place where a creek cut through the forest, and the moss grew deep. When I'd run from Damen a few days ago, it was the opposite direction. My thoughts had been in turmoil. It hadn't crossed my mind to seek out refuge there.

But this time I was prepared.

It wasn't so far. No one would ever know I'd left.

The sound grew louder as I stepped out into the small clearing.

It was a tiny space, no larger than one of the university's smaller lecture rooms, with thick foliage caging in the clearing on every side—almost as if they made up walls, separating this land from the outside world. In the center of the space, beside the creek, was an old hunting shack. It was barely more than faded two-by-fours and a tin roof, and no glass covered the small window, nor door on the rough doorframe. It looked old, as if a strong gust of wind would cause the entire framework to come tumbling down.

Despite the possibility of it collapsing on my head, I found myself drawn to it.

Moonlight filtered through the trees, and I picked my way toward the building. But the illumination didn't reach to the floor of the shack.

My heart was pounding in my ears, and there was a nervous energy in the air.

But still, I was curious. Bracing myself, I stepped into the darkness.

I'd only crossed three or so feet when my foot brushed against something soft. Whatever it was jerked back from me, throwing me off balance. The world tilted as the ground rushed up to meet me, and a strangled scream escaped my lips as I fell onto a warm, hard body.

The man let out a sound of alarm as his arms closed around my back, triggering the panic that had been hovering on the edge of my awareness.

But my voice had barely squeaked out before a hand pressed over my mouth, throwing me into helpless silence.

"Bianca?" Finn's sleepy voice broke through the blackness threatening to overwhelm my thoughts. As he pulled himself up, and me along with him, his hand dropped from my mouth. But he made no move to release my shoulders, and when he spoke next, his voice was only marginally more awake. "What in the world are you doing out here?"

"Finn!" My voice broke, my nerves still on edge, although my heart-rate was returning to normal and my breathing evened out. I glanced at him, and his shadowed eyes watched mine.

He wasn't himself, otherwise he would have let me go already. Physical affection had never been something we'd been comfortable with in the past. "Are you crazy? Why in the world is silencing me your first reaction?" And besides that, "What are you doing here? Why are you sleeping in woods?"

Damen *had* been displeased with him. Perhaps...

"Is Damen making you sleep out here?" I whispered, almost horrified. Because, really, that was a bit much, even for someone like Finn.

Finn's frown deepened as his eyes traveled over my face. Whatever he saw there caused his mouth to dip, and he pushed me from him, causing me to land on my side.

"No, he did not." Finn crossed his arms as I pushed to my knees. His bangs fell over his face, brushing the top rim of his glasses. But he continued to study me. "I came out here for another reason and fell asleep."

That was dangerous. It was chilly—he might have frozen to death. Not that it was important.

"Why would you come out here in the middle of the night?" I wondered.

Finn's lips pursed and his eyebrows slowly raised, there was judgment in his expression. "Really?" he asked, pointedly watching me.

My face heated.

"That's different!" I protested. I loathed this part of him—the times he'd call me out and make me feel six inches tall. "I was looking for an elephant!"

"An elephant," Finn repeated, the amusement fading from his voice. "Ah, yes. I had forgotten about your *plan*."

"Don't say it like that." The warmth spread down my chest. How dare he forget—he should have been spending every waking moment visualizing the moment of his doom. "Don't make fun of me!"

"Who says I'm making fun of you?" he drawled. "But, really, why are you out here? I'd have thought my brother wouldn't let you out of his sight. Why do you think he hasn't argued that you're sleeping with Miles?"

Damen. I narrowed my eyes.

Yes, that reminded me. I was quite annoyed with him. "Did you know he talks to himself in the mirror?"

"Damen?" Finn tilted his head. "Yes, he does that sometimes."

Funny, Finn didn't seem to be concerned. Was everyone in that family just very odd? "And you think this is normal? He seemed very angry."

He shrugged in response, something distant entering his expression. Then he pulled from me, moving to his feet. And without another word, he left the building.

I scrambled up, rushing after him.

Finn never walked away from a conversation. He wanted me to follow. And sure enough, he was already folding himself down into a cross-legged position at the edge of the water, uncaring about the damp ground as he shot me an expectant glance.

I moved next to him, my legs under me as I tucked the white gown around my knees.

"It works best with mirrors, or slow waters. But this'll work for a demonstration, I think," Finn replied, frowning at one of the small pools.

"What are you going to show me?" I leaned forward.

"One of the ways an onmyoji can scry." Finn pressed on my shoulder, forcing me back. "We can use it for fortunetelling."

"You see the future?" I couldn't keep the disbelief from my voice. "Since when?"

Finn shot me an even look. "Since always."

"You must not be very good." I mean, it was obvious. "Since you managed to miss the fact that I almost died. You do know I hate you?"

He sighed, his gaze returning to the water. "I've always known you were going to hate me, Bianca. But seers also don't know everything. We only glimpse at bits and pieces. But what happened at Professor Hamway's house *is* my fault. I should have been paying more attention."

My breath caught. "Is that an apology?"

"No." Finn didn't even hesitate.

I should have known. Finn would never apologize. But I still had to ask. "Were you wrong about lying to me?"

"I wasn't wrong," he responded.

My temper began to flare through me, and my face warmed. But then he glanced at me, his mouth pressed into a thin line. "But I do regret needing to do it."

The quasi-admission made me pause. It wasn't an apology. But from Finn, the statement was an olive branch.

Should I accept this attempt? I wasn't sure. This was one reason I'd been avoiding talking to him. His betrayal still ran thick through my blood. However, as the chapters unraveled, it was getting more difficult to keep him as the sole subject of my hatred.

"What is scrying?" I asked. At his surprised blink, I rushed to continue. "You've never told me anything about the paranormal. I don't even understand *what* you are outside of what Damen told me about himself."

"It's the practice of focusing your attention unto an object, to limit distractions from the outside world. When you're concentrating it becomes easier to use your third eye. It's easier for onmyoji to communicate between realms with reflective surfaces as well." Finn gestured toward the water. "I use water, usually in a dark bowl. Damen likes scrying with mirrors."

"So Damen really was talking to someone?" I asked.

"Sure," Finn replied, shrugging. "If he was angry, then it was probably Belial. He's a bit kinder to the other Overseers. But Belial and Damen fight a lot."

"Overseers? I thought you were…" I waved my hand. "Well, his next in command. What's an Overseer?"

"I'm Damen's Er Bashou." Finn squared his shoulders. "I'm an officer. My focus is in this realm. Four Overseers control the underworld since Damen resides here, but he checks in on them from time to time."

"The underworld?" Damen had mentioned this before. "Does he go to Hell frequently?"

"Not in this lifetime," Finn answered. "It takes a certain amount of power to transverse between realms, and he's been limited."

A sense of foreboding filled me. "Or he *was*."

Finn frowned, glaring out over the water. "He still is." He sounded sullen. "At least until we can test your bond with Kiania."

He was going to talk about Kiania? My fists tightened over my knees. "What about—"

"Damen is taking everything personally, and so he hasn't thought this through. What this bond has potentially *changed*," Finn continued. "I've been doing research myself over the last few days. You're a strategist, you always have been. But you've never been *clairvoyant* before."

"What in the world are you talking about?" I narrowed my eyes at him.

"'What should you do if you think you'll be used in a cannibalistic ritual'," Finn quoted. "Because of recent events, I've started second-guessing your browser history."

"That is *not* how I phrased it!" I couldn't believe he was bragging about this now. "And it was a real concern!"

"Why?" Finn asked. "What made you think something like that would happen?"

"There were reasons!" I didn't need to explain myself. Usually, I looked up the first thing that came to mind, but that was none of his business. My heart was racing as I panicked.

What else had I searched? Did he know about my illegal books?

Would I go to prison for downloading pirated comic books?

Although, the phone had been in *his* name. So, if justice was served, Finn would be the one to suffer.

"Focus." He snapped his fingers in my face. "This is why we're discussing scrying. I've another reason to bring you here besides Damen. I know Brayden is supposed to be going over working with your emphatic abilities. Granted, now that you're off your medication, you'll be *feeling* a lot. But I'm more concerned that you can see the future."

"I'm always right!" I argued.

"You're known for being *logical*." Finn pointed at me. "That's what *Mu* was known for. But your conclusions do not follow that thought pattern."

How dare he. "I'm still right."

"Then Damen said you thought they were monks, and I thought—"

I'd slapped my hand over his mouth, and my face engulfed in fire. "He *told* you?"

Finn's cheeks darkened, and he jerked away from my touch. "I heard them talking about it. He thought it was funny, especially since Tu was a priest in many past lives. He said—"

"Miles was a priest?" I gasped, covering my own mouth. "But he's a witch!" How could this be?

"He had also taken a vow chastity at one point in time." Finn shrugged. "That's why Damen and Titus were going to use your assumption to annoy him."

"Damen is picking on Miles?" My racing heart began to slow. And, for a moment, it felt like we were back in high school again—gossiping together on the roof of the school.

"And Titus too," Finn reminded me. "He's not happy about *The Hobbit*."

Damen was being influenced by his affiliation with unsavory demonic beings, I was sure of it. But then, if Miles worshipped Satan, how did that work? Wouldn't antagonizing Miles be a conflict of interest?

"This is exactly why you need to focus," Finn said. "You're already going off on a tangent. But without learning to harness your abilities, you're not going to be able to determine what is part of your sensitivity and what you should ignore."

I frowned. "Brayden said I need to compartmentalize my emotions. To distinguish my feelings and outside influences. I can't trust what I feel. Now you're saying I can't believe in what I *think*."

"No," Finn answered. "What you think is *you*, including your clairvoyance. But you'll need to know how to sort your thoughts, to determine which items need to be followed up on."

"But I research everything." I was already one step ahead of him.

He pinched the bridge of his nose. "I know."

"Is that a *problem* for you, Mr. Stalker?" I couldn't keep the derision from my voice. Why was he acting as though he was the one inconvenienced here. "No one asked you to sort through my search history."

Finn shot me a wary look, then cleared his throat. "That's why I'll teach you, first, how to meditate. I don't think I've ever seen you just be *still*."

"I'm *still* all the time." I didn't want Finn to be my teacher. The weather was becoming cold, and I'd catch pneumonia if he made me sit under any waterfalls. "Why can't Damen teach me? Julian won't like this."

"Do you honestly think Damen can sit near you and not be distracting?" Finn scoffed. "Would *you* be able to focus with him breathing down your neck? If you tell Julian what we're doing before you have control of it, he'll *make sure* Damen is the one to teach you."

A mental image of Damen holding Professor Hamway's ruler flashed through my mind. Yes, he would be very stern. When he snapped into his professional mode, he was quite scary.

It would probably be for the best that Damen didn't teach me a thing.

"Fine," I grumbled. "How does someone meditate?"

Chapter Twenty-Three

Bianca
Changes

Finn's instruction sucked.

I was bored after five minutes, and then he complained I was a terrible student. But Finn had no idea what he was doing, because I could *so* be calm and collected when the situation called for it. It wasn't my fault meditating was impossible.

"Clear your mind," he'd said. "Focus on breathing."

That was impossible. Any time I attempted to still my thoughts, *memories* resurfaced. When that happened, it got harder to breathe. And, after a second, it became impossible to miss the very strange patterns that the moss spread out in over the stone.

So really, I was observant. And that was a commendable trait.

Finn didn't understand. So it was almost a relief when he told me the lesson was over and to sneak back to bed.

Sunday passed with the same lackluster excitement as Saturday. The day began with a lesson with Brayden, during which neither of us brought up Kieran. Then there was a quiet lunch with Julian and Miles. Titus had been gone again, and the day ended with Damen *not quite* being ready to show me my new room.

Then Finn sent *Kiania* to wake me up in the middle of the night in order to meet him.

She didn't talk to me this time—just her appearance was enough to let me know that he was waiting. And the event led to a repeat of the night before.

It was almost depressing to consider I lacked the ability to not *think* about anything.

Then there was school.

Monday went by in a far less exciting manner than I'd expected. Bryce ignored me, people stared at me, and Xavier only gave me strange looks from a distance.

But I didn't even have a chance to worry about any of that—for once. The rest of the week had me in dire straits: trying to catch up on my missed work, avoiding the looks of my classmates, and seriously contemplating life as—with every French class—I grew to loathe the language even more.

At home, Damen had finished my bedroom by Monday night. Various shades of pink, green, and gray decorated the space, and an antique canopy bed stood in the middle of the grand room. Damen—and Bryce—had even set aside a space on my bed for the rabbit I'd sent the latter to fetch. My heart fluttered at their thoughtfulness.

Damen had been so excited to show me. Later, I was heavy with guilt that all I could muster in reaction was falling face-first into my mattress and sleeping straight through until my Tuesday morning class. We'd all been busy, hardly having a chance to talk as we all fought to catch up and settle into a routine.

Or maybe it was just me. But at least for now everyone had seemed to step back from prying answers out of me.

I had to catch up on my schoolwork. I was so far behind.

And every night, Finn sent for me. It became our routine.

I'd sneak out the window. We'd sit for five minutes while he lectured about the art of patience, and I tried not to call him out on his hypocrisy. Then I'd find something far more interesting than him to look at. Then he'd send me away only to do it all again the next day. He was so annoying.

By the time Friday came around, I was barely holding it together. The only positive to this week was that I'd managed to avoid seeing Do Yun, and no one had called me out on it.

Yet.

Bryce's attention flickered toward my hand as I entered the biology room. Every day, he checked to make sure I wore our mother's ring. But then he would ignore me the rest of the class. But I was used to that now.

It wasn't until French class when my routine had been broken.

Xavier had been absent.

I hardly had spoken to him, so I shouldn't really care about him missing class. Yet I couldn't quite get past the gross feeling crawling across my skin.

However, it wasn't until I'd left Miles after lunch that the proverbial hammer finally fell.

I had a short break before Geology. I took the opportunity to meander through the small courtyard between the Science and English buildings, before I heard the laughter. A gaggle of students, whispering voices, came from the shrubbery beside the red-bricked pathway. They were familiar, and when I finally located them, I knew why.

It was Heather, and the people who'd been with her when she'd taunted me in the lunchroom. Their backs were to me though, and their attention—and laughter—was focused on someone else entirely.

It wasn't difficult to figure out who. Sitting on a park bench—as she read a book in the center of the courtyard—was Jaiyi. She was wearing a black lace dress today, with mid-calf-length boots.

She didn't seem to have noticed Heather and her cronies.

But why were they making fun of her? I thought they were scared of her. Or were they the sort to prey on the weak, and gossip about everyone else?

In either case, I didn't like this.

Before I second-guessed myself, I'd closed the distance between us. And I shuffled nervously in front of the Lolita-dressed girl. "Jiayi…"

She glanced up, her ruby lips turning down. "Bianca. You're back at school?"

"Yes…" Wasn't it obvious? "Can I sit with you?" I glanced back from where I'd come. The group dispersed.

She shot me a strange look, but slowly moved over. "Is there something the matter?" she asked as I settled myself beside her.

"No." I tucked my bag behind my legs. "Why would you think that?"

Jiayi spoke slowly, as if she was weighing her words. "Your assignment as my roommate ended rather abruptly."

My face heated, and I covered my cheeks. I didn't even consider how she might feel about Bryce showing up to our room in the middle of the night.

Bryce wasn't the most sensitive person. The conversation between them was probably short and abrupt. He might have even made her *cry*.

I could imagine the whole scene now. How had the news been delivered to her?

"I'm sorry." I couldn't even look at her. "It wasn't anything you did."

"I know," she said. "Bryce explained everything."

Dear Lord. My eyes squeezed shut in horror.

"He told me the jig was up, that he was angry with me, and, *most surprisingly*, that you two were married. He's quite amusing when he's in a fluster," she said. "My favorite part, though, was him asking for your stuffed animal."

My head was starting to pound. But then her words registered through the horror, and I peeked at her through my fingers. "Why would it be amusing for us to be in love?"

"I'm sure you *are* in love." She smoothed the pages of her book down. "But not in that way. It's incest. Besides your thread of fate isn't connected to Bryce Dubois."

"Incest?" I'd given up trying to be cool and collected.

Jiayi shot me a patient look. "I *know*. I'm Damen's Tongjun, and I'm a fortune-teller." Before I could respond, she changed the subject. "I'm waiting for Xavier. He's supposed to help me. Have you seen him?"

My breath caught and conflict swirled inside me.

I wanted to be annoyed. Her earlier comment defending Finn made a lot more sense now.

But...

She needed my help. She was going to *Xavier*, and he was absent today. Since he was my underling, it was my *moral obligation* to assist her. This was my chance to prove myself. "Xavier missed class earlier, so I'm not sure he'll show. What do you need?"

"I'm going to curse someone, and I need information."

Whatever I expected, it wasn't that. I blinked at her—perhaps I'd misunderstood. "Pardon?"

"My revenge must be swift and deadly. But not quite enough to kill him completely." She tapped her chin, gazing off into the distance. "I want him mostly dead for a time. Perhaps with some permanent scarring."

"Why are you asking *Xavier* this?" I knew that folklore had stated the fae—and especially Unseelie—might be cruel, but surely such stories were exaggerations. Take me, for example. I didn't skip through life with death spells and plots hidden up my sleeves. Besides that, "Don't you have a witch in your quintet? Ask them."

She sighed. "Catalina is a softy. She's a firm believer of doing no harm. She'd not approve."

I blinked at her, did this mean Xavier *would*?

Jiayi ignored my open-mouthed stare. "Besides, this is Xavier's book, and it seemed promising. But I have questions."

I eyed the item in question, which now didn't seem quite so innocent. "What book is that?"

"Ah." She shut it, revealing the flesh-colored leather that bound the book. Scrawled across the top—in rusty brown letters I suspected might be blood—were the words: *The Practical Applications of Advanced Demonology*. "It's just a bit of light reading."

I was unsure of how to respond. I couldn't ask if it said anything exciting, not without compromising my morals.

"Does this scare you?" She frowned.

"I'm just surprised." I turned my stare to my knees. "You've always seemed so…" What was the word? "Poised and put together."

"I've been raised with certain expectations. In my family, women are seen rather than heard. And no matter what, we exist as something pretty to look at. I discovered my love for my fashion when I left for boarding school. It's the one thing I've done for myself," Jiayi answered. "Besides, it works out better this way."

I shot her a questioning glance.

"Lure in your prey with innocence and a pretty smile." She clenched her fists against her chest as she turned her eyes toward the sky. "Then you can *crush them*."

A shiver shot down my spine.

"Which brings us back to my curse," she continued, undisturbed. "It has to be something effective against witches, too. And needs to encourage a man to choose a side." She glanced at me. "Not that you would know about it. You allow everyone to walk all over you. I doubt there's a mean bone in your body—"

"Now wait a minute..." I began, ready to set the record straight. Hadn't I stood up to Finn? That had been mean.

But my words trailed off as a white cat stepped from the bushes and made her way toward us. Hadn't I seen this creature before?

"Cécile?" The amber-eyed feline stared at me, causing my skin to prickle.

"Ugh," Jiayi groaned, hiding the book and slipping into her backpack. "It's *you*. I suppose that's my cue to leave."

"Leave?" I frowned. "But why—"

"Miss Brosnan." Ms. Protean hobbled toward our bench. I wasn't sure if I was relieved or upset at her intrusion. "I've been waiting for your return. Another word, if you will?"

Jiayi, who'd been in the process of swinging her bag over her shoulder, made a sound of sympathy. "Someone's in trouble."

"Trouble?" My heart began to race. But I hadn't even done anything this time.

"Don't be dramatic, Miss Chou. Nobody is in trouble." Ms. Protean rolled her eyes as she braced her weight against her cane. Today she was wearing a floral dress that reached mid-calf, and a white sweater. "And if it's boils you need, Mr. Kelly is visiting today. He loves calamity. You'll find him lurking in the History department. But I warn you against messing with witches."

"Oh, thank you," Jiayi said, but then frowned sympathetically. "I'm sorry to hear about Mr. Weaver. I know you were close."

Ms. Protean's lips pursed. "I wouldn't write him off just yet."

I once again found myself in Ms. Protean's doily and lace-filled office. But this time, had no idea why she'd asked me to come.

Thankfully, I wasn't the only one confused about my presence here.

"What in the hell are *you* doing here?" Mr. Weaver glowered from the opposite end of the office.

I froze, starting at the ghost, and ignored Ms. Protean as she stepped around me to go to her desk.

He had been attempting to root through Ms. Protean's bookshelves. However, since ghosts couldn't always move physical items, he'd been failing at being able to explore much of anything. Yet at my arrival, he seemed to have gathered enough energy to tug a book out by the spine. But his victory was short-lived, and the book fell to the floor with a crash.

He turned his dark scowl to the thick, fallen volume, and a pang of longing stabbed at me.

Mr. Weaver was upset that he couldn't read? He didn't seem the scholarly sort.

"That's what I thought." Ms. Protean slumped into her chair, her weary gaze on dropped book. "He's always been this way."

My attention returned to her. "Sorry?"

"It's been over a week of this." She nodded her head toward her library. "I suspected he was haunting me, but I wasn't sure—"

"I'm not *haunting* her!" Caleb protested, uncaring that the woman couldn't hear him. He was watching me, uneasiness touching the air. "I'm a protector. I'm watching over the crazy old bat!"

"—Any time I ask for a sign of his presence, he goes silent." She crossed her hands under her chin, her eyes glowing. "It's rather annoying."

He'd been haunting her all this time? And wasn't this *during* the time he was supposed to be watching Michelle Nolan? "Don't tell me you were stalking Ms. Protean instead of watching Damen's suspect?" But why would he hide from her? "Are you *embarrassed*?"

Caleb Weaver had normal feelings?

"Stop analyzing me. And I am *offended* you would accuse me of not doing my job." Mr. Weaver floated above the fallen book, placing a hand to his chest. He was genuinely hurt. "My life has never revolved around an Abernathy spawn, and nor will my afterlife. I've always done my work to the best of my ability, which is better than anything you've done. You daft girl. Who the devil trained you?"

My lips pursed, irritation causing my blood to race. Technically you were supposed to respect your elders. But he was dead, so did that rule still apply?

"Is he insulting you?" Ms. Protean narrowed her eyes. "Don't pay him any mind. He's just an idiot. But don't feel bad about putting him in his place."

"I'm not an idiot!" Caleb protested.

My fury faded, and I sighed. I couldn't stay annoyed with someone who was clearly posturing. Being an empath had a way of making it difficult to separate yourself from the situation.

Why was I here? She'd still never told me. I was supposed to be on my way to Geology. I'd missed so much just missing one week, I wasn't sure how I'd ever catch up.

I was so stressed, even the pink-sweet décor and heavy peppermint scent that lingered over the room threatened to make me puke. And I liked pink and peppermint.

"Did you ask me here to confirm Mr. Weaver was haunting you, or…" I was too mentally exhausted to care much about *why* he was sticking around Ms. Protean. That was his business. "Why are you asking me? I'm sure you know Dr. Stephens sees ghosts, you're coworkers and they are brothers. Why didn't you ask for his help?"

Her elbow slipped, and she jerked upright into her chair. Redness brightened her weathered cheeks. "You want me to ask *Gregory*?" Her usually even voice squeaked. "No, thank you."

"Oh, here we go." Mr. Weaver groaned into his hands.

"I haven't spoken to him in a half-century, and will not start today. I have no intention of revisiting that old flame." With jerky movements, she snatched her knitting supplies from her desk drawer and spread them over her lap. "Yet he still watches me with that same disturbing dewy-eyed stare. It sends shivers through me."

Shivers? What kind of shivers? Was it a good thing, or bad?

I pressed my lips together, slowly looking between Mr. Weaver and Ms. Protean. He seemed almost mournful, and she was clearly flustered.

I was missing something.

The chagrin had completely faded from the ghost's expression as he watched the woman. And Ms. Protean, well… She had begun knitting with an intensity that was almost terrifying. It was as if she was trying to violently maim the sweater she was working on.

Could it be true? Had my original analysis of Mr. Weaver's death been correct? Or rather, partially so. He *had* been killed because of Daniel Cole's interference. But I did also surmise he and Dr. Stephens had been in love with the same woman.

I couldn't ignore what Finn had told me: I was a genius, and foresaw the future.

It explained so much.

Ghosts didn't linger anywhere there weren't strong emotional ties. And Ms. Protean did appear to be very angry at Dr. Stephens.

Were they ex-lovers? Was it possible *both* brothers had been involved with Ms. Protean? Could that be why they hated each other?

"Is there something on your mind?" Ms. Protean interrupted my thoughts, her expression returning her usual mildly-fascinated, and somewhat agitated, state. I was beginning to think this was her everyday expression.

What did they call it: resting bitch face?

It was actually more frightening on an old woman than a younger one. What had I been thinking? She was the least-grandmotherly figure I'd ever seen—her hobbies and style not-withstanding.

I was certain she'd have no hesitations about shifting and ripping out people's throats if she was angry enough.

"You've been standing there with your mouth open for a while now. Come sit down, you're making me nervous," she commanded.

"Um…" My thoughts raced as I settled into the chair across from her desk.

It wasn't like I could ask her about her romantic entanglements. She was probably a hundred. There was no way she'd had a scandalous affair in her youth. People in those days were known for their wholesome family values and well-behaved women.

It was one thing to press boundaries in the professional world. But anything else was unheard of.

"How are your classes going?" Ms. Protean raised her eyebrow, needles clicking together as she worked her craft.

Her question snapped me back to my earlier concern, and the feeling that had been following me around all day intensified. With the subject changed, my hands clenched into fists in my lap. "I don't think I can finish the semester. People are giggling at Bryce, and I've seen them looking at me. Plus, I wanted to drop French to take Chinese. I can't concentrate…"

I felt so stupid. Here I was, admitting my failures to a woman who'd made a name for herself in this school. She'd never understand.

"Why are people giggling at Bryce?" Mr. Weaver asked.

But I didn't respond, since Ms. Protean started speaking. "Don't waste your time and effort on something you're not interested in."

I bit my lip, touching my fingers together, choosing, for the moment, to ignore Mr. Weaver. It was difficult to carry on two conversations at once, especially when one party couldn't join in. "But I *am* interested in Botany."

"Then what's the problem?"

"I don't know what I want to do with the rest of my life." I didn't even know what was *expected* of me for the rest of my life. The others… did they even choose their own path, or was it decided for them?

And, as much as it shamed me to admit, being a research scientist didn't seem so enticing anymore. I'd never be able to relax. Not with Damen dodging bullets every day and walking into haunted crime scenes with no one except Kasai for company.

Who would protect him? I couldn't leave Damen's life in Norman's hands. I might as well send Damen off to his death.

"Poppycock!" Mr. Weaver was still in the corner, but strangely invested in our conversation. He was no longer paying attention to the books at all. "How can you not know what you want to do? You're almost sixteen already."

"I'm nineteen." I frowned at him.

"Ignore whatever Caleb is saying. *Most* people don't know what they want to do at your age." Ms. Protean finished a row and turned her work to begin the next, the shimmery white yarn pulled my attention as her words sunk into me.

"Did you?" Her admission emboldened me, and my racing heart calmed. Did she also go through this?

She nodded, pausing her actions briefly as she held my gaze, and my hopes quashed as my heart sank. "I knew what I wanted to do by the time I was five. But I'm not normal. Do you want to wait out the semester, or take a break and regain your bearings?"

"There's a lot going on in my personal life…" I bit my lip. "And I heard the school is strict with dropouts. What if they won't let me come back?"

Ms. Protean let out a low breath and set down her project on her desk. "First of all, I'm not a moron. I know exactly what you are to the Abernathy family—"

Caleb perked up. "Really? What's that?"

"—and should you decide to take a break, you would still be allowed to re-enroll next semester." She nodded. "Dean Abernathy would be a fool to pass on the opportunity to have *all* of the Xing graduate from his school."

Chapter Twenty-Four

Bianca

Drown

The room grew colder, and I almost forgot to breathe under the weight of her heavy stare. "What?"

This was bad. How did she know about me? Literally the whole point of being married to Bryce was to prevent this from happening.

"Pay attention. Don't let him leave," Ms. Protean said suddenly, her eyes flickering toward her bookshelves.

"But how—" I asked, glancing at Mr. Weaver. His skin had grown even paler—even for a ghost—and he'd frozen, mid-hover, and his wide-eyes were trained on me. But as our gazes locked, his appearance began to fade.

"Just tell him he needs to stay," Ms. Protean instructed.

My heart was thundering in my chest as panic raced through me, and it was quite possible I might faint. So instead of questioning her, I just reacted to her words. "Mr. Weaver, stay here."

Why did she want him to stay? This would be much easier if I didn't have to act as a mediator.

With that thought, he rematerialized. His shadowy form was more solid than before. And now there was no question Ms. Protean could see him as she glowered in his direction. "Just where did you think you were going?" Her tone was accusing.

"I cannot believe Gregory hasn't told me!" He pointed at her, disbelief still thick on his wrinkled face. His eyes flashed dangerously. "And stop telling her what to do. I didn't tell you these things for you to use them against me."

"Don't assume anything just yet." She looked toward me, resting her chin on her folded hands. "Tell him he can't talk to Gregory about this without your permission."

"Um…" I wasn't certain that was a good idea. Mr. Weaver was shaking with anger.

"Or does Gregory already know?" she asked, unconcerned by the man's fury.

I shrugged, my thoughts still muddled and hysteria still knotted in the base of my throat. As far as I knew, he didn't know anything about me. But then again, the boys never told me much of their interactions with Dr. Stephens.

Yet, he was Damen's mentor. So maybe?

"Please don't tell him?" My order was almost a question, and I glanced at Mr. Weaver, apologetic. "That is, if he doesn't know already."

"How can others know, but not him?" He glared at me. From his annoyed reaction, my words seemed to count as an order. If Mr. Weaver hadn't already been dead, I'd be worried he might have a heart attack. "Besides your quintet, he's the *first person* who should know!"

But, why?

"I'm guessing that's why you and Bryce are married." Ms. Protean touched her chin. "It's a diversion. Is it meant to throw people off the scent?"

"They're married?" Mr. Weaver's mouth dropped open, he sounded scandalized.

My nervousness grew as my stomach clenched. "But how did you—"

"I have eyes"—Ms. Protean rolled said eyes—"and a nose. Mr. Montrone isn't very subtle. And there was Mr. Abernathy—the both of them—stalking you in the library? You yourself mentioned being friends with Mr. Ducharme, and I've smelled Mr. Kohler on your clothing. Besides, I'm sure it's been explained higher ranking officials would be drawn to you. You seem to have met all three of yours: Bryce, Brayden, and Mr. Renouf."

At my blank look, she pursed her lips. "Xavier."

"It took a while after school started for them to notice me," I pointed out. "I've been in Bryce's class from the beginning. Xavier is in my French class." My thoughts were scrambling to find purchase and I wrung my hands in my lap. "Why do you call everyone else 'Mister,' and Bryce and Brayden by their names?"

"That's understandable. Unlike within a quintet, sometimes it takes an officer to make the connection. A bond between the officers and their Xing is based on submission and respect. As for your question, I take liberties with the Dubois family because I am your mother's godmother."

She had known my mother?

"Also, it's a sign of respect to address the Xing, in particular, formally. Most people will." She gazed at me, her golden eyes twinkling in mischief. "Should I call you Mrs. Dubois or would you still prefer Miss Brosnan?"

"Don't act nonchalant about this!" Mr. Weaver sputtered. "Bailey was the Xing, and he is dead. Besides, *I've* never felt any connection to her. And Gregory has been around her, too! How come *we* didn't notice?"

I blinked at Ms. Protean, trying to understand. This new information was coming at me so fast. "Why would Mr. Weaver and Dr. Stephens know?"

"Officers know," she explained, caution lacing her voice. When I didn't respond, she frowned. "You really don't know? Officers exist in *every* generation, while, depending on when they die, the Xing is reborn every two or three generations. Every generation is approximately thirty years. My parents' generation had the last Xing quintet. Officers in the off-generations are called proxies. Right now, you have two sets of proxies. We keep things running in between cycles, so when you're reborn you have magical guardians to look after you while your new officers are trained."

At my confused look, she sighed, waving between herself and Mr. Weaver. "Caleb and I are in the same quintet. We're the third level—Tongjun proxies."

I eyed Mr. Weaver, who was still glaring around the room. *He* was one of my magical guardians? What a nightmare.

"*You* were supposed to teach me?" It kind of served him right—remarking on my lack of education. This was his failure. Besides, what in the world did he specialize in? Evil curses, like Xavier?

I could see it.

"Don't look so disgusted." Mr. Weaver crossed his arms. "I feel quite the same about you."

"Gregory is in the Er Bashou of my generation," Ms. Protean said. "He'd have been one of your magical guardians. And Caleb…" Her attention drifted toward the ghost. "Caleb's first reaction to a connection is aggression. He doesn't open up easily, he's an empath. But if he wasn't intrigued, he wouldn't talk to you. Once he warms up to someone, he's fine. Think of him as a disgusting, greasy teddy bear. It's a vile creature, and you hate it. But at the same time, it's kind of adorable and you can't stay away."

"That is a lie!" Mr. Weaver protested, waving his hand in my direction. "She can't be *him*. She doesn't even know how to cook! I can't respect a person like that."

He had been rather horrible to me all this time. But according to Ms. Protean, that meant we were on the same wavelength and he actually liked me. Somehow. Yet knowing this didn't make him any more endearing.

"If this is true, do you really think Dr. Stephens doesn't know?" I asked. "I've been around him multiple times. He set me up with Damen in the first place."

Ms. Protean frowned, exchanging a glance with Mr. Weaver. And this time, the ghost dropped his angry expression for one of contemplation.

"It's difficult to say," Mr. Weaver said finally, stroking his scratchy-looking chin.

"If he's not involved in your plan, it's safe to assume that he doesn't know," Ms. Protean mused, pressing her project flat on the desk. She was frowning down at it, wariness in her voice. "And if he hasn't realized it right away, it means he's brushed you off and is ignoring any feelings he might have. He's terrible at self-reflection. It'll take ages for him to put the pieces together."

Wow. Dr. Stephens didn't sound very responsible.

"Don't worry about Gregory." Ms. Protean glanced back up, confidence returning to her voice. "He's brilliant, but odd."

"But you hate him," I said.

The serene expression dropped from her face, and she picked up her knitting. "Indeed."

"Is there a reason he *shouldn't* know?" Did it have anything to do with Mr. Weaver's still barely concealed anger.

"I personally don't care," Ms. Protean said. "But fae are very particular about their women. They rarely allow women to cross into this realm. And, historically, the majority of your officers are men. He hasn't said it yet, which surprises me, but I'm certain Caleb is having a spiritual coronary at the mere idea of *you*—Mu—being a female."

"It's too dangerous!" Mr. Weaver nodded. "She's delicate. It's not possible."

I narrowed my eyes at him, anger prickling my senses. *Now* I was delicate? He didn't seem to think so earlier.

"Gregory's attitude is only slightly better." She began to knit again. "The fae wouldn't know the first thing to do under female leadership. So, you see why the first female Xing being born fae is a comedic twist of fate."

"You're loving this." Mr. Weaver glared darkly at Ms. Protean.

"Maybe." The corner of her mouth lifted, and her gaze flashed over me.

"Do you think it's karma?" I offered, trying to distract from Mr. Weaver's tightening expression and the heavy tension descending on the room. "Because of the fae's uptight attitudes and outdated beliefs?"

She watched me, silent for a short moment longer, before she smiled. The expression softened the harsh lines of her face. "I think this will work fabulously."

"You'd say that," Mr. Weaver grumbled.

"We'll keep your secret. And don't worry about Gregory. See what the others have planned." She turned her attention back to her project. "In regards to our earlier discussion, I think it's safe to take off the semester—if you so wish. Afterward, if you should you decide that you have an interest in investigation, I may be open to taking on a protégée."

Chapter Twenty-Five

Miles
Pentacles

"You wanted to see us?" Abigail Geier stepped into the room, defiance written on her face, in the haughty way she crossed legs and in her refusal to meet my eyes.

Jonathan on the other hand silently followed after his wife, taking a seat in the empty chair beside her.

I'd skipped my afternoon classes—something that I would never tell Bianca—in order to make this meeting with her adoptive parents. Dean Abernathy had been kind enough to allow me to use his private office for the long-overdue confrontation.

He had only given me a glance, shaking his head, before he left—muttering under his breath about not wanting to be in their position.

I had no idea what he was talking about. Compared to the others and their rules… and their vengeance, I was the least intimidating of my group.

For example, my subjects never feared for their lives. The same couldn't be said of everyone else. Garrett Cole was an exception, not the rule.

So why would this confrontation be any different?

Why would Titus—upon hearing that I was going to meet with the two witches—ask me not to *kill* them?

Everyone was so dramatic. I didn't usually kill people.

I leaned over the desk, linking my fingers under my chin as the Geiers twitched under my gaze. They seemed nervous. What in the world did they think I was going to do?

"Do you know why I called you here?" I asked, turning my gaze to Jonathan.

It was Abigail who answered. "Yes…" She pressed her hands over her knees. "Hanah called us. But we already knew when Bianca was taken from the hospital."

"That wasn't a hospital," I pointed out. "That was a prison. Do you know *what* the nursing staff was doing behind Dr. Kohler's back? Do you even care?"

"Of course I care," she blinked, her fingernails digging into the arm of her chair. "She's my best friend's daughter. You didn't see what I saw—how she lived. She needed… still needs… help. She was somewhere she could relax. We paid good money—"

"You never even visited her!" The stirrings of fury twisted in my stomach. How dare she act concerned! Despite my anger, I fought to maintain my calm.

Abigail shifted in her seat, her attention on the files in front of me. "That's because…" Her voice had lost some of its earlier strength.

"Don't misunderstand." Jonathan leaned forward, grasping his wife's hand. "Abigail worries about Bianca, but she doesn't know how to interact with her. She's scared."

"Abigail, you were forced into early retirement because of the pressure you were under. We've even allowed the both of you to abandon your duties as proxies for the same reason. So what have you two been doing?" I rubbed my temples, trying desperately to keep the accusations from my thoughts. Flying off the handle wouldn't solve anything. It would only make things worse. Clearly, Abigail had never moved past her own issues.

Once, Abigail had been a powerful witch. She was not as influential as her husband, who outranked her, but she'd been strong enough.

But everything had changed when she lost her sanity.

At the moment, Bianca was fine. I needed to get to the heart of the matter, otherwise I could make the wrong decision. "How did you get pulled into the situation?"

"Jonathan tried to stop me. He said it wasn't safe." She watched her lap, twisting her fingers. "There was no one else available, and they needed help."

It sounded like the truth, but there was hesitance in her tone. I narrowed my eyes. "And?"

She glanced at her husband for help, but this time he didn't interject. Finally, she crossed her arms. Defiance—and a hint of apprehension—radiating from her. "I don't know. I can't explain why I decided to do it. I felt called to take the job. I *had* to."

I frowned, mentally filing that bit of information away for later. We were running out of time, and I had other places to be. "In any case, Bianca's abilities are growing stronger. Thankfully, you weren't able to stop her from growing."

She bit her lip, and Jonathan straightened. The air in the room seemed to still.

"I—" she began, the fear crossing both of their expressions.

"I don't have time to hear your excuses," I cut her off, my patience wearing thin. "Hanah already told me your reasons. We'll get into that later. I need time to decide what I'm going to do with the two of you. I need to pick up Bianca from class. I don't want you two anywhere near her unless she seeks you out, and you are to continue to keep her existence a secret. In the meantime, Titus has a job for you. If you want a chance to redeem yourselves, this is it."

Bianca's parents had been dealt with—at least for now. But the nurses that had been in charge of Bianca?

They hadn't escaped unscathed.

Earlier today, I'd stopped by the hospital. It was easy to track down those who'd taken care of Bianca, and I wasn't surprised to find they were all low-level witches, some of whom barely had any magical abilities at all. Of course they would be afraid of Bianca.

But that was no excuse.

Hopefully having their licenses revoked, and being supervised while on housekeeping and caregiving duties for the next five years might teach them proper bedside manner.

It wasn't enough. It was far from enough. But it would have to do… *for now*. We had other problems to deal with.

Crossing my arms, I glared at the laboratory door, mentally willing the class to end.

My heart was racing in anxiety, and my skin felt tight across my chest. Nothing was going to happen. Bianca was perfectly all right. I'd already peeked into the room earlier, so I had seen that for myself.

However, the sick feeling that rose in my chest during my talk with Abigail wouldn't recede. I couldn't wash the picture of her from my thoughts. The way she carried herself, the short temper, the paranoia—she reminded me of my mother.

She *honestly* thought she had been helping.

And what was Jonathan *doing*? I had never really known him, but his mother had been a proxy Er Bashou. Kathleen disappeared when I went to France, but she did what she could before I left.

Why was he enabling his wife?

Why did *I* feel *guilty*? What was I supposed to do about this?

And what in the world was taking so long? It was only a three-hour lab—whatever was on those petri dishes couldn't be all that fascinating.

Before I reached for the door again, I caught myself. I couldn't interrupt his class. Bryce would get all pissy, and now we had to live with him. I forced out a low breath.

Bianca was perfectly fine.

In fact, from the quick glimpse I'd gotten of her in the window, she seemed to be deep in thought but not panicked. That was a good sign, it meant Bryce must have been reining in his obnoxious impulses.

That, or married life agreed with him. It hadn't escaped my notice he had far fewer admirers today. In fact, every time he glanced at Bianca, there was even a slight skip to his step. The man almost looked *happy*.

Now, *that* was interesting. So my plan was helpful on more than one level, it seemed.

The door opened, jarring me out of my thoughts, and the gaggle of students stepping into the hallway fell from my vision as Bianca crossed the room to me, a wavering smile on her lips.

"Hi…" she said, but something was wrong. She wouldn't look me in the eyes, and she shifted her weight nervously from foot to foot.

"Bianca?" I reached for her. What was wrong? This was different than before. She wasn't on the verge of an anxiety attack. I didn't like this.

But Bianca didn't answer. Instead, she evaded my reach and made her way out of the building. She moved quickly, and it took a minute for me to regain my bearings enough to follow her. The crowd dwindled as we reached the library, and—as we rounded the corner of the building—I finally caught up.

"Bianca, what's wrong?" I tugged at her hand, pulling her to a stop beside me. The sun had set not long before, but the brick building protected us from the worst of the breeze.

"I want to quit school," was her reply.

I was stunned into silence. This wasn't what I was expecting. I was sure she'd tell me that Bryce had said something stupid again.

It wasn't until she shifted nervously and continued to stare at the sidewalk I realized I hadn't responded. "But why?" I asked. After all her lecturing about *my* classes, why would she want to drop out of college? Perhaps… "Did something happen today?"

We'd expected she might receive more attention, and we'd done our best to accommodate our schedules around hers. And when none of us were near, Kasai followed her. All the professors had gotten a memo she was married to Bryce, and rumors had spread across campus already. No one should have been bold enough to give her any trouble.

Maybe we'd missed something?

"I'm sorry." Her voice was soft, and she continued to avoid my gaze. "I know you had this plan… But I don't know *what* I want to do anymore, and I've been on edge all day. I don't think I'm ready to come back."

"I thought you wanted to work in research?" I cocked my head, fighting the urge to wrap my arms around her shaking form. After learning about her past, I'd only touched her in my weakest moments. There was no way to know what might trigger a fear-based reaction, and Damen had told us what had happened in the hospital.

Not all of us felt the same, but they also didn't understand. One of the worst things we could do right now would be to overwhelm her. While they were fine with pushing her boundaries and testing her limits, I wanted to become her safe place.

She shivered—guilt heavy in her expression—before she shocked me. Her small fingers wrapped around my wrist, and she held my hand between hers. "Are you angry?"

Had I misheard her? The surprise from her announcement faded as trepidation filled me. "Why would I be angry?"

If she wanted to take a break from school, it was *her* decision. It had nothing to do with me.

"Because you wanted to tutor me in French," she whispered, looking away. The guilt in her expression made my heart twist painfully. "Even before deciding this though, I already planned on switching to Chinese. Who cares what Damen says, he isn't my boss."

"Chinese?" But Mandarin was a far harder language to master than French.

Well, for people who aren't us.

She nodded, biting her lip. "Damen told me that when I remembered more about my past lives, I'll know how to understand it—"

"So Damen said you can't take Chinese because it's 'cheating'," I interrupted, nodding. I fought back a smile. This argument was familiar, at least. "Well, technically that is true. *But*"—I couldn't stand the crestfallen expression on her face—"he's the only one who really cares. He's just jealous."

"What do you mean?" The way she watched me caused my worry to fade. Her large hazel eyes were framed by a tiny amount of dark liner, and she blinked at me innocently.

There was no way she knew what that look could do to a man. At this exact second, if she were to ask me never to eat a danish again, I'd agree. She would be the end of me.

I almost forgot what we were talking about? But then she tilted her head, and clarity hit me.

She was waiting for an answer. I could daydream later.

"Damen took Spanish," I replied, focusing on my breathing.

It didn't help, because now her scent washed over me. She smelled like spring: roses and freshly-turned earth. My skin prickled and I fought back the urge to pull her to me.

Fuck my life. How could Titus stand this?

"Damen's dad pushes him to learn new things. To not rely on his past. We'll only recollect a few pieces of the languages we've known before. Our first life is the most powerful." I was trying not to breathe, but it wasn't working. "Nobody else cares what we study though. I've taken both French *and* Chinese. Julian took Chinese. Titus studied…" My words trailed off, as I tried to recall what he'd decided on. Titus was creepy, and was an overachiever. He focused on so many different things that I usually ignored him.

Wasn't he finishing *another* doctorate? Geology?

Show-off.

"What did Titus study?" she asked.

"He took Spanish, this time…" I muttered. "But he's studied other languages too. He says it's fun. I think he knows Arabic, Japanese, and he has a weird obsession with ancient Egyptian hieroglyphics."

"He studies languages *for fun*?" Bianca choked. "Who *does* that?"

"Weird people," I muttered. "Overachievers." Hadn't she realized yet that Titus was a nerd? Where did she think he spent most of his time? If he wasn't dealing with business, he was either ripping apart mechanics and putting them back together, or was holed up in the library, *studying*.

Julian studied because he wanted to be a doctor. And while I spent a lot of time in the library, it wasn't for *fun*. When I studied, it was a means to an end. I had a plan.

My environmental advocacy firm wasn't going to start itself. It was my responsibility to start a movement in this life, to change the world.

But that was for work. And Titus wasn't normal. He was obsessed.

Normal people found enjoyment in the simple pleasures of life.

What was better than taking a meditative journey to soak in the light of the full moon?

Then there was gardening—feeling the freshly turned earth beneath your hands. To work with the life there, and pride in seeing your seedlings come to life. Harvesting herbs, and allowing the medicinal and magical energies to wash over you.

The last was an activity I'd always shared with Mu.

Then there was cooking. The feeling of satisfaction of creating something entirely from scratch.

Mu had always been a good assistant chef. Of course Bianca would be the same.

What else was fun?

Relaxing by a summer's brook. Allowing the cool water to wash over my bare feet as I worked on my grimoire. Or, even better, read. Reading was supposed to be a pleasurable activity.

Non-fiction rarely held any interest for me. Early fiction on the other hand? We all had our favorite genres. Mine personally though, I could never tell another soul. Not even Mu.

Most people would never understand Andreina Bellini, and the heart-wrenching realness of mindful erotica. *Sinful Response* was a masterpiece beyond compare. Just the thought of being alone with my secret library caused my heart to race.

"There's nothing wrong with taking a break," I repeated, petting her head. One day, when she'd moved past the trauma of her childhood, perhaps we could read Andreina together. "I'm not angry at you, nor do I mind if you don't want to take French. Considering everything that's happened, I believe it makes sense. However, I do have one suggestion…"

Her nervousness touched the air between us, and her voice was breathy when she asked. "Yes?"

"You need to tell Titus yourself," I warned. "He won't be angry. But he'll be hurt if you do this without letting him know. Especially because he's been worried about how to protect you."

Chapter Twenty-Six

Titus

Swords

The jewels sparkled under the light, and I studied the new setting that my mother's heirloom laid in.

The previous piece had all but been destroyed after it'd been thrown into the fire, and even though Bianca never mentioned it, I could tell it worried her. She wouldn't have tried to claw her way to save it otherwise, even as she was so injured.

She wouldn't continue to look at me with such guilt.

I wasn't angry at her—though I was disappointed that the original gold was destroyed. But that was far from her fault.

But bringing it up without something to offer as closure would probably cause her to become even more anxious. She didn't seem like the kind of person to accept reassurances at face value.

So I had to approach this in a different way.

"Titus?"

Her voice cut through my concentration, and I dropped the ring, spinning to face the intruder.

We were in my garage—mine because no one else cared about cars besides riding around in the most expensive models. But the maintenance and upgrades of said vehicles always fell to me, if they didn't bypass me and take them into the shop, anyway. I sat at my desk, where I was currently working. I'd been in the process of rebuilding a computer. So my work surface, and the room as a whole, was shamefully disorganized.

Bianca stood in the doorway, nervously shuffling as she watched me. And now that I'd noticed her, it was alarming that my attention had lapsed so much that I'd missed her entrance.

"Bianca?" This was embarrassing. "When did you get in here?"

Miles was retreating to the main part of the house. He must have brought her. And Bryce was still practicing his forms in the adjacent workroom. His movements hadn't paused, so he didn't seem to have heard his sister.

"Just now…" She sounded so unsure, and she stepped into the room, biting her lip. "Can I talk to you?"

A deep sense of foreboding twisted in my guts at the hesitance in her voice, and my instincts stirred at the fear in her eyes.

There was no reason for her to *ever* have that expression around me.

My gift to her was still in plain view on the table, and I dropped an unused cloth over the surface. I crossed my arms, facing her. "Is something wrong?" Why would Miles bring her to me *here*? I thought she didn't like messes.

"I'm not…" she began, but her attention drifted to the table. My heart began to race as she asked, "What are you working on?"

"Nothing." It was a battle to keep my voice calm. There was only one way out of this now—one tactic. She was too scary when she had her focus on something.

"No." She frowned. "It was something."

I had to distract her. Before I knew it, I'd crossed the room, pulling her to me and turning us away from the table. But now what? It wasn't like I could dip and kiss her like we lived in some sort of fairy tale.

I needed to divert her attention, not terrify her.

What should I do?

"Is that Damen's Jaguar?" she asked.

I blinked, my nervous energy receding and interest piquing at the sudden gleam in her eyes. It almost felt as though she was *judging* me.

"Why did you rip apart Damen's car?"

She *was* judging me!

"That's *my* car." Not that it mattered. I had ripped apart Damen's car more than once. "Mine is darker."

"Why do you have a Jaguar?" she asked, squinting her eyes at the vehicle. "I thought you had a Range Rover. And that Harley. Though, I couldn't place the model." She shivered, and guilt rushed over me. Was she recollecting our first meeting?

I'd never misjudged a situation so badly in my life.

I would give almost anything to go back to the past and redo that moment. But for now, this worked to distract her. She seemed to know a bit about this topic; she'd payed enough attention to remember the vehicle models. "Are you interested in cars?"

She blinked, turning her attention to me.

"Not building them or anything..." she muttered, gesturing around the room. "But I like looking."

"You like looking at cars?" Like car shows? The fact that she was interested in this topic at all was a bit of a surprise. Although, it did seem like various fetishes ran in her family. "Why?"

Caleb Weaver had been a mechanic once. Meanwhile, Gregory Stephens and Declan Dubois both collected vintage vehicles—a show was where Bianca's parents had met. Then there was Bryce, who had a fondness for gambling at races. He wasn't responsible with his money, and he lost more often than won.

She pressed her hands to her cheeks. "I can imagine what I want! I'm not hurting anyone."

I raised my eyebrow, wary now. What was she *imagining*?

Her imagination was genius, but also a little bit scary. I had to figure out what she was thinking, otherwise she might do something without me there to protect her. "Imagine *what*?"

She covered her eyes, the thready scent of panic filling the room.

Why was she panicking? Was there something she wanted, and she was afraid to ask?

"Princess." I pulled her hands from her face, and my mouth went dry at her embarrassed expression. How could I make her happy? "What are you imagining? Do you even have your license? Would you like to take a drive in the Rover? If you want me to buy you your own car, I—"

"No." The redness faded from her cheeks. "I don't have my license. I don't care about passenger cars. They are boring." Her gaze drifted toward my modest bike collection across the room.

A sense of foreboding filled me, and it became harder to breathe. "You want a *motorcycle*?"

"They seem fun," she said.

"But…" My mind raced. While the thought of Bianca and me riding together was exciting, there was also the worry that she'd get hurt. Especially if she went out on her own. Plus, it didn't make any sense! She was logical, she knew how dangerous motorcycles could be. She was terrified of most things that wouldn't scare anyone.

Why would *this* be the thing that didn't frighten her? "Are you not afraid of the danger?"

She gave me a look that indicated she thought I was an idiot. "Why would I be afraid?"

But... *how?*

I pulled at my hair, unsure of how to respond. I was thrilled she wasn't scared. But for the first time, I was left wondering how she'd come to *this* conclusion. Usually I understood her, we were always on the same page.

It was usually us against the world.

"Well, a bike like that wouldn't be practical for all your needs," I finally said. "You should still get your license first. It might be more difficult for you to commute to school on a bike, or go shopping."

Guilt twisted across her expression, and my mind raced back over my words. Had I said something accusing? I didn't think so.

"I'm quitting school."

I blinked at her wide-eyed expression and pulled at my ear. Did she just say... But hadn't she threatened to beat up Miles for missing class?

He had been so scared. It was hilarious.

"Pardon?" I asked.

"I'm going to t-t-take off for the rest of the s-s-semester," she stuttered through the words. "I don't k-k-know what I want to do anymore." Her voice washed away my disbelief, and a sudden seething anger burned in my chest.

It was the sound of her fear.

None of us had missed her occasional stuttering. The first time I heard it—at the hospital after Daniel Cole had attacked her—I assumed it was from shock. But I was wrong.

Julian had glanced at Bianca's medical records. We'd spoken to Finn. Miles had even forced Abigail and Jonathan into a meeting.

And they shared the same story.

Bianca's stuttering had developed when she was young, most likely due to the trauma she lived through before Abigail Geier found her. Trinity Kohler noted that Bianca had been able to move past the stuttering with extensive speech therapy. However, it could be triggered when she wasn't focusing, or if she was thrown back into a negative mindset.

It was a struggle to force my expression to remain blank. But Bianca didn't need me to storm from the room and rip apart another punching bag. First, I doubted she wanted to see Bryce. Second, she'd probably misunderstand my anger and believe it was directed toward her.

My instincts pulled me in different directions. Vengeance filled me, but also the need to comfort. I'd never felt like this before.

I'd been in love with Mu for countless lifetimes, but we were never mates. If he was hurt, or wronged, it had been easy to detach in order to focus on my duties.

It was different now.

Bianca's essence was the same—she was, after all, Mu reborn. But something about her had fundamentally changed, and it wasn't only her gender. She was different in a way I couldn't explain, and it seemed as though I was the only one to notice.

Perhaps this change was what triggered the mate bond?

It didn't matter. I couldn't walk away from her while she was like this—not even to get angry on her behalf or to defend her. The thought of it was physically painful.

This could, potentially, become an issue in my work. It would be dangerous if certain groups were to discover this weakness.

But she was shaking, watching me with watery eyes. And I no longer cared about any of that.

"Why are you upset?" I asked, pulling her to me.

"Are you angry?" she asked instead of answering, burying her face in my chest.

My arms tightened over her shoulders. "Why would I be angry?"

"Because everyone says you're really smart." Her voice was almost a whisper. "And you've lectured me about school before. I know you have all these degrees, and you're really ambitious, and—"

"You do what you want," I interrupted, forcing my heart to stop racing. "I go to school because I *enjoy* it. I've pressured you to go to classes because—while you're working a program you enjoy—I want to help you succeed. If you need to take a semester off, then do it. You're not going to do your best work struggling through something if you're not confident about it."

"Oh…" Her voice sounded so small.

But I wondered, "Why do you want to take a break? Did something happen?"

"Not really," she answered. "I'm just unsure of my major, and there's a lot going on."

I nodded even though she couldn't see me. That made sense. A break might be good. But if she was anything like her old self, it would be better for her to have something to focus on. "What are you going to do with your break?"

"I don't know…"

This wasn't good. She already sounded lost. Mu always turned sullen and angry when he had nothing to do. I had to think of something.

I blurted out the first thing that came to mind. "Do you want me to teach you how to drive?"

Her sniffling subsided, and she pushed back from me, meeting my eyes. "What?" Her eyes flickered toward the motorcycles again. "But—"

Why was this my life?

"Do you want me to teach you how to drive a motorcycle?" The words were almost painful.

"No," she said. "I don't want to drive it. When did I say that?"

I paused, going over our conversation. No, she hadn't said that.

But then, "Then what—"

"Sidecar racing." She raised her finger. "I've seen videos on the internet. It looks exciting."

"You don't want to drive." Please let this be a nightmare. "Does that mean you want—"

"I want to be the passenger!" She sounded happier now, and her eyes twinkled with excitement. And despite my initial reaction, her mood was contagious. "I've watched *so* many videos on cornering, I'm practically a master already!"

My mood dipped slightly. "Well…" One did not become a master of something by watching videos.

"And it'll be safe because *you'll* be the driver." She beamed as she grasped my hands. "It could be *our thing*."

My heartbeat echoed in my ear and my skin grew warm. First thing tomorrow, I would be ordering a sidecar racer.

Chapter Twenty-Seven

Bianca
Defeat

Titus and I had barely crossed into Damen's living room before Bryce—who'd apparently finished working out and had been waiting for us—started his antics.

"I challenge you," he said, pointing at me.

My breath hitched, and conversation in the room halted. Anthony was visiting, conversing with Julian in the window seat. Finn was on the couches with Damen and Miles.

Meanwhile Brayden, who'd been sitting cross-legged on the floor, turned to Bryce in horror. "What are you talking about?"

"Yes, do explain." Damen stood, his fists clenched at his sides. "You have no right to—"

"I'm not challenging her *position*, you moron." Bryce rolled his eyes but didn't spare Damen a glance. His attention was still fixated on me. "She owes me." He pointed at the television. "We have a deal!"

I sighed—I'd forgotten about this. "*Fine.*"

Why he'd waited until now to bring this up, when I'd had the console for a week already, I didn't know. But if he wanted his butt kicked in front of all these witnesses, who was I to argue?

Damen was still frowning at Bryce. "I still don't have—"

"I'd like to change the terms," Bryce interrupted with a wave of his hand. "I overheard you talking to Titus earlier, and I don't approve. No one in the Dubois family is a quitter. If I win, you need to stay in school. If I lose, I won't protest and you can still keep your stupid system."

"You can't tell me what to do anyway." I wasn't sure if my fists were shaking from fury or from being thrown off guard. The last thing I expected was this sudden bit of drama.

"I'm not finished," he continued. "You've skipped all your appointments with Do Yun this week. You need to go."

"No."

Bryce shrugged. "Well, if you win, it'll be your choice. And I won't ever mention it again."

"Fine." All my pent-up anger and frustration was causing my vision to bleed red. He'd been pushing my buttons for *weeks* now, and now it was time to murder him.

"Hold on." Brayden stood between us, hands outstretched. "What is this challenge?"

"We're going to battle it out," I answered, pushing up my sleeves. "First-person shooter style."

Finn, who'd been watching the scene with barely concealed curiosity, almost fell from his seat. However, he regained his bearings quickly enough and moved to us. But when he spoke, his focus was on my brother. "Bryce, you really don't want to—"

"Shut up, Finn." I pushed past him, stalking toward the television. "No one asked you."

Everyone else, I'd noticed, only stood back. Watching, but—outside of Damen's initial outburst—not interfering.

Apparently, they'd decided to let me deal with Bryce. At least, so long as I was handling the situation. Good. My heart swelled at the knowledge that they thought I was capable.

How *dare* Bryce listen in on a private conversation between me and Titus. Who did he think he was? And did it mean he'd been *stalking* me?

This was not going to fly.

My anger quietly built as Brayden, still wearing his befuddled expression, handed me a game system controller and proceeded to instruct me on how to use it. I was barely listening. My focus remained zeroed in on Bryce, who'd plopped himself elegantly on an ottoman wearing an expression as if he was so perfectly brilliant.

I was going to throw my controller at his head.

"You got that, Bianca?" Brayden's question cut through my silent rant, and I blinked at him.

"Yeah, thanks." I tried to smile. At least he was *trying* to be nice.

Bryce scoffed, and my hatred flared again.

Then the game was starting.

I'd never played this edition. The controls were essentially the same, so it only took a few minutes to pick things up. And yet, no one had protested—not even when Bryce's avatar had chased mine across an ivy-covered bridge and shot it in the back.

I'd lost a life, but that was fine. And the fact I was being trusted to handle Bryce in my own way made me feel powerful.

Then Bryce snickered as we waited for my character to respawn, and all bets were off.

"I am going to murder you," I growled.

The snickering stopped, and the instant my controls allowed, I was after him.

"What the hell?" Bryce protested after his avatar died ten seconds later. He didn't even have time to spot me before it happened. His relaxed pose shifted, and suddenly he was leaning forward in his seat, holding the controller out in front of him in mild panic. And after he lost another two of his ten lives, the laugher had left his voice. "Stop doing that!"

"I don't know what you're talking about." I'd found the perfect vantage point, and once Bryce's character was in view again, took him out.

"You're camping!" he complained. "That's cheating."

What a sore loser. "If it were cheating, it wouldn't be possible. This is a computer game."

"You can still cheat! Anyone can play a sniper."

I sighed. Since he was being such a baby, it wouldn't be fun to destroy him this way. Then he'd only whine forever.

So I gave in to his demands and moved to stalking him over the map.

Of course, he would still complain. "How are you doing this?" Bryce had resorted to button-mashing, but it made no difference. He was defeated, and this time his character was killed with a knife in the chest.

"Only a fool writes off their opponent as having no value," I replied. I'd cornered him once more, and once again, Bryce was forced to respawn. "Let this be a lesson to you, lest you are tempted to forget."

"Do they even remember they're playing a video game?" Brayden was speaking to someone behind us.

"I don't know, but I'm so turned on right now," Miles responded.

"I don't want to hear that," Brayden said.

"Don't distract me!" I tossed a grenade after Bryce's fleeing soldier. "He still has lives left!"

"I don't want to play anymore." Bryce sounded upset.

"I don't care," I said. "No one in the Dubois family is a quitter."

"Don't mock me!"

As much as his distress thrilled me, the fun was soon over. "It doesn't matter anymore," I pointed out. "You're dead, and I win."

The screen darkened and the final score flashed across the top, proving my point. As if there were any question.

"This isn't fair." Bryce was pouting.

In comparison, almost everyone else was staring at me, open-mouthed. "What?"

"What was *that*?" Miles asked, stepping toward me. There was a look of wonder on his face—almost as if he couldn't decide whether to hug me or run away.

I glanced at the controller in my hand, then back to him, frowning. "A first-person shooter game. Some people play them to relieve stress. Others because they have repressed violent natures and want to kill something. I just think it's fun."

Miles pinched his nose. "That's not what I meant."

"Baby girl." Damen knelt in front of me, his eyes twinkling in an alarming way. "When did you—"

I pointed at Finn, interrupting his question.

"ElvenEdgeLord69." He buried his face in his hands. "That's her handle. She has had a lot of free time."

"*She's* ElvenEdgeLord69?" Brayden covered his mouth. "But he's a legend! He's one of the top ten players in the country. All this time I thought it was *you*."

"Does it *look* like I have time to play video games?" Finn glared at him. "No, I just let her use my information for her account. She needed an outlet. I disabled chat and the microphones."

"What are you talking about?" I asked. What chats? What in the world was there to talk about in these games? The only objective was to go in and kill people. But as he pursed his lips, I waved my hand in the air. I probably wouldn't like the answer anyway.

"Never mind. Listen, can we transfer my account to this system?" I asked. "I really miss my custom skins." There were all manner of items I needed. Hopefully this edition had the same downloadable attachments. My *Hello Kitty* VPAR was greatly missed. "ElvenEdgeLord69 has all the cool stuff."

"Okay, you are all going to need to stop saying 'ElvenEdgeLord69'." Julian held out his hands. "How did you even come up with that handle?" he asked, looking at me. "Why the…" He hesitated only briefly. "Sixty-nine?"

Wasn't it *obvious*? So many other players had gotten the reference. It was a number I'd seen often throughout my gaming career.

"The yin-yang symbol!" How could they not know this? Why did everyone—except Finn—seem so confused? "Think about it. They fit together so perfectly. And the bubble-part of the number holds the dot, and they wrap around each other…" My words trailed off at Julian's look of confusion. "Do I need to draw it out for you?"

"No!" Julian sounded alarmed, and his eyes had widened almost comically.

"Please don't."

Now I was confused, and my gaze narrowed on the others. Clearly, I was missing something. Perhaps I had been misled.

"Fine." I pulled out my phone. "Just give me a moment."

"No! Don't Google it." This time it was Damen who interrupted, pulling the phone out of my hands. He turned his narrowed gaze to Finn. "What did you do?"

"Don't ask me!" Finn was staring at me in horror. "I had nothing to do with this one."

"What is it?" I asked, my face was burning in embarrassment. I loathed the uncomfortable looks of pity on their faces. And my heart twisted painfully at the knowledge that I, surely, sounded so stupid to them right now.

"I had no idea it was this bad." Bryce was rubbing his temples. "Someone should have warned me."

"Warned *you*?" I rounded on him, my pulse roaring in my ears. The stress of the week pulled at me, and exhaustion shredded my final hold on restraint. Distantly, I caught Julian reaching for me. I saw his mouth move, but his words didn't register.

"Why would anyone do that?" The words tore from me. "All of this is your fault!"

The moment seemed to freeze in time, my awareness shifted. There was only Bryce, pale—yet still slightly black and blue—staring at me with eyes that matched my own.

He was normally so annoying, so smug. But not anymore.

I witnessed the exact second his expression broke; when the first hint of real, genuine emotion—other than fury—filled his features.

Pain.

It was masked over within an instant, but I had seen it. My breath caught, and guilt washed over me.

What was I doing? I was the most horrible person in the world.

"Fine." Bryce got to his feet, brushing off his jeans. He would no longer meet my eyes. "I'll just get out of your way then."

And before I could protest, he stalked from the room.

The heaviness in the room lifted, and I sucked in a breath. "I'm terrible."

Julian wrapped his arms around me, and as I pressed my face into his chest, the comforting blanket of his presence washed over me.

"No, you're not," he said.

"And you're not wrong." Damen was still on the floor, glaring at the place where Bryce had retreated. "Let him wallow."

"It *was* kind of harsh. Whether you believe it or not, he *does* care." Brayden stood between me and the door, glancing at it, and me, nervously. "I should probably—"

"No." I sighed. Gathering my composure, I pushed away from Julian. Though my gaze locked with Brayden only for a moment, I didn't miss the surprise, and pride, in my brother's eyes.

His acceptance made me feel better about my next actions.

"I'll go talk to him myself."

Bryce's door was open still, just a crack. And I took the opportunity to peek through the gap. My heart pounded, and I couldn't stop my stomach from twisting.

I'd never meant to push him this far, to hurt him. But he'd been mean, and I'd been embarrassed. I'd only wanted to make him feel the same way he'd made me feel.

I never thought it would feel this bad though.

The light on his side table was on, and the dim glow threw his face into shadows as he sat on the side of his small bed. His face was buried in his hands, and his shoulders slumped. And if I held my breath and listened hard enough, I could hear him muttering under his breath.

It felt like I was spying on him, and my breath caught. Guilt was guiding my actions now, and I pushed the door open. "Bryce?"

His head snapped up, eyes wild and unrestrained. "What are you doing here?"

"I'm sorry..." I bit my lip, locking my hands together at my back. "I didn't mean it that way."

"What?" He sounded confused at first, but then cleared his throat. "Oh, that." He sighed. "No worries, I didn't take it personally. Brayden said you might lash out, and I'm not known for being great with people."

That was an understatement. But I was the same way, so I couldn't judge.

"I didn't hurt your feelings?" I asked.

"No," Bryce replied, a frown heavy in his voice. "I needed a moment to think."

Relief swelled in my chest. I hadn't hurt his feelings. Bryce was tough and heartless. He drank poison for fun and probably had no soul. It would take a bulldozer to move his emotions. "What were you thinking about?"

"Our mother," he said. "You reminded me of her. She would have liked you."

His response floored me, and I tore my gaze from the ground. Of course, people thought about their parents all the time, that was to be expected. At least, I thought that was normal. I tried not to think about the couple who'd adopted me, and I knew almost nothing about the ones biologically related to me.

I didn't even know their names.

But it wasn't that which surprised me.

He'd said *our* mother. Why did he keep saying it this way? He hardly knew me.

How was it so easy for him? I'd tried to call him my brother in my head, but it was difficult. It felt strange, so I avoided focusing on it.

In the same way I'd been trying not to face reality. My worst fears had come true—my birth mother was dead.

But it was stupid to settle for not having information. The answers to my questions had been in front of me all this time.

And his statement. How could he know? "Why do you think she'd like me?"

"She always wanted a girl, and she'd thought she'd never have one. Women aren't commonly born in the higher ranking fae families. You're a lot like her," Bryce replied. "She loathed being sheltered and being told what to do. She'd put up with it but found small ways to rebel. Despite that, she was beautiful and graceful and feminine…" His words trailed off as his eyes ran over me critically.

My face was warm. This was the first time he'd said anything remotely nice to me—

"Well, there *are* differences," he said. "I'm not certain that last part applies."

I frowned, the warm feeling spreading through my chest vanished. "You're mean." Should I ask? It felt stupid to bring it up now, and the worst he could do would be to refuse to answer...

He sighed, sitting back on the mattress. "What is it?"

My voice was smaller than I hoped, but I couldn't help myself. "What was her name?"

Bryce blinked at me and his mouth dipped. My nervousness made it difficult to stand in one spot, and when he finally answered, his voice echoed in my spiraling thoughts. "Alyssa."

The name registered, and so did the connotations. I frowned at him. "Alyssa."

"Yes..." Confusion flickered across his expression. "Is something wrong?"

Oh, nothing out of the ordinary. Only that I was going to kill Finn. Again.

"Excuse me, I need to go see Finn for a moment." I hoped he was having a grand time discussing my handle in my absence. They may even be having some laughs over it.

I hoped they were.

He should enjoy himself, because he had only moments of joviality remaining before I strangled him with my bare hands.

Not until the life faded from his eyes would I be victorious.

Bryce slowly moved to his feet. "Why? Do you need help?"

Good call. Bryce should be there when I murdered Finn. Finn played an essential part in Bryce's quintet, so he should witness the hand of justice.

As for Finn's role in this world, we would replace him soon enough. Perhaps, even, with Norman. The red-headed man was an ambitious person. "Follow me."

Chapter Twenty-Eight

Bianca
Burn

Everyone was still lingering when I stalked into the living room. However, what they were doing, I wasn't sure, because only Finn's startled form remained locked in my sight.

"You!" I pointed at him. He'd said he regretted everything. What a liar.

I'd show him regret.

"She's more pissed than before!" Brayden had been sitting beside Finn. But at my entrance, jumped back from the blond. His voice was thick with accusation. "Finn, what did you do?"

Titus, Julian, and Damen had also gotten to their feet at my arrival. But Finn ignored them, answering Brayden instead. "Why does everyone blame me for everything? How the hell should I know what happened?" He sounded slightly panicked. "I was here the whole time."

"Bianca?" Julian reached for me, concern heavy in his question. "What's wrong?"

I sidestepped Julian's reach, my finger still pointed at Finn. "Alyssa."

Finn paled, his eyes widening.

My blood ran hot, and my breathing became forced. How dare he look innocent? He'd done this to himself.

But then I spotted the fear in his expression.

Good.

He had better be afraid. I was going to rip off his head and pull his intestines out through his chest. Then I'd feed his remains to some free-range cattle. I wasn't aware of where a farm might be, but we were in a remote area so there was bound to be something.

If there was no farm, I'd leave him out for the werewolves to eat. Surely Ms. Protean's pack might enjoy some spiced jerky.

I lunged for him, but Damen caught me mid-leap.

"Hold on now, baby girl." His voice was mild, and he wrapped his arms around my shoulders. "You can't kill my brother without cause. He's my Er Bashou, and I've only recently gotten his cooperation."

He held me tightly against him, but I was still able to meet his eyes. I glared at him, my anger pulsing through me. If Damen knew what was good for him, he'd mind his own business.

"Only Julian or I can kill him," he amended, frowning. His grip loosened enough for my breathing to even. "What's wrong?"

"When I first met Finn, I didn't have a middle name," I explained, twisting my fingers in the front of his shirt.

Damen's frown twisted, confusion heavy in his expression, and he cocked his head to the side. "And?"

"He gave me one..." My chest swelled with emotion. There was no way it was a coincidence. "He named me after *her*." I glowered in Finn's direction. "How long have you known?"

A flicker of guilt passed through Finn's expression, along with a hint of self-doubt. My throat closed, and the edges of my fury faded.

I'd always hated upsetting him.

But the look lasted only for an instant, and then it was gone.

"The first time I saw you…" Finn glanced away. "You resembled the pictures I'd seen of her. And Kiania told me who you were."

"That's interesting," Bryce mused. He was leaning against the frame of the door, his finger to his chin. "And to think your middle name is actually Alyssa."

"Oh please. It's not like it was difficult to guess," Finn snapped, glaring at Bryce.

"Is that an insult?" Bryce raised his eyebrow. "Your family isn't much better."

"Both of you shut up." Julian was rubbing his temples, and when he turned his attention to Finn, the temperature of the room seemed to drop ten degrees. "I understand why you didn't say anything *after* Kiania bonded with Bianca. I don't agree with your decision to stay silent, but upon retrospection, I do admit it wasn't entirely your choice. That being said, if you knew who Bianca was before any of that, why didn't you come forward then?"

Finn paled, and when he spoke next, his tone was slightly hesitant. "I couldn't…"

"Why not?" Damen stepped forward, looking genuinely curious.

The blond's eyes met mine for a moment, and my breath caught. He watched me with a faintly familiar expression—I hadn't seen that look since the first time he'd offered me his hand.

"Never mind…" I muttered, breaking the connection between us. Did we really have to discuss this? Perhaps I was overreacting.

What did it matter why he never said anything sooner? It's not like it would have changed anything.

"I don't care anymore," I lied. And with that, I ignored the imploring looks of the others and left the room.

A breeze brushed over my face, pulling me out of my sleep. And I cracked my eyes open to see who'd woken me up—not that it was difficult to guess.

"I'm not going." I turned over, pulling the blankets over my head. "You can tell him that I'm over it."

'You can't be 'over it',' Kiania's voice echoed through my mind. The ethereal quality of it caused the hair on the back of my neck to stand up. This was the first time she'd spoken to me since last week's confrontation. *'And it's not like you to run away from a problem.'*

I wanted to laugh at the audacity of her statement. Who did she think she was? She didn't know me. I was the *master* of running away.

'You really aren't,' she said. *'It's not your style. But—in this life—that's all you've ever done.'*

My heart began to beat furiously in my chest. Who did she think she was?

'Well, we were friends once. A long time ago. Friends are honest with each other, even if the truth hurts.'

And who was she to talk? She hadn't been honest at all.

"Then why did you avoid me in my other lives?" I snuggled in my sheets but turned—only enough to spot her through a gap in the blankets. "That's not *friendly*. And neither is tricking me into this bond, thing, we have."

'*We* were *friends*.' The tiger cocked her head, golden eyes reflecting off the light of my small lamp. She changed the subject. '*But you're not the same. When the moon isn't out, you can't even sleep alone in the dark.*'

"I can so!" My voice was low, and I pulled the covers around my face. I didn't need a light—most nights. I once thought I'd gotten past that. Outside, in the forest where nature surrounded me, there was no issue. There was a natural light there, even in the night. But lately, when trying to sleep inside, it felt like the night threatened to swallow me whole.

I expected her to remark on my lie. After all, she seemed to be able to read my mind.

But, instead, she said something I didn't expect.

'*Don't run from Finn.*' She sounded further away. '*He had a moment of human weakness, but—throughout this—he's been your greatest ally. If our past together means anything to you, you'll consider my words.*'

I ignored her. After all, how I felt about Finn was none of her business.

'*Out of everyone in his circle, you should understand his actions, considering.*'

I sat up in my bed, my racing heartbeat echoing loudly in my ears. The forest from my dream flashed across my thoughts. It'd felt so real—I could almost smell the wet moss, hear the wind moving through the trees.

She'd said something similar there. Was it a coincidence?

"Hey…" My words trailed off—she was already gone. The darkness surrounded me once again.

Saturday morning brought Finn avoiding me at breakfast. And he disappeared shortly thereafter. Apparently, he was having a private meeting with Damen. But I didn't care, I was far from ready to talk to him again anyway. The coursing heat of his betrayal still flooded through my system, along with something new.

It felt suspiciously like guilt, which couldn't be true.

Curse that stupid white tiger. She was the one who didn't understand.

I'd been named after my mother, and she was dead. The entire time, my *ex-best friend* knew about this! He'd hid this from me. How was I supposed to feel?

He also said that I looked like her. Bryce did too, but it was expected that he knew what his own mother look like. She had been in his life. But what really stuck with me was that *Finn* knew, too.

And—outside of a vague reference to look in the mirror—I still had no idea.

How much more was I supposed to take?

I couldn't face anyone, not right now. Now that Damen had given me a refuge, I didn't need to. Instead of socializing, I spent the morning setting up base. And really, my new room was quite pretty. I had been too exhausted, and distracted, to notice the smaller details of Damen's craftsmanship. Such as the inlaid gold in the crown molding—Damen was truly terrible with money. Either that, or it was fake.

Either way, I hadn't technically accepted this finery as a gift. I was simply a resident of this establishment. So there was no reason to *not* enjoy the riches life had bestowed upon me.

There was even an adult-sized, fuzzy beanbag chair and a corner library. How could I ever repay him?

I was quitting school Monday—no more French class for me. I had a space all to myself. I had money—no matter that I couldn't access it yet. Finally, my little introverted heart was at peace. And, now, for the first time in a long time, no prying eyes stalked my every movement.

As I lay back on my beanbag chair, I studied the strange cherubic patterns on my ceiling. They almost seemed like something from an art history book. Did Damen hire a painter, too?

I should probably ask him, but then he might flirt with me. Some of the creatures were naked, and I'd rather not bring attention to that aspect. Anything with nudity and Damen should be avoided at all costs. What if he grinned in that lopsided way of his and he tempted me to kiss him again? Now that I was aware of the Curse of Empaths, I had to be ever vigilant.

Ignoring these things was for the best. Life was bliss—

"Bianca." Bryce knocked on my door only once before popping his head into my room. He wore his usual commanding look, and it was obvious he wouldn't take no for an answer. "I need to talk to you."

I raised my eyebrow, disappointed at the rudeness. Was it not clear that I was busy?

"Brayden would like to talk to you, too," he added, and the other man smiled at me apologetically, stepping into the room.

Brayden did? If Brayden needed something, it might be important.

I turned to my stomach, watching them as they stepped into my space.

"You've been hiding in your room all day." Bryce gestured toward a settee tucked under my window. "We've been waiting for you to come out. Go sit there so you're not sprawled all over the floor."

"I'm not on the floor," I argued. "And what do you mean 'all day'? We just had breakfast an hour ago, *and* I was sleeping before that. I haven't been hiding."

"You were sleeping?" Bryce scowled, his eyes tailing over me in disapproval. "That's even worse. Is that why you're still wearing those unsightly pajamas?"

"Finn was there," I said, not commenting on his lack of fashion sense. "Doesn't he have stuff to do with Damen? So it wasn't that late."

"Finn was there because he was waiting to see you." Brayden rolled his eyes.

"Which, by the way, was also something I wanted to talk to you about." Bryce crossed his arms, bracing himself on the corner of my vanity. "Nobody outside of the family should be seeing you in your pajamas."

I made a face at him, noting the warning look that Brayden shot in his direction, but decided not to comment.

It didn't matter if Finn was there or not. He hadn't even looked at me anyway.

As for the others—Bryce had better step down real quick or I'd ask Titus to eat him.

"Who cares." Bryce changed the subject as he gestured toward me.

Sighing, as there was nothing better to do, and the more quickly we got this over with, the faster he'd leave, I dutifully went to the window seat. "Brayden and I were discussing some of our previous oversights regarding you—"

My eyes widened as my alertness sharpened.

Had they really? I hoped they accounted for them all. I might have to go over the list with them; I had noted at least ten transgressions already, not disregarding the pompous way he spoke to me.

Plus, he had the audacity to poke fun at my pajamas. These were vintage!

"—and we realized that in all the confusion, neither one of us had *actually* thought to go over the basics with you."

Oh. So he planned on lecturing me about something? My stomach knotted—I hated showing weakness to him. "What do you mean?"

"Our family." Brayden sat on the bench beside me. "Until yesterday, we didn't realize that we never told you anything about our family or our life. You didn't even know about our mother."

The last of my annoyance faded away, and my hands twisted in my skirt. It was a wonder I wasn't shaking.

"Why didn't you *ask*, Bianca?" Brayden face turned sad, and his hand gripped mine.

Bryce stood still, his arms crossed and expression expectant. Meanwhile, Brayden watched me, his gaze unwavering. Sympathy swirled in his gaze, and it caused a shameful heat to fill me.

"You know," Brayden began. "Father wants to—"

I cut him off. "I don't want to talk about him." Regardless of the reason, a tiny part of me still felt as though he'd betrayed me.

The large room seemed to shrink around us. Even the naked angels on the ceiling were laughing at my cowardice.

But I didn't care. I wasn't ready to talk about my father.

Brayden's brows furrowed, and he glanced at Bryce.

"Tell me about my mother." I latched on to their offering of another topic. This was information I was too shy to seek out on my own, but now they were here, trying to reach out.

This, I could handle.

"What do you want to know?" Brayden tilted his head.

"Everything."

Wasn't it obvious?

"Um…" He looked at Bryce again.

"Her name was Alyssa Titania Dubois, maiden name Stephens. Her brother's name is Arthur, and her parents are Oliver and Marianne," Bryce said. "Our mother loved music and art. And she loved plants. She made up all sorts of home remedies. She was soft-spoken, gentle, kind, and was the embodiment of feminine grace."

My heart filled with warmth and the room seemed to brighten. I could imagine her now—such elegance and poise. She was perfect—everything I imagined a fairy princess to be.

Brayden coughed out a laugh.

"What?" Bryce frowned at him.

He shot his brother an incredulous look. "Are you joking?"

"She was all of those things!" Bryce protested. "At least to me!"

Brayden rolled his eyes, as he held both my hands between his and turned to me.

"Ignore his theatrics," he said. "I don't remember much about her, but Bryce *is* right. She was *all* those things. However, from what I understand, she was also rebellious—"

"Don't encourage it!" Bryce interjected.

"Shut up." Brayden continued watching my face. "She was the most god-awful cook known to mankind. She loved playing pranks on people. And while she was hard to anger, when she finally had enough of someone, she didn't hesitate to kick ass."

I blinked at him, stunned into silence. Yet, he spoke again—somehow, there was more.

"Gloria was her godmother, and they adored each other. Once Mother was old enough, she spent her summers here, trailing after her. She loved solving mysteries and getting into trouble. Grandfather hated it."

That sounded kind of fun. "Why did he hate it?"

"She was only allowed out because Grandmother and Gloria are best friends and because of her position. It's dangerous for a female fae in this world," Bryce cut in, petulant. "You've seen what can happen!"

Brayden shot him a scathing look, but I was hardly paying enough attention to care.

I had all this new information... She *wasn't* a fairy princess.

She was *better*.

This was everything I'd ever imagined. But there was still...

I bit my lip, glancing at Brayden. I wanted to ask.

"What is it?" he prodded.

I squeezed my eyes shut, trying to ignore the heat warming my face. "Do you have a picture of her?" My voice warbled, and it was a miracle any of those words were understood.

But they had been.

"Of course." Brayden tugged at my hands, waiting for me to open my eyes. And when I did, he smiled. "You only had to ask."

Bryce cleared his throat, and my attention turned to him. He reached into his pocket, pulling out a heart-shaped locket. By the time he'd finished opening it, the edges of my vision had turned black and the sound of my heartbeat was all I heard.

I couldn't speak, I pulled my hands from Brayden, holding them out in front of me as Bryce handed me the small frame. The gold felt hot against my skin, and the nervous excitement flooded my body. As my attention wandered to the picture itself, my breathing shook. A long-haired brunette woman with rosy pink lips and large eyes smiled back at me.

It was at that instant my world stopped.

The sound of my name echoed through my awareness—Brayden calling for me. First as a question, and then in alarm. More commotion pressed in from every direction, fuzzy details in a background that continued to fade from my awareness. Julian was here now, but it didn't matter.

My body felt numb. It was so cold.

Nothing mattered anymore. I wanted to respond, to scream. But I couldn't, I was trapped in my own mind, the face of Alyssa Dubois staring back at me.

Judgment heavy in her gaze.

Someone tried to pull the picture away, but I reflexively held it against my pounding chest. I'd let go of her once, and I couldn't do it again.

It was my fault. How could I have been so stupid? Why hadn't I realized?

The things she'd told me, the things she knew about me. The way she'd sing to comfort me in the dark.

I should have made the connection.

Bryce had been wrong.

Her physical death might not have been my fault, but the destruction of her soul had been.

Chapter Twenty-Nine

Damen
Wands

Finn and I were having a past-due conversation about the merits of open communication when Julian's shout echoed through the upstairs. His tone was enough to cause my alarm to flare to life. Before I realized what was happening, I'd abandoned my brother and raced into Bianca's room in time to witness the other man smacking her on the face.

"What the fuck, Julian?" I moved between them, horror and alarm battling for dominance inside me. I barely restrained myself from lashing out—only resisting with the unsettling knowledge that something was deeply, *terribly* wrong.

Though I'd forced him back, Julian hadn't even attempted to respond to my question. Panic was heavy in his expression, and he was already on his feet, pushing past me.

"Move!" he demanded, and without thought, I stepped aside.

Finn stumbled into the room a second later, a wildly confused look in his eyes. And there was Bryce—and Brayden—standing to the side, fear radiating from their every pore.

Then I saw Bianca, and my heart twisted painfully.

She'd been thrown to the settee at my arrival, and Julian was only just forcing her back into a lounging position. Her expression was dazed, emotionless, and she had no reaction to Julian's frantic questions. Nor was she acknowledging a thing. It was as if she wasn't here at all.

My throat closed—I'd seen this once before, during my undergraduate years.

"What happened?" I turned toward Bryce. "What did you do?" He'd pushed her too far, and too fast. This was his fault.

"Nothing!" Bryce threw his hands into the air. For once, there was no snark in his tone. "She was upset about not knowing our mother, so Brayden and I brought her a photo. Then she went like this."

That didn't make any sense. "Why would that—"

"What in the world are you plotting?" Julian had taken up a defensive position at Finn's arrival, and was now glaring at him.

I was about to defend him—Finn had been with me, after all, so there was no way he'd done anything to contribute to this—when I noticed his expression.

"Finn?" I asked.

He blinked, turning his startled gaze toward me. "I was thinking." He sounded younger than his age, almost unsure. "This is the look she'd get when we'd talk about her first ghost. Except, this time, it's worse."

My heart jerked, and my attention returned to the woman in front of me.

When she wasn't afraid, her blue-green eyes would sparkle with a quiet inquisitiveness. They shone when she was happy, which was never often enough. But usually, they would shine with dark mischief. That, I'd learned, was when she'd plot. And when she was angry, her eyes would turn into a dark green. Like furious waves cresting in against a boulder.

I was beginning to live for those expressions.

But now her gaze held nothing but a dull emptiness that haunted me. What it meant terrified me on a foundational level, and my thoughts turned to dread.

She held a locket tightly against her chest, almost as if it were her only lifeline. Inside it, according to Bryce, was a picture of their mother.

Shit.

My heart fell, and I prayed with every fiber of my being that my suspicions were wrong.

But I doubted I was.

"You don't think…" Brayden began, his voice unsure.

"Alyssa died right after Bianca was born." I ran my hand over my face. How could we not have guessed this? "There's a high possibility that the first spirit Bianca ever encountered was her own mother's."

"I'm glad you called me." Dr. Kohler stepped from the room, closing Bianca's bedroom door behind her. Julian remained inside—much to my everlasting annoyance—while the rest of us, including Miles and Titus, had been sequestered in the hallway.

I'd been excluded in my own home. It was difficult to not take offense. But this was more important—

"What do you think?" I asked, pushing myself from the wall.

She shot me a derisive look. "Damen, I know you've seen catatonic patients before. The study of psychological disorders is one of Gregory's specialties."

"I know that!" My face heated, and I ignored the looks the others gave me. "I just pay attention to—"

"The parts that interest you." She sighed. "I know."

"That's not what I meant!" I protested. "I know what dissociation looks like. I just didn't want to assume…"

"You'd be right to assume," she said, her expression troubled. "She's suffering from a severe dissociative episode. It's been two hours, and right now, she's not responding to any external stimuli." Dr. Kohler turned to Bryce. "If the situation doesn't change, I'm going to insist that she go to the hospital."

"You can't do that!" Titus and Miles had moved to protest, but I spoke up first. I felt sick at the thought. "She's scared of hospitals. Especially after what happened last time. It might make it worse."

Dr. Kohler held her clipboard to her chest, frowning as she squared her shoulders. "Damen, she is not even responding enough to eat or drink. I've already started her on an IV, so she'll get fluids. But that is not a good sign. If it were anyone else, I would have already admitted her. She needs to be monitored."

Bryce seemed to contemplate this. "Do you think—"

"No!" I pointed at him, seething hatred burning through me. How dare he even consider this option. "This is your fault to begin with. Don't you dare make it worse!"

Bryce glanced at Finn.

"Don't look at me." Finn shrugged. "You're the one who married her. You wanted this responsibility."

"I haven't forgotten that you offered." Bryce gritted his teeth. Surprise chased away my anger. "You've known her longer than the rest of us," he continued. "What do you think we should do?"

Finn frowned, his gaze turning to the floor.

He had offered to marry Bianca? When did that happen? Miles didn't look surprised, but Titus was now eyeing my brother warily as well.

Despite the situation, jealousy churned in my stomach. He was an Er Bashou, *my* Er Bashou. He had no rights to her.

"If you put her in the hospital, she'll never trust you again." His shoulders slumped. "It won't matter that it's for her own good. It's probably the worst possible thing you could do right now."

He was speaking from experience, obviously.

Well, he deserved it.

"No." Bryce crossed his arms, turning to face Dr. Kohler. "What other options do we have?"

Dr. Kohler turned her gaze heavenward, pausing a moment before she responded. "You're *eventually* not going to have a choice. But for now, keep her under observation. Try to talk to her, it might bring her out of it. But if nothing changes in forty-eight hours, I am admitting her."

Bryce opened his mouth to argue, but she cut him off. "If I am forced to do so, I will go to your father. Don't test me."

The next two days passed slowly, and Bianca was never left alone. Occasionally, she'd sleep. But when she woke, there was no change to her condition. Bryce had hired a private aid, and she made sure Bianca stayed clean. But outside of that, we were the only people in the room.

Finn's fiddling had been getting on my nerves. Between his nervousness and Julian's sullen attitude toward him, I couldn't stand it anymore.

By the thirtieth hour, I'd sent him off to deal with Belial. Normally, I would never let even my Er Bashou communicate directly with the Overseers. But this was an emergency. The demon had been vying for my attention, and I didn't have the patience to talk business with him.

I hadn't seen him since—but Kiania was still near and not alarmed. Which meant that Belial had, most likely, started telling Finn his entire life's story, and my brother had passed out from boredom.

It was quite possible. The Overseers were almost my age. So their stories were quite long.

Then it no longer mattered.

I'd sat with Bianca. We all had. I spent hours stroking her hair, talking to her. Just trying to get her to *respond*. But there had been no change, and it was coming close to the time when Dr. Kohler would make good on her promise.

"What are we supposed to do?" Brayden sat, wringing his hands.

"I have an idea…" Miles began, his tone tentative. But then he glanced to Julian—who was taking his turn on the bed with Bianca—and he frowned. "Never mind…" he muttered.

I glanced between him and Julian—who didn't even seem to notice Miles's statement. But I had a suspicion as to what he'd been about to say. "I—"

A loud sound blared through the room, causing us all to jump and glare at the culprit.

"Could you think of a more obnoxious tone?" Miles stalked across the room, snatching my phone from the top of Bianca's vanity. He threw it at me.

"It's Gregory," I protested, glancing down at the screen. I'd missed a call already. "And since I don't always know where my phone is, I need to make sure I can hear it."

"Then put it somewhere you'll remember," Miles said. "So you don't deafen us all."

"It's Gregory!" Excitement coursed through me, electrifying my nerves. I was so stupid. Why didn't I think of this sooner? And it was perfect because—according to my clock—he was due to arrive at any moment.

I knew this would work out!

"You just said that." Bryce shot me a barely concealed look of concern.

"He can help us, you idiot." I lowered my phone, glaring at him. "He meets me on Mondays so we can go over the schedule for the week."

"It's Monday?" Bryce sounded unsure, although I'd just told him. "I didn't realize."

"Did you seriously abandon your classes all day and not post a warning?" Brayden frowned at his brother.

Bryce shot him an annoyed look. "I've had other things on my mind."

"True…" Brayden didn't argue.

Miles seemed to catch on to my excitement, and he jumped to his feet. "When is he supposed to be here?"

"Now…" Titus had been sitting on an armchair, and at his statement, rested his chin on his folded arms.

"That's right." The doorbell echoed through the room. "I'll be right back. Don't go anywhere!"

"Where are we supposed to go?" Brayden called after me, but I ignored him.

We only had a short amount of time before Dr. Kohler came back. Every second counted.

"Gregory!" I pulled the older man through the door without another word.

He blinked at me, barely regaining his footing in time to prevent a fall. "Mr. Damen?" he asked. "What in the world—?"

But I was already dragging him up the stairs before he even had a chance to respond.

We didn't have a lot of time.

"Bryce and Bianca got married. Then Bryce triggered her, and now she's unresponsive." I breathed, pulling him onto the landing after me. "Dr. Kohler wants to admit her to the hospital. But we can't do that. So now you need to stop her."

By the time I'd finished my explanation, we were in front of Bianca's room.

"See!" I threw open the door. "Now do something."

Gregory had taken a deep breath, barely glancing into the room before he rubbed his temples. "Again, I say, *what in the world?* Happy nuptials," he added, glancing at Bryce, his expression filled with judgment.

Bryce flushed. "I—"

"Now move out of the way." He wasted no further time before taking charge. He approached the bed, noting—and making use of—the medical equipment that remained on the bedside table.

And at least *he* didn't kick us out.

"What exactly am I looking for?" he asked, his attentions moving over Bianca clinically. He didn't even stop to shoo Julian away or remark on the fact that he was holding her. "She's catatonic! Just how long has she been like this?"

"Almost two days," Julian choked out.

"And Trinity wants to admit her?" Gregory stood, shooting me an even glare. "What do you want from me?"

"Think of another way besides hospitalization." This should be easy. He knew everyone.

"No."

My hope began to dwindle, and despair began to rise. "But why?"

"First of all"—Gregory pinched the bridge of his nose—"she is not my patient. So even though Miss Bianca—or rather, Mrs. Dubois—interests me, I'm not going to intervene. Besides, I won't tell you any differently than what Trinity already has. If she wants to hospitalize Miss Bianca, listen to her. She's an excellent doctor."

"Uncle Gregory, it's *her*," Brayden interrupted. "We can't let them take her away. That's why we *need* your opinion. You have an obligation to your family. This is your responsibility."

"You two are driving me up the wall," Gregory snapped. "Will you stop talking in riddles? I haven't the foggiest idea who…" But then his words trailed off, and his eyes opened, shooting to Bryce. "Are you serious?"

Bryce crossed his arms and nodded. "Completely."

Gregory frowned, and a strange expression passed over him. It was an emotion that I couldn't quite place but, for some reason, wanted to defend Bianca from.

I hadn't considered this when asking him for help crossed my mind.

"You're not going to tell the council." I stepped forward—it wasn't a question.

Gregory had been my mentor since I was young, taking on Uncle Michael's responsibility. The man had done his best to fulfill multiple roles, even though he was under no obligation to do so.

Then, after we'd grown, he'd stayed with me—with the four of us—continuing to offer his advice and guidance. Not only as a teacher, but as a friend.

And although I'd grown to like him, my darker instincts couldn't be ignored.

No matter who I had to hurt, my loyalty didn't extend to anyone who might pose a threat to Bianca. If he even *thought* about hurting her, I would kill him.

"*What?*" His narrowed gaze darted to me, the sharpness of his voice returning. "Mr. Damen, I suggest you erase that terrible expression from your face before your features freeze that way. It's unbecoming. And while you're at it, return to your senses. *Those people* are crazy, why would I tell them anything?"

It wasn't so far-fetched. "But you *were* a councilmember…"

"Insufferable fools, the lot of them," he said. "I'm offended you'd think that lowly of me." His annoyed look lingered on me for another long moment before he turned his attention back to Bryce. "And as for *you*. Why in the world would you *marry* her? Is there something addled in your brain?"

"That's the least of our concerns at the moment!" Bryce growled, inclining his head toward Bianca's unmoving form.

Julian stroked her hair. "What do you think we should do?" His voice was soft. "She won't want to go to the hospital."

A thoughtful look crossed Gregory's expression, and he moved to the foot of the bed. "It's been two days. She *should* be hospitalized. But she's been getting fluids, at least." He nodded at the IV. "Does Declan know about her?"

Alarm caused my breath to catch at the mention of Declan Dubois—Bianca's father.

"Why?" A million panicked scenarios raced through my mind. I hadn't seen him in a long time, but I remembered his eccentric behavior. From a child's perspective, he'd been both fun and scary. "What do you think he's going to do?"

"Declan?" Gregory raised his eyebrows. "It really depends on what he knows, and his mood. Knowing she's alive and where she is would probably having him jumping for joy. However, if he knew about *this*... I wouldn't be surprised if he had her forcibly relocated to a specially made wing in Whisperwind."

My fists clenched, anger coursing through me. He had no right to interfere.

Then there was fear. It made me lightheaded and my thoughts muddled. The thought of Bianca being taken *anywhere* again, somewhere far from where we could protect her...

I wouldn't allow it.

A growl reverberated throughout the room—Titus. Declan Dubois wouldn't stand a chance.

"Oh, stop being dramatic." Gregory sliced his hand through the air, shooting the four of us exasperated looks. "If you plan on continuing this ridiculous charade much longer, you're all going to need to curb your baser instincts. I'm only telling you this because your best chance is to work *with* him. He will be insufferable when he knows she's here. Don't push his buttons. He's been in a frenzy lately."

"She doesn't want to see Declan," Miles said, his voice low. He still stood near the door, bracing his weight against it. "She wants nothing to do with him."

"He's staying away. He doesn't want to force her into anything. But he *does* know she's here," Brayden whispered. "He's scared of overwhelming her. Especially with her past."

"What happened in her past?" Gregory asked, the tension in the room growing thick. "Declan isn't one to back off lightly. Does this have anything to do with his sudden murderous rampage elsewhere? What am I missing?"

Brayden's expression blanked and his gaze drifted toward his brother, who had the audacity to look guilty. But neither made any move to speak.

"Answer me." His tone was reminiscent of when we were young and he was training us. He'd always been imposing in those days. "I need to know what we're dealing with."

"She wasn't always with Kieran…" Brayden turned his attention back to Bianca. His gaze softened, and sadness seemed to fill the room.

A burning fury coursed through me. I hoped they choked on that guilt.

Brayden continued speaking, "After that, we're not entirely sure how she ended up in that situation. It's just that—"

"She was *five* and ended up being sold as game. It was Abigail Grier who found her, during one of her *missions*." I couldn't keep the bite from my voice. "She had been there for *years*."

Gregory paled, and ran his hand over his mouth. His attention remained on Bianca.

"And Declan knows about this?" he asked finally. "What triggered his episode?"

Bryce nodded. "He knows. We have a name, but it's not much help."

"He's been working with Maria," Titus interjected, his voice gruff from disuse.

I glanced at him, surprised. "What?"

"That's also where Abigail and Jonathan have been." Titus squared his shoulders, his gaze still never leaving the bed. "They don't want to face Bianca—though she doesn't want to see them anyway. And they needed something to do. So we put them to work."

"Why didn't you say something?" Betrayal shot through me, fueling my seething anger. "That's not your call to make."

"It keeps them busy," Titus growled. "And out of *our hair*. And we gain traction on our investigations. You told me to 'look into it', and I feel better knowing where everyone is. You were busy elsewhere and had no vision in mind. What else do you want from me?"

I opened my mouth, ready to argue, when Miles stepped between us.

"This is not the time to fight!" he said. "Both of you should be ashamed of yourselves."

"He's right," Brayden interjected. "And Father is more than happy to work together."

"You knew!" I accused, flashing my teeth at Brayden then glancing at Bryce. He didn't even look ashamed. "You too!"

"Of course I knew." Bryce shrugged. "If you honestly believe we wouldn't have thrown the full weight of our family ties into this, you're a fool."

"That's what you've all been doing!" I'd been distracted by one smaller catastrophe after another, and no one had thought to inform me. Who the hell did they think they were? "How could you not tell me?"

"Will you shut up?" Julian's tone washed over me like ice, and my fury stilled. "What happened to your meditations? You're only continuing to prove you can't act like a grown-ass man."

I blinked at him, offended. That wasn't true. "I—"

"You don't care that they're working together." Julian was glaring at me, though he still cradled Bianca against him. Because of that, his voice came out a scathing whisper. Yet his words seemed to echo though the room. "You *want* them to succeed, because you can't wait to get your hands on the culprit. I know you've been planning out your every action. No," he hissed. "You're pissed because you've been left out. When are you going to learn life is *not* about *you*?"

"That's not why I'm mad!" I couldn't explain it. It was getting harder to ignore my thirst for vengeance.

Mu had been my closest friend. In past lives, he'd taken blows for me. I'd trusted him like no other. But now I wanted more than our games and conversation. It was getting harder to ignore the pull of Bianca's presence. The pull to take care of *her*.

Why didn't anyone understand? Why didn't they trust me? Things were different now!

"I don't care about your petty arguments," Gregory said, his accusing tone cutting through the air like a knife. "I'm talking about *Bianca*. What in the world caused her to enter this state?"

Julian's flush made me feel marginally better about my own outburst, and it was him who responded. "She saw a picture of Alyssa."

Brayden nodded, and Gregory's frown deepened.

"That's it?" he asked.

"We think she knew her," Julian said. He was gazing at Bianca again, brushing the hair away from her brow. She continued to blankly stare in front of her, and my heart twisted as the last of my anger faded away.

"Why do you think that?" Gregory sounded genuinely curious.

"I haven't felt anything, if that's what you mean," Julian answered. "And I'm not reading anything from her, emotionally. She's just... *here*. Damen and... Finn suggested it. We all agree. She fears her first spiritual encounter, and Alyssa had died right after she was born."

"Well, you could know for sure." Gregory stroked his chin. "Why not look into her memories? You could even pull her out."

There was a collective intake of breath as the older man broached the subject. We'd all been avoiding this because we knew how it would end. But from the expectant looks around the room, we were all in agreement.

Except one.

"I can't!" Julian's expression twisted and his dark gaze focused on Gregory. His voice was menacing, causing the hair on my arms to rise. "I'm not doing that!"

"Technically, you *can*." Gregory seemed nonplussed by Julian's reaction. "But you don't seem inclined to do so."

Julian blinked, some of the force diminishing. No one had ever pressed him before. "I can't!" he said again. "I made a promise to her just last week—"

"Actually, you said you wouldn't look *unless* her life was in danger." Miles stepped forward.

He'd been waiting for this—the moment to press his luck.

Julian's suspicious gaze turned to Miles, and he pulled Bianca closer to him. "Her life *isn't* in danger."

"Not yet," Gregory said. "But soon it may very well be. She'll need to be hospitalized, and unlike you, I'm not overly sensitive to her wishes. Not in a situation like this. Do you really want to wait until she's at a critical point?"

"You said she could snap out of it!" Julian protested, panic lacing his voice.

"She could, but it hasn't happened yet. When are you planning on intervening?" Gregory narrowed his eyes at Julian. "Are you waiting for someone to stick a tube into her stomach first? She'll need to eat somehow."

"No!" Julian protested. "I don't want to see that either."

Gregory glanced at Bryce, and the two of them shared a long look before he spoke again. "If you don't do it soon, we're setting up at Whisperwind. This dump you call a home is far from an ideal medical environment," he added, giving me a pointed look. "Whisperwind is another option."

My blood turned to ice. "We called you here to help. To keep her *out* of the hospital."

"Whisperwind is not a hospital," Gregory argued, his position unchanged.

I could see the panic crossing Julian's expression, and Titus had gone unnaturally still in his seat.

"But," Julian protested weakly, "she could still snap out of it."

"Julian, think about this." Miles sat down on the bed, his voice a calmness in the storm. "*You* would know if she was even close to coming around. Her heart would speed up, and her breathing would change. Have you noticed either of those signs?"

Julian's expression turned pained, and his attention returned to Bianca. Even before he responded, I knew his answer.

"No," he said. "She's not waking up."

Chapter Thirty

Julian
Cups

"How much longer do you plan on waiting?" Miles asked, and his tone told me everything I needed to know.

When Miles used his abilities to cajole, he did it in one of two ways. There was the dark force of his anger. It was rare, but something that did happen on occasion. He had a wildness to him. I hadn't been there when he'd gotten angry at Finn on Bianca's behalf, but Damen had said it was almost frightening. It seemed only Bianca's presence had been enough to keep him from crossing the line.

But then there was his dark side. When he was controlled but his displeasure was a tangible thing in the air. Like his anger at Garrett Cole.

But Miles also used his abilities another way. He was extremely persuasive. He could talk his way around almost any situation and make people see his point of view. I knew he was manipulating me—this entire plan. But I couldn't argue with him. Mu had always been the only one able to out-logic Tu.

Damn it.

Bryce was already wearing a contemplative look that didn't bode well for my protests. We'd trapped ourselves into this corner, giving Bryce the power to make medical decisions on Bianca's behalf. Now we were going to have to learn to deal with it.

"What if I don't…" My words trailed off.

"I'll give it until Dr. Kohler gets here, then we'll go to Whisperwind," Bryce said. "I don't like the idea as much as anyone, but Miles—and Uncle Gregory—are right. We need to do something. There's no other choice."

"Fine." My voice came out as a growl, barely discernable through over the pounding of my heart. "But don't think I'm happy about this." I glared around the room. "And I'm not going to be forgiving any of you anytime soon."

Miles grimaced before his expression steeled over and he nodded. "It'll work."

"It better." I shifted Bianca in my arms until she was facing me. She offered no resistance as I studied her face one last time, trying to catch any flicker of emotion.

But there was nothing. She was seeing me, but nothing was registering in her mind.

"It helped *me*," Miles said softly. My gaze tore from Bianca, lifting to Miles. Guilt flooded through me, making it hard to breathe.

"You're right…" I muttered, the edges of my anger fading away as, for the first time, I took note of the stressed lines of Miles's expression. Out of everyone, he wouldn't suggest this lightly. And how was he feeling right now, seeing Bianca like this?

She was the strong one, the one who kept him grounded. And he…

Miles had been in a similar situation not so many years ago.

How could I have forgotten? "Sorry."

"Besides, you can control it," Miles continued. "I'll help you."

The statement was so absurd that I was sure I'd misheard. However, when Damen and Titus also made sounds of confusion, I knew I hadn't imagined it.

Tu *never* used his abilities with mine—excluding preparing the items I needed for rituals.

My powers were invasive, and—when unleashed—unpredictable. Once I began, I never knew which memories would be conjured. I'd start with a direction, but I'd always see more than my intentions. In my practice, it generally didn't matter—the privacy and wellbeing of my victims weren't priority. And the others, besides Mu, never cared for their secrets.

Betraying Bianca's trust was my biggest fear.

But if there was a way to control my ability, to help her through what pertained to her *at this moment*, then I could do this without guilt.

Well, mostly. But how—

"I'll come with you," Miles continued, contemplation on his expression as he answered my unspoken question.

If my hands had been free, I'd have pinched my nose. So he had no plan. "We have no idea how this works. You might not be able to use your abilities at all."

"He might," Damen interjected, stepping toward the bed. "Bianca was able to do it when she went into Lily's memories with you."

"She did *what?*" Gregory asked, but Damen waved him off.

"You're the one who confirmed she was using her abilities." Damen sounded almost accusing as he crossed his arms. "Why did we never think to combine them before?"

"Because it's dangerous and completely illogical. It could have seriously harmed her." My heart raced at the recollection. "We had no reason to assume it *would* work."

I'd never been so afraid before. When she crossed the room, holding on to me at the worst possible moment, my world had stopped. Until the darkness cleared, I had no idea what had happened to her. And when I arrived at the other realm with Bianca was safe beside me, it was as if a thousand pounds had been lifted from my shoulders.

"We can do it." Miles sat down at Bianca's other side. He raised his hand, brushing back a lock of her hair. Even though he spoke to me, his attention was all for her. His expression might have made me jealous in any other situation, but because it was him, I wasn't. "Do your work, and I'll keep you on track."

It felt strange standing over Bianca's sleeping form intending to use my abilities on her. She looked vulnerable, and—since she was sleeping again—almost peaceful. Knowing that I would invade a world that would not match that added to my inner conflict.

I had *promised*.

But she was suffering. She was all alone, facing her demons with no one beside her.

But not for much longer.

"Ready?" Miles stood beside me, holding my blade. I'd already suffered the bitter-tasting drink. Such ritual was unnecessary, of course. I could invade a person's thoughts by only my effort. But Miles's concoctions helped my focus, in hopefully the same manner that his presence would continue to do.

"As I'll ever be." I sighed, taking the knife. My focus was growing sharper, colors brighter. A faint buzzing had begun in my ears.

"Get in, find Bianca, and get out." Titus was straddling the chair at Bianca's vanity, his arms linked over the back and his gaze unwavering from us. He'd been silent throughout most of the conversation and our planning, but now he seemed inclined to join.

Damen frowned at him. "That's what they are going to do."

"And no snooping around," Titus continued, ignoring Damen. "You made a promise. She'll probably be angry at you."

My jaw locked. The heavy sensation of my power washed over me.

"I know." It felt as though I was underwater. The world was sluggish—a familiar sensation for when I drew upon my abilities. "I'm not Damen."

"Hey!" Damen protested, but there was no chance to respond.

I glanced back to Bianca, resolution settling in. A dark wave crashed over my senses as I drew the blade across my palm.

There was no pain, only the euphotic pulse of power. The words came naturally to me, the ritualistic phrases unnecessary but habitual.

A breath later, the room faded around me.

After the darkness cleared and the ground steadied under my feet, my gaze was immediately drawn toward the only living inhabitant of the room.

Bianca.

She was young in this memory, no older than four. And I knew it was her upon sight, even with her back to me. She played with a small doll with button eyes and red yarn for hair, and she hummed under her breath.

There were voices barely discernable from elsewhere in the house. But I couldn't make out anything they said. Not that it mattered, not in this moment. That wasn't why I was here.

"Where is this?" Miles said mildly, not sounding perturbed to be travelling in a memory for the first time in his life.

I ignored him. It was Bianca who held my complete focus. Before I realized it, I was beside her.

Nausea stuck at the base of my throat. She was going to be so angry. But it was too late to back out now.

"It's fine." Miles stood behind me. "You're in control, right?"

I nodded. From the beginning of this, all my focus—my attention—had been on locating a memory that would benefit Bianca's current predicament.

But it still didn't make the guilt easier to bear.

However, the sight in front of me helped slightly. My heart slowed and panic receded.

She looked and acted *normal*. This wasn't anything like what I'd imagined.

Titus told us about Kieran. She'd been *relatively* safe before he died.

But it was different seeing her before the events of her life had broken her.

Bianca giggled and rocked the doll. She was smiling so widely that her face seemed to glow. A stone seemed to settle in my stomach and my breathing caught. Miles also hissed in a breath, so he'd seen it too.

She never smiled like that around us.

"Bianca," a woman's voice rang through the room. And as I looked, a presence shimmered into focus some feet away. This was a memory, and these moments were the only time where I could experience abilities besides my own.

She had waist-length, curly brown hair, and an elegant posture. And I knew without question that I was looking at the spirit of Alyssa Dubois.

"Aly!" Bianca smiled at her mother, dropping the doll on the floor as she jumped to her feet.

She crossed the room with her arms outstretched, but stopped when Alyssa held out her hand. The woman wore a stern expression and my heart ached as Bianca's steps slowed, disappointment heavy in her expression as her gaze turned to the floor.

"Sorry," she said.

Alyssa sighed, sadness softening the stern set of her jaw. "Don't be sorry, little one." She crossed the room, kneeling in front of Bianca. Her hands raised, as if she was going to touch her daughter's shoulders but then she bit her lip and dropped her hands to her sides. "Just remember, no touching."

Why was she lying? Alyssa Dubois knew Bianca would be able to touch, and be touched, by spirits. It was an ability that Mu had always had from birth.

Then Alyssa spoke, her voice leaving a heavy weight in the room. "What are the rules?"

"You were gone a long time." Bianca sniffled. "I missed you."

"I know Bianca, and I've missed you too." Alyssa folded her hands into her lap. "But that's not what I asked. Before we play, I need to know you understand this. Look at me," she demanded, waiting until Bianca's watery eyes raised to meet her own.

"What are the rules?" she asked again.

"Don't touch." Her little fists clenched in front of her as she repeated Alyssa's earlier statement.

"That's right. You must *never* touch a ghost, and don't ever let them touch you." Alyssa nodded.

"But why?" Bianca tilted her head, the tears drying up.

"What's the second rule?" Alyssa ignored her question.

"Not all ghosts are good," Bianca responded. "If one feels scary, run away."

"That's right," Alyssa said. "A normal spirit will feel non-threatening. But there are those who can hurt you. And you're not old enough to defend yourself."

"Who will hurt me?" Bianca asked, frowning.

"You'll learn as you get older. Kieran will teach you." Alyssa's gaze never wavered from her daughter. "But until you're taught, it's safest to assume that all non-human spirits are demons. Don't ever trust them."

Well, that explained her feelings toward Kasai and Kiania.

"Now, what's the third rule?" Alyssa asked.

Bianca bit her lip, glancing down at her doll before looking back to Alyssa. "I want to play."

"In a minute, Bianca." There was a frown in her voice. "Now tell me, what's the third rule?"

I cursed as the ground fell out from under me when Bianca opened her mouth to answer. I wouldn't count on Bianca coming forward with the 'rules' she'd been given any time soon. But the memory was over—I'd gotten what I'd come for. Bianca had known her mother, even though she hadn't been aware.

Before I could lose my focus, I grasped the next thread of light.

It was raining. The sun was setting, and in the distance, a small, white farmhouse stood alone in the middle of a sloping landscape. Mountains and woods, with an explosion of color, surrounded the area. It was autumn, and the leaves were changing. Frost covered the grass.

However, this was a memory, so Miles and I were unaffected by the chilly air. The rain, also, we were unable to feel.

But the sudden fear that caused my heart to jerk painfully was enough.

"Bianca!" Miles moved to step past me, only stopping when I grabbed at him.

"This isn't reality," I reminded him. "There's nothing you can do about what happens next."

Miles hissed in a breath, his arm shaking under my hold. "Fuck your abilities," he muttered.

I silently agreed. Now, more than any other time in my recollections, I wanted to intervene.

Bianca stood at the edge of a pond, enamoured. She watched the surface as the darkness grew. But what she couldn't see—what was so clear to Miles and myself—was the demon standing across the water.

We could only hear the music because *she* could, otherwise the sound would have been unnoticeable to us. Adults, after all, were unaware of the call of the piper. The water rippled from where Bianca stood, and I knew—from legends—that she was captivated by the creature's illusions.

There were many demons that lured children to their deaths, and every one had their own reasons. Lonliness, revenge, or evil intentions. I wasn't certain of this one's history—this fell more into Bianca and Damen's realms of expertise—but it was easy to see that it wanted Bianca dead. And once it achieved its goal, it would devour her soul. Add it to his collection.

I glanced around the darkening space, fury lacing though me. Where was Kieran? Hadn't someone else been in the house, too? Multiple people had been speaking in Bianca's earlier memory.

Why was she out here alone? He was supposed to be protecting her!

Bianca moved, dipping her toe into the water and remaining unaware of the danger she was in. My heart raced.

I couldn't do anything. It wouldn't matter even if I tried. Everything had already happened, and she was alive now.

This was only a memory.

But then—unlike any other entranced child—Bianca paused. A second later, she glanced up. There was no fear in her gaze, only mild curiousity as she spoke to the giant, long-limbed kappa. "Why?"

The creature's yellow eyes popped open, and it lowered the reed flute. It's shoulders dropped as it's mouth thinned. Clearly it'd never been questioned before. "You can see me?"

"You're lonely," Bianca said, clutching the doll to her chest. "But you have people with you. So why are you sad?"

"It's not enough," he said, raising the flute back to his lips. "I have to fulfill my contract." He seemed to say the second statement more for himself than her and after, began to play the instrument once more.

But to Bianca, the magic had been lost. Possibly because she was aware of his presence.

"I can't go with you," Bianca interrupted his song. "I'm not allowed. I need to go home now."

He paused, eyes narrowing, limbs tensing.

"I'm sorry you're sad though," she said, turning away from the demon. "Goodbye."

She hadn't even taken a step before the monster moved. The flute was thrown aside, and he lunged across the surface of the water, claw-like fingers reaching for Bianca.

"I only need one more," he screeched. "Just the one. I'll drag you with me myself, I don't care."

My throat closed, and I stepped forward despite myself as the demon reached Bianca and wrapped his fingers around her neck. He couldn't have known it would work, his reaction reeked of desperation. There was no way he'd have known he could touch her.

However, he didn't let his surprise stop him from continuing his assault.

Instead, he smiled.

She dropped the doll, reaching for the hands that held her. Fear barely had time to enter her expression before she was pulled backward into the shallow end of the water.

She was drowning.

Everything else fell from existance as the kappa's face transformed into something even far more sinister and dark. The creature remained unmoved as Bianca flailed, trying to escape. To breathe.

I held my breath as her movements slowed and his teeth bared.

He didn't win. Bianca was—relatively—safe with us, in the present.

But how? No one was here to help her. Any longer and—

A whirlwind of movement rushed past us, and the demon was thrown back. A second later, Alyssa carried Bianca to the shore, throwing a dark glance in the direction where the creature had fallen.

But when it didn't resurface, she turned her focus back toward her daughter.

"Bianca..." She slapped the smaller girl's cheek, unable to attempt anything else. "Bianca, you're okay? Wake up." Her statement came out as both a desperate question and command.

At first, Bianca didn't stir. Then even though I expected it, I let out a sigh of relief as she finally gagged and began to cough.

Next to me, Miles started cursing under his breath.

Alyssa's hands shook, and she dropped all pretenses as she threw herself at her daughter, pulling the smaller girl into her lap. "You're okay, baby," she kept repeating. "You're okay."

Bianca's eyes slowly blinked open, and she looked up. "Aly?"

"I love you so much." Alyssa peppered Bianca's face with kisses. "I love you."

Bianca brows furrowed in confusion. She seemed too disoriented to even notice that Alyssa was holding her. "I was bad."

"No, you weren't, baby," Alyssa insisted. "It's not your fault."

"But—"

"I love you." Alyssa held Bianca back from her. "Now, go back and find Kieran. He's still bespelled. Wake him up and—"

Her sentence cut off with a gasp. She didn't need to breathe, of course, but demons could feel spirits as easily as one human could touch another. And having a hand thrust through your back would shock anyone.

Bianca blinked, still dazed as she stared up at her mother. "Aly?"

"I only need one more," the kappa growled, pulling his hand back. With the movement, Alyssa was thrown from Bianca, who had been released in that moment. The demon snatched the spirit's limp form in midair, smiling his toothy grin. "And I don't care who it is anymore."

Then he dove under the water, taking the spirit of Alyssa Dubois with him.

I had no control of when my abilities decided to shift between memories. My work relied on following the thought patterns of my subjects. The longer I stayed in someone's mind, the more difficult it was to focus—to control the direction of my power.

The echo of a thousand memories passed over me, overlapping as they all fought for my attention. The threads of each memory surrounded me—all equally important. What was I looking for? I didn't remember.

But why was I hesitating? Why was my heart aching?

The noise grew louder, almost painful against the pounding in my head. The memories brushed against my senses. What was I supposed to do?

I reached for one. But my chest felt heavy, and my finger twitched.

Why was I hesitating?

"Stay focused," Miles's voice thundered through my head. With it, walls rose from the ground, enclosing the flow of my abilities, and I was no longer free.

My bearings returned, and the thread pulled from my grip, fading away. The buzzing began to fade until I, at last, stood alone with Miles. The barriers fell.

"I did it…" My throat felt raw. I'd never resisted a memory before—usually a session ended when there were no questions left, or—in cases of working with older remains and objects—there was nothing left that could be told.

"With my help," Miles pointed out.

Now that clarity had returned, shame filled me. The memory I'd been about to enter had nothing to do with why we were here. Of course, I wouldn't know what it entailed until I'd actually seen it. But I knew it in my heart.

"Thank you." I pressed my head against Miles shoulder. "I couldn't have done it without you."

He cleared his throat and stumbled over his words. As if he was surprised I'd actually thanked him at all. "No problem. Are we done? I want to get out of here."

"Yes." The pinpricks of lights still tempted me, but I could hold back my power now. There was nothing left that stood out as being helpful for our purpose. I touched Miles's shoulder, meeting his gaze.

He looked tired.

"We'll go back together," I told him. "Let me just…"

My words trailed off and his eyes widened as the dark space flashed in an explosion of white. An electric sensation passed over me, and when the brightness faded, he was gone.

And so was the emptiness. Now the space had been filled with life: trees, moss—wildness.

"Miles?" My limbs felt strange, and my voice different. I glanced at my hands—they were lighter, and the skin scarred across the knuckles. But it still took another moment for me to reorient myself, to fall back into the familiarity of my first form.

Well, this hadn't happened in a while. But why now?

"I sent him back first." The familiar words of our ancient language washed over me, and the words were almost accusing. "Did you find what you were searching for?"

Mu.

My heart jumped into my throat, and guilt filled me at the presence of the other man.

I shouldn't have been surprised that he was here, this was his consciousness, too. But I hadn't been ready. And thousands of years later, the sound of his voice still caused a shiver to run down my spine.

A gentle breeze blew through the glen, causing his long chestnut hair to gently sway behind him. His emerald robes contrasted brightly against his pale skin. And his jade eyes knowingly—and judgmentally—held mine.

His thick brows furrowed and he frowned. "We had an agreement."

"I apologize." The accusation stabbed at me. "I was running out of options. I needed to see—"

"I know what you needed." Mu's response was curt, but then his jaw tightened. A look that I knew to be regret lined his face. "And in this case, exceptions had to be made…"

My heart began to race.

Normally, Mu would have lectured me at the very least. Or at least pouted a while. But now he seemed resigned. This was unlike him. "You're not angry?"

"Not at you," he said, studying his hand. "This was just… unexpected. Though it changes nothing. Once again, you've pushed me outside of my comfort zone, and you were right for it. You usually are."

This was new.

"But you know, you need to keep pushing me. I'm not going to break," Mu said lightly. "I could never hold a grudge against you for very long. You're one of the few who seems to be immune to that."

"I'm not worried about that," I replied. Although it was a lie, because I was worried. Yet there was another reason why I'd been avoiding this moment. "It's just that—"

"You think *she'll* break," Mu said knowingly. "You know, we *are* the same person."

"It's not the same as dealing with you…" How could he say such a thing? "She's tiny, frail, and has been through so much—"

"That's correct." Mu nodded. "But she's stronger than you credit her. We've survived without your meddling for years."

I flinched. His statement almost sounded like an accusation. Especially since Bianca had said the same thing herself.

She didn't *need* us to survive. She'd already proven that.

"You've been up to something." This might be my only chance to ask for a while. "Tell me what you're hiding. Let me in, and I can help…"

Mu's smile caused me to trail off.

There was something almost broken in that expression, but his eyes glittered with a hint of his ever-present mischievousness. "I don't think so. I've gotten it under control."

That tipped me off, and realization dawned. "You *chose* to be born as a female…"

"Well, we *can* choose aspects of our forms." He raised his eyebrows.

"But *why*?" At the curious tilt of his head, my words continued to stumble out. It was embarrassing, and heat raised to my face. "Not that I'm complaining, I rather *like* your current form. But I assumed it was a random accident. You're *fae*. You know how women are seen in your world. What possessed you to come back as one?"

"Prophecies are tricky things…" he mused, his attention drifting past me. "And sometimes change can be good for everyone involved."

I frowned, my every sense on high alert. I loathed when he got into these moods. "What are you plotting?"

"You know who doesn't like change?" Mu continued, ignoring my question. "Quite a few people actually. Dragons especially."

"So why are you a woman? To fulfill the prophecy, or to annoy Jin?" I asked.

"No, I'll leave that to Tu. He and Jin secretly enjoy their bickering." Mu waved his hand in the air, unperturbed. Then his mood shifted, and his eyes flashed. "But be serious, who do you think my new form throws off the most?"

Suddenly, it made sense and my jaw locked. "Huo. What are you plotting?"

I asked again, annoyance flaring through me. He'd come back as Bianca to annoy *Damen*?

"You're going to need to let go of that resentment." Mu frowned.

He was in no position to judge me. "Only when he stops acting like this," I replied.

"Your hatred of him is affecting how you treat other onmyoji." He pointed out, not incorrectly. "Which clouds your judgement in regards to myself."

Finn's smug expression flashed across my mind, and the urge to murder him swelled within me. "I don't want to."

He'd lied to Bianca. He hurt her—and I didn't care about his reasons. He made her *cry*. There was no excuse. The only way he could be forgiven was after his skewered head stood on display. And then, only maybe.

Chapter Thirty-One

Bianca
Tower

I was slowly falling through a bottomless space. It seemed like forever and the weight of the air kept me in stasis. I was trapped inside of my own mind.

I felt nothing—no embarrassment or discomfort. Instead my body and thoughts were numb. I was aware of existence, but just. Nothing mattered.

My emotions were locked away in a safe place and nothing painful or sad could reach me here.

"Bianca."

My eyes drifted open, and a spark of recognition broke through the static. Why was this voice familiar? A feeling swelled in my chest—curiosity. But at the same time, I almost was afraid to learn more.

"What are you still doing here?" A warmth surrounded me, and the voice echoed through the space—formless and disjoined.

My heart raced at the accusation in his tone and feeling seeping back into me. An anger swelled in my chest—annoyance flaring toward the entity which threatened my peace. "Leave me alone."

"You're stagnating," Mu said, causing another shiver to rush through me. "This is not what we were born to become."

"Mind your own business." I was arguing with myself. Or was I?

We weren't the same, and I wasn't him. Damen had said so earlier. Even if we were reincarnations, I was still *me*. And I wasn't strong enough to—

"Yes, you are *you*," Mu said. Somehow, I could almost visualize him. He probably looked like a *Lord of the Rings* elf—all regal and beautiful. Possibly all-knowing and wise.

What a pretentious jerk.

"But you were born with the knowledge, hopes, and dreams of every Wood Xing that has ever existed." If he knew my thoughts, he ignored them. "You're you, and you're also all of us."

"That's stupid…" I muttered. "And extremely confusing."

"Focus," he demanded, and the space shifted.

I blinked, studying the ground that had risen up under my feet.

Yes, this was definitely Mu's doing. The stupid man seemed to have a propensity for fairy-land forests. The mossier the better. He stood in front of me, the sight familiar and startling.

Was he wearing a crown? And those billowing clothes. They were green, of course, and with what appeared to be golden, leaf-patterned trim along the hems. But even more important was the length of his hair. I had thought Kiania's seemed hard to manage.

"You've come to claim your birthright," he said.

So, he was a drama queen. I was so not surprised.

I glanced down at myself—I'd been cloaked in the same ridiculous outfit, except it was swimming on me. But that was far from a concern at the moment.

"I don't think so." I frowned. After sampling a taste of his power before, I was no longer interested. I was more than happy to just stay with the boys, hiding in obscurity.

I would stay married to Bryce forever.

"You really don't have a choice," Mu said, dropping his hand back to his side. "One of the hardest things is to watch everyone else make a mess. The others need you."

Darn it. My shoulders dropped as the argument fell from me.

"They are pretty clueless," I grumbled, remembering Damen's terrible plans. Then there was Bryce, who just needed so much guidance. And Miles. Poor Miles who needed someone to push him to be his best self.

Yet doubt filled me, causing my chest to ache.

"I can't help anyone." I looked at Mu. "I'm not *you*, I'm damaged. I'm not brave enough. I can't go back." But why couldn't I go back? I couldn't remember. What happened?

But if Mu *was* in my head, if he had been my whole life, it meant something else too.

I couldn't trust him.

"Why didn't you stop it?" I asked.

So much had been packed into that question I was afraid he'd not understand.

But I didn't need to explain further. From the slight downturn of his lips and the lowering of his head, he knew.

"Why didn't you just take over, or whatever it was that you did when I was fighting Daniel Cole?" I accused. "You could have saved me, and now I'm all messed up. This is all *your* fault."

"You are *you*," he repeated in that sage-like way that made me want to punch him in the face. "No matter which life, we're limited in how much we can assist. Because you're *us*."

"But—" That made absolutely zero sense.

"When you fought against the witch, I only helped." Mu tilted his head, studying me. "But you surely know that. When do you plan to tell the others?"

"Tell them what?" I snapped.

He didn't seem to take offense. "That you know how to fight. Kieran taught you basic exercises. I may have started it, but you carried out the movements in the end."

My face flooded with heat, and I pressed my hands against my cheeks. No one had known, not even after seeing the video.

I felt so guilty.

"I'm not very good at it." I glanced at the floor. "It's been a long time. I was only five when—"

"It's enough," Mu responded. "There's the potential for something more. Just like Spring."

I glanced at him. "Pardon?"

"*Mu*," he replied, holding out his hand. In it was a dead daffodil. But as I watched, it regained its yellow color and sprung back to life. "Wood. *Us*. We're the representative of Spring. Rebirth, flexibility, strength, and life. It's not in your nature to be stagnant."

"I'm not stagnant." How offensive. I'd worked so very hard to avoid that accusation. "I've moved on with my life. I'm *fine*. It's everyone else who seems to have a problem. Not me."

"You're okay?" Mu open his hand, dropping the flower. It disappeared before it hit the ground. "Is that why Shui is rummaging around in your head?"

"He's *what*?" I covered my mouth, but it wasn't enough to prevent my squeaky outburst. "What if he sees something secret? You're in my head too, right?" I glared at him. How could he allow this? "Go smite him. Get him out."

"He hasn't seen anything besides what you'd share if you could, but currently cannot communicate." Mu tilted his head, studying me. "Don't worry, I've locked away our deepest thoughts. Everything else remains a mystery, and he won't search anymore. He's gotten what he needed."

I was going to throttle Julian.

"Which was *what*?" I growled. "Why am I here?"

"That's the question. Why *are* you here, if you've moved on?" Mu asked. "Avoiding the problem isn't healing, and it causes the issue to fester in your mind and poison your soul. Before you can truly move on, you need to confront your past."

The bravado seeped from me. What was he saying? "I can't…"

"Take it one day at a time." He waved his hand and the ground faded from beneath my feet. However, instead of falling, this time I floated in place. "Confrontation of the current issue is a good place to begin, I think."

And with that, the white lights faded to black.

This time I found myself in a circular room. Stone walls surrounded me on all sides, barring a tiny window to my right. There were no doors, and—upon peeking out the window—no way down from this tower besides a disastrous-looking fall.

There was no point in jumping, this time I doubted I'd float.

"My own subconscious is trying to kill me…" I fell to my knees in front of the low window, and from this position I could see the happy looking sky above my prison.

Stupid Mu. Why would he trap me here? I hated him. Perhaps there was a way to purge him from my soul.

"Bianca?" Julian's voice drifted up to me.

At first, I was certain I'd misheard. But at his second attempt, I pushed myself up, pulling my upper body out of the window in order to see the base of the tower.

"Julian?" He was frowning up at me, and I blinked at him. What was this? Were we still in my head? Was he?

That sounded weird.

"Why are you up there?" he asked.

"I'm stargazing," I said, narrowing my eyes. I hadn't forgotten that he'd jumped into my memories. Lord only knew what he'd seen. It was too humiliating to face him, and anger still burned in me. "Seemed like a good idea at the time."

His gaze turned to the cloudless sky, before finally returning to me. "Darling…" His voice was unsure. "That's not the real sky. Secondly… Well, it's daytime."

"I know that!" My face heated and I ducked under the edge of the window. Pressing my cheek against the stones, I began to count my breaths.

I couldn't face him. He had seen—

"Bianca, can you look at me please?" His voice had returned to the measured calm with which I was so familiar. "I want to talk to you."

"No. I don't want to talk to you." My racing heart was echoing with force in my throat. Mu was a moron. I didn't have to face anything. "I'm just going to stay up here forever."

"You will, if you don't snap out of it." Julian's tone changed slightly. There was something darker, more commanding in his voice that had never been present in the past. "You've locked yourself away, trying to escape the world around you. But you can't hide for the rest of your life."

"Watch me." The coldness of the rough stones began to numb my face. "You're not even supposed to be here anyway," I muttered, closing my eyes.

A scratching sound pulled at the edge of my senses, but I didn't move. I was just so tired.

"You're not allowed to hide from me."

Julian's voice came from above me, and I screamed, jumping back from the wall. I landed ungracefully on my butt as I clutched at my chest, willing my heart to slow.

He had, *somehow*, scaled the building. And now was crouched in the window, his head tilted as he studied me. "Are you all right?"

"You scared me! How in the world did you climb up here?"

He raised his eyebrow, briefly glancing behind him, down the tower, before he returned his attention to me. "I'm an assassin," he said slowly.

"That's what you say." I didn't believe it. Outside of him punching Finn, I'd yet to see him harm even a fly. Besides, he was a vegetarian—which meant that he held some regard for all living things. "So that means you can climb walls like a *ninja*?"

His lips pressed in a line and he remained in silence, his eyebrow slowly rising as he continued to watch me in that same unnerving way. And now that he was here, it was easier to tell.

It was Julian in front of me, yet it wasn't fully him either. There was something dark in his gaze, something deep and ancient. Different than the Julian I'd come to know.

"Who are you?" I asked.

"Julian." His voice moved over me, deep and melodious. "But, at the moment, I'm also Shui. The veil that separates us is thinner in the astral realm."

"How can that—"

"Have you spoken with Mu? Being here would make it easier for him to connect to you." He tilted his head. "You seem braver now."

"I am not brave," I protested, crossing my arms. I was still on the floor, my feet straight out in front of me and the skirt of the green robes bunched around my knees.

"You are," he said, a hint of the old Julian returning to his voice. "Before, you would never argue with me, but now you're not afraid."

"Why are you in my head?" I frowned at him. Did he think I was going to rush into his arms after he'd done the exact opposite of what he promised? "I know what you did. I am very angry at you. I am going to push you right out of that window."

"You're extremely violent when you're not scared." Julian stroked his chin, studying me. "Now we need to take that energy and redirect it to your real life. Do you remember why you ran away?"

What was he talking about?

"I—" I'd started to protest, but then recollection slammed into me, taking my breath away.

Ah.

All this time, I'd known my mother. And I'd never known. From my earliest memories, she'd been there. She was the one who taught me everything I knew about spirits—despite being one herself. She saved me.

Then she was devoured by a demon because I hadn't been strong enough. She'd told me to never follow a bad spirit, but I hadn't even noticed until it was too late.

I could never go back. I couldn't face Bryce and Brayden. And there was no way I could meet my biological father now, even if I wanted to. How could I ever tell my family that my mother's spirit *wasn't* at peace, and it was entirely my fault?

Julian's presence washed over me, and I blinked back the dots of darkness that had been swarming in my vision. I'd been on the verge of fainting, and I hadn't even realized.

Was it even possible to faint right now?

"It's not your fault," he whispered in my ear. "No one is going to blame you."

The force of his words resonated through me. Both humiliation and fear warred for dominance. He sounded so certain—he'd been looking through my memories.

What did he see?

"Julian?" I was almost afraid to ask.

"Miles helped me," he explained, his hands rubbing circles on my back. "I searched only for the memories to help you pull out of this. It's something your subconsciousness wanted to communicate but couldn't."

That didn't make me feel any better, and I pressed my cheek against his chest. His heartbeat echoed loudly against my ear—he was nervous. Possibly more than me. It was that knowledge which steadied my emotions.

When I didn't respond, he continued, his voice unsure. "We saw a scene where Alyssa met you and went over some rules." He paused, but only briefly. "Then we saw what happened that night, with the water demon."

"That's what it was?" I felt numb again. "I wasn't sure."

"It was a kappa, technically," Julian responded. "This particular one was a cross between a water demon and one that collected children. It probably had another contract elsewhere. It would lure children to their deaths and eat their souls. You broke out of his spell, which even being *you*, was unheard of. No one has ever escaped."

"So, she really is gone." I'd never seen her after that day, so I'd always assumed. "She's been eaten."

His movements slowed, and his voice was soft. "Possibly," he answered, and I was thankful he wouldn't lie. "But we didn't see what happened after the demon left. Was there anything else?"

I shook my head, pressing my face into his chest.

I would never forget that night. I watched the water for what felt like forever. And it wasn't until the moon was high before Kieran came rushing to my side.

He'd only been that angry on one other occasion.

"I'm still mad at you," I muttered, my thoughts distracted.

"I'm sorry, but it's been two days," Julian said. "You weren't getting any better. Gregory has been told who you are, and he and Bryce were on the verge of taking you to the hospital—or to Whisperwind, your family's home. We were trying to think of anything we could do to prevent that. It was becoming a life-or-death situation."

I shivered. The *hospital?* Waking up there would have killed me.

And even if I had pulled myself out of this, they would want to know what happened. I wasn't even sure I could put my experience into words.

So really, this was a safe, logical fix. I'd even given Julian permission to jump into my memories before, sort of. Yet it was so hard to move forward.

"I'm still mad"—my resolve had weakened—"but I'll get over it."

I should be used to disappointment. Nobody was perfect, not even these men. It made sense I'd get hurt eventually. Maybe it wasn't on purpose, but I couldn't stop how I felt.

Julian swallowed and his frame trembled. "Bianca—"

"I don't care anymore," I lied, pushing against his chest. "Let's go back."

"Bianca, I'm sorry." He sounded tortured. But was he really? They had wanted to know about my past. "We didn't know what else to do. Look at me, please."

His voice pulled at me, and I glanced up, opening myself for whatever he might have to say. I was so tired of fighting.

If we were going to be stuck together for the rest of our lives, I would have to talk to him at some point. So, really, there was no harm in hearing him out.

But when my gaze locked with Julian's, everything around us faded.

A shiver shot down my spine, and a hundred thousand feelings washed over me.

Julian's emotions.

Brayden had warned me this would happen, but why now?

My pondering faded away as the warmth of adoration—love—warmed my skin. There was a genuine, compassionate sincerity to his feelings, which ran so deep they almost took my breath away.

However, he also radiated self-loathing and doubt. My chest felt heavy from the weight of it.

How could I have thought so little of him? I was used to being lied to and manipulated. It was something I expected. But with Julian, there was no dishonesty or darkness in his motives.

This was Julian—raw and exposed. He held nothing back, and his presence filled me with a strength I normally wouldn't possess. He didn't care if this openness made him vulnerable.

His face wavered in my vision.

No—my breath caught—he wasn't entirely benevolent either. While he held no ill intentions toward me, I could now sense the part of him he'd so carefully concealed.

He was powerful, but there was a loneliness and zealous nature to him, held at a depth that couldn't be reached by the light. He didn't want to do the things he'd done, but he would suffer through them—for me.

"It's okay." The last of my anger faded. I pushed to my knees, never breaking eye-contact, and touched his face. "I understand. I'm not angry." And this time, I meant it.

"Bianca, I love you," he said, running his hands down my arms. His tone was desperate, and the pain of it sunk into my bones, and his anxiety was almost contagious. "In every life we've shared, I've felt this way. I only want you safe. If it helps, I can—"

My heart raced as our lips collided and his warmth washed over me. His hair was soft and his sensual mouth moved like silk under mine.

Again, I had made the first move on one of the boys. But Julian's earnest plea had been impossible to ignore. My body, and my heart, had been pulled toward him at the flood of his emotions. My fingers tangled in his curly hair. He tasted like the ocean, and the sensation of his chest against mine was electrifying. I poured the last ounce of courage into this moment.

Because it wasn't something I could repeat anytime soon. Butterflies fluttered in my stomach, but—already—the skin at the back of my neck prickled.

With that—as awareness stirred in Julian and his touch, which had moved to my shoulders, dropped away—I pushed back.

His cheeks had darkened, and his expression was clouded in a sense of bewilderment. But through that, wariness and concern radiated from him. "Bianca—"

"Stop." I pressed my fingers to his lips. My pulse soared. His admission continued to ring through my head. "It's fine, I can feel you."

Chapter Thirty-Two

Bianca
Emotion

"You can really feel my emotions? I'd hoped…" Julian's uncertainty fled, and barely restrained joy filled its place. "You decided to accept your role?"

"What do you mean?" Hadn't I always?

Nothing had changed in the last ten minutes. I'd only decided to stop running.

"The empath of the quintet completes the group," Julian said. "It is when they accept their position they're able to pick up on the other's emotions."

I frowned at him, feeling slightly hurt. That wasn't fair, I'd been accepting from the beginning. "I've always been on board."

Julian shook his head, his eyes fierce. "You need to *trust* your quintet. To expose a part of yourself that you never normally would. You haven't been ready for that step, but we were waiting for you to settle before discussing it."

This was both good and bad. Brayden was right on how this feeling worked. It *was* easy to distinguish Julian's emotions from my own. They were something that radiated *at* me, rather than from in me. And it was different than the brush of emotions that one experienced from a spirit.

But seriously, I might not be ready for this.

"How is this different than what you do?" I wondered.

Julian cocked his head. "A Water elemental can read emotions by sensing and interpreting the body's reaction to a situation. We need to be touching the person we are reading. So, technically, we are empaths—in a way. But your work isn't tied to the physical body like mine is. Your focus is another level of existence. That's why you can feel the emotions of people you're spiritually linked to, and ghosts."

I wasn't used to this. And Brayden had said I would need to master my own emotions first. "Am I going to feel everyone's emotions now?"

"No." Julian emanated glee though his expression was masked. "You have to make a connection with each person, individually. It looks like I'm the first."

"Lucky you." I never took him for the childish sort, but he didn't even try to hide his pride. "You're not going to go brag about it, are you?"

"No." He was lying, and his mouth curled up in the corner. "I won't say a word."

Somehow, I had a feeling he wouldn't have to *say* anything.

My thoughts drifted back to my make-out session with Damen. And my heart dropped. There was another hurdle to overcome—because now I couldn't blame him for that promiscuous display. That had been *all* me.

Darn it.

And then, what would Damen—and the others—think about this new development?

"I don't want anyone to get jealous," I warned him.

He sighed and pulled me into his arms—ignoring my squeak of protest. "They'll get over it," he muttered into my hair. "They should be used to it, anyway. I've always been the first. Without you, there's literally no other reason for me to exist."

I clenched my fist against his chest and fought the butterflies in my stomach. Because while the admission was romantic, well…

Wasn't this the very definition of codependency? "That's not very healthy."

He grinned against my ear. "Yes, you've never been one for flowery words. I've been amusing myself lately, imagining what you've been really thinking about Damen's flirtations—"

Well, that wasn't fair. I only thought kind things.

"—and it brings me great joy to know that aspect of you hasn't changed."

I could hear the racing of his heart, and my cheek was warm as I rested my face against his chest. It was quiet, and the room grew darker as the daylight turned to dusk. How long had we even been here?

But the air between us soothed with contentment, and I didn't want this peace to end.

"We should go back." Julian sighed, running his fingers through my hair. "The others are probably worried."

Why did he have to ruin everything?

"I'm scared," I admitted.

"I know." Julian's movements stopped, concern heavy in his voice. "What are you scared of?" Before I could answer, he had already continued. "Do you think they'll blame you?"

I nodded. "You said it's not my fault, but—"

"Bianca," he interrupted. "What do you feel from me?"

Goose bumps broke out over me, and I shivered. It was cold, and I closed my eyes, pushing myself further into Julian's embrace. His pulse raced under my cheek, and I listened to his soft breath as my thoughts tentatively travelled over the emotions pouring off him.

But no matter how hard I focused; I couldn't find it.

Where was the disgust? The blame? Yet—

"You're angry," I pointed out. "You don't even look angry."

"I'm not angry at you," he said. "I'm angry at the situation. I'm angry that you were in that position, and at the creature responsible. I'm *extremely* angry about what's happened to you, and not only about what happened with Alyssa Dubois."

I shivered. Why was he continuing to ruin everything?

"I am not angry at *you*," he repeated. He sounded so certain, and his resolve echoed through me. "I know I don't look angry, and it's for a good reason. I've practice in hiding my feelings. I need to for my work. But don't think I'm hiding from you, because I'm not. And know this, no one—including Bryce and Brayden, or anyone else in that family—is going to blame you for what happened."

There was no hesitation or doubt. But still, I was concerned. "Are you sure?"

"I can't stop you from blaming yourself," he said—correctly guessing those concerns hadn't been driven from my mind. "But I *can* promise you they'll be more upset with *themselves* about the situation than they are with you."

But that wasn't fair—no one besides me had been there. "But—"

"The only way you'll know is by confronting it," Julian said, rising to his feet and pulling me with him. "Isn't it scarier to wonder what *might* happen rather than face what *will* happen? In most cases, a person's imagination is far harsher than reality."

Since when was *he* so wise? "Yes…" I grumbled.

"Like Bryce," Julian pointed out. "He's not so bad once you get used to him."

I shot him a dubious look—surely Julian wasn't trying to reassure me using *Bryce* as an example. "We still have our issues…"

He made a sound under his breath, and his smugness pulled at me. There were very few people in the world who were more annoying than Bryce.

Speaking of—

"What about Finn?" I rebutted. "He grows on you—like a strain of incredibly invasive bacteria destroying its host. I didn't even realize I'd been infected for the longest time. Are you saying he's not as bad as we imagined?"

Kiania had been telling me something of the sort.

The humor fled from Julian's expression, and there was no denying the coursing, hot anger that filled the air.

"No." His voice was clipped. "Finn is far worse than you can imagine. Damen has him around for monitoring purposes, but I want you to stay away from him. You've only witnessed a portion of what he's like when he loses control. And with the bond with Kiania the way it is, who knows how this has affected him."

That didn't make any sense. I'd seen Finn angry before. What could be worse? "What—"

My question was cut off as the world fell out from under my feet.

I woke with a gasp, choking as a coughing fit ransacked my body. Warm hands moved over me, and someone pulled me into a seated position as they pounded on my back. Then once my breathing had evened out, the hands proceeded to poke and prod at me.

The bright light hurt my eyes, and I covered my face. "S-s-stop!"

There was a rustle, and suddenly Damen's warm skin pressed against mine. He'd crawled onto the bed, pulling me against him.

Everything hurt.

My throat was raw, and my skin felt dry and brittle. I'd been changed into another nightgown at some point, and the fabric was rough against my skin.

It felt as though I'd been dragged over gravel. It hadn't been like this the last time Julian used his powers.

"Welcome back." Dr. Reed's dry greeting was the only other sound in the room. "Especially considering the circumstances. Just how long were you expecting to be gone?" She sounded almost disappointed, and terribly angry.

I'd never heard her sound like this toward *me* before.

I lowered my hands, peeking at her over my fingers, to note that she hadn't been talking to me at all. Instead, her attention was on Julian, who was blearily blinking himself into wakefulness in a plush red chair at the foot of the bed.

What happened? When Julian used his powers before, it didn't seem like any time had passed. But from Dr. Reed's sharp words, that wasn't the case this time. And—unlike then, Julian was dazed too.

Confusion rippled through the space between us, and our gazes briefly locked. His blue eyes were uncharacteristically brighter than usual as the remnants of his power faded. "How long—"

"I arrived shortly after you began." Dr. Reed pursed her lips as she put her hands on her hips, the room chilled under the force of her anger. "Then Miles woke up, and you didn't. We had no idea what happened. It's been *hours*."

Julian opened his mouth to speak, but she turned to me, her stern expression fading. "And *you*." She pressed her lips in a thin line. "You've had us worried to death. What in the world happened?"

My breath caught, and on the tip of my tongue was my usual denial: 'Nothing happened', 'Everything is okay', or even 'It doesn't matter'. I could refuse to talk about it.

I could go back to my usual self, refusing to accept the reality directly in front of me, and live in fear of what might be.

But I was tired of living like that. I wanted to change.

"I'm sorry…" The audience was wider than I'd preferred, but there was no better moment. Besides, it would make it easier, not having to explain the same thing a million times. For the moment, the others faded from the room and I looked at Bryce, and despite what Julian had assured me, I was certain he'd blame me.

He stood a short distance away, halfway between the door and the bed. Watching me with a dispassionate indifference that caused my blood to grow colder.

I was certain he hated me. Well, even more than usual.

This went far beyond our rivalry.

"I didn't know until you showed me her picture," I said, hiding my shaking hands under the blankets. I felt exposed, as if a single harsh remark could shatter me. "But I met our mother before. She taught me about ghosts and gave me rules. She told me how to hide. She never told me who she was."

A crease had formed on his forehead, and his face darkened with ire. The first hint of emotion had broken through the surface of his blank expression. He was going to say something mean, I knew it. But I continued before he could interject.

I needed him to know *everything*.

"She was…" I wasn't even sure how to describe what happened: killed *again*, delivered to hell? "…eaten." Bryce's frown deepened, and my stomach lurched. "It was my fault. Something tried to kill me, and—"

"I know," he said. "Miles told us. That's not your fault."

"It's not," Brayden interjected, also crossing his arms and nodding sharply. The entire time, he'd been hovering near to his brother.

My words trailed off, and I blinked at them. I didn't need to explain?

"Her soul might still be safe." Dr. Stephens scratched his cheek, and my heart leapt into my throat. I hadn't even noticed him. He stood by Dr. Reed and, after his statement, stepped away from my bed. He didn't look at me as he pulled on his tweed jacket. "The entire situation doesn't sound right. Collectors usually work toward a greater purpose. They aren't destroyers."

"They kill children," Damen said dryly, still holding me against him.

Dr. Stephens shrugged. "That's not what I'm talking about. They don't care about destroying *souls*." His attention turned to me, and I shivered in response. Did this mean he knew? What was going to happen now?

My reaction hadn't gone unnoticed by Damen, who tightened his grip over my shoulders.

But Dr. Stephens only watched me curiously for an instant. Then he cocked his head and said with a disinterested tone, "You and I have a lot to discuss."

"You can have your discussion later." Dr. Reed stepped between us, blocking him from my view. "She only just woke up. And if you're quite finished hijacking my patient, I want all of you to get out."

Damen hissed in a breath, and I peeked at him. His angular jaw was covered with a dark stubble of unshaven days, and his expression was stubbornly set into a refusal. But despite that, his face was lined with the heavy lines of exhaustion.

The other men seemed similarly worn.

Julian still hadn't gathered his bearings, and his exhaustion was a tangible thing, broadcasted through the room. Miles was seated on the floor at his feet, dark circles under his eyes. Titus had been watching me since I'd woken up, but turned to Dr. Reed with an intense look that made me worry he might try to rip off her face.

They all looked ready to pass out, but Julian the most.

"And Julian, go to bed," Dr. Reed commanded, also noticing Julian's state.

Julian shook his head, instantly appearing more alert. "I'm not tired."

"Yes, he is. He's just pretending to be fine." I spoke before thinking of the implications.

The room seemed to hold its breath, and a long moment passed as everyone's attention returned to me. I shifted nervously, realizing my mistake a second too late. "It's true though," I protested, my voice wavering.

What else was I supposed to do? I just didn't want anyone to get jealous. Damen was already beginning to shake.

"Julian is my son," Dr. Reed said finally, brows furrowing and brown eyes gleaming. "I know when he's lying. But you—"

"You've accepted the bond!" Miles jumped to his feet, pushing past Dr. Reed as he almost jumped onto the bed. "That's awesome! I'll go next." He held out his wrist for me, eyes glistening with newfound excitement.

"Um…" I glanced at his wrist, then back to his face. What was he expecting me to do? I wasn't going to bite him. Besides, everyone was watching and it was embarrassing. This was supposed to be a private moment. "Can we talk about it later?"

"Sure…" His grin wavered, and the confidence leaked from his voice. He dropped his arm back to his side. "We can do it later."

Guilt washed over me—I hadn't meant to hurt his feelings! "Miles—"

But he'd already turned from me, slipping out of the room without another word.

"That's not what I meant!" I protested, looking to Damen for help. Hurting Miles was the last thing I wanted. "What should I do?"

"Give him time," Damen said, watching after Miles's retreat. And although he was speaking to me, it felt as though his mind wasn't present. "He'd been looking forward to this for a while. And he's on edge lately. His power isn't at a stable place."

I looked at Titus, trying to find an ally. Julian was too tired to be much help, and Damen clearly had other things on his mind.

And me? I could barely move.

But I couldn't leave things with Miles like this. "What—"

"He's overly-sensitive right now. I'll go talk to him." Titus rolled his shoulders and stretched before making his way to the bed. He ignored the fact that we had witnesses, and leaned down, brushing his lips over my forehead.

"I'm glad you're awake," he said, and then he, too, left the room.

"Now get out!" Dr. Reed repeated, glaring at the rest of the room's inhabitants and pointing at the door with a harsh movement. "All of you," she added, narrowing her eyes at Damen, as if indicating that she meant him specifically. "You're going to be in my way."

Bryce and Brayden slipped out the door without argument, and the room already felt larger. Then, sighing, Julian got to his feet before he looked expectantly in my direction. At Damen.

The onmyoji hesitated briefly before his grip loosened from my shoulders. "Fine," he muttered, his lips turning down into a pout. "But I'm not happy about it."

"Duly noted," Dr. Reed chirped. It didn't sound like she cared. "Now move it."

Once they'd left, the space felt cold with only me, Dr. Reed, and Dr. Stephens present.

The older man remained near my second armchair, rooting through a bag.

She turned to him, narrowing her eyes. "I'm talking to you too."

"I think not." Dr. Stephens shot her a bored look and raised his eyebrow in challenge. "Without guardians present, she's my responsibility."

"Not anymore she's not," Dr. Reed responded, squaring her shoulders. "Or have you missed that she's married to Bryce."

The blasé façade faded and he openly scowled. "Please don't remind me." He touched his tie, and I could easily imagine him to be a pearl-clutcher. "Wait until Caleb finds out. He'll be insufferable."

"Um…" I raised my finger, attempting to interject, but they ignored me.

"It's your fault anyway—whatever it was that you did. I know you're behind this. So you can't complain, because the reason you're stuck with *Bryce* is because Abigail forced him to act," Dr. Reed said.

"That's between Bianca and myself. Besides, I'm a doctor," Dr. Stephens pointed out. "And as qualified as you are with mental health, I am *more*."

I glanced between the two of them. The air in the room was tight with tension.

But at the same time, it was almost interesting.

"You're a quack," Dr. Reed said, pulling the scope of her stethoscope from behind the lapel of her white coat. "Why would you approve of such a stunt? You've jeopardized the health and wellbeing of my son and Bianca. I—on the other hand—am an *actual* medical professional. Which medical school did you go to again?"

"They are *fine*. He's *your* son, and she's *Alyssa's* daughter. Do you really think they can't handle a minor astral adventure? You're usually so agreeable, but now you're surprisingly hostile. There's nothing *here* that is a threat to them." Dr. Stephens's frown deepened and he straightened. He turned toward Dr. Reed, mock-concern on his face. "Is the stress getting to you? What are you so worried about?"

"I'm okay!" I squeaked, waving my hands in front of me and cutting into their heated argument. She was worried? Was that why her face was flushed and her movements frazzled? I held out my arm and tried to smile. It was kind of unsteady, but I managed. "Why don't you see, Dr. Reed? I'll be fine."

Dr. Reed turned from Dr. Stephens, blinking at me. Then she let out a slow breath, and—tentatively—reached for my hand.

I held my breath—this was the first time she'd hesitated before touching me. Usually, she had complete confidence in her actions.

Her initial reluctance confirmed what Julian had already told me—she could read my emotions by touch. She'd been doing it all along, and I'd never noticed.

Had she really been trying to help me? Or was I being stupid for thinking I could trust her?

No. She had been *trying* to help. I could feel it. It was my paranoia making me have this fear now.

I glanced at my blanket-covered feet, keeping my arm raised in her direction. "I don't know what to call you…" The question had been present in my mind since Julian announced she was his mother, but I hadn't been sure how to approach the subject.

"Trinity." Her fingers closed over my wrist, her grip firm despite the insecure tenor of her statement. "Or Dr. Kohler, if you'd prefer. 'Reed' was once my married name. We legally changed it after I left my husband."

"Dr. Kohler…" This might not be so bad—a herald for a new beginning. "Thank you…" My skin grew warm, and my confidence wavered. What if I couldn't see her in a new light? All these years, she'd been a source of fear. Even now, it was difficult to face her.

But still, I couldn't run away.

This wasn't like the past. Failure didn't have to mean pain or death. Life wasn't always like that. Even if I had a bad moment, or a bad day, it would be okay.

That's what everyone had been trying to teach me.

"Actually, I think you're right." Dr. Kohler's voice broke through my thoughts. I glanced at her, startled, and she smiled. "You'll be just fine."

Epilogue

Bianca

Ink

It was now one minute before midnight, and I was wide awake. Having slept for so long already, or at least having been not myself, had left me with extra energy to burn.

Dr. Kohler had ordered me to stay in my room the rest of the day, until tomorrow. After she left, most of the boys had visited me, one by one, to keep me company.

Damen had brought me food. Bryce and Brayden had even stopped by, with Finn sulking in the background.

But there was an absence that had caused my heart to twist, and I couldn't stop the nagging feeling that something wasn't right. Titus had said not to worry—that he'd spoken to Miles and he'd seemed just fine.

Yet, why was I uneasy?

As soon as the clock chimed twelve, I jumped from my bed. It was morning and I wasn't breaking any promises.

The room swayed, and I barely managed to grasp the bedpost. But the dizziness passed, and a moment later, I was ready.

Miles had better be ready. I did say I needed to talk to him, and I never specified a place or a time. Constant vigilance was something we all must learn.

It took a shamefully long time to make it to his room, and I couldn't help but notice that only a small light shone from under the gap in his door. Was he asleep? I'd hurt his feelings earlier. There was no way he was sleeping soundly. Did it mean he had *cried* himself to sleep? He had only wanted acceptance, and I had rejected him.

What kind of person did that make me?

"Miles?" I knocked on the door, trying to keep my voice at a whisper. If he was awake, he should hear me. If not, then I'd wake him up anyway.

This needed resolution. I'd do anything he wanted, even if it meant biting his wrist. I wasn't sure if witches drank blood in this universe, but it seemed to have some significance for him.

But he didn't answer, and the silence seemed to swallow my shallow breaths.

"Miles?" I tried again, slightly louder. "Can I talk to you?"

Still nothing.

What should I do? There was no way I could allow him to wallow in self-pity any longer. We had to clear the air between us. And if it meant I had to be the brave one, I could totally do that. I'd been brave a lot recently.

"I'm coming in," I muttered, pushing open the door. I stepped into the room, swallowing back the nagging worry that Miles now hated me. We were adults, and we would handle the situation as adults should.

But my stomach sank and my chest constricted at the sight in front of me.

Miles was nowhere to be seen. His clothes had been picked up, and room was utterly spotless. Under the tiny desk lamp rested a single white paper.

Mon rêve,

I'm afraid I am not worthy of you, so I've left to learn how to be a better man. Don't wait for me. When the time is right, the fates will allow us to meet once again.

♥ *Miles*

To Be Continued:

Book Five: Balance

The Author

Lyla Oweds is a paranormal romance author who resides in the beautiful Pocono Mountains, Pennsylvania. She grew up near Gettysburg, Pennsylvania and is a native of Baltimore, Maryland, and has a deep appreciation for the paranormal, hauntings, and Edgar Allan Poe. As such, she loves all things fantasy, mystery, crime, and horror.

She is the author of the Paranormal Reverse Harem series, The Grimm Cases and related novellas. She has also published the first book of Gloria Protean's story, The Red Trilogy. You can find out more about her current and upcoming works at her website, http://lylaoweds.com.

When not reading, writing, or working as a web programmer, Lyla can be found doing adult-y things such as being a single mom to a toddler and a bird. She also frequently enjoys makeup videos, massages, wine, and coffee.

Printed in Great Britain
by Amazon